LEO TOLSTOY

Short Novels

LEO
TOLSTOY
Short Novels

*Stories of Love, Seduction,
and Peasant Life*

VOLUME ONE

Selected *and* Introduced *by*

ERNEST J. SIMMONS

*The Modern Library
New York*

Acknowledgments. For permission to reprint the following short novels, the editor wishes to thank:
The World's Classics for "Two Hussars," "A Landlord's Morning," and "Polikúshka" from *Nine Stories;* for "The Cossacks: A Tale of 1852" from *Tales of Army Life,* translated by Louise and Aylmer Maude; and for "Family Happiness," translated by J. D. Duff, from *The Kreutzer Sonata and Other Tales.* Published by Oxford University Press.

THE MODERN LIBRARY
is published by
RANDOM HOUSE, INC.

Manufactured in the United States of America

INTRODUCTION

During Tolstoy's early literary period, before he embarked, in 1863, on his first major work, *War and Peace,* he experimented with a fictional form longer than the short story yet considerably shorter than a full-length novel. The Russians have a felicitous word for this genre, *povest,* which is defined in their dictionaries as: "A literary work of a narrative nature, in size less than a novel." We employ several designations for it: "long short story," "novelette," "short novel," and, quite improperly, "novella." With some arbitrariness I have chosen the term "short novel" for the five pieces brought together in this collection, for it seems to describe best their form and content, and it also suggests that in these tales Tolstoy was consciously preparing himself to undertake the full-length novel.

Two Hussars, A Landlord's Morning, Family Happiness, Polikúshka, and *The Cossacks* are Tolstoy's only short novels during these early years, with the exception of *Childhood, Boyhood,* and *Youth.* These last three, however, are interrelated narratives and taken together—the form in which they are so frequently published—must be regarded as a full-length novel. With this exception, these five short novels, in addition to fourteen tales printed in a companion volume (*Leo Tolstoy's Short Stories,* Modern Library, 1964), constitute all the completed fiction that Tolstoy wrote between 1851-63, his first literary period.

Though Tolstoy excelled in the short-story form from the beginning of his writing career, the artistic restrictions of this form were alien to the natural bent of his expansive genius. Hence his early efforts in the short novel, often brilliantly realized, represent a transition to the more artistically congenial, spacious, and complex world of *War and Peace* and

Anna Karenina. In the narratives of this collection we begin to perceive for the first time that no novelist was more acutely aware of the reality around him than Tolstoy or more exhaustively absorbed, through the intellect and senses, in all its manifestations.

In *Two Hussars,* the earliest of this group of short novels and Tolstoy's first piece of fiction based on a theme outside his personal experience, one is immediately aware, in comparison with his previous writing, of maturing artistic powers. The juxtaposition of two generations reflecting alternating contrasts in the personalities and adventures of father and son became a favorite fictional device which Tolstoy later used in his long novels on a much more elaborate scale to create an illusion of ceaseless movement involving a variety of actions, people, and moods. Count Fëdor Túrbin, a handsome, fire-eating young hussar, appears for one night in a provincial town and throws its society into a turmoil by his fearlessness, drinking, and wild escapades, and before he leaves he seduces a pretty young widow. Yet no one is shocked by his behavior, for his daring, generosity, and noble nature win the admiration of all.

Twenty years later another young hussar officer, the son of Count Fëdor Túrbin, who has been killed in a duel, arrives with his troops in the same provincial town. By chance he is quartered in the widow's house and unsuccessfully attempts to seduce her pretty daughter. The son, a calculating, materialistic prig, is entirely unlike his lovable scapegrace of a father. The contrast between them, as well as between the two generations they represent, is deliberate. In the son Tolstoy is condemning his own generation in favor of an older one for which he had a familiar nostalgic hankering. But in so doing the portrayal of the son is much less convincing than that of his father, an artistic fault which Tolstoy seemed to recognize. For in his diary he noted a friend's remark that the son is described without love, and he commented in his notebook at this time: "The first condition of an author's popularity, that is, the way to make himself loved, is the love with which he treats all his characters." It was a mistake he rarely made later, for even in his most negative characters he nearly always discovers some good, which was also his abiding principle with the real men and women he knew. He learned, in observing the human condition, that man does not go through the wringer of life and emerge all white. "Every man," he declared in *Resurrection*, "carries in himself the germ of every human quality, but sometimes it is one quality that manifests itself and sometimes another."

Actually, Tolstoy was greatly attracted, in real life as well as in fiction, to strong, bold, intense personalities like that of the father in *Two Hussars* or Eróshka in *The Cossacks*, and he willingly forgives their violent actions and moral lapses when committed out of an excess of their passionate natures. Some of the scenes in *Two Hussars* are extremely well handled, such as the party at the gypsies' and the poetic dreams of the widow's charming daughter, Lisa, as she stands at the window in the moonlight, an early preview of the famous scene of Natasha in *War and Peace* when she contemplates from her bedroom window the moonlit beauty of a perfect spring night.

In *A Landlord's Morning* and *Polikúshka*, Tolstoy for the first time is mainly concerned with peasants, a class that played an important role in his later fiction. And in *A Landlord's Morning* he also returns to the events of his personal life which had furnished themes for so much of his previous fiction. His initial intention, which he abandoned, was to write a full-length novel about a landowner's experiences with his peasants, and the present short novel appears to be the self-contained opening section of this project. At the beginning of it the nineteen-year-old Nekhlyúdov writes his aunt that he has given up his studies at the University, in order to devote himself to the affairs of his estate and especially to trying to remedy the pitiable and impoverished conditions of his hundreds of peasants. He explains, in a spirit of high idealism, that it is his sacred duty to care for their welfare, and that to guide his endeavors he has written down rules of conduct for himself.

At the age of nineteen Tolstoy also left the University to live on his estate, Yasnaya Polyana, in order to fulfill a new humanitarian "purpose in life"—to improve the lot of his many serfs over whom he was then absolute master. And he too, like Nekhlyúdov, wrote out rules of conduct. In doing good for the peasantry he was convinced that he would find real happiness.

Unfortunately we have no definite information about Tolstoy's activities in this first attempt to reform his fellow men. Several years later a diary note on the plan of the proposed novel suggests what his intentions had been in this experiment and the consequences that followed: "The hero searches for the realization of an ideal of happiness and justice in a country existence. Not finding it, he becomes disillusioned and wishes to search for his ideal in family life. His friend introduces him to the thought that happiness does not consist of an ideal but may be found in continued vital work that has for its purpose the happiness of others."

It may be assumed that Tolstoy's course of action paralleled that of his hero in *A Landlord's Morning*. Nekhlyúdov, who refuses to regard the poverty of his peasants an unavoidable evil, abolishes corporal punishment and provides schooling and medical aid for them. Like a ministering angel, he visits their wretched, filthy hovels described by Tolstoy with that saturation of precise detail which became a hallmark of his realism. In simple-hearted fashion Nekhlyúdov pours out his willingness to devote his life to their happiness. But his first fine rapture does not last long. Despite all his efforts, the peasants remain poor, shirk education, and do not improve morally. Somehow his plans all come to nothing. The peasants are endlessly suspicious and regard his offer of aid as just another trick on the part of the master to get more work out of them. Perplexed in the extreme and sadly disillusioned, he finally abandons his experiment.

If the young Tolstoy's similar efforts at Yasnaya Polyana were equally feckless, he was not above subjecting his motives to acute self-criticism in the response of Nekhlyúdov's aunt to his undertaking. One does not believe in arguments and rules but only in experience, she writes, and experience tells her that his plans are childish. "You always wished to appear original," she declares, "but your originality is really nothing but excessive self-esteem."

Turgenev, in a letter to a friend, argues that *A Landlord's Morning* conveys the unpleasant impression that all efforts of landowners to improve conditions of the peasantry lead to nothing. The real moral of the work, however, is that so long as serfdom exists the master will be unable to better the lot of his peasants, despite disinterested endeavors to do so. Tolstoy clearly recognized this fact and one may perceive a connection between *A Landlord's Morning* and his attempt, in the course of the year it was published (1856), to free his own serfs. But they rejected his offer, which was carefully contrived to protect his interests in the land, perhaps because he once again failed to take into consideration the innate hostility for the master that centuries of serfdom had implanted in the peasantry. Rather bitterly he commented in his diary: "Two powerful men are joined with a sharp chain; it hurts both of them, and when one of them moves, he involuntarily cuts the other, and neither has room to work." *A Landlord's Morning* gives effective artistic expression to this profound antagonism and at the same time illuminates with striking clarity the nature of the Russian peasant and the unbelievably shocking conditions under which he lived.

Though *Polikúshka* was published after the emancipation of the serfs in 1861, it is concerned, like *A Landlord's Morning*, with peasant existence before they obtained their freedom. But here the emphasis is quite different. There is no autobiographical element, no personal thesis to develop. Tolstoy's concentration is entirely upon telling a gripping story of peasant life and he does it with infinite art. The result is a masterpiece in the genre of the short novel.

Tolstoy's maturing artistic powers are much in evidence in this tale. Here he accepts the real world and his picture of it is fresh and interesting because he sees so much more of it than his readers, yet its commonplaces, observed through the prism of his imagination, take on new meaning. That is, he is able to perceive genuine poetry in the average which so

often embodies man's dreams and hopes. The wretched peasant Polikúshka, who drinks too much, is a liar, and cannot
keep his pickers and feelers off the loose property of anyone,
joyfully dreams of justifying his mistress' faith in him by
safely fulfilling her commission to bring a package of money
from town. His terrible despair over the collapse of his hopes
because of the accidental loss of the money on the way home
is compounded by the realization that no one will believe him
if he tells the truth. To kill himself seems the only way out of
his impossible dilemma.

Tolstoy adds convincingness to this tragic incident by placing it in a setting of remarkably described peasant existence:
the subtly handled relations of the mistress of the estate to her
steward and his to the peasants of the village; the superb picture of the superstitious terror of these simple people over
Polikúshka's suicide; old Dútlov's similar fear that the found
money, which had been given to him by his mistress, is the
evil money of the devil; and the splendid, almost Dostoevskian
scene in the tavern where old Dútlov, who uses the "evil
money" to buy up a substitute for his nephew conscripted into
the army, bows down before the young man, who has offended
him, and asks his forgiveness.

No wonder that Turgenev, who at this time had little reason
to be well disposed toward his irascible friend Tolstoy, wrote
the poet Fet that after reading *Polikúshka* he "marveled at the
strength of his [Tolstoy's] huge talent. But he has used up too
much material, and it is a pity he drowned the son. It makes
it too terrible. But there are pages that are truly wonderful.
It makes a cold shudder run down even my back, and you
know my back has grown thick and coarse. He is a master, a
master!"

Tolstoy had indeed become a master. Without being ten-
dentious, *Polikúshka* exposes the hard features of peasant life.
The tone of refined humor that aimed to ridicule the false and
insincere in art appeared for the first time in his fiction. On
this same high level of performance, he continued to write
about the peasant and his relation to the landowner in brilliant sections of *War and Peace* and *Anna Karenina*.

Family Happiness is a most interesting example of the manner in which Tolstoy transposes the facts of real life into the substance of art. It will be remembered that in his plan for a novel about a Russian landowner, of which *A Landlord's Morning* is all he completed, the hero, after his disillusionment in reforming his peasants, seeks a new ideal in family life. Tolstoy himself long pursued this ideal of family happiness, and during 1856-57 he actively sought the realization of it in courting pretty Valérya Arséneva, much younger than himself, who lived on an estate not far from Yasnaya Polyana. Somewhat like Sergey Mikháylych in *Family Happiness,* Tolstoy had easy access to the young lady's house as the guardian of her brother. And again like the hero of the short novel, he employed an imaginary second-self to explain his feelings to Valérya, urged her to practice his favorite piano pieces, and grew wrathful over her fondness for high society.

Although Tolstoy allowed himself to become deeply committed to Valérya, in the end, unlike Sergey Mikháylych in the story, he shrank from marriage with her because he lost faith in it as an ideal of happiness. "I never loved her with real love," he wrote a family friend. "I was carried away by the reprehensible desire to inspire love. This gave me a delight I had never before experienced. . . . I have behaved very badly."

No doubt a felt need to justify his shabby conduct and purge his mind of the whole episode drove Tolstoy to write *Family Happiness,* in which he tries to prove that if he and Valérya had married, their different views of what made for happiness in such a relationship would have led to unhappiness for both. But by the witchery of his art he transforms the experience of real life, in the first part of the tale, into a charming, poetic narrative of the dawning love of a sensitive seventeen-year-old girl for a man twice her age, a contemporary of her father, and also her guardian. All we know of Tolstoy's relations with Valérya comes from his letters and diary entries. In his short novel the challenge of art compels Tolstoy to tell the story of the love of Másha and her guardian as it is seen through the eyes of this young girl. It is a delicate psychological study in depth, a worthy forerunner of the exquisitely told love stories of his great novels. Except perhaps for the conclusion, he never appears to hover over the destiny of Másha and Sergéy Mikháylych; they exercise free choice in working out their fate so that what they do seems to be psychologically necessary. Like his style, Tolstoy's psychological insights create in the reader a sense of intimacy with the characters, for in his analysis of thought, feeling, and action his points of reference are nearly always the reality of life and not abstractions. "You can invent anything you please," he once said of Gorky's fiction, "but it is impossible to invent psychology." We observe how the mysterious chemistry of love gradually and insensibly alters the nature of the youthful, inexperienced Másha and reveals to her "a whole new world of joys in the present, without changing anything in my life, without adding anything except himself to each impression of my mind. All that had surrounded me from childhood, without saying anything to me, suddenly came to life. The mere sight of him made everything begin to speak and press for admittance to my heart, filling it with happiness."

The radiant poetic atmosphere of the first part of the story is dissipated in the second part by the familiar stresses and strains of married life. Másha eventually grows impatient with the uneventfulness of country existence with her husband and craves the movement and excitement of high society in the city. Although he has lived this kind of social life himself and is aware of its shallowness, he bows to the wishes of his young wife. Her social success and eager willingness to sacrifice to it the values he prized most in her soon bring about an estrangement in their relations. At this point Tolstoy may be accused of introducing into his story a didactic puritanical element. Quite clearly he wished to suggest that the disparities in years, experience, and tastes inevitably erode the family happiness of Másha and her husband just as they would have done if he had married Valérya. The conclusion of the story, however, saves the situation by a solution that does not appear to be false either to the reality of things or to the demands of art. Tormented by the conviction that she has lost his love, Másha at last confronts her husband with an anguished plea for an explanation. They sit on the veranda of her old house, and here the reluctant husband, prompted by tender memories of their first ecstasies and the antiphonal responses of nature as gentle summer rain clouds shadow the setting sun, offers a clarification. She accuses him of not continuing to love her as at the beginning of their marriage and of failing to exercise his authority and greater experience to save her from the mistakes she made in pursuing the illusion of social success. She had to learn this by her own experience, he tells her, and if their early passionate love has vanished this was inevitable anyway. It can now be replaced, he adds, by another kind of peaceful love. "Don't let us try to repeat life," he declares. "Don't let us make pretences to ourselves. Let us be thankful that there is an end of the old emotions and excitements. The excitement of searching is over for us; our quest is done, and happiness enough has fallen to our lot. Now we must stand aside and make room for him," he concluded, pointing to their infant son whom the nurse was carrying out to the veranda for their nightly blessing.

The Cossacks, the last and longest of the pieces in this collection, was planned as the first part of a three-part novel which Tolstoy never completed, but the work as it stands has a beginning, middle, and end and the inner unity of a well-rounded short novel. He began it in 1852 during his stay in the Caucasus as a cadet in the Russian army fighting the local hill tribes, but because of many interruptions he did not finish it until ten years later, shortly after his marriage in 1862. In fact, if he had not felt obliged to the publisher, for an advance of a thousand roubles to pay off a gambling debt, it is possible that he might never have completed *The Cossacks.*

As the subtitle indicates, the story concerns events of 1852. At that time, when not off on a campaign, Tolstoy was quartered in the Grebénsk Cossack village of Starogládkov and lived more or less the life vividly described in *The Cossacks.* Though it is unwise to push autobiographical correspondences too far, certain obvious sources are worth pointing out. Tolstoy stayed in the house of the old Cossack Epíshka Sékhin, who is quite faithfully portrayed as the remarkable Daddy Eróshka in the tale. And in her way the equally impressive Maryánka was modeled on the beautiful Starogládkov Cossack girl Solomónida, as impervious to Tolstoy's attentions as the heroine is to Olénin's. Both girls preferred a dashing young Cossack like Lukáshka who in the story killed Chéchens, stole horses, got drunk, and at night climbed in the window of his sweetheart without thinking who he was or why he existed.

This ambivalence of Olénin, a struggle in him between the social and moral claims of the cultured society into which he had been born and the simple, amoral way of life of these Cossack children of nature, reflects in part Tolstoy's struggle during his more than two years of service in the Caucasus. Under the impressions of his new surroundings Olénin learns to condemn artificial civilization, yet he finds it difficult to accept whole-heartedly the views of Daddy Eróshka who thinks all religion is a fraud and declares: "God has made everything for the joy of man. There is no sin in any of it." But Olénin definitely regards it as a sin when this old reprobate offers to provide a beauty for him. "A sin?" he shouts. "Where's the sin? A sin to look at a nice girl? A sin to have some fun with her? Or is it a sin to love her? Is that so in your parts? . . . No, my dear fellow, it's not a sin, it's salvation! God made you and God made the girl too. He made it all; so it is no sin to look at a nice girl. That's what she was made for: to be loved and to give joy."

The natural beauty of Cossack existence transforms Olénin into a philosophical reasoner searching for personal happiness, a kind of Rousseauistic "natural man," a type that became a favorite of Tolstoy in later fiction. For such characters, and Olénin is no exception, reality turns out to be something different from what they hope and dream; life often disappoints them because they confuse the imagined with the real. Olénin's conception of the romantic existence of the Cossacks is shattered by the reality of it. Under the impact of these people, unspoiled by civilization, he envisages his personal pursuit of happiness in terms of self-sacrifice and love for others. But this romantic ideal is shattered by his passionate love for Maryánka, who is utterly inaccessible to him as a non-Cossack incapable of ever identifying himself with their emancipated life.

The Cossacks is the final work of Tolstoy's first literary period, and no doubt it is his finest during these twelve years. Turgenev did not hesitate to declare it "the best story that has been written in our language." Though there are artistic flaws in the portrait of Olénin, the principal Cossack characters, Eróshka, Lukáshka, and Maryánka, are among the most memorable of Tolstoy's creations. With them one experiences that baffling impression, which is the quintessence of his realism, that somehow these characters are telling their own stories without the author's intervention beyond that of acting as an occasional commentator. And that inner truth of a work of fiction, which must come from life itself, seems more fully developed in *The Cossacks* than in any other tale of Tolstoy's first literary period.*

Ernest J. Simmons

---

* All the numbered footnotes in the text have been contributed by the translator Aylmer Maude.

CONTENTS

LEO TOLSTOY

Short Novels

TWO HUSSARS

'Jomini and Jomini—
Not half a word of vodka.'—D. DAVÝDOV.[1]

Early in the nineteenth century, when there were as yet no
railways or macadamized roads, no gaslight, no stearine
candles, no low couches with sprung cushions, no unvar-
nished furniture, no disillusioned youths with eye-glasses, no
liberalizing women philosophers, nor any charming *dames
aux camélias* of whom there are so many in our times, in those
naïve days, when leaving Moscow for Petersburg in a coach
or carriage provided with a kitchenful of home-made provisions one travelled for eight days along a soft, dusty, or
muddy road and believed in chopped cutlets, sledge-bells,
and plain rolls; when in the long autumn evenings the tallow
candles, around which family groups of twenty or thirty people gathered, had to be snuffed; when ball-rooms were illuminated by candelabra with wax or spermaceti candles,
when furniture was arranged symmetrically, when our fathers
were still young and proved it not only by the absence of
wrinkles and grey hair but by fighting duels for the sake of a
woman and rushing from the opposite corner of a room to
pick up a bit of a handkerchief purposely or accidentally
dropped; when our mothers wore short-waisted dresses and
enormous sleeves and decided family affairs by drawing lots,
when the charming *dames aux camélias* hid from the light of
day—in those naïve days of Masonic lodges,[2] Martinists,[3] and

---

[1] From *The Song of an old Hussar,* in which the great days of the
past are contrasted with the trivial present. D. V. Davýdov is referred to in *War and Peace.*

[2] Freemasonry in Russia was a secret association, the original pur-

Tugendbunds,[4] the days of Milorádoviches[5] and Davýdovs[6] and Púshkins—a meeting of landed proprietors was held in the Government town of K——, and the nobility elections[7] were being concluded.

I

'Well, never mind, the saloon will do,' said a young officer in a fur cloak and hussar's cap, who had just got out of a post-sledge and was entering the best hotel in the town of K——.

'The assembly, your Excellency, is enormous,' said the boots, who had already managed to learn from the orderly that the hussar's name was Count Túrbin, and therefore addressed him as 'your Excellency'.

'The proprietress of Afrémovo with her daughters has said she is leaving this evening, so No. 11 will be at your disposal as soon as they go,' continued the boots, stepping softly be-

---

pose of which was the moral perfecting of people on the basis of equality and universal brotherhood. Commencing as a mystical-religious movement in the eighteenth century, it became political during the reign of Alexander I and was suppressed in 1822.

[3] The Martinists were a society of Russian Freemasons founded in 1780 and named after the French theosophist, Louis Claude Saint-Martin.

[4] The Tugendbund (League of Virtue) was a German association founded in 1808 with the acknowledged purpose of cultivating patriotism, reorganizing the army, and encouraging education, and with the secret aim of throwing off the French yoke. Dissolved on Napoleon's demand in 1809, it continued to exist secretly, and exerted great influence in 1812. It was suspected of having revolutionary tendencies, and was in very bad odor with the Russian government at the time of the Holy Alliance.

[5] M. H. Milorádovich (1770-1825) distinguished himself in the Napoleonic war, became Governor-General of Petersburg, and was killed when suppressing the 'Decembrist' mutiny in 1825. He appears in *War and Peace*.

[6] D. V. Davýdov (1784-1839), a popular poet, and leader of a guerrilla force in the war of 1812. A. S. Púshkin (1799-1837), the greatest of Russian poets, was his contemporary.

[7] The *nobility* included not merely those who had titles, but all who in England would be called the gentry.

fore the count along the passage and continually looking round.

In the general saloon at a little table under the dingy full-length portrait of the Emperor Alexander the First, several men, probably belonging to the local nobility, sat drinking champagne, while at another side of the room sat some travellers—tradesmen in blue, fur-lined cloaks.

Entering the room and calling in Blücher, a gigantic grey mastiff he had brought with him, the count threw off his cloak, the collar of which was still covered with hoar-frost, called for vodka, sat down at the table in his blue satin Cossack jacket, and entered into conversation with the gentlemen there.

The handsome open countenance of the newcomer immediately predisposed them in his favour and they offered him a glass of champagne. The count first drank a glass of vodka and then ordered another bottle of champagne to treat his new acquaintances. The sledge-driver came in to ask for a tip.

'Sáshka!' shouted the count. 'Give him something!'

The driver went out with Sáshka but came back again with the money in his hand.

'Look here, y'r 'xcelence, haven't I done my very best for y'r honour? Didn't you promise me half a ruble, and he's only given me a quarter!'

'Give him a ruble, Sáshka.'

Sáshka cast down his eyes and looked at the driver's feet.

'He's had enough!' he said, in a bass voice. 'And besides, I have no more money.'

The count drew from his pocket-book the two five-ruble notes which were all it contained, and gave one of them to the driver, who kissed his hand and went off.

'I've run it pretty close!' said the count. 'These are my last five rubles.'

'Real hussar fashion, Count,' said one of the nobles who from his moustache, voice, and a certain energetic freedom about his legs, was evidently a retired cavalryman. 'Are you staying here some time, Count?'

'I must get some money. I shouldn't have stayed here at all but for that. And there are no rooms to be had, devil take them, in this accursed pub.'

'Permit me, Count,' said the cavalryman. 'Will you not join me? My room is No. 7. . . . If you do not mind, just for the night. And then you'll stay a couple of days with us? It happens that the *Maréchal de la Noblesse* is giving a ball to-night. You would make him very happy by going.'

'Yes, Count, do stay,' said another, a handsome young man. 'You have surely no reason to hurry away! You know this only comes once in three years—the elections, I mean. You should at least have a look at our young ladies, Count!'

'Sáshka, get my clean linen ready. I am going to the bath,' [1] said the count, rising, 'and from there perhaps I may look in at the Marshal's.'

Then, having called the waiter and whispered something to him to which the latter replied with a smile, 'That can all be arranged,' he went out.[2]

'So I'll order my trunk to be taken to your room, old fellow,' shouted the count from the passage.

'Please do, I shall be most happy,' replied the cavalryman, running to the door. 'No. 7—don't forget.'

When the count's footsteps could no longer be heard the cavalryman returned to his place and sitting close to one of the group—a Government official—and looking him straight in the face with smiling eyes, said:

'It is the very man, you know!'

'No!'

'I tell you it is! It is the very same duellist hussar—the famous Túrbin. He knew me—I bet you anything he knew me. Why, he and I went on the spree for three weeks without a break when I was at Lebedyáni[3] for remounts. There was one thing he and I did together. . . . He's a fine fellow, eh?'

---

[1] For a Russian bath, as for a Turkish bath, one goes to a public establishment and subjects oneself to heat that produces profuse perspiration.

[2] It was not unusual at the bath to associate with a woman.

[3] A town in the Tambóv province noted for its horse fair.

'A splendid fellow. And so pleasant in his manner! Doesn't show a grain of—what d'you call it?' answered the handsome young man. 'How quickly we became intimate. . . . He's not more than twenty-five, is he?'

'Oh no, that's what he looks but he is more than that. One has to get to know him, you know. Who abducted Migúnova? He. It was he who killed Sáblin. It was he who dropped Matnëv out of the window by his legs. It was he who won three hundred thousand rubles from Prince Néstorov. He is a regular dare-devil, you know: a gambler, a duellist, a se-ducer, but a jewel of an hussar—a real jewel. The rumours that are afloat about us are nothing to the reality—if anyone knew what a true hussar is! Ah yes, those were times!'

And the cavalryman told his interlocutor of such a spree with the count in Lebedyáni as not only never had, but never even could have, taken place.

It could not have done so, first because he had never seen the count till that day and had left the army two years before the count entered it; and secondly because the cavalryman had never really served in the cavalry at all, but had for four years been the humblest of cadets in the Belévski regi-ment, and retired as soon as ever he became ensign. But ten years ago he had inherited some money and had really been in Lebedyáni where he squandered seven hundred rubles with some officers who were there buying remounts. He had even gone so far as to have an uhlan uniform made with orange facings, meaning to enter an uhlan regiment. This de-sire to enter the cavalry, and the three weeks spent with the remount officers at Lebedyáni, remained the brightest and happiest memories of his life, so he transformed the desire first into a reality and then into a reminiscence and came to be-lieve firmly in his past as a cavalry officer—all of which did not prevent his being, as to gentleness and honesty, a most worthy man.

'Yes, those who have never served in the cavalry will never understand us fellows.'

He sat astride a chair and thrusting out his lower jaw began to speak in a bass voice. 'You ride at the head of your squadron, not a horse but the devil incarnate prancing about under you, and you just sit in devil-may-care style. The squadron commander rides up to review: "Lieutenant," he says. "We can't get on without you—please lead the squadron to parade." "All right," you say, and there you are: you turn round, shout to your moustached fellows. . . . Ah, devil take it, those were times!'

The count returned from the bath-house very red and with wet hair, and went straight to No. 7, where the cavalry-man was already sitting in his dressing-gown smoking a pipe and considering with pleasure, and not without some appre-hension, the happiness that had befallen him of sharing a room with the celebrated Túrbin. 'Now suppose,' he thought, 'that he suddenly takes me, strips me naked, drives me to the town gates and sets me in the snow, or . . . tars me, or sim-ply. . . . But no,' he consoled himself, 'he wouldn't do that to a comrade.'

'Sáshka, feed Blücher!' shouted the count.

Sáshka, who had taken a tumbler of vodka to refresh him-self after the journey and was decidedly tipsy, came in.

'What, already! You've been drinking, you rascal! . . . Feed Blücher!'

'He won't starve anyway: see how sleek he is!' answered Sáshka, stroking the dog.

'Silence! Be off and feed him!'

'You want the dog to be fed, but when a man drinks a glass you reproach him.'

'Hey! I'll thrash you!' shouted the count in a voice that made the window-panes rattle and even frightened the caval-ryman a bit.

'You should ask if Sáshka has had a bite to-day!. Yes, beat me if you think more of a dog than of a man,' muttered Sáshka.

But here he received such a terrible blow in the face from the count's fist that he fell, knocked his head against the par-tition, and clutching his nose fled from the room and fell on a settee in the passage.

'He's knocked my teeth out,' grunted Sáshka, wiping his bleeding nose with one hand while with the other he scratched the back of Blücher, who was licking himself. 'He's knocked my teeth out, Blüchy, but still he's my count and I'd go through fire for him—I would! Because he—is my count. Do you understand, Blüchy? Want your dinner, eh?'

After lying still for a while he rose, fed the dog, and then, almost sobered, went in to wait on his count and to offer him some tea.

'I shall really feel hurt,' the cavalryman was saying meekly, as he stood before the count who was lying on the other's bed with his legs up against the partition. 'You see I also am an old army man and, if I may say so, a comrade. Why should you borrow from anyone else when I shall be delighted to lend you a couple of hundred rubles? I haven't got them just now—only a hundred rubles—but I'll get the rest to-day. You would really hurt my feelings, Count.'

'Thank you, old man,' said the count, instantly discerning what kind of relations had to be established between them, and slapping the cavalryman on the shoulder: 'Thanks! Well then, we'll go to the ball if it must be so. But what are we to do now? Tell me what you have in your town. What pretty girls? What men fit for a spree? What gaming?'

The cavalryman explained that there would be an abundance of pretty creatures at the ball, that Kólkov, who had been re-elected Captain of Police, was the best hand at a spree, only he lacked the true hussar go—otherwise he was a good sort of a chap; that the Ilyúshin gipsy chorus had been singing in the town since the elections began, Stëshka leading, and that everybody meant to go to hear them after leaving the Marshal's that evening.

'And there's a devilish lot of card-playing too,' he went on. 'Lúkhnov plays. He has money and is staying here to break his journey, and Ilyín, an uhlan cornet who has room No. 8, has lost a lot. They have already begun in his room. They play every evening. And what a fine fellow that Ilyín is! I tell you, Count, he's not mean—he'll let his last shirt go.'

'Well then, let us go to his room. Let's see what sort of people they are,' said the count.

'Yes do—pray do. They'll be devilish glad.'

II

The uhlan cornet, Ilyín, had not long been awake. The evening before he had sat down to cards at eight o'clock and had lost pretty steadily for fifteen hours on end—till eleven in the morning. He had lost a considerable sum, but did not know exactly how much, because he had about three thousand rubles of his own, and fifteen thousand of Crown money which had long since got mixed up with his own, and he feared to count lest his fears that some of the Crown money was already gone should be confirmed. It was nearly noon when he fell asleep and he had slept that heavy dreamless sleep which only very young men sleep after a heavy loss. Waking at six o'clock (just when Count Túrbin arrived at the hotel), and seeing the floor all around strewn with cards and bits of chalk, and the chalk-marked tables in the middle of the room, he recalled with horror last night's play, and the last card—a knave on which he lost five hundred rubles; but not yet quite convinced of the reality of all this, he drew his money from under the pillow and began to count it. He recognized some notes which had passed from hand to hand several times with 'corners' and 'transports', and he recalled the whole course of the game. He had none of his own three thousand rubles left, and some two thousand five hundred of the Government money was also gone.

Ilyín had been playing for four nights running.

He had come from Moscow where the Crown money had been entrusted to him, and at K—— had been detained by the superintendent of the post-house on the pretext that there were no horses, but really because the superintendent had an agreement with the hotel-keeper to detain all travellers for a day. The uhlan, a bright young lad who had just received three thousand rubles from his parents in Moscow for his equipment on entering his regiment, was glad to spend a

few days in the town of K—— during the elections, and hoped
to enjoy himself thoroughly. He knew one of the landed gentry there who had a family, and he was thinking of looking
them up and flirting with the daughters, when the cavalryman turned up to make his acquaintance. Without any evil
intention the cavalryman introduced him that same evening, in the general saloon or common room of the hotel, to
his acquaintances, Lúkhnov and other gamblers. And ever
since then the uhlan had been playing cards, not asking at
the post-station for horses, much less going to visit his acquaintance the landed proprietor, and not even leaving his
room for four days on end.

Having dressed and drunk tea he went to the window. He
felt that he would like to go for a stroll to get rid of the recollections that haunted him, and he put on his cloak and went
out into the street. The sun was already hidden behind the
white houses with their red roofs and it was getting dusk. It
was warm for winter. Large wet snowflakes were falling slowly
into the muddy street. Suddenly at the thought that he had
slept all through the day now ending, a feeling of intolerable
sadness overcame him.

'This day, now past, can never be recovered,' he thought.

'I have ruined my youth!' he suddenly said to himself, not
because he really thought he had ruined his youth—he did not
even think about it—but because the phrase happened to occur to him.

'And what am I to do now?' thought he. 'Borrow from someone and go away?' A lady passed him along the pavement.
'There's a stupid woman,' thought he for some reason. 'There's
no one to borrow from . . . I have ruined my youth!' He
came to the bazaar. A tradesman in a fox-fur cloak stood at
the door of his shop touting for customers. 'If I had not with-
drawn that eight I should have recovered my losses.' An old
beggar-woman followed him whimpering. 'There's no one to
borrow from.' A man drove past in a bearskin cloak; a policeman was standing at his post. 'What unusual thing could I do?
Fire at them? No, its dull . . . I have ruined my youth! . . .
Ah, those are fine horse-collars and trappings hanging there!

Ah, if only I could drive in a tróyka: Gee-up, beauties! . . .
I'll go back. Lúkhnov will come soon, and we'll play.'

He returned to the hotel and again counted his money. No,
he had made no mistake the first time: there were still two
thousand five hundred rubles of Crown money missing. 'I'll
stake twenty-five rubles, then make a "corner" . . . seven-
fold it, fifteen-fold, thirty, sixty . . . three thousand rubles.
Then I'll buy the horse-collars and be off. He won't let me, the
rascal! I have ruined my youth!'

That is what was going on in the uhlan's head when Lúkhnov actually entered the room.

'Have you been up long, Michael Vasílich?' asked Lúkhnov slowly removing the gold spectacles from his skinny
nose and carefully wiping them with a red silk handkerchief.

'No, I've only just got up—I slept uncommonly well.'

'Some hussar or other has arrived. He has put up with
Zavalshévski—had you heard?'

'No, I hadn't. But how is it no one else is here yet?'

'They must have gone to Pryákhin's. They'll be here directly.'

And sure enough a little later there came into the room a
garrison officer who always accompanied Lúkhnov; a Greek
merchant with an enormous brown hooked nose and sunken
black eyes, and a fat puffy landowner, the proprietor of a
distillery, who played whole nights, always staking 'simples'
of half a ruble each. Everybody wished to begin playing as
soon as possible, but the principal gamesters, especially Lúkhnov who was telling about a robbery in Moscow in an exceedingly calm manner, did not refer to the subject.

'Just fancy,' he said, 'a city like Moscow, the historic capital,
a metropolis, and men dressed up as devils go about there
with crooks, frighten stupid people and rob the passers-by—
and that's the end of it! What are the police about? That's the
question.'

The uhlan listened attentively to the story about the robbers, but when a pause came he rose and quietly ordered
cards to be brought. The fat landowner was the first to speak
out.

'Well, gentlemen, why lose precious time? If we mean business let's begin.'

'Yes, you walked off with a pile of half-rubles last night so
you like it,' said the Greek.

'I think we might start,' said the garrison officer.

Ilyín looked at Lúkhnov. Lúkhnov looking him in the eye
quietly continued his story about robbers dressed up like
devils with claws.

'Will you keep the bank?' asked the uhlan.

'Isn't it too early?'

'Belóv!' shouted the uhlan, blushing for some unknown reason, 'bring me some dinner—I haven't had anything to eat yet,
gentlemen—and a bottle of champagne and some cards.'

At this moment the count and Zavalshévski entered the
room. It turned out that Túrbin and Ilyín belonged to the same
division. They took to one another at once, clinked glasses,
drank champagne together, and were on intimate terms in five
minutes. The count seemed to like Ilyín very much; he looked
smilingly at him and teased him about his youth.

'There's an uhlan of the right sort!' he said. 'What moustaches! Dear me, what moustaches!'

Even what little down there was on Ilyín's lip was quite
white.

'I suppose you are going to play?' said the count: 'Well, I
wish you luck, Ilyín! I should think you are a master at it,' he
added with a smile.

'Yes, they mean to start,' said Lúkhnov, tearing open a bundle of a dozen packs of cards, 'and you'll join in too, Count,
won't you?'

'No, not to-day. I should clear you all out if I did. When I
begin "cornering" in earnest the bank begins to crack! But I
have nothing to play with—I was cleaned out at a station near
Volochók. I met some infantry fellow there with rings on his
fingers—a sharper I should think—and he plucked me clean.'

'Why, did you stay at that station long?' asked Ilyín.

'I sat there for twenty-two hours. I shan't forget that accursed station! And the superintendent won't forget me either . . .'

'How's that?'

'I drive up, you know; out rushes the superintendent looking a regular brigand. "No horses!" says he. Now I must tell you that it's my rule, if there are no horses I don't take off my fur cloak but go into the superintendent's own room—not into the public room but into his private room—and I have all the doors and windows opened on the ground that it's smoky. Well, that's just what I did there. You remember what frosts we had last month? About twenty degrees! [1] The superintendent began to argue, I punched his head. There was an old woman there, and girls and other women; they kicked up a row, snatched up their pots and pans and were rushing off to the village. . . . I went to the door and said, "Let me have horses and I'll be off. If not, no one shall go out: I'll freeze you all!" '

'That's an infernally good plan!' said the puffy squire, rolling with laughter. 'It's the way they freeze out cockroaches . . .'

'But I didn't watch carefully enough and the superintendent got away with the women. Only one old woman remained in pawn on the top of the stove; she kept sneezing and saying her prayers. Afterwards we began negotiating: the superintendent came and from a distance began persuading me to let the old woman go, but I set Blücher at him a bit. Blücher's splendid at tackling superintendents! But still the rascal didn't let me have horses until the next morning. Meanwhile that infantry fellow came along. I joined him in another room, and we began to play. You have seen Blücher? . . . Blücher! . . .' and he gave a whistle.

Blücher rushed in, and the players condescendingly paid some attention to him though it was evident that they wished to attend to quite other matters.

'But why don't you play, gentlemen? Please don't let me prevent you. I am a chatterbox, you see,' said Túrbin. 'Play is play whether one likes it or not.'

---

[1] Réaumur = thirteen below zero Fahrenheit.

III

Lúkhnov drew two candles nearer to him, took out a large brown pocket-book full of paper money, and slowly, as if performing some rite, opened it on the table, took out two one-hundred ruble notes and placed them under the cards.

'Two hundred for the bank, the same as yesterday,' said he, adjusting his spectacles and opening a pack of cards.

'Very well,' said Ilyín, continuing his conversation with Túrbin without looking at Lúkhnov.

The game[1] started. Lúkhnov dealt the cards with machine-like precision, stopping now and then and deliberately jotting something down, or looking sternly over his spectacles and saying in low tones, 'Pass up!' The fat landowner spoke louder than anyone else, audibly deliberating with himself and wetting his plump fingers when he turned down the corner of a card. The garrison officer silently and neatly noted the amount of his stake on his card and bent down small corners under the table. The Greek sat beside the banker watching the game attentively with his sunken black eyes, and seemed to be waiting for something. Zavalshévski standing by the table would suddenly begin to fidget all over, take a red or blue bank-note[2] out of his trouser pocket, lay a card on it, slap it with his palm and say: 'Little seven, pull me through!' Then he would bite his moustache, shift from foot to foot, and keep fidgeting till his card was dealt. Ilyín sat eating veal and pickled cucumbers, which were placed beside him on the horsehair sofa, and

---

[1] The game referred to was *shtos*. The players selected cards for themselves from packs on the table, and placed their stakes on or under their cards. The banker had a pack from which he dealt to right and left alternately. Cards dealt to the right won for him, those dealt to the left won for the players. 'Pass up' was a reminder to the players to hand up stakes due to the bank. 'Simples' were single stakes. By turning down 'corners' of his card a player increased his stake two- or three-fold. A 'transport' increased it six-fold. *Shtos* has long gone out of fashion and been replaced by other forms of gambling.

[2] Five-ruble notes were blue and ten-ruble notes red.

hastily wiping his hands on his coat laid down one card after another. Túrbin, who at first was sitting on the sofa, quickly saw how matters stood. Lúkhnov did not look at or speak to Ilyín, only now and then his spectacles would turn for a moment towards the latter's hand, but most of Ilyín's cards lost.

'There now, I'd like to beat that card,' said Lúkhnov of a card the fat landowner, who was staking half-rubles, had put down.

"You beat Ilyín's, never mind me!' remarked the squire.

And indeed Ilyín's cards lost more often than any of the others. He would tear up the losing card nervously under the table and choose another with trembling fingers. Túrbin rose from the sofa and asked the Greek to let him sit by the banker. The Greek moved to another place, the count took his chair and began watching Lúkhnov's hands attentively, not taking his eyes off them.

'Ilyín!' he suddenly said in his usual voice, which quite unintentionally drowned all the others. 'Why do you keep to a routine? You don't know how to play.'

'It's all the same how one plays.'

'But you're sure to lose that way. Let me play for you.'

'No, please excuse me. I always do it myself. Play for yourself if you like.'

'I said I should not play for myself, but I should like to play for you. I am vexed that you are losing.'

'I suppose it's my fate.'

The count was silent, but leaning on his elbows he again gazed intently at the banker's hands.

'Abominable!' he suddenly said in a loud, long-drawn tone. Lúkhnov glanced at him.

'Abominable, quite abominable!' he repeated still louder, looking straight into Lúkhnov's eyes.

The game continued.

'It is not right!' Túrbin remarked again, just as Lúkhnov beat a heavily-backed card of Ilyín's.

'What is it you don't like, Count?' inquired the banker with polite indifference.

'This!—that you let Ilyín win his simples and beat his corners. That's what's bad.'

Lúkhnov made a slight movement with his brows and shoulders, expressing the advisability of submitting to fate in everything, and continued to play.

'Blücher!' shouted the count, rising and whistling to the dog. 'At him!' he added quickly.

Blücher, bumping his back against the sofa as he leapt from under it and nearly upsetting the garrison officer, ran to his master and growled, looking round at everyone and moving his tail as if asking, 'Who is misbehaving here, eh?'

Lúkhnov put down his cards and moved his chair to one side.

'One can't play like that,' he said. 'I hate dogs. What kind of a game is it when you bring a whole pack of hounds in here?'

'Especially a dog like that. I believe they are called "leeches",' chimed in the garrison officer.

'Well, are we going to play or not, Michael Vasílich?' said Lúkhnov to their host.

'Please don't interfere with us, Count,' said Ilyín, turning to Túrbin.

'Come here a minute,' said Túrbin, taking Ilyín's arm and going behind the partition with him.

The count's words, spoken in his usual tone, were distinctly audible from there. His voice always carried across three rooms.

'Are you daft, eh? Don't you see that that gentleman in spectacles is a sharper of the first water?'

'Come now, enough! What are you saying?'

'No enough about it! Stop playing, I tell you. It's nothing to me. Another time I'd pluck you myself, but somehow I'm sorry to see you fleeced. And maybe you have Crown money too?'

'No . . . why do you imagine such things?'

'Ah, my lad, I've been that way myself so I know all those sharpers' tricks. I tell you the one in spectacles is a sharper. Stop playing! I ask you as a comrade.'

'Well then, I'll only finish this one deal.'

'I know what "one deal" means. Well, we'll see.'

They went back. In that one deal Ilyín put down so many cards and so many of them were beaten that he lost a large amount.

Túrbin put his hands in the middle of the table. 'Now stop it! Come along.'

'No, I can't. Leave me alone, do!' said Ilyín, irritably shuffling some bent cards without looking at Túrbin.

'Well, go to the devil! Go on losing for certain, if that pleases you. It's time for me to be off. Let's go to the Marshal's, Zavalshévski.'

They went out. All remained silent and Lúkhnov dealt no more cards until the sound of their steps and of Blücher's claws on the passage floor had died away.

'What a devil of a fellow!' said the landowner laughing.

'Well, he won't interfere now,' remarked the garrison officer hastily, and still in a whisper.

And the play continued.

IV

The band, composed of some of the Marshal's serfs standing in the pantry—which had been cleared out for the occasion—with their coat-sleeves turned up ready, had at a given signal struck up the old polonaise, 'Alexander, 'Lizabeth', and under the bright soft light of the wax-candles a Governor-General of Catherine's days, with a star on his breast, arm-in-arm with the Marshal's skinny wife, and the rest of the local grandees with their partners, had begun slowly gliding over the parquet floor of the large dancing-room in various combinations and variations, when Zavalshévski entered, wearing stockings and pumps and a blue swallow-tail coat with an immense and padded collar, and exhaling a strong smell of the frangipane with which the facings of his coat, his handkerchief, and his moustaches, were abundantly sprinkled. The handsome hussar who came with him wore tight-fitting light-blue riding-breeches and a gold-embroidered scarlet coat on which a Vladímir cross and an 1812 medal[1] were fastened. The count was not tall but remarkably well built. His clear blue and exceedingly brilliant eyes, and thick, closely curling, dark-brown hair, gave a remarkable character to his beauty. His arrival at the ball was expected, for the handsome young man who had seen him at the hotel had already prepared the Marshal for it. Various impressions had been produced by the news, for the most part not altogether pleasant.

'It's not unlikely that this youngster will hold us up to ridicule,' was the opinion of the men and of the older women. 'What if he should run away with me?' was more or less in the minds of the younger ladies, married or unmarried.

As soon as the polonaise was over and the couples after bowing to one another had separated—the women into one group and the men into another—Zavalshévski, proud and happy, introduced the count to their hostess.

The Marshal's wife, feeling an inner trepidation lest this hussar should treat her in some scandalous manner before everybody, turned away haughtily and contemptuously as she said: 'Very pleased, I hope you will dance,' and then gave him a distrustful look that said, 'Now, if you offend a woman it will show me that you are a perfect villain.' The count however soon conquered her prejudices by his amiability, attentive manner, and handsome gay appearance, so that five minutes later the expression on the face of the Marshal's wife told the company: 'I know how to manage such gentlemen. He immediately understood with whom he had to deal, and now he'll be charming to me for the rest of the evening.' Moreover at that moment the governor of the town, who had known the count's father, came up to him and very affably took him aside for a talk, which still further calmed the provincial public and raised the count in its estimation. After that Zavalshévski introduced the count to his sister, a plump young widow whose large black eyes had not left the count from the moment he entered. The count asked her to dance the waltz the

---

[1] That is to say, a medal gained in the defence of his country against Napoleon.

band had just commenced, and the general prejudice was finally dispersed by the masterly way in which he danced.

'What a splendid dancer!' said a fat landed proprietress, watching his legs in their blue riding-breeches as they flitted across the room, and mentally counting 'one, two, three—one, two, three—splendid!'

'There he goes—jig, jig, jig,' said another, a visitor in the town whom local society did not consider genteel. 'How does he manage not to entangle his spurs? Wonderfully clever!'

The count's artistic dancing eclipsed the three best dancers of the province: the tall fair-haired adjutant of the governor, noted for the rapidity with which he danced and for holding his partner very close to him; the cavalryman, famous for the graceful swaying motion with which he waltzed and for the frequent but light tapping of his heels; and a civilian, of whom everybody said that though he was not very intellectual he was a first-rate dancer and the soul of every ball. In fact, from its very commencement this civilian would ask all the ladies in turn to dance, in the order in which they were sitting,[2] and never stopped for a moment except occasionally to wipe the perspiration from his weary but cheerful face with a very wet cambric handkerchief. The count eclipsed them all and danced with the three principal ladies: the tall one, rich, handsome, stupid; the one of middle height, thin and not very pretty but splendidly dressed; and the little one, who was plain but very clever. He danced with others too—with all the pretty ones, and there were many of these—but it was Zavalshévski's sister, the little widow, who pleased him best. With her he danced a quadrille, an *écossaise,* and a mazurka. When they were sitting down during the quadrille he began paying her many compliments; comparing her to Venus and Diana, to a rose, and to some other flower. But all these compliments only made the widow bend her white neck, lower her eyes and look at her white muslin dress, or pass her fan from hand to hand. But when she said: 'Don't, you're only joking, Count,'

---

[2] The custom was, not to dance a whole dance with one lady but to take a few turns round the room, conduct her to her seat, bow to her, thank her, and seek a fresh partner.

and other words to that effect, there was a note of such naïve simplicity and amusing silliness in her slightly guttural voice, that looking at her it really seemed that this was not a woman but a flower, and not a rose, but some gorgeous scentless rosy-white wild flower that had grown all alone out of a snowdrift in some very remote land.

This combination of naïveté and unconventionality with her fresh beauty created such a peculiar impression on the count that several times during the intervals of conversation, when gazing silently into her eyes or at the beautful outline of her neck and arms, the desire to seize her in his arms and cover her with kisses assailed him with such force that he had to make a serious effort to resist it. The widow noticed with pleasure the effect she was producing, yet something in the count's behaviour began to frighten and excite her, though the young hussar, despite his insinuating amiability, was respectful to a degree that in our days would be considered cloying. He ran to fetch almond-milk for her, picked up her handkerchief, snatched a chair from the hands of a scrofulous young squire who danced attendance on her, to hand it her more quickly, and so forth.

When he noticed that the society attentions of the day had little effect on the lady he tried to amuse her by telling her funny stories and assured her that he was ready to stand on his head, to crow like a cock, to jump out of the window or plunge into the water through a hole in the ice, if she ordered him to do so. This proved quite a success. The widow brightened up and burst into peals of laughter, showing lovely white teeth, and was quite satisfied with her cavalier. The count liked her more and more every minute, so that by the end of the quadrille he was seriously in love with her.

When, after the quadrille, her eighteen-year-old adorer of long standing came up to the widow (he was the same scrofulous young man from whom Túrbin had snatched the chair—a son of the richest local landed proprietor and not yet in government service) she received him with extreme coolness and did not show one-tenth of the confusion she had experienced with the count.

'Well, you are a fine fellow!' she said, looking all the time at Túrbin's back and unconsciously considering how many yards of gold cord it had taken to embroider his whole jacket. 'You are a good one! You promised to call and fetch me for a drive and bring me some comfits.'

'I did come, Anna Fëdorovna, but you had already gone, and I left some of the very best comfits for you,' said the young man, who—despite his tallness—spoke in a very high-pitched voice.

'You always find excuses! . . . I don't want your bonbons. Please don't imagine—'

'I see, Anna Fëdorovna, that you have changed towards me and I know why. But it's not right,' he added, evidently unable to finish his speech because a strong inward agitation caused his lips to quiver in a very strange and rapid manner.

Anna Fëdorovna did not listen to him, but continued to follow Túrbin with her eyes.

The master of the house, the stout, toothless, stately old Marshal, came up to the count, took him by the arm, and invited him into the study for a smoke and a drink. As soon as Túrbin left the room Anna Fëdorovna felt that there was absolutely nothing to do there and went out into the dressing-room arm-in-arm with a friend of hers, a bony, elderly, maiden lady.

'Well, is he nice?' asked the maiden lady.

'Only he bothers so!' Anna Fëdorovna replied walking up to the mirror and looking at herself.

Her face brightened, her eyes laughed, she even blushed, and suddenly, imitating the ballet-dancers she had seen during the elections, she twirled round on one foot, then laughed her guttural but pleasant laugh and even bent her knees and gave a jump.

'Just fancy, what a man! He actually asked me for a keepsake,' she said to her friend, 'but he will get no-o-o-thing.' She sang the last word and held up one finger in her kid glove which reached to her elbow.

In the study, where the Marshal had taken Túrbin, stood bottles of different sorts of vodka, liqueurs, champagne, and *zakúska.*[3] The nobility, walking about or sitting in a cloud of tobacco smoke, were talking about the elections.

'When the whole worshipful society of our nobility has honoured him by their choice,' said the newly elected Captain of Police who had already imbibed freely, 'he should on no account transgress in the face of the whole society—he ought never . . .'

The count's entrance interrupted the conversation. Everybody wished to be introduced to him and the Captain of Police especially kept pressing the count's hand between his own for a long time, and repeatedly asked him not to refuse to accompany him to the new restaurant where he was going to treat the gentlemen after the ball, and where the gipsies were going to sing. The count promised to come without fail, and drank some glasses of champagne with him.

'But why are you not dancing, gentlemen?' said the count, as he was about to leave the room.

'We are not dancers,' replied the Captain of Police, laughing. 'Wine is more in our line, Count. . . . And besides, I have seen all those young ladies grow up, Count! But I can walk through an *écossaise* now and then, Count . . . I can do it, Count.'

'Then come and walk through one now,' said Túrbin. 'It will brighten us up before going to hear the gipsies.'

'Very well, gentlemen! Let's come and gratify our host.'

And three or four of the noblemen who had been drinking in the study since the commencement of the ball, put on gloves of black kid or knitted silk, and with red faces were just about to follow the count into the ball-room when they were stopped by the scrofulous young man who, pale and hardly able to restrain his tears, accosted Túrbin.

'You think that because you are a count you can jostle peo-

---

[3] The *zakúska* ('little bite') consists of a choice of snacks: caviare, salt-fish, cheese, radishes, or what not, with small glasses of vodka or other spirits. It is sometimes served alone, but usually forms an appetizer laid out on a side table and partaken of immediately before dinner or supper. It answers somewhat to the *hors-d'oeuvre* of an English dinner.

ple about as if you were in the market-place,' he said, breathing with difficulty, 'but that is impolite . . .'

And again, do what he would, his quivering lips checked the flow of his words.

'What?' cried Túrbin, suddenly frowning. 'What? . . . You brat!' he cried, seizing him by the arms and squeezing them so that the blood rushed to the young man's head not so much from vexation as from fear. 'What? Do you want to fight? I am at your service!'

Hardly had Túrbin released the arms he had been squeezing so hard, than two nobles caught hold of them and dragged the young man towards the back door.

'What! Are you out of your mind? You must be tipsy! Suppose we were to tell your papa! What's the matter with you?' they said to him.

'No, I'm not tipsy, but he jostles one and does not apologize. He's a swine, that's what he is!' squealed the young man, now quite in tears.

But they did not listen to him and someone took him home.

On the other side the Captain of Police and Zavalshévski were exhorting Túrbin: 'Never mind him, Count, he's only a child. He still gets whipped, he's only sixteen. . . . What can have happened to him? What bee has stung him? And his father such a respectable man—and our candidate.'

'Well, let him go to the devil if he does not wish . . .'

And the count returned to the ball-room and danced the *écossaise* with the pretty widow as gaily as before, laughed with all his heart as he watched the steps performed by the gentlemen who had come with him out of the study, and burst into peals of laughter that rang across the room when the Captain of Police slipped and measured his full length in the midst of the dancers.

V

While the count was in the study Anna Fëdorovna had approached her brother, and supposing that she ought to pretend to be very little interested in the count began by asking:

'Who is that hussar who was dancing with me? Can you tell me, brother?'

The cavalryman explained to his sister as well as he could what a great man the hussar was, and told her at the same time that the count was only stopping in the town because his money had been stolen on the way, and that he himself had lent him a hundred rubles, but that that was not enough, so that perhaps 'sister' would lend another couple of hundred. Only Zavalshévski asked her on no account to mention the matter to anyone—especially not to the count. Anna Fëdorovna promised to send her brother the money that very day and to keep the affair secret, but somehow during the *écossaise* she felt a great longing herself to offer the count as much money as he wanted. She took a long time making up her mind, and blushed, but at last with a great effort broached the subject as follows:

'My brother tells me that a misfortune befell you on the road, Count, and that you have no money by you. If you need any, won't you take it from me? I should be so glad.'

But having said this, Anna Fëdorovna suddenly felt frightened of something and blushed. All gaiety instantly left the count's face.

'Your brother is a fool!' he said abruptly. 'You know when a man insults another man they fight; but when a woman insults a man, what does he do then—do you know?'

Poor Anna Fëdorovna's neck and ears grew red with confusion. She lowered her eyes and said nothing.

'He kisses the woman in public,' said the count in a low voice, leaning towards her ear. 'Allow me at least to kiss your little hand,' he added in a whisper after a prolonged silence, taking pity on his partner's confusion.

'But not now!' said Anna Fëdorovna, with a deep sigh.

'When then? I am leaving early to-morrow and you owe it me.'

'Well then it's impossible,' said Anna Fëdorovna with a smile.

'Only allow me a chance to meet you to-night to kiss your hand. I shall not fail to find an opportunity.'

'How can you find it?'

'That is not your business. In order to see you everything is possible. . . . It's agreed?'

'Agreed.'

The *écossaise* ended. After that they danced a mazurka and the count was quite wonderful: catching handkerchiefs, kneeling on one knee, striking his spurs together in a quite special Warsaw manner, so that all the old people left their game of boston and flocked into the ball-room to see, and the cavalryman, their best dancer, confessed himself eclipsed. Then they had supper after which they danced the 'Grandfather', and the ball began to break up. The count never took his eyes off the little widow. It was not pretence when he said he was ready to jump through a hole in the ice for her sake. Whether it was whim, or love, or obstinacy, all his mental powers that evening were concentrated on the one desire—to meet and love her. As soon as he noticed that Anna Fëdorovna was taking leave of her hostess he ran out to the footmen's room, and thence—without his fur cloak—into the courtyard to the place where the carriages stood.

'Anna Fëdorovna Záytseva's carriage!' he shouted.

A high four-seated closed carriage with lamps burning moved from its place and approached the porch.

'Stop!' he called to the coachman, and plunging knee-deep into the snow ran to the carriage.

'What do you want?' said the coachman.

'I want to get into the carriage,' replied the count opening the door and trying to get in while the carriage was moving. 'Stop, I tell you, you fool!'

'Stop, Váska!' shouted the coachman to the postilion, and pulled up the horses. 'What are you getting into other people's carriages for? This carriage belongs to my mistress, to Anna Fëdorovna, and not to your honour.'

'Shut up, you blockhead! Here's a ruble for you; get down and close the door,' said the count. But as the coachman did not stir he lifted the steps himself and, lowering the window, managed somehow to close the door. In the carriage, as in all old carriages, especially in those in which yellow galloon is

used, there was a musty odour something like the smell of de-
cayed and burnt bristles. The count's legs were wet with
snow up to the knees and felt very cold in his thin boots and
riding-breeches; in fact the winter cold penetrated his whole
body. The coachman grumbled on the box and seemed to be
preparing to get down. But the count neither heard nor felt
anything. His face was aflame and his heart beat fast. In his
nervous tension he seized the yellow window strap and leant
out of the side window, and all his being merged into one feeling of expectation.

This expectancy did not last long. Someone called from the
porch: 'Záytseva's carriage!' The coachman shook the reins,
the body of the carriage swayed on its high springs, and the
illuminated windows of the house ran one after another past
the carriage windows.

'Mind, fellow,' said the count to the coachman, putting his
head out of the front window, 'if you tell the footman I'm here,
I'll thrash you, but hold your tongue and you shall have another ten rubles.'

Hardly had he time to close the window before the body of
the carriage shook more violently and then stopped. He
pressed close into the corner, held his breath, and even shut
his eyes, so terrified was he lest anything should balk his passionate expectation. The door opened, the carriage steps fell
noisily one after the other, he heard the rustle of a woman's
dress, a smell of frangipane perfume filled the musty carriage,
quick little feet ran up the carriage steps, and Anna Fëdorovna, brushing the count's leg with the skirt of her cloak
which had come open, sank silently onto the seat beside him
breathing heavily.

Whether she saw him or not no one could tell, not even
Anna Fëdorovna herself, but when he took her hand and said:
'Well, now I will kiss your little hand,' [1] she showed very little
fear, gave no reply, but yielded her arm to him, which he
covered much higher than the top of her glove with kisses. The
carriage started.

---

[1] The same word (*ruká*) stands for hand or arm in Russian.

'Say something! Art thou angry?' he said.

She silently pressed into her corner, but suddenly something caused her to burst into tears and of her own accord she let her head fall on his breast.

VI

The newly elected Captain of Police and his guests the cavalryman and other nobles had long been listening to the gipsies and drinking in the new restaurant when the count, wearing a blue cloth cloak lined with bearskin which had belonged to Anna Fëdorovna's late husband, joined them.

'Sure, your excellency, we have been awaiting you impatiently!' said a dark cross-eyed gipsy, showing his white teeth, as he met the count at the very entrance and rushed to help him off with his cloak. 'We have not seen you since the fair at Lebedyáni . . . Stëshka is quite pining away for you.'

Stëshka, a young, graceful little gipsy with a brick-red glow on her brown face and deep, sparkling black eyes shaded by long lashes, also ran out to meet him.

'Ah, little Count! Dearest! Jewel! This is a joy!' she murmured between her teeth, smiling merrily.

Ilyúshka himself ran out to greet him, pretending to be very glad to see him. The old women, matrons, and maids, jumped from their places and surrounded the guest, some claiming him as a fellow godfather, some as brother by baptism.[1]

Túrbin kissed all the young gipsy girls on their lips; the old women and the men kissed him on his shoulder or hand. The noblemen were also glad of their visitor's arrival, especially as the carousal, having reached its zenith, was beginning to flag, and everyone was beginning to feel satiated. The wine having lost its stimulating effect on the nerves merely weighed on the stomach. Each one had already let off his store of swagger, and they were getting tired of one another; the songs had all been sung and had got mixed in everyone's head, leaving a

---

[1] In Russia god-parents and their god-children, and people having the same god-father or god-mother, were considered to be related.

noisy, dissolute impression behind. No matter what strange or dashing thing anyone did, it began to occur to everyone that there was nothing agreeable or funny in it. The Captain of Police, who lay in a shocking state on the floor at the feet of an old woman, began wriggling his legs and shouting: 'Champagne! . . . The Count's come! . . . Champagne! . . . He's come . . . now then, champagne! . . . I'll have a champagne bath and bathe in it! Noble gentlemen! . . . I love the society of our brave old nobility . . . Stëshka, sing *The Pathway.*'

The cavalryman was also rather tipsy, but in another way. He sat on a sofa in the corner very close to a tall handsome gipsy girl, Lyubásha; and feeling his eyes misty with drink he kept blinking and shaking his head and, repeating the same words over and over again in a whisper, besought the gipsy to fly with him somewhere. Lyubásha, smiling and listening as if what he said were very amusing and yet rather sad, glanced occasionally at her husband—the cross-eyed Sáshka who was standing behind the chair opposite her—and in reply to the cavalryman's declarations of love, stooped and whispering in his ear asked him to buy her some scent and ribbons on the quiet, so that the others should not notice.

'Hurrah!' cried the cavalryman when the count entered.

The handsome young man was pacing up and down the room with laboriously steady steps and a careworn expression on his face, warbling an air from *Il Seraglio.*

An elderly paterfamilias, who had been tempted by the persistent entreaties of the nobles to come and hear the gipsies, as they said that without him the thing would be worthless and it would be better not to go at all, was lying on a sofa where he had sunk as soon as he arrived, and no one was taking any notice of him. Some official or other who was also there had taken off his swallow-tail coat and was sitting up on the table, feet and all, ruffling his hair, and thereby showing that he was very much on the spree. As soon as the count entered, this official unbuttoned the collar of his shirt and got still farther onto the table. In general on Túrbin's arrival the carousal revived.

The gipsy girls, who had been wandering about the room, again gathered and sat down in a circle. The count took Stëshka, the leading singer, on his knee, and ordered more champagne.

Ilyúshka came and stood in front of Stëshka with his guitar, and the 'dance' commenced, i.e., the gipsy songs, *When you go along the Street, O Hussars!, Do you hear, do you know?*, and so on in a definite order. Stëshka sang admirably. The flexible sonorous contralto that flowed from her very chest, her smiles while singing, her laughing passionate eyes, and her foot that moved involuntarily in measure with the song, her wild shriek at the commencement of the chorus—all touched some powerful but rarely-reached chord. It was evident that she lived only in the song she was singing. Ilyúshka accompanied her on the guitar—his back, legs, smile, and whole being, expressing sympathy with the song—and eagerly watching her, raised and lowered his head as attentive and engrossed as though he heard the song for the first time. Then at the last melodious note he suddenly drew himself up, and as if feeling himself superior to everyone in the world, proudly and resolutely threw up his guitar with his foot, twirled it about, stamped, tossed back his hair, and looked round at the choir with a frown. His whole body from neck to heels began dancing in every muscle—and twenty energetic, powerful voices each trying to chime in more strongly and more strangely than the rest, rang through the air. The old women bobbed up and down on their chairs waving their handkerchiefs, showing their teeth, and vying with one another in their harmonious and measured shouts. The basses with strained necks and heads bent to one side boomed while standing behind the chairs.

When Stëshka took a high note Ilyúshka brought his guitar closer to her as if wishing to help her, and the handsome young man screamed with rapture, saying that now they were beginning the *bémols*.[2]

---

[2] *Bémol* is French for a flat; but in Russia many people knowing nothing of musical technicalities imagined it to have something to do with excellence in music.

When a dance was struck up and Dunyásha, advancing with quivering shoulders and bosom, twirled round in front of the count and glided onwards, Túrbin leapt up, threw off his jacket, and in his red shirt stepped jauntily with her in precise and measured step, accomplishing such things with his legs that the gipsies smiled with approval and glanced at one another.

The Captain of Police sat down like a Turk, beat his breast with his fist, and cried 'vivat!' and then, having caught hold of the count's leg, began to tell him that of two thousand rubles he now had only five hundred left, but that he could do anything he liked if only the count would allow it. The elderly paterfamilias awoke and wished to go away, but was not allowed to do so. The handsome young man began persuading a gipsy to waltz with him. The cavalryman, wishing to show off his intimacy with the count, rose and embraced Túrbin. 'Ah, my dear fellow,' he said, 'why didst thou leave us, eh?' The count was silent, evidently thinking of something else. 'Where did you go to? Ah, you rogue of a count, I know where you went to!'

For some reason this familiarity displeased Túrbin. Without a smile he looked silently into the cavalryman's face and suddenly launched at him such terrible and rude abuse that the cavalryman was pained, and for a while could not make up his mind whether to take the offence as a joke or seriously. At last he decided to take it as a joke, smiled, and went back to his gipsy, assuring her that he would certainly marry her after Easter. They sang another song and another, danced again, and 'hailed the guests', and everyone continued to imagine that he was enjoying it. There was no end to the champagne. The count drank a great deal. His eyes seemed to grow moist, but he was not unsteady. He danced even better than before, spoke firmly, even joined in the chorus extremely well, and chimed in when Stëshka sang *Friendship's Tender Emotions*. In the midst of a dance the landlord came in to ask the guests to return to their homes as it was getting on for three in the morning.

The count seized the landlord by the scruff of his neck and

ordered him to dance the Russian dance. The landlord refused. The count snatched up a bottle of champagne and having stood the landlord on his head and had him held in that
position, amidst general laughter, slowly emptied the bottle
over him.

It was beginning to dawn. Everyone looked pale and ex-
hausted except the count.

'Well, I must be starting for Moscow,' said he, suddenly
rising. 'Come along, all of you! Come and see me off . . . and
we'll have some tea together.'

All agreed except the paterfamilias (who was left behind
asleep), and crowding into three large sledges that stood at
the door, they all drove off to the hotel.

VII

'Get horses ready!' cried the count as he entered the saloon of
his hotel followed by the guests and gipsies. 'Sáshka!—not
gipsy Sáshka but my Sáshka—tell the superintendent I'll
thrash him if he gives me bad horses. And get us some tea.
Zavalshévski, look after the tea: I'm going to have a look at
Ilyín and see how he's getting on . . .' added Túrbin, and
went along the passage towards the uhlan's room.

Ilyín had just finished playing, and having lost his last
kopék was lying face downwards on the sofa, pulling one hair
after another from its torn horse-hair cover, putting them in his
mouth, biting them in two and spitting them out again.

Two tallow candles, one of which had burnt down to the
paper in the socket, stood on the card-strewn table and feebly
wrestled with the morning light that crept in through the
window. There were no ideas in Ilyín's head: a dense mist of
gambling passion shrouded all his faculties, he did not even
feel penitent. He made one attempt to think of what he should
do now: how being penniless he could get away, how he
could repay the fifteen thousand rubles of Crown money,
what his regimental commander would say, what his mother
and his comrades would say, and he felt such terror and dis-

gust with himself that wishing to forget himself he rose and
began pacing up and down the room trying to step only where
the floor-boards joined, and began, once more, vividly to recall
every slightest detail of the course of play. He vividly imagined how he had begun to win back his money, how he with-
drew a nine and placed the king of spades over two thousand
rubles. A queen was dealt to the right, an ace to the left,
then the king of diamonds to the right and all was lost; but if,
say, a six had been dealt to the right and the king of diamonds to the left, he would have won everything back, would
have played once more double or quits, would have won fifteen thousand rubles, and would then have bought himself an
ambler from his regimental commander and another pair of
horses besides, and a phaeton. Well, and what then?—Well it
would have been a splendid, splendid thing!

And he lay down on the sofa again and began chewing the
horse-hair.

'Why are they singing in No. 7?' thought he. 'There must
be a spree on at Túrbin's. Shall I go in and have a good
drink?'

At this moment the count entered.

'Well, old fellow, cleaned out, are you? Eh?' cried he.

'I'll pretend to be asleep,' thought Ilyín, 'or else I shall have
to speak to him, and I want to sleep.'

Túrbin, however, came up and stroked his head.

'Well, my dear friend, cleaned out—lost everything? Tell
me.'

Ilyín gave no answer.

The count pulled his arm.

'I have lost. But what is that to you?' muttered Ilyín in a
sleepy, indifferent, discontented voice, without changing his
position.

'Everything?'

'Well—yes. What of it? Everything. What is it to you?'

'Listen. Tell me the truth as to a comrade,' said the count,
inclined to tenderness by the influence of the wine he had
drunk and continuing to stroke Ilyín's hair. 'I have really taken
a liking to you. Tell me the truth. If you have lost Crown

money I'll get you out of your scrape: it will soon be too late.
. . . Had you Crown money?'

Ilyín jumped up from the sofa.

'Well then, if you wish me to tell you, don't speak to me,
because . . . please don't speak to me. . . . To shoot myself is the only thing!' said Ilyín, with real despair, and his
head fell on his hands and he burst into tears, though but a
moment before he had been calmly thinking about amblers.

'What pretty girlishness! Where's the man who has not done
the like? It's not such a calamity; perhaps we can mend it.
Wait for me here.'

The count left the room.

'Where is Squire Lúkhnov's room?' he asked the boots.

The boots offered to show him the way. In spite of the
valet's remark that his master had only just returned and was
undressing, the count went in. Lúkhnov was sitting at a table
in his dressing-gown counting several packets of paper money
that lay before him. A bottle of Rhine wine, of which he was
very fond, stood on the table. After winning he permitted himself that pleasure. Lúkhnov looked coldly and sternly through
his spectacles at the count as though not recognizing him.

'You don't recognize me, I think?' said the count, resolutely
stepping up to the table.

Lúkhnov made a gesture of recognition, and said: 'What is
it you want?'

'I should like to play with you,' said Túrbin, sitting down on
the sofa.

'Now?'

'Yes.'

'Another time with pleasure, Count! But now I am tired and
am going to bed. Won't you have a glass of wine? It is famous
wine.'

'But I want to play a little—now.'

'I don't intend to play any more to-night. Perhaps some of
the other gentlemen will, but I won't. You must please excuse
me, Count.'

'Then you won't?'

Lúkhnov shrugged his shoulders to express his regret at his inability to comply with the count's desire.

'Not on any account?'

The same shrug.

'But I particularly request it. . . . Well, will you play?'

Silence.

'Will you play?' the count asked again. 'Mind!'

The same silence and a rapid glance over the spectacles at the count's face which was beginning to frown.

'Will you play?' shouted the count very loud, striking the table with his hand so that the bottle toppled over and the wine was spilt. 'You know you did not win fairly. . . . Will you play? I ask you for the third time.'

'I said I would not. This is really strange, Count! And it is not at all proper to come and hold a knife to a man's throat,' remarked Lúkhnov, not raising his eyes. A momentary silence followed during which the count's face grew paler and paler. Suddenly a terrible blow on the head stupefied Lúkhnov. He fell on the sofa trying to seize the money and uttered such a piercingly despairing cry as no one could have expected from so calm and imposing a person. Túrbin gathered up what money lay on the table, pushed aside the servant who ran in to his master's assistance, and left the room with rapid strides.

'If you want satisfaction I am at your service! I shall be in my room for another half-hour,' said the count, returning to Lúkhnov's door.

'Thief! Robber! I'll have the law on you . . .' was all that was audible from the room.

Ilyín, who had paid no attention to the count's promise to help him, still lay as before on the sofa in his room choking with tears of despair. Consciousness of what had really happened, which the count's caresses and sympathy had evoked from behind the strange tangle of feelings, thoughts, and memories filling his soul, did not leave him. His youth, rich with hope, his honour, the respect of society, his dreams of love and friendship—all were utterly lost. The source of his tears began to run dry, a too passive feeling of hopelessness overcame him more and more, and thoughts of suicide, no longer arousing revulsion or horror, claimed his attention with increasing frequency. Just then the count's firm footsteps were heard.

In Túrbin's face traces of anger could still be seen, his hands shook a little, but his eyes beamed with kindly merriment and self-satisfaction.

'Here you are, it's won back!' he said, throwing several bundles of paper money on the table. 'See if it's all there and then make haste and come into the saloon. I am just leaving,' he added, as though not noticing the joy and gratitude and extreme agitation on Ilyín's face, and whistling a gipsy song he left the room.

VIII

Sáshka, with a sash tied round his waist, announced that the horses were ready, but insisted that the count's cloak, which, he said, with its fur collar was worth three hundred rubles, should be recovered, and the shabby blue one returned to the rascal who had changed it for the count's at the Marshal's; but Túrbin told him there was no need to look for the cloak, and went to his room to change his clothes.

The cavalryman kept hiccoughing as he sat silent beside his gipsy girl. The Captain of Police called for vodka, and invited everyone to come at once and have breakfast with him, promising that his wife would certainly dance with the gipsies. The handsome young man was profoundly explaining to Ilyúshka that there is more soulfulness in pianoforte music, and that it is not possible to play *bémols* on a guitar. The official sat in a corner sadly drinking his tea, and in the daylight seemed ashamed of his debauchery. The gipsies were disputing among themselves in their own tongue as to 'hailing the guests' again, which Stëshka opposed, saying that the *baroráy* (in gipsy language count or prince or, more literally, 'great gentleman') would be angry. In general the last embers of the debauch were dying down in everyone.

'Well, one farewell song, and then off home!' said the count, entering the parlour in travelling dress, fresh, merry, and handsomer than ever.

The gipsies again formed their circle and were just ready to begin when Ilyín entered with a packet of paper money in his hand and took the count aside.

'I only had fifteen thousand rubles of Crown money and you have given me sixteen thousand three hundred,' he said, 'so this is yours.'

'That's a good thing. Give it here!'

Ilyín gave him the money and, looking timidly at the count, opened his lips to say something, but only blushed till tears came into his eyes and seizing the count's hand began to press it.

'You be off! . . . Ilyúshka! Listen! Here's some money for you, but you must accompany me out of the town with songs!' and he threw onto the guitar the thirteen hundred rubles Ilyín had brought him. But the count quite forgot to repay the hundred rubles he had borrowed of the cavalryman the day before.

It was already ten o'clock in the morning. The sun had risen above the roofs of the houses. People were moving about in the streets. The tradesmen had long since opened their shops. Noblemen and officials were driving through the streets and ladies were shopping in the bazaar, when the whole gipsy band, with the Captain of Police, the cavalryman, the handsome young man, Ilyín, and the count in the blue bearskin cloak, came out into the hotel porch.

It was a sunny day and a thaw had set in. The large postsledges, each drawn by three horses with their tails tied up tight, drove up to the porch splashing through the mud and the whole lively party took their places. The count, Ilyín, Stëshka, and Ilyúshka, with Sáshka the count's orderly, got into the first sledge. Blücher was beside himself, and wagged his tail, barking at the shaft-horse. The other gentlemen got into the two other sledges with the rest of the gipsy men and women. The tróykas got abreast as they left the hotel and the gipsies struck up in chorus.

The tróykas with their songs and bells—forcing every vehicle they met right onto the pavements—dashed through the whole town right to the town gates.

The tradesmen and passers-by who did not know them, and especially those who did, were not a little astonished when they saw the noblemen driving through the streets in broad daylight with gipsy girls and tipsy gipsy men, singing.

When they had passed the town gates the tróykas stopped and everyone began bidding the count farewell.

Ilyín, who had drunk a good deal at the leave-taking and had himself been driving the sledge all the way, suddenly became very sad, begged the count to stay another day, and when he found that this was not possible, rushed quite unexpectedly at his new friend, kissed him and promised with tears to try to exchange into the hussar regiment the count was serving in as soon as he got back. The count was particularly gay; he tumbled the calvaryman, who had become very familiar in the morning, into a snowdrift; set Blücher at the Captain of Police, took Stëshka in his arms and wished to carry her off to Moscow, and finally jumped into his sledge and made Blücher, who wanted to stand up in the middle, sit down by his side. Sáshka jumped on the box after having again asked the cavalryman to recover the count's cloak from *them,* and to send it on. The count cried, 'Go!', took off his cap, waved it over his head, and whistled to the horses like a post-boy. The tróykas drove off in their different directions.

A monotonous snow-covered plain stretched far in front with a dirty yellowish road winding through it. The bright sunshine—playfully sparkling on the thawing snow which was coated with a transparent crust of ice—was pleasantly warm to one's face and back. Steam rose thickly from the sweating horses. The bell tinkled merrily. A peasant with a loaded sledge that kept gliding to the side of the road, got hurriedly out of the way, jerking his rope reins and plashing with his wet bast shoes as he ran along the thawing road. A fat red-faced peasant woman, with a baby wrapped in the bosom of her sheepskin cloak, sat in another laden sledge, urging on a thin-tailed, jaded white horse with the ends of the reins. The count suddenly thought of Anna Fëdorovna.

'Turn back!' he shouted.

The driver did not at once understand.

'Turn back! Back to town! Be quick!'

The tróyka passed the town gates once more, and drove briskly up to the wooden porch of Anna Fëdorovna's house. The count ran quickly up the steps, passed through the vestibule and the drawing-room, and having found the widow still asleep, took her in his arms, lifted her out of bed, kissed her sleepy eyes, and ran quickly back. Anna Fëdorovna, only half awake, licked her lips and asked, 'What has happened?' The count jumped into his sledge, shouted to the driver, and with no further delay and without even a thought of Lúkhnov, or the widow, or Stëshka, but only of what awaited him in Moscow, left the town of K—— for ever.

❄   ❄   ❄   ❄

IX

More than twenty years had gone by. Much water had flowed away, many people had died, many been born, many had grown up or grown old; still more ideas had been born and had died, much that was old and beautiful and much that was old and bad had perished; much that was beautiful and new had grown up and still more that was immature, monstrous, and new, had come into God's world.

Count Fëdor Túrbin had been killed long ago in a duel by some foreigner he had horse-whipped in the street. His son, physically as like him as one drop of water to another, was a handsome young man already twenty-three years old and serving in the Horse Guards. But morally the young Túrbin did not in the least resemble his father. There was not a shade of the impetuous, passionate and, to speak frankly, depraved propensities of the past age. Together with his intelligence, culture, and the gifted nature he had inherited a love of propriety and the comforts of life; a practical way of looking at men and affairs, reasonableness and prudence were his dis-

tinguishing characteristics. The young count had got on well
in the service and at twenty-three was already a lieutenant. At
the commencement of the war he made up his mind that he
would be more likely to secure promotion if he exchanged into
the active army, and so he entered an hussar regiment as captain and was soon in command of a squadron.

In May 1848[1] the S—— hussar regiment was marching to
the campaign through the province of K——, and the very
squadron young Count Túrbin commanded had to spend the
night in the village of Morózovka, Anna Fëdorovna's estate.

Anna Fëdorovna was still living, but was already so far
from young that she did not even consider herself young,
which means a good deal for a woman. She had grown very
fat, which is said to make a woman look younger, but deep
soft wrinkles were apparent on her white plumpness. She
never went to town now, it was an effort for her even to get
into her carriage, but she was still just as kind-hearted and as
silly as ever (now that her beauty no longer biases one, the
truth may be told). With her lived her twenty-three-year-old
daughter Lisa, a Russian country belle, and her brother—
our acquaintance the cavalryman—who had good-naturedly
squandered the whole of his small fortune and had found a
home for his old age with Anna Fëdorovna. His hair was quite
grey and his upper lip had fallen in, but the moustache above
it was still carefully blackened. His back was bent, and not
only his forehead and cheeks but even his nose and neck were
wrinkled, yet in the movements of his feeble crooked legs the
manner of a cavalryman was still perceptible.

The family and household sat in the small drawing-room of
the old house, with an open door leading out onto the veranda, and open windows overlooking the ancient star-shaped
garden with its lime-trees. Grey-haired Anna Fëdorovna, wearing a lilac jacket, sat on the sofa laying out cards on a round
mahogany table. Her old brother in his clean white trousers
and a blue coat had settled himself by the window and was

---

[1] Tolstóy seems here to antedate Russia's intervention in the Hungarian insurrection. The Russian army did not enter Hungary till
May 1849 and the war lasted till the end of September that year.

plaiting a cord out of white cotton with the aid of a wooden
fork—a pastime his niece had taught him and which he liked
very much, as he could no longer do anything and his eyes
were too weak for newspaper reading, his favourite occupation. Pímochka, Anna Fëdorovna's ward, sat by him learning a
lesson—Lisa helping her and at the same time making a goat's-
wool stocking for her uncle with wooden knitting needles. The
last rays of the setting sun, as usual at that hour, shone
through the lime-tree avenue and threw slanting gleams on
the farthest window and the what-not standing near it. It was
so quiet in the garden and the room that one could hear the
swift flutter of a swallow's wings outside the window, and
Anna Fëdorovna's soft sigh or the old man's slight groan as he
crossed his legs.

'How do they go? Show me, Lisa! I always forget,' said
Anna Fëdorovna, at a standstill in laying out her cards for
patience.

Without stopping her work Lisa went to her mother and
glanced at the cards:

'Ah, you've muddled them all, mamma dear!' she said, rearranging them. 'That's the way they should go. And what
you are trying your fortune about will still come true,' she
added, withdrawing a card so that it was not noticed.

'Ah yes, you always deceive me and say it has come out.'

'No really, it means . . . you'll succeed. It has come out."

'All right, all right, you sly puss! But isn't it time we had
tea?'

'I have ordered the samovar to be lit. I'll see to it at once.
Do you want to have it here? . . . Be quick and finish your
lesson, Pímochka, and let's have a run.'

And Lisa went to the door.

'Lisa, Lizzie!' said her uncle, looking intently at his fork. 'I
think I've dropped a stitch again—pick it up for me, there's a
dear.'

'Directly, directly! But I must give out a loaf of sugar to be
broken up.'

And really, three minutes later she ran back, went to her
uncle and pinched his ear.

'That's for dropping your stitches!' she said laughing, 'and you haven't done your task!'

'Well, well, never mind, never mind. Put it right—there's a little knot or something.'

Lisa took the fork, drew a pin out of her tippet—which thereupon the breeze coming in at the door blew slightly open —and managing somehow to pick up the stitch with the pin, pulled two loops through, and returned the fork to her uncle.

'Now give me a kiss for it,' she said, holding out her rosy cheek to him and pinning up her tippet. 'You shall have rum with your tea to-day. It's Friday, you know.'

And she again went into the tea-room.

'Come here and look, uncle, the hussars are coming!' she called from there in her clear voice.

Anna Fëdorovna came with her brother into the tea-room, the windows of which overlooked the village, to see the hussars. Very little was visible from the windows—only a crowd moving in a cloud of dust.

'It's a pity we have so little room, sister, and that the wing is not yet finished,' said the old man to Anna Fëdorovna. 'We might have invited the officers. Hussar officers are such splendid, gay young fellows, you know. It would have been good to see something of them.'

'Why of course, I should have been only too glad, brother; but you know yourself we have no room. There's my bedroom, Lisa's room, the drawing-room, and this room of yours, and that's all. Really now, where could we put them? The village elder's hut has been cleaned up for them: Michael Matvéev says it's quite clean now.'

'And we could have chosen a bridegroom for you from among them, Lizzie—a fine hussar!'

'I don't want an hussar; I'd rather have an uhlan. Weren't you in the uhlans, uncle? . . . I don't want to have anything to do with these hussars. They are all said to be desperate fellows.' And Lisa blushed a little but again laughed her musical laugh.

'Here comes Ustyúshka running; we must ask her what she has seen,' she added.

Anna Fëdorovna told her to call Ustyúshka.

'It's not in you to keep to your work, you must needs run off to see the soldiers,' said Anna Fëdorovna. 'Well, where have the officers put up?'

'In Erómkin's house, mistress. There are two of them, such handsome ones. One's a count, they say!'

'And what's his name?'

'Kazárov or Turbínov. . . . I'm sorry—I've forgotten.'

'What a fool; can't so much as tell us anything. You might at least have found out the name.'

'Well, I'll run back.'

'Yes, I know you're first-rate at that sort of thing. . . . No, let Daniel go. Tell him to go and ask whether the officers want anything, brother. One ought to show them some politeness after all. Say the mistress sent to inquire.'

The old people again sat down in the tea-room and Lisa went to the servants' room to put into a box the sugar that had been broken up. Ustyúshka was there telling about the hussars.

'Darling miss, what a handsome man that count is!' she said. 'A regular cherubim with black eyebrows. There now, if you had a bridegroom like that you would be a couple of the right sort.'

The other maids smiled approvingly; the old nurse sighed as she sat knitting at a window and even whispered a prayer, drawing in her breath.

'So you liked the hussars very much?' said Lisa. 'And you're a good one at telling what you've seen. Go, please, and bring some of the cranberry juice, Ustyúshka, to give the hussars something sour to drink.'

And Lisa, laughing, went out with the sugar basin in her hands.

'I should really like to have seen what that hussar is like,' she thought, 'brown or fair? And he would have been glad to make our acquaintance I should think. . . . And if he goes away he'll never know that I was here and thought about him. And how many such have already passed me by? Who sees me here except uncle and Ustyúshka? Whichever way I do my hair, whatever sleeves I put on, no one looks at me with pleasure,' she thought with a sigh as she looked at her plump white arm. 'I suppose he is tall, with large eyes, and certainly small black moustaches. . . . Here am I, more than twenty-two, and no one has fallen in love with me except pock-marked Iván Ipátich, and four years ago I was even prettier. . . . And so my girlhood has passed without gladdening anyone. Oh, poor, poor country lass that I am!'

Her mother's voice, calling her to pour out tea, roused the country lass from this momentary meditation. She lifted her head with a start and went into the tea-room.

The best results are often obtained accidentally, and the more one tries the worse things turn out. In the country, people rarely try to educate their children and therefore unwittingly usually give them an excellent education. This was particularly so in Lisa's case. Anna Fëdorovna, with her limited intellect and careless temperament, gave Lisa no education— did not teach her music or that very useful French language —but having accidentally borne a healthy pretty child by her deceased husband she gave her little daughter over to a wet-nurse and a dry-nurse, fed her, dressed her in cotton prints and goat-skin shoes, sent her out to walk and gather mushrooms and wild berries, engaged a student from the seminary to teach her reading, writing, and arithmetic, and when sixteen years had passed she casually found in Lisa a friend, an ever-kind-hearted, ever-cheerful soul, and an active housekeeper. Anna Fëdorovna, being kind-hearted, always had some children to bring up—either serf children or foundlings. Lisa began looking after them when she was ten years old: teaching them, dressing them, taking them to church, and checking them when they played too many pranks. Later on the decrepit kindly uncle, who had to be tended like a child, appeared on the scene. Then the servants and peasants came to the young lady with various requests and with their ailments, which latter she treated with elderberry, peppermint, and camphorated spirits. Then there was the household management which all fell on her shoulders of itself. Then an unsatisfied longing for love awoke and found its outlet only in Nature and religion. And Lisa accidentally grew into an active, good-natured, cheerful, self-reliant, pure, and deeply religious woman. It is true that she suffered a little from vanity when she saw neighbours standing by her in church wearing fashionable bonnets brought from K——, and sometimes she was vexed to tears by her old mother's whims and grumbling. She had dreams of love, too, in most absurd and sometimes crude forms, but these were dispersed by her useful activity which had grown into a necessity, and at the age of twenty-two there was not one spot or sting of remorse in the clear calm soul of the physically and morally beautifully developed maiden. Lisa was of medium height, plump rather than thin, her eyes were hazel, not large, and had slight shadows on the lower lids, and she had a long light-brown plait of hair. She walked with big steps and with a slight sway—a 'duck's waddle' as the saying is. Her face, when she was occupied and not agitated by anything in particular, seemed to say to everyone who looked into it: 'It is a joy to live in the world when one has someone to love and a clear conscience.' Even in moments of vexation, perplexity, alarm, or sorrow, in spite of herself there shone—through the tear in her eye, her frowning left eyebrow and her compressed lips—a kind straightforward spirit unspoilt by the intellect; it shone in the dimples of her cheeks, in the corners of her mouth, and in her beaming eyes accustomed to smile and to rejoice in life.

X

The air was still hot though the sun was setting when the squadron entered Morózovka. In front of them along the dusty village street trotted a brindled cow separated from its herd, looking round and now and then stopping and lowing, but never suspecting that all she had to do was to turn aside. The peasants—old men, women, and children, and the servants from the manor-house, crowded on both sides of the street and eagerly watched the hussars as the latter rode through a thick cloud of dust, curbing their horses which occasionally stamped and snorted. On the right of the squadron were two officers who sat their fine black horses carelessly. One was

Count Túrbin, the commander, the other a very young man
recently promoted from cadet, whose name was Pólozov.

An hussar in a white linen jacket came out of the best of
the huts, raised his cap, and went up to the officers.

'Where are the quarters assigned us?'

'For your Excellency?' answered the quartermaster-sergeant, with a start of his whole body. 'The village elder's
hut has been cleaned out. I wanted to get 'quarters at the
manor-house, but they say there is no room there. The proprietress is such a vixen.'

'All right!' said the count, dismounting and stretching his
legs as he reached the village elder's hut. 'And has my phaeton
arrived?'

'It has deigned to arrive, your Excellency!' answered the
quartermaster-sergeant, pointing with his cap to the leather
body of a carriage visible through the gateway, and rushing
forward to the entrance of the hut, which was thronged with
members of the peasant family collected to look at the officer.
He even pushed one old woman over as he briskly opened the
door of the freshly cleaned hut and stepped aside to let
the count pass.

The hut was fairly large and roomy but not very clean. The
German valet, dressed like a gentleman, stood inside sorting
the linen in a portmanteau after having set up an iron bed-
stead and made the bed.

'Faugh, what filthy lodgings!' said the count with vexation.
'Couldn't you have found anything better at some gentleman's house, Dyádenko?'

'If your Excellency desires it I will try at the manor-house,'
answered the quartermaster-sergeant, 'but it isn't up to much
—doesn't look much better than a hut.'

'Never mind now. Go away.'

And the count lay down on the bed and threw his arms
behind his head.

'Johann!' he called to his valet. 'You've made a lump in
the middle again! How is it you can't make a bed properly?'

Johann came up to put it right.

'No, never mind now. But where is my dressing-gown?' said the count in a dissatisfied tone.

The valet handed him the dressing-gown. Before putting it on the count examined the front.

'I thought so, that spot is not cleaned off. Could anyone be a worse servant than you?' he added, pulling the dressing-gown out of the valet's hands and putting it on. 'Tell me, do you do it on purpose? . . . Is the tea ready?'

'I have not had time,' said Johann.

'Fool!'

After that the count took up the French novel placed ready for him and read for some time in silence: Johann went out into the passage to prepare the samovar. The count was obviously in a bad temper, probably caused by fatigue, a dusty face, tight clothing, and an empty stomach.

'Johann!' he cried again, 'bring me the account for those ten rubles. What did you buy in the town?'

He looked over the account handed him, and made some dissatisfied remarks about the dearness of the things purchased.

'Serve rum with my tea.'

'I didn't buy any rum,' said Johann.

'That's good! . . . How many times have I told you to have rum?'

'I hadn't enough money.'

'Then why didn't Pólozov buy some? You should have got some from his man.'

'Cornet Pólozov? I don't know. He bought the tea and the sugar.'

'Idiot! . . . Get out! . . . You are the only man who knows how to make me lose my patience. . . . You know that on a march I always have rum with my tea.'

'Here are two letters for you from the staff,' said the valet.

The count opened his letters and began reading them without rising. The cornet, having quartered the squadron, came in with a merry face.

'Well, how is it, Túrbin? It seems very nice here. But I must confess I'm tired. It was hot.'

'Very nice! . . . A filthy stinking hut, and thanks to your lordship no rum; your blockhead didn't buy any, nor did this one. You might at least have mentioned it.'

And he continued to read his letter. When he had finished he rolled it into a ball and threw it on the floor.

In the passage the cornet was meanwhile saying to his orderly in a whisper: 'Why didn't you buy any rum? You had money enough, you know.'

'But why should we buy everything? As it is I pay for everything, while his German does nothing but smoke his pipe.'

It was evident that the count's second letter was not unpleasant, for he smiled as he read it.

'Who is it from?' asked Pólozov, returning to the room and beginning to arrange a sleeping-place for himself on some boards by the oven.

'From Mina,' answered the count gaily, handing him the letter. 'Do you want to see it? What a delightful woman she is! . . . Really she's much better than our young ladies. . . . Just see how much feeling and wit there is in that letter. Only one thing is bad—she's asking for money.'

'Yes, that's bad,' said the cornet.

'It's true I promised her some, but then this campaign came on, and besides. . . . However if I remain in command of the squadron another three months I'll send her some. It's worth it, really; such a charming creature, eh?' said he, watching the expression on Pólozov's face as he read the letter.

'Dreadfully ungrammatical, but very nice, and it seems as if she really loves you,' said the cornet.

'H'm . . . I should think so! It's only women of that kind who love sincerely when once they do love.'

'And who was the other letter from?' asked the cornet, handing back the one he had read.

'Oh, that . . . there's a man, a nasty beast who won from me at cards, and he's reminding me of it for the third time. . . . I can't let him have it at present. . . . A stupid letter!' said the count, evidently vexed at the recollection.

After this both officers were silent for a while. The cornet, who was evidently under the count's influence, glanced now and then at the handsome though clouded countenance of Túrbin—who was looking fixedly through the window—and drank his tea in silence, not venturing to start a conversation.

'But d'you know, it may turn out capitally,' said the count, suddenly turning to Pólozov with a shake of his head. 'Supposing we get promotions by seniority this year, and take part in an action besides, I may get ahead of my own captains in the Guards.'

The conversation was still on the same topic and they were drinking their second tumblers of tea, when old Daniel entered and delivered Anna Fëdorovna's message.

'And I was also to inquire if you are not Count Fëdor Iványch Túrbin's son?' added Daniel on his own account, having learnt the count's name and remembering the deceased count's sojourn in the town of K——. 'Our mistress, Anna Fëdorovna, was very well acquainted with him.'

'He was my father. And tell your mistress I am very much obliged to her. We want nothing, but say we told you to ask whether we could not have a cleaner room somewhere—in the manor-house, or anywhere.'

'Now, why did you do that?' asked Pólozov when Daniel had gone. 'What does it matter? Just for one night—what does it matter? And they will be inconveniencing themselves.'

'What an idea! I think we've had our share of smoky huts! . . . It's easy to see you're not a practical man. Why not seize the opportunity when we can, and live like human beings for at least one night? And on the contrary they will be very pleased to have us. . . . The worst of it is, if this lady really knew my father . . .' continued the count with a smile which displayed his glistening white teeth. 'I always have to feel ashamed of my departed papa. There is always some scandalous story or other, or some debt he has left. That is why I hate meeting these acquaintances of my father's. However that was the way in those days,' he added, growing serious.

'Did I ever tell you,' said Pólozov, 'I once met an uhlan

brigade-commander, Ilyín? He was very anxious to meet you. He is awfully fond of your father.'

'That Ilyín is an awful good-for-nothing, I believe. But the worst of it is that these good people, who assure me that they knew my father in order to make my acquaintance, while pretending to be very pleasant, relate such tales about my father as make me ashamed to listen. It is true—I don't deceive myself, but look at things dispassionately—that he had too ardent a nature and sometimes did things that were not nice. However that was the way in those times. In our days he might have turned out a very successful man, for to do him justice he had extraordinary capacities.'

A quarter of an hour later the servant came back with a request from the proprietress that they would be so good as to spend the night at her house.

XI

Having heard that the hussar officer was the son of Count Fëdor Túrbin, Anna Fëdorovna was all in a flutter.

'Oh, dear me! The darling boy! . . . Daniel, run quickly and say your mistress asks them to her house!' she began, jumping up and hurrying with quick steps to the servants' room. 'Lizzie! Ustyúshka! . . . Your room must be got ready, Lisa, you can move into your uncle's room. And you, brother, you won't mind sleeping in the drawing-room, will you? It's only for one night.'

'I don't mind, sister. I can sleep on the floor.'

'He must be handsome if he's like his father. Only to have a look at him, the darling. . . . You must have a good look at him, Lisa! The father *was* handsome. . . . Where are you taking that table to? Leave it here,' said Anna Fëdorovna, bustling about. 'Bring two beds—take one from the foreman's —and get the crystal candlestick, the one my brother gave me on my birthday—it's on the what-not—and put a stearine candle in it.'

At last everything was ready. In spite of her mother's interference Lisa arranged the room for the two officers her own way. She took out clean bed-clothes scented with mignon-ette, made the beds, had candles and a bottle of water placed on a small table near by, fumigated the servants' room with scented paper, and moved her own little bed into her uncle's room. Anna Fëdorovna quieted down a little, settled in her own place, and even took up the cards again, but instead of laying them out she leaned her plump elbow on the table and grew thoughtful.

'Ah, time, time, how it flies!' she whispered to herself. 'Is it so long ago? It is as if I could see him now. Ah, he was a madcap! . . .' and tears came into her eyes. 'And now there's Lizzie . . . but still, she's not what I was at her age—she's a nice girl but she's not like that . . .'

'Lisa you should put on your *mousseline-de-laine* dress for the evening.'

'Why, mother, you are not going to ask them in to see us? Better not,' said Lisa, unable to master her excitement at the thought of meeting the officers: 'Better not, mamma!'

And really her desire to see them was less strong than her fear of the agitating joy she imagined awaited her.

'Maybe they themselves will wish to make our acquaintance, Lizzie!' said Anna Fëdorovna, stroking her head and thinking: 'No, her hair is not what mine was at her age. . . . Oh, Lizzie, how I should like you to. . . .' And she really did very earnestly desire something for her daughter. But she could not imagine a marriage with the count, and she could not desire for her daughter relations such as she had had with the father; but still she did desire something very much. She may have longed to relive in the soul of her daughter what she had experienced with him who was dead.

The old cavalryman was also somewhat excited by the arrival of the count. He locked himself into his room and emerged a quarter of an hour later in a Hungarian jacket and pale-blue trousers, and entered the room prepared for the visitors with the bashfully pleased expression of a girl who puts on a ball-dress for the first time in her life.

"I'll have a look at the hussars of to-day, sister! The late count was indeed a true hussar. I'll see, I'll see!'

The officers had already reached the room assigned to them through the back entrance.

'There, you see! Isn't this better than that hut with the cock-roaches?' said the count, lying down as he was in his dusty boots, on the bed that had been prepared for him.

'Of course it's better, but still, to be indebted to the propri-etress . . .'

'Oh, what nonsense! One must be practical in all things. They're awfully pleased, I'm sure . . . Eh, you there!' he cried. 'Ask for something to hang over this window, or it will be draughty in the night.'

At this moment the old man came in to make the officers' acquaintance. Of course, though he did it with a slight blush, he did not omit to say that he and the old count had been comrades, that he had enjoyed the count's favour, and he even added that he had more than once been under obliga-tions to the deceased. What obligations he referred to, whether it was the count's omission to repay the hundred ru-bles he had borrowed, or his throwing him into a snow-heap, or swearing at him, the old man quite omitted to ex-plain. The young count was very polite to the old cavalryman and thanked him for the night's lodging.

'You must excuse us if it is not luxurious, Count,' (he very nearly said 'your Excellency', so unaccustomed had he be-come to conversing with important persons), 'my sister's house is so small. But we'll hang something up there directly and it will be all right,' added the old man, and on the plea of seeing about a curtain, but mainly because he was in a hurry to give an account of the officers, he bowed and left the room.

The pretty Ustyúshka came in with her mistress's shawl to cover the window, and besides, the mistress had told her to ask if the gentlemen would not like some tea.

The pleasant surroundings seemed to have a good influence on the count's spirits. He smiled merrily, joked with Ustyúshka in such a way that she even called him a scamp, asked whether her young lady was pretty, and in answer to her question whether they would have any tea he said she might bring them some tea, but the chief thing was that, their own supper not being ready yet, perhaps they might have some vodka and something to eat, and some sherry if there was any.

The uncle was in raptures over the young count's politeness, and praised the new generation of officers to the skies, saying that the present men were incomparably superior to the former generation.

Anna Fëdorovna did not agree—no one could be superior to Count Fëdor Iványch Túrbin—and at last she grew seriously angry and drily remarked, 'The one who has last stroked you, brother, is always the best. . . . Of course people are cleverer nowadays, but Count Fëdor Iványch danced the *écossaise* in such a way and was so amiable that everybody lost their heads about him, though he paid attention to no one but me. So you see, there were good people in the old days too.'

Here came the news of the demand for vodka, light refreshments, and sherry.

'There now, brother, you never do the right thing; you should have ordered supper,' began Anna Fëdorovna. 'Lisa, see to it, dear!'

Lisa ran to the larder to get some pickled mushrooms and fresh butter, and the cook was ordered to make rissoles.

'But how about sherry? Have you any left, brother?'

'No sister, I never had any.'

'How's that? Why, what is it you take with your tea?'

'That's rum, Anna Fëdorovna.'

'Isn't it all the same? Give them some of that—it's all the same. But wouldn't it after all be best to ask them in here, brother? You know all about it—I don't think they would take offence.'

The cavalryman declared he would warrant that the count was too good-natured to refuse and that he would certainly fetch them. Anna Fëdorovna went and put on a silk dress and a new cap for some reason, but Lisa was so busy that she had no time to change her pink gingham dress with the wide sleeves. Besides, she was terribly excited; she felt as if something wonderful was awaiting her and as if a low black cloud

hung over her soul. It seemed to her that this handsome hussar
count must be a perfectly new, incomprehensible, but beautiful being. His character, his habits, his speech, must all be so
unusual, so different from anything she had ever met. All he
thinks or says must be wise and right, all he does must be
honourable, his whole appearance must be beautiful. She
never doubted that. Had he asked not merely for refreshments and sherry, but for a bath of sage-brandy and perfume, she would not have been surprised and would not have
blamed him, but would have been firmly convinced that it
was right and necessary.

The count at once agreed when the cavalryman informed
them of his sister's wish. He brushed his hair, put on his uniform, and took his cigar-case.

'Come along,' he said to Pólozov.

'Really it would be better not to go,' answered the cornet.
'*Ils feront des frais pour nous recevoir.*' [1]

'Nonsense, they will be only too happy! Besides, I have
made some inquiries: there is a pretty daughter. . . . Come
along!' said the count, speaking in French.

'*Je vous en prie, messieurs!*' [2] said the cavalryman, merely to
make the officers feel that he also knew French and had understood what they had said.

XII

Lisa, afraid to look at the officers, blushed and cast down her
eyes and pretended to be busy filling the teapot when they
entered the room. Anna Fëdorovna on the contrary jumped
up hurriedly, bowed, and not taking her eyes off the count,
began talking to him—now saying how unusually like his
father he was, now introducing her daughter to him, now offering him tea, jam, or home-made sweetmeats. No one paid
any attention to the cornet because of his modest appearance,
and he was very glad of it, for he was, as far as propriety al-

---

[1] They will be putting themselves to expense on our account.
[2] If you please, gentlemen.

lowed, gazing at Lisa and minutely examining her beauty which evidently took him by surprise. The uncle, listening to his sister's conversation with the count, awaited, with the words ready on his lips, an opportunity to narrate his cavalry reminiscences. During tea the count lit a cigar and Lisa found it difficult to prevent herself from coughing. He was very talkative and amiable, at first slipping his stories into the intervals of Anna Fëdorovna's ever-flowing speech, but at last monopolizing the conversation. One thing struck his hearers as strange; in his stories he often used words not considered improper in the society he belonged to, but which here sounded rather too bold and somewhat frightened Anna Fëdorovna and made Lisa blush to her ears; but the count did not notice it and remained calmly natural and amiable.

Lisa silently filled the tumblers, which she did not give into the visitors' hands but placed on the table near them, not having quite recovered from her excitement, and she listened eagerly to the count's remarks. His stories, which were not very deep, and the hesitation in his speech gradually calmed her. She did not hear from him the very clever things she had expected, nor did she see that elegance in everything which she had vaguely expected to find in him. At the third glass of tea, after her bashful eyes had once met his and he had not looked down but had continued to look at her too quietly and with a slight smile, she even felt rather inimically disposed towards him, and soon found that not only was there nothing especial about him but that he was in no wise different from other people she had met, that there was no need to be afraid of him though his nails were long and clean, and that there was not even any special beauty in him. Lisa suddenly relinquished her dream, not without some inward pain, and grew calmer, and only the gaze of the taciturn cornet which she felt fixed upon her, disquieted her.

'Perhaps it's not this one, but that one!' she thought.

XIII

After tea the old lady asked the visitors into the drawing-room and again sat down in her old place.

'But wouldn't you like to rest, Count?' she asked, and after receiving an answer in the negative continued: 'What can I do to entertain our dear guests? Do you play cards, Count? There now, brother, you should arrange something; arrange a set—'

'But you yourself play *préférence*,' [1] answered the cavalry-man. 'Why not all play? Will you play, Count? And you too?'

The officers expressed their readiness to do whatever their kind hosts desired.

Lisa brought her old pack of cards which she used for divining when her mother's swollen face would get well, whether her uncle would return the same day when he went to town, whether a neighbour would call to-day, and so on. These cards, though she had used them for a couple of months, were cleaner than those Anna Fëdorovna used to tell fortunes.

'But perhaps you won't play for small stakes?' inquired the uncle. 'Anna Fëdorovna and I play for half-kopeks. . . . And even so she wins all our money.'

'Oh any stakes you like—I shall be delighted,' replied the count.

'Well then, one kopek "assignats" [2] just for once, in honour

---

[1] In *préférence* partners play together as in whist. There is a method of scoring 'with tables' which increases the gains and losses of the players. The players compete in declaring the number of tricks the cards they hold will enable them to make. The highest bidder decides which suit is to be trumps and has to make the number of tricks he has declared, or be fined. A player declaring *misère* undertakes to make no tricks, and is fined (puts on a *remise*) for each trick he or she takes. 'Ace and king blank' means that a player holds the two highest cards and no others of a given suit.

[2] At the time of this story two currencies were in use simultaneously —the depreciated 'assignats' and the 'silver rubles', which like the 'assignats' were usually paper. The assignats had been introduced in Russia in 1768 and by the end of the Napoleonic wars were much depreciated. They fluctuated till 1841, when a new 'silver ruble' was introduced, the value of which was about 38 pence.

of our dear visitors! Let them beat me, an old woman!' said
Anna Fëdorovna, settling down in her arm-chair and arranging
her mantilla. 'And perhaps I'll win a ruble or so from them,'
thought she, having developed a slight passion for cards in her
old age.

'If you like, I'll teach you to play with "tables" and "*misère*",' said the count. 'It is capital.'

Everyone liked the new Petersburg way. The uncle was
even sure he knew it; it was just the same as 'boston' used to
be, only he had forgotten it a bit. But Anna Fëdorovna could
not understand it at all, and failed to understand it for so long
that at last, with a smile and a nod of approval, she felt
herself obliged to assert that now she understood it and that
all was quite clear to her. There was not a little laughter during the game when Anna Fëdorovna, holding ace and king
blank, declared *misère*, and was left with six tricks. She even
became confused and began to smile shyly and hurriedly
explain that she had not got quite used to the new way. But
they scored against her all the same, especially as the count,
being used to playing a careful game for high stakes, was
cautious, skilfully played through his opponents' hands, and
refused to understand the shoves the cornet gave him under
the table with his foot, or the mistakes the latter made when
they were partners.

Lisa brought more sweets, three kinds of jam, and some specially prepared apples that had been kept since last season,
and stood behind her mother's back watching the game and
occasionally looking at the officers and especially at the
count's white hands with their rosy well-kept nails, which
threw the cards and took up the tricks in so practised, assured, and elegant a manner.

Again Anna Fëdorovna, rather irritably outbidding the
others, declared seven tricks, made only four, and was fined

Paper 'silver rubles' were exchangeable for coin at par, and it was
decreed that the assignats would be redeemed at the rate of 3½ assignats for one 'silver ruble'. In out-of-the-way provincial districts
the assignats were still in general use.

accordingly, and having very clumsily noted down, on her brother's demand, the points she had lost, became quite confused and flustered.

'Never mind, mamma, you'll win it back!' smilingly remarked Lisa, wishing to help her mother out of the ridiculous situation. 'Let uncle make a forfeit, and then he'll be caught.'

'If you would only help me, Lisa dear!' said Anna Fëdorovna, with a frightened glance at her daughter. 'I don't know how this is . . .'

'But I don't know this way either,' Lisa answered, mentally reckoning up her mother's losses. 'You will lose a lot that way, mamma! There will be nothing left for Pímochka's new dress,' she added in jest.

'Yes, this way one may easily lose ten silver rubles,' said the cornet looking at Lisa and anxious to enter into conversation with her.

'Aren't we playing for "assignats"?' said Anna Fëdorovna, looking round at them all.

'I don't know how we are playing, but I can't reckon in "assignats",' said the count. 'What is it? I mean, what are "assignats"?'

'Why, nowadays nobody counts in "assignats" any longer,' remarked the uncle who had played very cautiously and had been winning.

The old lady ordered some sparkling home-made wine to be brought, drank two glasses, became very red, and seemed to resign herself to any fate. A lock of her grey hair escaped from under her cap and she did not even put it right. No doubt it seemed to her as if she had lost millions and it was all up with her. The cornet touched the count with his foot more and more often. The count scored down the old lady's losses. At last the game ended, and in spite of Anna Fëdorovna's wicked attempts to add to her score by pretending to make mistakes in adding it up, in spite of her horror at the amount of her losses, it turned out at last that she had lost 920 points. 'That's nine "assignats"?' she asked several times, and did not comprehend the full extent of her loss until her brother told her, to her horror, that she had lost more than thirty-two 'assignats' and that she must certainly pay.

The count did not even add up his winnings, but rose immediately the game was over, went over to the window at which Lisa was arranging the *zakúska* and turning pickled mushrooms out of a jar onto a plate for supper, and there quite quietly and simply did what the cornet had all that evening so longed, but failed, to do—entered into conversation with her about the weather.

Meanwhile the cornet was in a very unpleasant position. In the absence of the count, and more especially of Lisa, who had been keeping her in good humour, Anna Fëdorovna became frankly angry.

'Really, it's too bad that we should win from you like this,' said Pólozov in order to say something. 'It is a real shame!'

'Well, of course, if you go and invent some kind of "tables" and *"miseres"* and I don't know how to play them. . . . Well then, how much does it come to in "assignats"?' she asked.

'Thirty-two rubles, thirty-two and a quarter,' repeated the cavalryman who under the influence of his success was in a playful mood. 'Hand over the money, sister; pay up!'

'I'll pay it all, but you won't catch me again. No! . . . I shall not win this back as long as I live.'

And Anna Fëdorovna went off to her room, hurriedly swaying from side to side, and came back bringing nine 'assignats'. It was only on the old man's insistent demand that she eventually paid the whole amount.

Pólozov was seized with fear lest Anna Fëdorovna should scold him if he spoke to her. He silently and quietly left her and joined the count and Lisa who were talking at the open window.

On the table spread for supper stood two tallow candles. Now and then the soft fresh breath of the May night caused the flames to flicker. Outside the window, which opened onto the garden, it was also light but it was a quite different light. The moon, which was almost full and already losing its golden tinge, floated above the tops of the tall lindens and more and more lit up the thin white clouds which veiled it at intervals. Frogs were croaking loudly by the pond, the surface of which, silvered in one place by the moon, was visible through the avenue. Some little birds fluttered slightly or lightly hopped from bough to bough in a sweet-scented lilac-bush whose dewy branches occasionally swayed gently close to the window.

'What wonderful weather!' the count said as he approached Lisa and sat down on the low window-sill. 'I suppose you walk a good deal?'

'Yes,' said Lisa, not feeling the least shyness in speaking with the count. 'In the morning about seven o'clock I look after what has to be attended to on the estate and take my mother's ward, Pimochka, with me for a walk.'

'It is pleasant to live in the country!' said the count, putting his eye-glass to his eye and looking now at the garden, now at Lisa. 'And don't you ever go out at night, by moonlight?'

'No. But two years ago uncle and I used to walk every moonlight night. He was troubled with a strange complaint—insomnia. When there was a full moon he could not fall asleep. His little room—that one—looks straight out into it.'

'That's strange: I thought that was your room,' said the count.

'No, I only sleep there to-night. You have my room.'

'Is it possible? Dear me, I shall never forgive myself for having disturbed you in such a way!' said the count letting the monocle fall from his eye in proof of the sincerity of his feelings. 'If I had known that I was troubling you . . .'

'It's no trouble! On the contrary I am very glad; uncle's is such a charming room, so bright, and the window is so low. I shall sit there till I fall asleep, or else I shall climb out into the garden and walk about a bit before going to bed.'

'What a splendid girl!' thought the count, replacing his eyeglass and looking at her and trying to touch her foot with his own while pretending to seat himself more comfortably on the window-sill. 'And how cleverly she has let me know that I may see her in the garden at the window if I like!' Lisa even lost much of her charm in his eyes—the conquest seemed so easy.

'And how delightful it must be,' he said, looking thoughtfully at the dark avenue of trees, 'to spend a night like this in the garden with a beloved one.'

Lisa was embarrassed by these words and by the repeated, seemingly accidental, touch of his foot. Anxious to hide her confusion she said without thinking: 'Yes, it is nice to walk in the moonlight.' She was beginning to feel rather uncomfortable. She had tied up the jar out of which she had taken the mushrooms, and was going away from the window, when the cornet joined them and she felt a wish to see what kind of man he was.

'What a lovely night!' he said.

'Why, they talk of nothing but the weather,' thought Lisa.

'What a wonderful view!' continued the cornet. 'But I suppose you are tired of it,' he added, having a curious propensity to say rather unpleasant things to people he liked very much.

'Why do you think so? The same kind of food or the same dress one may get tired of, but not of a beautiful garden if one is fond of walking—especially when the moon is still higher. From uncle's window the whole pond can be seen. I shall look at it to-night.'

'But I don't think you have any nightingales?' said the count, much dissatisfied that the cornet had come and prevented his ascertaining more definitely the terms of the rendezvous.

'No, but there always were until last year when some sportsman caught one, and this year one began to sing beautifully only last week but the police-officer came here and his carriage-bells frightened it away. Two years ago uncle and I used to sit in the covered alley and listen to them for two hours or more at a time.'

'What is this chatterbox telling you?' said her uncle coming up to them. 'Won't you come and have something to eat?'

After supper, during which the count by praising the food and by his appetite had somewhat dispelled the hostess's

ill humour, the officers said good-night and went into their
room. The count shook hands with the uncle and to Anna
Fëdorovna's surprise shook her hand also without kissing it,
and even shook Lisa's looking straight into her eyes the while
and slightly smiling his pleasant smile. This look again
abashed the girl.

'He is very good-looking,' she thought, 'but he thinks too
much of himself.'

XIV

'I say, aren't you ashamed of yourself?' said Pólozov when
they were in their room. 'I purposely tried to lose, and kept
touching you under the table. Aren't you ashamed? The old
lady was quite upset, you know.'

The count laughed very heartily.

'She was awfully funny, that old lady. . . . How offended she was! . . .'

And he again began laughing so merrily that even Johann,
who stood in front of him, cast down his eyes and turned away
with a slight smile.

'And with the son of a friend of the family! Ha-ha-ha! . . .'
the count continued to laugh.

'No, really it was too bad. I was quite sorry for her,' said
the cornet.

'What nonsense! How young you still are! Why, did you
wish me to lose? Why should one lose? I used to lose before
I knew how to play! Ten rubles may come in useful, my
dear fellow. You must look at life practically or you'll always
be left in the lurch.'

Pólozov was silenced; besides, he wished to be quiet and
to think about Lisa who seemed to him an unusually pure
and beautiful creature. He undressed and lay down in the
soft clean bed prepared for him.

'What nonsense all this military honour and glory is!' he
thought, looking at the window curtained by the shawl
through which the white moonbeams stole in. 'It would be

happiness to live in a quiet nook with a dear, wise, simple-hearted wife—yes, that is true and lasting happiness!'

But for some reason he did not communicate these reflections to his friend and did not even refer to the country lass, though he was convinced that the count too was thinking of her.

'Why don't you undress?' he asked the count who was walking up and down the room.

'I don't feel sleepy yet, somehow. You can put out the candle if you like. I shall lie down as I am.'

And he continued to pace up and down.

'Don't feel sleepy yet somehow,' repeated Pólozov, who after this last evening felt more dissatisfied than ever with the count's influence over him and was inclined to rebel against it. 'I can imagine,' he thought, addressing himself mentally to Túrbin, 'what is now passing through that well-brushed head of yours! I saw how you admired her. But you are not capable of understanding such a simple honest creature: you want a Mina and a colonel's epaulettes. . . . I really must ask him how he liked her.'

And Pólozov turned towards him—but changed his mind. He felt he would not be able to hold his own with the count, if the latter's opinion of Lisa were what he supposed it to be, and that he would even be unable to avoid agreeing with him so accustomed was he to bow to the count's influence, which he felt more and more every day to be oppressive and unjust.

'Where are you going?' he asked, when the count put on his cap and went to the door.

'I'm going to see if things are all right in the stables.'

'Strange!' thought the cornet, but put out the candle and turned over on his other side, trying to drive away the absurdly jealous and hostile thoughts that crowded into his head concerning his former friend.

Anna Fëdorovna meanwhile, having as usual kissed her brother, daughter, and ward, and made the sign of the cross over each of them, had also retired to her room. It was long since the old lady had experienced so many strong impressions in one day and she could not even pray quietly: she could not rid herself of the sad and vivid memories of the deceased count and of the young dandy who had plundered her so unmercifully. However she undressed as usual, drank half a tumbler of *kvas*[1] that stood ready for her on a little table by her bed, and lay down. Her favourite cat crept softly into the room. Anna Fëdorovna called her up and began to stroke her and listened to her purring, but could not fall asleep.

'It's the cat that keeps me awake,' she thought and drove her away. The cat fell softly on the floor and gently moving her bushy tail leapt onto the stove. And now the maid, who always slept in Anna Fëdorovna's room, came and spread the piece of felt that served her for a mattress, put out the candle, and lit the lamp before the icon. At last the maid began to snore, but still sleep would not come to soothe Anna Fëdorovna's excited imagination. When she closed her eyes the hussar's face appeared to her, and she seemed to see it in the room in various guises when she opened her eyes and by the dim light of the lamp looked at the chest of drawers, the table, or a white dress that was hanging up. Now she felt very hot on the feather bed, now her watch ticked unbearably on the little table, and the maid snored unendurably through her nose. She woke her up and told her not to snore. Again thoughts of her daughter, of the old count and the young one, and of the *préférence*, became curiously mixed in her head. Now she saw herself waltzing with the old count, saw her own round white shoulders, felt someone's kisses on them, and then saw her daughter in the arms of the young count. Ustyúshka again began to snore.

'No, people are not the same nowadays. The other one was ready to leap into the fire for me—and not without cause. But this one is sleeping like a fool, no fear, glad to have won—no love-making about him. . . . How the other one said on his knees, "What do you wish me to do? I'll kill my-

---

[1] Kvas is a non-intoxicating drink usually made from rye-malt and rye-flour.

self on the spot, or do anything you like!" And he would have killed himself had I told him to.'

Suddenly she heard a patter of bare feet in the passage and Lisa, with a shawl thrown over her, ran in pale and trembling and almost fell onto her mother's bed.

After saying good-night to her mother that evening Lisa had gone alone to the room her uncle generally slept in. She put on a white dressing-jacket and covering her long thick plait with a kerchief, extinguished the candle, opened the window, and sat down on a chair, drawing her feet up and fixing her pensive eyes on the pond now all glittering in the silvery light.

All her accustomed occupations and interests suddenly appeared to her in a new light; her capricious old mother, uncritical love for whom had become part of her soul; her decrepit but amiable old uncle; the domestic and village serfs who worshipped their young mistress; the milch cows and the calves, and all this Nature which had died and been renewed so many times and amid which she had grown up loving and beloved—all this that had given such light and pleasant tranquillity to her soul suddenly seemed unsatisfactory; it seemed dull and unnecessary. It was as if someone had said to her: 'Little fool, little fool, for twenty years you have been trifling, serving someone without knowing why, and without knowing what life and happiness are!' As she gazed into the depths of the moonlit, motionless garden she thought this more intensely, far more intensely, than ever before. And what caused these thoughts? Not any sudden love for the count as one might have supposed. On the contrary she did not like him. She could have been interested in the cornet more easily, but he was plain, poor fellow, and silent. She kept involuntarily forgetting him and recalling the image of the count with anger and annoyance. 'No, that's not it,' she said to herself. Her ideal had been so beautiful. It was an ideal that could have been loved on such a night amid this Nature without impairing its beauty—an ideal never abridged to fit it to some coarse reality.

Formerly, solitude and the absence of anyone who might have attracted her attention had caused the power of love, which Providence has given impartially to each of us, to rest intact and tranquil in her bosom, and now she had lived too long in the melancholy happiness of feeling within her the presence of this something, and of now and again opening the secret chalice of her heart to contemplate its riches, to be able to lavish its contents thoughtlessly on anyone. God grant she may enjoy to her grave this chary bliss! Who knows whether it be not the best and strongest, and whether it is not the only true and possible happiness?

'O Lord my God,' she thought, 'can it be that I have lost my youth and happiness in vain and that it will never be . . . never be? Can that be true?' And she looked into the depths of the sky lit up by the moon and covered by light fleecy clouds that, veiling the stars, crept nearer to the moon. 'If that highest white cloudlet touches the moon it will be a sign that it is true,' thought she. The mist-like smoky strip ran across the bottom half of the bright disk and little by little the light on the grass, on the tops of the limes, and on the pond, grew dimmer and the black shadows of the trees grew less distinct. As if to harmonize with the gloomy shadows that spread over the world outside, a light wind ran through the leaves and brought to the window the odour of dewy leaves, of moist earth, and of blooming lilacs.

'But it is not true,' she consoled herself. 'There now, if the nightingale sings to-night it will be a sign that what I'm thinking is all nonsense, and that I need not despair,' thought she. And she sat a long while in silence waiting for something, while again all became bright and full of life and again and again the cloudlets ran across the moon making everything dim. She was beginning to fall asleep as she sat by the window, when the quivering trills of a nightingale came ringing from below across the pond and awoke her. The country maiden opened her eyes. And once more her soul was renewed with fresh joy by its mysterious union with Nature which spread out so calmly and brightly before her. She leant on both arms. A sweet, languid sensation of sadness oppressed her heart, and tears of pure wide-spreading love, thirsting to be satisfied—good comforting tears—filled her eyes. She folded her arms on the window-sill and laid her head on them. Her favourite prayer rose to her mind and she fell asleep with her eyes still moist.

The touch of someone's hand aroused her. She awoke. But the touch was light and pleasant. The hand pressed hers more closely. Suddenly she became alive to reality, screamed, jumped up, and trying to persuade herself that she had not recognized the count who was standing under the window bathed in the moonlight, she ran out of the room. . . .

XV

And it really was the count. When he heard the girl's cry and a husky sound from the watchman behind the fence, who had been roused by that cry, he rushed headlong across the wet dewy grass into the depths of the garden feeling like a detected thief. 'Fool that I am!' he repeated unconsciously, 'I frightened her. I ought to have roused her gently by speaking to her. Awkward brute that I am!' He stopped and listened: the watchman came into the garden through the gateway, dragging his stick along the sandy path. It was necessary to hide and the count went down by the pond. The frogs made him start as they plumped from beneath his feet into the water. Though his boots were wet through, he squatted down and began to recall all he had done: how he had climbed the fence, looked for her window, and at last espied a white shadow; how, listening to the faintest rustle, he had several times approached the window and gone back again: how at one moment he felt sure she was waiting, vexed at his tardiness, and the next, that it was impossible she should so readily have agreed to a rendezvous: how at last, persuading himself that it was only the bashfulness of a country-bred girl that made her pretend to be asleep, he went up resolutely and distinctly saw how she sat, but then for some reason ran away again and only after severely taunting himself for cowardice boldly drew near to her and touched her hand.

The watchman again made a husky sound and the gate creaked as he left the garden. The girl's window was slammed to and a shutter fastened from inside. This was very provoking. The count would have given a good deal for a chance to begin all over again; he would not have acted so stupidly now. . . . 'And she is a wonderful girl—so fresh—quite charming! And I have let her slip through my fingers. . . . Awkward fool that I am!' He did not want to sleep now and went at random, with the firm tread of one who has been crossed, along the covered lime-tree avenue.

And here the night brought to him also its peaceful gifts of soothing sadness and the need of love. The straight pale beams of the moon threw spots of light through the thick foliage of the limes onto the clay path, where a few blades of grass grew, or a dead branch lay here and there. The light falling on one side of a bent bough made it seem as if covered with white moss. The silvered leaves whispered now and then. There were no lights in the house and all was silent; the voice of the nightingale alone seemed to fill the bright, still, limitless space. 'O God, what a night! What a wonderful night!' thought the count, inhaling the fragrant freshness of the garden. 'Yet I feel a kind of regret—as if I were discontented with myself and with others, discontented with life generally. A splendid, sweet girl! Perhaps she was really hurt. . . .' Here his dreams became mixed: he imagined himself in this garden with the country-bred girl in various extraordinary situations. Then the role of the girl was taken by his beloved Mina. 'Eh, what a fool I was! I ought simply to have caught her round the waist and kissed her.' And regretting that he had not done so, the count returned to his room.

The cornet was still awake. He at once turned in his bed and faced the count.

'Not asleep yet?' asked the count.

'No.'

'Shall I tell you what has happened?'

'Well?'

'No, I'd better not, or . . . all right, I'll tell you—draw in your legs.'

And the count having mentally abandoned the intrigue that had miscarried, sat down on his comrade's bed with an animated smile.

'Would you believe it, that young lady gave me a rendez-vous!'

'What are you saying?' cried Pólozov, jumping out of bed.

'No, but listen.'

'But how? When? It's impossible!'

'Why, while you were adding up after we had played *préférence*, she told me she would sit at the window in the night and that one could get in at the window. There, you see what it is to. be practical! While you were calculating with the old woman, I arranged that little matter. Why, you heard her say in your presence that she would sit by the window to-night and look at the pond.'

'Yes, but she didn't mean anything of the kind.'

'Well, that's just what I can't make out: did she say it intentionally or not? Maybe she didn't really wish to agree so suddenly, but it looked very like it. It turned out horribly. I quite played the fool,' he added, smiling contemptuously at himself.

'What do you mean? Where have you been?'

The count, omitting his manifold irresolute approaches, related everything as it had happened.

'I spoilt it myself: I ought to have been bolder. She screamed and ran from the window.'

'So she screamed and ran away,' said the cornet, smiling uneasily in answer to the count's smile, which for such a long time had had so strong an influence over him.

'Yes, but it's time to go to sleep.'

The cornet again turned his back to the door and lay silent for about ten minutes. Heaven knows what went on in his soul, but when he turned again, his face bore an expression of suffering and resolve.

'Count Túrbin!' he said abruptly.

'Are you delirious?' quietly replied the count. '. . . What is it, Cornet Pólozov?'

'Count Túrbin, you are a scoundrel!' cried Pólozov, and again jumped out of bed.

XVI

The squadron left next day. The two officers did not see their hosts again and did not bid them farewell. Neither did they speak to one another. They intended to fight a duel at the first halting-place. But Captain Schulz, a good comrade and splendid horseman, beloved by everyone in the regiment and chosen by the count to act as his second, managed to settle the affair so well that not only did they not fight but no one in the regiment knew anything about the matter, and Túrbin and Pólozov, though no longer on the old friendly footing, still continued to speak in familiar terms to one another and to meet at dinners and card-parties.

A LANDLORD'S MORNING

(Part of an unfinished novel A Russian Landlord, 1852)

CHAPTER I

Prince Nekhlyúdov was nineteen years old when, at the end
of his Third Course at the University, he came to his estate
for the summer vacation and spent the whole summer there by
himself. That autumn, in his unformed boyish hand, he wrote
the following letter to his aunt, Countess Belorétski, whom he
considered to be his best friend and the cleverest woman in
the world. It was in French, and ran as follows:

'My dear Aunt,

'I have made a resolution which will affect my destiny for
life. I am leaving the university to devote myself to life on
my estate, because I feel that I was born for it. For heaven's
sake, dear Aunt, don't laugh at me. You will say that I am
young; perhaps I really am still a child, but that does not prevent me from feeling my vocation—from wishing to do good,
and from loving goodness.

'As I wrote you before, I found affairs here in indescribable
disorder. Wishing to put them in order and understand them,
I discovered that the chief evil lies in the very pitiable and
impoverished condition of the peasants, and that this is an
evil that can be remedied only by work and patience. If you
could only see two of my peasants, David and Iván, and the

way they and their families live, I am sure that the mere sight of those two unfortunates would do more to convince you than anything I can say to explain my intention. Is it not my sacred and direct duty to care for the welfare of these seven hundred men for whom I must be responsible to God? Would it not be a sin, for the sake of pleasure or ambition, to abandon them to the caprice of harsh elders and stewards? And why should I seek other opportunities of being useful and doing good, when such a noble, brilliant, and immediate duty lies at hand? I feel that I am capable of being a good landlord; and to be so, as I understand the word, one needs neither university diplomas nor official rank, such as you desire for me. Dear Aunt, don't make ambitious plans for me; accustom yourself to the thought that I have chosen quite a special path, but a good one which I feel will yield me happiness. I have thought much, very much, about my future duties, and have written down rules of conduct for myself; and if God only grants me life and strength, I shall succeed in my undertaking.

'Don't show my brother Vásya this letter: I am afraid of his ridicule. He is accustomed to domineer over me and I am accustomed to submit to him. Ványa even if he does not approve of my intentions will at least understand them.'

The countess answered with the following letter, which is here also translated from the French:

'Your letter, my dear Dmítri, proved nothing to me except that you have an admirable heart, of which I was always convinced. But, my dear boy, our good qualities do us more harm in life than our bad ones. I must not tell you that you are doing a foolish thing and that your action grieves me; I will try to influence you only by persuasion. Let us consider the matter, my dear. You say you feel a vocation for country life, that you wish to make your serfs happy, and hope to be a good proprietor. I must tell you: first, that we feel our vocation only after we have once mistaken it, secondly, that it is easier to make oneself happy than others, and thirdly, that to be a good landlord one must be a cold and austere man, which you will scarcely be, though you may try to make believe that you are.

'You think your arguments irrefutable and even accept them as rules for the conduct of life, but at my age, my dear, one does not believe in arguments and rules but only in experience; and experience tells me that your plans are childish. I am getting on for fifty and have known many fine men, but have never heard of a young man of good family and ability burying himself in the country in order to do good. You always wished to appear original, but your originality is really nothing but excessive self-esteem. Believe me, my dear, it is better to choose the trodden paths. They lead more easily to success, and success, even if you don't want it for yourself, is indispensable to enable you to do the good you desire.

'The poverty of some peasants is an unavoidable evil or one which can be remedied without forgetting all your obligations to society, to your relations, and to yourself. With your intelligence, your heart, and your love of goodness, there is no career in which you would not obtain success; but choose at any rate one worthy of you and which will bring you honour.

'I believe in your sincerity when you say you are free from ambition, but you are deceiving yourself. At your age and with your capacity ambition is a virtue, though it becomes a defect and a vulgarity when a man is no longer able to satisfy that passion, and you will experience this if you do not change your intention.

'Goodbye, dear Dmítri. It seems to me that I love you more than ever for your absurd, but noble and magnanimous plan. Do as you think best, but I confess that I cannot agree with you.'

Having received this letter the young man considered it for a long time, and at last, having come to the conclusion that even the cleverest woman may make mistakes, sent in his petition for discharge from the university, and settled down on his estate.

CHAPTER II

The young landowner, as he had written to his aunt, had
drawn up rules for his estate management and for his life in
general, and had allotted his hours, days, and months to different occupations. Sundays were fixed for receiving peti-
tioners—the domestic and other serfs—for visiting the allotments of the poorest peasants and giving them assistance
with the assent of the village Commune (the *mir*) which
met each Sunday evening and decided how much help
should be distributed and to whom.

More than a year had passed in such activities and the
young man was no longer quite a novice either in practical or
theoretical knowledge of estate management.

It was a bright Sunday in June when Nekhlyúdov, having
drunk his coffee and glanced through a chapter of *Maison
Rustique*, put a note-book and a packet of ruble notes in the
pocket of his light overcoat, and started out from the large
wooden house with its colonnades and verandas, in which he
occupied one small room downstairs, and went along the un-
swept weed-grown paths of the old English garden, towards
the village which lay along both sides of the high road. Nekhlyúdov was a tall well-knit young man, with a mass of thick
curly brown hair, a bright sparkle in his dark eyes, a fresh
complexion, and rosy lips above which the first down of young
manhood was just appearing. Youthful strength, energy, and
good-natured self-satisfaction were apparent in his gait and
every movement. The peasants, dressed in their Sunday best,
were returning from church in motley groups—old men, maidens, children, and women with babies in their arms—and dis-
persing into their homes, bowing low to the master and stepping out of his way. After going some way along the street
Nekhlyúdov stopped, took out his note-book, and looked at the
last page, on which in his unformed hand he had written
the names of several peasants, with comments: 'Iván Chúris
asks for props', he read, and went up to the gate of the
second hut on his right.

The Chúrises' domicile consisted of a half-rotten log building, mouldy at the corners, sloping to one side, and so sunk in
the ground that a small, broken sash window, with its shutter
half torn off, and a still smaller casement window stopped
up with tow, were only just above the manure heap. Attached
to the principal hut were a boarded passage with a low door
and a rotten threshold, another small building, still older, and
even lower than the passage, a gate, and a wattled shed. All
this had once been covered by one irregular roof, but the
thick, black, rotting thatch now hung only over the eaves, so
that in places the rafters and laths were visible. In the front of
the yard was a well with dilapidated sides and the remains of
a post and pulley, and a dirty cattle-trampled puddle in which
ducks were splashing. Near the well stood two ancient willows
that were split and had scanty pale-green shoots. Under one of
these willows, which witnessed to the fact that there had been
a time when someone had cared to beautify the place, sat a
fair-haired little girl, about eight years old, making a two-year-
old baby girl crawl round her. A puppy playing beside them,
seeing Nekhlyúdov, rushed headlong under the gate and burst
into frightened, quivering barking.

'Is Iván at home?' asked Nekhlyúdov.

The elder girl seemed petrified by the question and opened
her eyes wider and wider without answering. The younger
one opened her mouth and prepared to cry. A little, old-
looking woman in a tattered check gown with an old red
girdle tied low down, looked out from behind the door, but
did not answer either. Nekhlyúdov went up to the door and
repeated his question.

'He is, master,' said the old woman in a tremulous voice,
bowing low and growing more and more frightened and agitated.

When Nekhlyúdov, having greeted her, passed through
the passage into the narrow yard, the old woman went up
to the door and, resting her chin on her hand and not taking
her eyes off the master, began slowly to shake her head.

The yard was a wretched place. Here and there lay old
blackened manure left after carting, and on this lay in disorder

a rotting block, a pitchfork, and two harrows. The penthouse round the yard had almost no thatch left on the roof, and one side had fallen in so that the rafters no longer lay on the fork-posts but on the manure. On the other side stood a wooden plough, a cart lacking a wheel, and a heap of empty, useless beehives piled one on another. Chúris, with the edge and head of his axe, was getting the wattle wall clear from the roof which had crushed it. Iván Chúris was a peasant of about fifty, below the average height. His tanned, oval face, surrounded by a dark brown beard streaked with grey and thick hair of the same colour, was handsome and expressive. His dark blue half-closed eyes were intelligent and carelessly good-natured, and when he smiled his small regular mouth, sharply defined under his scanty brown moustache, expressed calm self-confidence and a certain ironical indifference to his surroundings. The coarseness of his skin, his deep wrinkles, the sharply marked sinews of his neck, face, and arms, the unnatural stoop of his shoulders, and his crooked bandy legs, showed that his life had been spent in labour beyond his strength. He wore thick white hempen trousers patched with blue on the knees, a dirty shirt of the same material torn at the back and arms, and a low girdle of tape, from which hung a brass key.

'Good-day', said Nekhlyúdov as he entered the yard.

Chúris looked round and then continued his work, and only when he had cleared the wattle from under the roof by an energetic effort did he stick his axe into a log, adjust his girdle, and come out into the middle of the yard.

'A pleasant holiday, your honour!' he said, bowing low and then shaking back his hair.

'Thank you, friend. You see I've come to look at your allotment,' said Nekhlyúdov, looking at the peasant's garb with boyish friendliness and timidity. 'Let me see why you want those props you asked me for at the meeting of the Commune.'

'The props? Why, you know what props are for, your honour! I'd like to prop things up a bit: there, please see for yourself. Only the other day this corner fell in—but thank God the cattle were not inside at the time. Things hardly hold together,' said Chúris, looking contemptuously at his unthatched, crooked, and dilapidated sheds. 'The rafters, gable-ends, and cross-pieces now, if you only touch them you won't find a single piece of timber that's any use. And where's a man to get timber from nowadays—you know yourself.'

'Then what use would five props be to you, when one shed has fallen in and the others will soon do so? You don't need props, but new rafters, cross-pieces, and uprights,' said the master, evidently parading his knowledge of the subject.

Chúris was silent.

'So what you need is timber and not props. You should have said so.'

'Of course I want timber, but there's nowhere to get it. It won't do to keep going to the master's house! If the likes of us were allowed to get into the habit of coming to your honour's house for everything we need, what sort of serfs should we be? But if you will be merciful concerning the oak posts that are lying unused on your threshing-floor,' he added, bowing and shifting from foot to foot, 'I might be able to change some of the pieces, cut away others, and fix things up somehow with the old stuff.'

'With the old stuff? Don't you yourself say that it's all old and rotten? To-day this corner falls in, to-morrow that, the day after a third: so if you are to do anything you must rebuild it altogether that the work may not be wasted. Tell me, do you think your place could stand through this winter or not?'

'Who can tell?'

'But what do you think? Will it fall in or not?'

Chúris considered.

'It will all fall in,' he said suddenly.

'There, you see you should have said at the meeting that you need to rebuild the whole homestead, and not only put in a few props. You know I should be glad to help you . . .'

'We're very grateful for your favour,' Chúris replied suspiciously, and without looking at the master. 'If you would only favour me with four beams and some props I could perhaps fix things up myself; and the rotten wood I'd take out and use for supports in the hut.'

'Then is your hut in a bad state too?'

'My old woman and I are expecting from day to day that it will crush someone,' Chúris remarked indifferently. 'The other day she did get crushed by a strut from the ceiling.'

'Crushed? What do you mean?'

'Why, your honour, it hit her on the back so that she lay more dead than alive till night-time.'

'Well, and has she recovered?'

'Yes, she's recovered, but she's always ailing. It's true that she's been sickly since her birth.'

'What, are you ill?' Nekhlyúdov asked the woman who was still standing in the doorway and had begun groaning as soon as her husband mentioned her.

'Just here it never leaves me,' she said, pointing to her dirty emaciated chest.

'Again!' said Nekhlyúdov, shrugging his shoulders with vexation. 'Why don't you go to the dispensary when you're ill? That's what the dispensary is for. Haven't you been told of it?'

'We have, master, but I've no time. There's the obligatory work on the estate, our own work, and the children, and I'm all alone. We are lone people.'

CHAPTER III

Nekhlyúdov went into the hut. The uneven smoke-begrimed walls of one end of the room had all sorts of rags and clothing hanging up on them, and the best corner was literally covered with reddish cockroaches that had collected round the icon and the benches. In the middle of the black, smelly, fourteen-foot-square hovel, there was a large crack in the ceiling, which though propped up in two places was bulging so that it threatened to collapse at any moment.

'Yes, the hut is very bad,' said Nekhlyúdov, looking straight at Chúris, who did not seem inclined to begin speaking about this state of things.

'It will crush us and will crush the children,' muttered the woman in a tearful voice, leaning against the brick oven under the bunks.

'Don't you talk,' Chúris said sternly, and with a subtle smile showing slightly under his moustache he turned to the master. 'I can't think what could be done to it, your honour—to the hut. I have put up props and boards, but nothing can be done.'

'How are we to live through the winter here? Oh, oh, oh!' said the woman.

'If we put up some more props and new struts,' her husband interrupted her with a quiet businesslike expression, 'and changed one of the rafters, we might somehow get through the winter. We might get along—only the props will crowd the hut, that's all. But if we touch it, there won't be a sound bit left. It's only as long as it's not touched that it holds together,' he concluded, evidently well pleased to have realized that fact.

Nekhlyúdov was vexed and grieved that Chúris had let himself come to such a pass and had not applied to him sooner, for ever since his arrival he had never refused help to a peasant, and only tried to get them to come straight to him with their troubles. He even felt a sort of animosity against Chúris, and angrily shrugged his shoulders and frowned; but the sight of the wretchedness around him and Chúris's quiet, self-satisfied appearance in the midst of it, changed his vexation into a melancholy feeling of hopelessness.

'Now why didn't you tell me sooner, Iván?' he said reproachfully, sitting down on the dirty crooked bench.

'I daren't, your honour,' Chúris replied with the same barely perceptible smile, shifting from one dirty bare foot to the other on the uneven earth floor, but he said this so boldly and calmly that it was hard to believe that he had not dared to apply to his master.

'We are only peasants: how can we dare . . .' began the woman with a sob.

'Hold your jabber,' Chúris addressed her again.

'It's impossible for you to live in this hut. It's nonsense!' said

Nekhlyúdov after a pause. 'Now this is what we'll do, friend . . .'

'Yes, sir,' Chúris replied.

'You've seen those brick cottages with hollow walls that I have been building in the new village?'

'Of course I have,' answered Chúris, showing his still sound and white teeth in a smile. 'We were quite surprised at the way they were laid. Tricky cottages! The children were laughing and asked if they were going to be store-houses, and the walls filled in to keep the rats out. . . . Grand cottages!' he finished, shaking his head with a look of ironical perplexity. 'Just like jails!'

'Yes, they are fine cottages, warm and dry, and not so likely to catch on fire,' said the master with a frown on his young face, evidently annoyed by the peasant's irony.

'No gainsaying, your honour—grand cottages!'

'Well then, one of them is quite ready. It is twenty-three feet square, with a passage and a larder, and is quite ready. I might let you have it at cost price and you could pay me when you can,' said the master with a self-satisfied smile which he could not control at the thought of his benevolence. 'You can pull down this old one and use it to build a granary, and we will move the yard buildings too. There is good water there. I will allot you fresh land for your vegetable plots and you will have arable land quite close. You'll soon live well. Now, don't you like it?' he added, noticing that as soon as he spoke of settling somewhere else, Chúris stood quite motionless and looked at the ground no longer smiling.

'It's as your honour pleases,' he said without looking up.

The old woman came forward as if touched to the quick, and prepared to say something, but her husband forestalled her.

'It's as your honour pleases,' he replied, firmly and yet submissively, looking up at his master and tossing back his hair, 'but it won't do for us to live in the new village.'

'Why not?'

'No, your honour. If you move us there—we're in a bad way as it is, but there we should never be proper peasants. What

sort of peasants should we be there? Why, a man couldn't possibly live there . . . but just as you please.'

'Why not?'

'We should be quite ruined, your honour.'

'But why couldn't a man live there?'

'What kind of life would it be? Just think. The place has
never been lived in, the water not tested, and there's no pasture. Our hemp plots here have been manured from olden
times, but what is there there? There's nothing! All bare! No
wattles, no corn-kilns, no sheds—nothing at all. We shall be
ruined, your honour, if you drive us there, we shall be ruined
completely. The place is new, unknown . . .' he repeated
thoughtfully but shaking his head decisively.

Nekhlyúdov began to argue that the change would on the
contrary be very advantageous for him, that wattles and sheds
would be erected, that the water was good there, and so on;
but Chúris's dull silence confused him and he felt he was not
saying the right things. Chúris did not reply, but when his
master stopped, remarked with a slight smile that it would be
better to house the old domestic serfs and Alëshka, the fool, in
the new village, to watch over the grain there.

'That would be fine,' he remarked, and laughed calmly. 'No,
it's a hopeless business, your honour!'

'Well, what if the place *is* uninhabited?' Nekhlyúdov insisted patiently. 'This place was uninhabited once, but now
people live here; and you will be the first to settle in the new
village and will bring luck. . . . You must certainly settle
there . . .'

'Oh sir, your honour, how can they be compared?' said
Chúris with animation, as if afraid the master might take a
definite decision. 'Here we are in the Commune—it's lively,
and we're accustomed to it. We have the road, and the pond
here for the wife to wash the clothes and water the cattle, and
our whole peasant establishment here from days of old: the
threshing-floor and little vegetable plot, and these willows
that my parents planted. My grandfather and father breathed
their last here and if only I can end my days here, your honour, I don't ask anything more. If you will have the goodness

to let my hut be mended, we shall be very grateful for your kindness. If not, we'll manage to live somehow in the old one to the end of our days. Let us pray for you all our lives,' he continued, bowing low. 'Don't turn us from our nest, master. . . .'

While Chúris was speaking, louder and louder sobs came from the place under the bunks where his wife stood, and when her husband said 'master' she unexpectedly sprang forward and threw herself on her knees at Nekhlyúdov's feet, weeping bitterly.

'Don't ruin us, benefactor! You are like father and mother to us! How could we move? We are old, lonely people. As God, so you . . .' and she began her lamentations again.

Nekhlyúdov jumped up from the bench to raise the old woman, but she beat her head on the earthen floor in a kind of passionate despair and pushed away his hand.

'What are you doing? Please get up. If you don't wish to go, you needn't. I won't force you,' he said, waving his arms and stepping towards the door.

When Nekhlyúdov had again sat down on the bench and the silence in the hut was only interrupted by the wailing of the woman who had retired under the bunk and stood there wiping her tears with the sleeve of her smock, he realized for the first time what the tumbledown hovel, the broken-down well with the muddy puddle, the rotting sheds and outhouse, and the broken willows which he saw through the crooked window, meant to Chúris and his wife, and he felt depressed, sad, and without knowing why, ashamed.

'Why didn't you tell the Commune last Sunday that you needed a cottage, Iván? I don't know now how to help you. I told you all at the first meeting that I have settled on the estate to devote my life to you; and I was ready to deprive myself of everything to make you contented and happy, and I swear before God that I will keep my word,' said the young proprietor, ignorant of the fact that outpourings of that kind are ill adapted to arouse faith in anyone, and least of all in a Russian, who likes not words but deeds, and dislikes the expression of feelings however fine.

But the simple-hearted young man was so pleased with the
feeling he experienced that he could not help pouring it out.

Chúris bent his head to one side, and blinking slowly listened to his master with forced attention, as to one who had to
be listened to though he was saying things that were not very
nice, and did not at all concern 'us'.

'But I can't give everybody all I am asked for. If I did not
refuse some who ask me for timber, I should soon not have any
left myself and should be unable to give to those who really
need it. That is why I gave the "Crown wood" for the better-
ment of the peasants' buildings, and handed it over completely to the Commune. That wood is now not mine, but belongs to you peasants. I can no longer dispose of it, but the
Commune does what it sees fit with it. Come to the meeting to-
night. I will tell them of your request, and if they resolve to
give you wood for a new hut it will be all right, but I have
no timber now. I wish to help you with all my heart, but if
you don't want to move, the matter is not in my hands but
rests with the Commune. Do you understand me?'

'We are very grateful for your kindness, your honour,' answered Chúris, abashed. 'If you will oblige us with the timber
for the building, we will get straight that way. . . . Anyhow,
what's the Commune? Everybody knows. . . .'

'No, you must come.'

'Yes, I'll come. Why not? But all the same I won't beg of
the Commune.'

CHAPTER IV

The young landlord evidently wished to ask the couple something more; he did not rise from the bench but looked hesitatingly now at Chúris and now at the empty unheated brick
oven.

'Have you had dinner?' he asked at last.

A mocking smile showed under Chúris's moustache, as if it
amused him that the master should ask such a silly question,
and he did not answer.

'What dinner, benefactor?' said the woman with a deep sigh. 'We've eaten bread—that's our dinner. We had no time to get sorrel to-day, so I had nothing to make soup of, and what kvas there was I gave the children.'

'To-day we have a strict fast, your honour,' said Chúris, explaining his wife's words. 'Bread and onions—that's our peasant food. Thank the Lord we have grain, by your honour's kindness—for many of our peasants haven't even that. The onions failed everywhere this year. Michael the gardener asked two kopeks[1] a bunch when we sent to him the other day, so there's nowhere the likes of us can buy any. Since Easter we haven't been to Church. We can't even afford a candle to put in front of St. Nicholas's icon.'

Nekhlyúdov had long known, not by hearsay or by trusting to other people's words, but by personal observation, the extreme poverty in which his serfs lived; but that reality was in such contrast with his whole upbringing, his bent of mind, and the course of his life, that he involuntarily kept forgetting it, and whenever he was forcibly reminded of it, as now, he felt intolerably depressed and sad, as though he were tormented by a reminder of some crime committed and unatoned for.

'Why are you so poor?' he asked, involuntarily uttering his thought.

'What else could we be but poor, master, your honour? What is our land like? As you know, it's clay and mounds, and we must have angered God, for since the cholera year the crops won't grow. And we have less meadow and less arable land now; some have been taken into the owner's farm and some added to his fields. I am a lonely man and old. . . . I'd be glad to bestir myself but I haven't the strength. My wife is ailing, and hardly a year passes without another girl baby, and they all have to be fed. Here am I working alone, and there are seven of us at home. I often sin before God, thinking that if He took some of them soon, things would be easier, and it would be better for them than suffering here. . . .'

---

[1] Two kopeks were about a halfpenny.

'O-oh!' the woman sighed aloud, as if confirming her husband's words.

'Here's all the help I have,' Chúris continued, pointing to an unkempt flaxen-haired boy of seven with an enormous belly, who had just then come in timidly, making the door creak, and who now, holding onto his father's shirt with both his little hands, stood gazing with astonished eyes from under his brow at the master. 'All the help I have is this,' Chúris continued in his deep voice, stroking the child's flaxen hair with his rough hand. 'How long shall I have to wait for him? The work is getting beyond me. It's not so much my age as the rupture that is getting the best of me. In bad weather I'm ready to scream, and by rights I ought to be released from serf-labour on account of my age.[2] There's Dútlov, Dëmkin, Zyábrev—all younger than me—who have long since stopped working on the land. But I have no one to work for me—that's the trouble. We have to eat, so I am struggling on, your honour.'

'I should really be glad to help you. But what can I do?' said the young master, looking compassionately at the serf.

'How can it be helped? Of course if a man holds land he must work for his master—we know that well enough. I'll have somehow to wait for my lad to grow up. Only, if you'll be so good, excuse him from school! The other day the clerk came round and said that your honour ordered him to go to school. Do let him off, your honour. What sense has he got? He's too young to understand anything.'

'Oh, no, friend. Say what you will, your boy can understand,' replied Nekhlyúdov, 'and it's time for him to be learning. I'm saying it for your own good. Just think: when he grows up and is head of the house he'll be able to read and write, and to read in Church too—with God's help everything will go right in the home,' he added, trying to express himself so as to be understood, but yet blushing and hesitating without knowing why.

'There's no denying it, your honour, you don't wish us any

---

[2] Under serfdom a man and his wife had to work some days each week for the owner, and they were reckoned as one unit.

harm, but there's no one to stay at home when my wife and I go to work on the owner's land; of course he's small, but still he's useful to drive in the cattle, and water the horses. Such as he is, still he's a peasant,' and Chúris smiled and took hold of the child's nose with his thick fingers and blew it for him.

'All the same, send him when you are at home and he has time. Do you hear? Be sure to send him.'

Chúris sighed deeply and gave no reply.

CHAPTER V

'Yes, and I wanted to ask why your manure has not been carted,' continued Nekhlyúdov.

'What manure have I got, sir, your honour? There's nothing to cart. What live-stock have I got? I have a little mare and a foal. The heifer I sold to the inn-keeper as a calf last autumn. That's all the live-stock I have.'

'How is that? You haven't enough cattle, yet you sold a heifer as a calf?' the master asked with surprise.

'But what could I feed it on?'

'Haven't you enough straw to feed a cow? Others have enough.'

'Others have manured land, but mine is nothing but clay. I can't do anything with it.'

'Well then dress it, so that it should not be all clay, then it will yield grain and there'll be something to feed the cattle on.'

'But I have no cattle, so how can there be any manure?'

'This is a strange vicious circle,' thought Nekhlyúdov, but could not imagine how to advise the peasant.

'And then again, your honour,' Chúris went on, 'it is not manure that makes the corn grow, but only God. Last year I got six ricks from an unmanured plot, but from the manured land we got almost nothing. It's only God!' he added with a sigh. 'And then cattle do not thrive in our yard. This is the sixth year they have died. Last year one calf died, the other I sold, as we had nothing to live on, and the year before last a fine cow perished: she was driven home from the pasture all right, then suddenly she staggered and staggered and died. Just my bad luck!'

'Well friend, so that you should not say you have no cattle because you have no fodder, and no fodder because you have no cattle, here's something to buy a cow with,' said Nekhlyúdov, blushing as he took some crumpled paper money out of his trouser pocket and began sorting it. 'Buy yourself a cow, and I wish you luck; and you can have fodder from the threshing ground; I'll give orders. Mind you have a cow by next Sunday. I'll look in.'

Chúris stood so long smiling and shifting from foot to foot without stretching out his hand for the money, that Nekhlyúdov at last put it on the table, blushing still more.

'We are greatly satisfied with your kindness,' Chúris said with his usual rather sarcastic smile.

His wife stood under the bunks sighing heavily, and seemed to be saying a prayer.

The young master felt embarrassed; he hurriedly rose from his seat, went out into the passage, and called Chúris to follow. The sight of the man he was befriending was so pleasant that he did not wish to part from him at once.

'I am glad to help you,' he said, stopping by the well. 'I can help you because I know you are not lazy. If you take pains I'll help you, and with God's aid you'll get straight.'

'It's not a case of getting straight, your honour,' said Chúris, his face suddenly assuming a serious and even stern expression as if quite dissatisfied that the master should suppose he could get straight. 'In my father's time I lived with my brothers and we did not know any want, but when he died and we broke up, everything went from bad to worse. It's all from being alone!'

'Why did you separate?'

'All because of our wives, your honour. Your grandfather was not living then. In his time we should not have dared to, there used to be real order then. Like yourself he looked into everything, and we should not have dared to think of separating. Your grandfather did not like to let the peasants get into

bad ways. But after him Andrew Ilých managed us. God forgive him! He's left different memories behind—he was a
drunken and unreliable man. We went to ask him once and
again. "The women make life impossible," we said, "allow us
to separate." Well he had us thrashed once and again, but in
the end the women got their way and the families separated
and lived apart. Of course everyone knows what a one-man
home is! Besides there was no kind of order. Andrew Ilých
ruled us as he pleased. "See that you have everything that's
needed,"—but how a peasant was to get it he didn't ask. Then
the poll-tax was increased, and more provisions were requisi-
tioned and we had less land, and the crops began to fail. And
when the time came for re-allotting the land, he took away
from our manured land to add to the owner's—the rascal—and
did for us altogether. We might as well die! Your father—the
kingdom of heaven be his!—was a kind master, but we rarely
had sight of him; he always lived in Moscow, and of course we
had to cart more produce there. Sometimes when a thaw set
in and the roads were impassable and we had no fodder left
we still had to cart! The master could not do without it. We
dare not complain of that, but there was no order. Now that
your honour lets every peasant come to you, we are a different
people and the steward is a different man. At least we know
now that we have a master. And it's impossible to say how
grateful the peasants are to your honour! During the time you
were under guardianship we had no real master. Everybody
was master—your guardian and Ilých, and his wife was mistress, and the clerk from the police-office was a master too. At
that time we peasants suffered a great deal—oh God! How
much sorrow!'

Again Nekhlyúdov experienced something like shame or remorse. He raised his hat and went his way.

CHAPTER VI

'Epifán Wiseman wishes to sell a horse,' Nekhlyúdov read in
his note-book, and he crossed the street to Epifán's home.

This hut was carefully thatched with straw from the thresh-ing-floor of the estate, and was built of light grey aspen timber —also from the master's forest. It had two red painted shutters to each window, a little roofed porch, and board railings with fancy patterns cut in them. The passage and unheated portion of the house were also sound; but the general look of well-being and sufficiency was rather marred by a shed with an un-finished wattle wall and unthatched roof adjoining the gate-way. Just as Nekhlyúdov reached the porch from one side, two women came up from the other carrying between them a full tub slung from a pole. One was Epifán Wiseman's wife, the other his mother. The former was a sturdy red-cheeked woman with a very fully developed bosom and broad fleshy cheeks. She wore a clean smock with embroidered sleeves and collar, an apron with similar embroidery, a new linen skirt, shoes, glass beads and a smart square head-dress embroidered with red cotton and spangles.

The end of the pole did not sway but lay firmly on her broad solid shoulder. The easy effort noticeable in her red face, in the curve of her back, and the measured movement of her arms and legs, indicated excellent health and extraordinary masculine strength.

Epifán's mother who carried the other end of the pole was, on the contrary, one of those elderly women who seem to have reached the utmost limit of age and decrepitude possible to a living person. Her bony figure, clad in a dirty torn smock and discoloured skirt, was so bent that the pole rested rather on her back than on her shoulder. Her hands were of a dark red-brown colour, with crooked fingers which seemed unable to unbend and with which she seemed to clutch the pole for sup-port. Her drooping head, wrapped in some clout, bore the un-sightly evidence of want and great age. From under her low forehead, furrowed in all directions by deep wrinkles, her two red, lashless eyes looked dimly on the ground. One yellow tooth protruded from under her sunken upper lip and, con-stantly moving, touched at times her pointed chin. The folds on the lower part of her face and throat were like bags that swung with every movement. She breathed heavily and

hoarsely, but her bare deformed feet, though they dragged
along the ground with effort, moved evenly one after the
other.

CHAPTER VII

Having almost collided with the master, the young woman
looked abashed, briskly set down the tub, bowed, glanced at
him with sparkling eyes from under her brow, and clattering
with her shoes ran up the steps, trying to hide a slight smile
with the embroidered sleeve of her smock.

'You go and take the yoke back to Aunt Nastásya, mother,'
she said to the old woman, pausing at the door.

The modest young man looked attentively but sternly at
the rosy-faced woman, frowned, and turned to the old one,
who having disengaged the yoke from the tub with her rough
hands and lifted it onto her shoulders, was submissively direct-
ing her steps towards the neighbouring hut.

'Is your son at home?' the master asked.

The old woman, bending still lower, bowed and was about
to speak, but lifting her hand to her mouth began coughing so
that Nekhlyúdov did not wait, but went into the hut.

Epifán, who was sitting on the bench in the best corner,
rushed to the oven when he saw his master, as if trying to
hide from him, hurriedly shoved something onto the bunk, and
with mouth and eyes twitching, pressed himself against the
wall as if to make way for the master.

Epifán was a man of about thirty, slender, well set, with
brown hair and a young pointed beard, he would have been
rather good-looking had it not been for the evasive little brown
eyes that looked unpleasantly from under his puckered brows,
and for the absence of two front teeth, which at once caught
the eye as his lips were short and constantly moving. He had
on a holiday shirt with bright red gussets, striped cotton trousers, and heavy boots with wrinkled legs. The interior of his
hut was not so crowded and gloomy as Chúris's, though it was
also stuffy, smelt of smoke and sheepskin coats, and was lit-

tered in the same untidy way with peasant garments and im-
plements. Two things struck one as strange: a small dented
samovar which stood on a shelf, and the portrait of an archimandrite with a red nose and six fingers, that hung near the
icon with its brass facings, in a black frame with the remnant
of a dirty piece of glass. Nekhlyúdov looked with dissatisfaction at the samovar, the archimandrite's portrait, and the bunk
where the end of a brass-mounted pipe protruded from under
some rags, and addressed the peasant.

'Good morning, Epifán,' he said, looking into his eyes.

Epifán bowed and muttered, 'Hope you're well, y'r Ex'-
cency,' pronouncing the last word with peculiar tenderness
while his eyes ran rapidly over his master's whole figure, the
hut, the floor, and the ceiling, not resting on anything. Then
he hurriedly went to the bunk and pulled down from it a coat
which he began putting on.

'Why are you doing that?' said Nekhlyúdov, sitting down
on the bench and trying to look at Epifán as sternly as possible.

'What else could I do, y'r Ex'cency? I think we know our
place. . . .'

'I have come to ask what you need to sell a horse for, and
how many horses you have, and which horse you want to sell,'
said Nekhlyúdov drily, evidently repeating questions he had
prepared.

'We are very pleased that y'r Ex'cency deigns to come to
peasants like us,' replied Epifán with a rapid glance at the
archimandrite's portrait, at the oven, at Nekhlyúdov's boots,
and at everything except his master's face. 'We always pray
God for y'r Ex'cency. . . .'

'Why must you sell a horse?' Nekhlyúdov repeated, raising
his voice and clearing his throat.

Epifán sighed, shook back his hair, his glance again roving
over the whole hut, and noticing a cat that lay quietly purring
on the bench, shouted to it, 'Sss, get away, beast!' and hurriedly turned to the master.

'It's a horse, y'r Ex'cency, that's no good. . . . If it were a
good beast I wouldn't sell it, y'r Ex'cency.'

'And how many horses have you?'

'Three horses, y'r Ex'cency.'

'And no foals?'

'Why certainly, y'r Ex'cency, I have a foal too.'

CHAPTER VIII

'Come, let me see your horses. Are they in the yard?'

'Exactly so, y'r Ex'cency. I have done as I was ordered, y'r Ex'cency. As if we could disobey y'r Ex'cency! Jacob Alpátych told me not to let the horses out into the field. "The prince will look at them," he said, so we did not let them out. We dare not disobey y'r Ex'cency.'

As Nekhlyúdov was passing out of the hut, Epifán snatched his pipe from the bunk and shoved it behind the oven; his lips continued to move restlessly even when the master was not looking at him.

A lean little grey mare was rummaging among some rotten straw under the penthouse, and a two-months-old long-legged foal of some nondescript colour, with bluish legs and muzzle, kept close to her thin tail which was full of burrs. In the middle of the yard, with its eyes shut and pensively hanging its head, stood a thick-bellied sorrel gelding—by his appearance a good peasant horse.

'Are these all the horses you have?'

'No, sir, y'r Ex'cency, there's also the mare and the foal,' Epifán said, pointing to the horses which his master could not have helped seeing.

'I see. And which of them do you want to sell?'

'Why, this one, y'r Ex'cency,' replied Epifán, shaking the skirt of his coat towards the drowsy gelding and continually blinking and twitching his lips. The gelding opened its eyes and lazily turned its tail to him.

'He doesn't look old and is a sturdy horse,' said Nekhlyúdov. 'Just catch him, and let me see his teeth. I can tell if he is old.'

'It's impossible for one person to catch him, Ex'cency. The beast is not worth a penny and has a temper—he bites and kicks, Ex'cency,' replied Epifán, smiling gaily and letting his eyes rove in all directions.

'What nonsense! Catch him, I tell you.'

Epifán smiled for a long time, shuffling from foot to foot, and only when Nekhlyúdov cried angrily: 'Well, what are you about?' did he rush under the penthouse, bring out a halter, and begin running after the horse, frightening it and following it.

The young master was evidently weary of seeing this, and perhaps wished to show his skill.

'Let me have the halter!' he said.

'I beg your pardon, how can y'r Ex'cency? Please don't. . . .'

But Nekhlyúdov went up to the horse's head and suddenly seized it by the ears with such force that the gelding, which was after all a very quiet peasant horse, swayed and snorted, trying to get away. When Nekhlyúdov noticed that it was quite unnecessary to use such force, and looked at Epifán who continued to smile, the idea—most humiliating to one of his age—occurred to him that Epifán was making fun of him and regarded him as a child. He flushed, let go of the horse's ears, and without making use of the halter opened its mouth and examined its teeth: the eye-teeth were sound and the double teeth full—which the young master knew the meaning of. Of course the horse was a young one.

Meanwhile Epifán had gone to the penthouse, and noticing that a harrow was not lying in its place, moved it and stood it up against the wattle wall.

'Come here!' cried Nekhlyúdov with an expression of child-ish annoyance on his face and a voice almost tearful with vex-ation and anger. 'Now, is this horse old?'

'Please, y'r Ex'cency, very old. It must be twenty. . . . Some horses . . .'

'Silence! You're a liar and a good-for-nothing! A decent peasant does not lie—he has no need to!' said Nekhlyúdov, choking with angry tears. He stopped, in order not to disgrace himself by bursting into tears before the peasant. Epifán too was silent, and looking as if he would begin to cry at any mo-ment, sniffed and slightly jerked his head.

'Tell me, what will you plough with if you sell this horse?' Nekhlyúdov went on when he had calmed down sufficiently to speak in his ordinary tone. 'You are being sent to do work on foot so as to let your horses be in better condition for the ploughing, and you want to sell your last one? And above all, why do you tell lies?'

As soon as his master grew calm Epifán quieted down too. He stood straight, still twitching his lips and his eyes roaming from one object to another.

'We'll come out to work for y'r Ex'cency no worse than the others.'

'But what will you plough with?'

'Don't trouble about that, we'll get y'r Ex'cency's work done!' said Epifán, shooing at the horse and driving it away. 'If I didn't need the money would I sell him?'

'What do you need the money for?'

'We have no flour left, y'r Ex'cency, and I must pay my debts to other peasants, y'r Ex'cency.'

'No flour? How is it that others with families still have flour, while you without a family have none? What have you done with it?'

'Eaten it up, y'r Ex'cency, and now there's none left at all. I'll buy a horse before the autumn, y'r Ex'cency.'

'Don't dare to think of selling the horse!'

'But if I don't sell it, y'r Ex'cency, what kind of a life will ours be, when we've no flour and daren't sell anything . . .', replied Epifán turning aside, twitching his lips, and suddenly casting an insolent look at his master's face—'it means we're to starve!'

'Mind, my man!' Nekhlyúdov shouted, pale with anger and experiencing a feeling of personal animosity towards the peasant. 'I won't keep such peasants as you. It will go ill with you.'

'That's as you wish, if I've not satisfied y'r Ex'cency,' replied Epifán, closing his eyes with an expression of feigned humility, 'but it seems that no fault has been noticed in me. Of course if y'r Ex'cency doesn't like me, it's all in your power: but I don't know what I am to be punished for.'

'For this: that your sheds are not thatched, your wattle

walls are broken, your manure is not ploughed in, and you sit at home smoking a pipe and not working; and because you don't give your mother, who turned the whole farm over to you, a bit of bread, but let your wife beat her so that she has to come to me with complaints.'

'Oh no, y'r Ex'cency, I don't even know what a pipe is!' replied Epifán in confusion, apparently hurt most of all by being accused of smoking a pipe. 'It is possible to say anything about a man . . .'

'There you are, lying again! I saw it myself.'

'How should I dare to lie to y'r Ex'cency?'

Nekhlyúdov bit his lip silently and began pacing up and down the yard. Epifán stood in one spot and without lifting his eyes watched his master's feet.

'Listen, Epifán!' said Nekhlyúdov suddenly in a voice of childlike gentleness, stopping in front of the peasant, and trying to conceal his excitement. 'You can't live like that—you will ruin your life. Bethink yourself. If you want to be a good peasant change your way of life, give up your bad habits, stop lying, don't get drunk, and respect your mother. You see I know all about you. Attend to your allotment, don't steal from the Crown forest, and stop going to the tavern. What good is all that?—just think. If you need anything come to me and ask straight out for what you want, and tell me why you want it. Don't lie, but tell the whole truth, and then I shan't refuse anything I can do for you.'

'Excuse me, y'r Ex'cency, I think we can understand y'r Ex'cency!' Epifán replied smiling, as if he quite understood the excellence of the master's joke.

That smile and that reply completely disillusioned Nekhlyúdov of his hope of touching Epifán and bringing him to the right path by persuasion. Moreover he felt all the time as if it were indecorous for him, who had authority, to persuade his own serf, as if all that he had said was not at all what he ought to have said. He sadly bowed his head and went into the passage. The old woman was sitting on the threshold groaning aloud, as if to show her sympathy with the master's words which she had overheard.

'Here is something to buy yourself bread with,' Nekhlyúdov whispered, giving her a ruble note. 'But buy it yourself, and don't give it to Epifán or he will drink it.'

The old woman took hold of the door-post with her bony hand, trying to rise and thank the master, but her head began shaking, and Nekhlyúdov had already crossed the road before she had got to her feet.

CHAPTER IX

'White David wants grain and posts,' was the next entry in Nekhlyúdov's note-book.

After passing several homesteads, he met his steward, Jacob Alpátych, at the corner of the lane. The latter having seen his master in the distance had removed his oilskin cap, produced a foulard kerchief, and begun wiping his fat red face.

'Put on your cap, Jacob! Put it on I tell you. . . .'

'Where has your Excellency been pleased to go?' said Jacob, holding up his cap to shade the sun, but not putting it on.

'I've been to see Wiseman. Now tell me, why has he become like that?' asked the master continuing on his way.

'Like what, your Excellency?' replied the steward, who followed his master at a respectful distance and having put on his cap was smoothing his moustache.

'What indeed! He is a perfect scamp—lazy, a thief, a liar, ill-treats his mother, and seems to be such a confirmed good-for-nothing that there is no reforming him.'

'I don't know, your Excellency, why he has displeased you so. . . .'

'And his wife too,' his master interrupted him, 'seems to be a horrid creature. The mother is dressed worse than any beggar and has nothing to eat, but the wife is all dressed up, and so is he. I don't at all know what to do with him.'

Jacob grew visibly confused when Nekhlyúdov mentioned Epifán's wife.

'Well if he has let himself go like that,' he began, 'we ought to take measures. It's true he's poor, like all one-man householders, but unlike some others he does keep himself in hand a bit. He's intelligent, can read and write, and seems pretty honest. He is always sent round to collect the poll-tax, and he has been village elder for three years while I have been here, and nothing wrong has been noticed. Three years ago it pleased your guardian to dismiss him, but he was all right also when he worked on the estate. Only he has taken rather to drink, having lived at the Post Station in town, so measures should be taken against that. When he misbehaved in the past we used to threaten him with a flogging and he'd come to his senses, and it was good for him and there was peace in the family; but as you don't approve of such measures, I really don't know what we are to do with him. I know he has let himself go pretty badly. He can't be sent as a soldier because he has lost two teeth, as you will have noticed. He knocked them out purposely a long time ago.[1] But he is not the only one, if I may take the liberty of reporting to your Excellence, who has got quite out of hand.'

'Let that matter alone, Jacob!' said Nekhlyúdov with a slight smile. 'We have discussed it over and over again. You know what I think about it, and say what you will I shall still not change my mind. . . .'[2]

'Of course your Excellence knows best,' said Jacob, shrugging his shoulders and gazing at his master from behind as if what he saw boded no good. 'As to the old woman, you are pleased to trouble about her needlessly,' he continued. 'It's true she brought up her fatherless children, and raised Epifán and married him off and all that; but among the peasants it is the custom, when a mother or father hands over the homestead to a son, that the son and his wife become the masters and the old woman has to earn her bread as best she can. Of course they have no delicate feelings, but it is the usual way among the peasants. So I make bold to say that the old woman has troubled you needlessly. She is an intelligent woman and a good housekeeper, but why trouble the master

---

[1] The proprietors had to send a certain proportion of their serfs to serve in the army, but they had to be fit men with sound teeth.

[2] As to the desirability of flogging the peasants.

about every trifle? Well, she had a dispute with her daughter-in-law, and the daughter-in-law may have pushed her—those are women's affairs! They might have made it up again instead of troubling you. And besides, you take it all too much to heart,' added the steward, looking with fatherly tenderness and condescension at his master who was walking silently up the street before him with long strides.

'Are you going home, sir?' he asked.

'No, to see White David, or the Goat . . . how is he called?'

'Now that's another sluggard, let me tell you. The whole Goat family are like that. Whatever you may do with him nothing helps. I drove over the peasant fields yesterday, and he has not even sown his buckwheat. What is one to do with such people? If only the old man at least taught his son, but he is just such a sluggard himself—whether it's for himself or for the owner he always bungles it. . . . Both your guardian and I—what have we not done to them? He's been sent to the police-station, and been flogged at home—which is what you are pleased to disapprove of. . . .'

'Who? Surely not the old man?'

'The old man, sir. Your guardian has many a time had him flogged before the whole Commune. But would your Excellence believe it, it had no effect! He would give himself a shake, go home, and behave just the same. And I must admit that David is a quiet peasant and not stupid; he doesn't smoke or drink, that is,' Jacob explained, 'but yet you see he's worse than some drunkards. The only thing would be to conscript him, or exile him—nothing else can be done. The whole Goat family are like that. Matryúshka, who lives in that hovel, is of the same family and is a damned sluggard too. But your Excellence does not require me?' added the steward, noticing that his master was not listening to him.

'No, you may go,' replied Nekhlyúdov absent-mindedly, and went on towards White David's hut.

David's hut stood crooked and solitary at the end of the village. It had no yard, no kiln, and no barn; only some dirty cattle sheds clung to one side of it while on the other brush-

wood and beams, prepared for outbuildings, lay all in a heap.
Tall green grass was growing where there had once been a
yard. There was not a living being near the hut, except a pig
that lay grunting in a puddle by the threshold.

Nekhlyúdov knocked at a broken window, but as no one
answered he went into the entry and shouted, 'Hullo there!'
but got no reply to this either. He entered the passage, looked
into the empty cattle stalls, and entered the open door of the
hut. An old red cock and two hens, jerking their crops and
clattering with their claws, were strutting about the floor and
benches. Seeing a man they spread their wings and, cackling
desperately, flew against the walls, one of them jumping up on
the oven. The hut, which was not quite fourteen-foot square,
was almost filled by the brick oven with its broken chimney, a
weaving loom that had not been put away though it was summer, and a blackened table with a warped and cracked top.

Though it was dry outside there was still a dirty puddle inside near the threshold, which had been formed by a leak in
the roof and ceiling during previous rain. There were no beds.
It was difficult to believe that the place was inhabited—there
was such an appearance of absolute neglect and disorder both
within the hut and outside. Yet White David and his whole
family lived there, and at that very moment, though it was a
hot June day, David, wrapped head and all in his sheepskin,
lay huddled in a corner on the top of the oven fast asleep. The
frightened hen that had alighted there and had not yet quieted
down was walking over his back without waking him.

Not seeing anyone in the hut Nekhlyúdov was about to
leave, when a long-drawn slobbering sigh betrayed the sleep-
er's presence.

'Hullo, who's there?' shouted the master.

Another long-drawn sigh came from the oven.

'Who is there? Come here!'

Another sigh, a moan, and a loud yawn replied to the master's call.

'Well, what are you about?'

Something moved slowly on the oven. The skirt of a worn-
out sheepskin coat appeared, one big foot in a tattered bast

shoe came down, and then another, and finally the whole of
White David appeared, sitting on the oven and lazily and dis-
contentedly rubbing his eyes with his big fist. Slowly bending
his head he looked round the hut with a yawn, and, seeing
his master, began to move a little quicker than before, but still
so slowly that Nekhlyúdov had time to walk some three times
from the puddle to the loom and back while David was getting
down from the oven.

White David was really white: his hair, body, and face were
all quite white. He was tall and very stout, but stout as peasants are—that is, his whole body was stout and not only his
stomach—but it was a flabby and unhealthy stoutness. His
rather comely face, with pale blue quiet eyes and broad, full
beard, bore the impress of ill-health: there was no vestige of
sunburn or colour in it; it was all of a pale yellowish tint with
a purple shadow under the eyes, and seemed swollen and
bloated. His hands were puffy and yellow, like those of people
suffering from dropsy, and were covered with fine white hair.
He was so drowsy that he could hardly open his eyes or stand
without staggering and yawning.

'How is it you are not ashamed,' Nekhlyúdov began, 'to
sleep in broad daylight when you ought to be building your
out-houses and when you are short of grain. . . .'

As soon as David came to his senses and began to realize
that his master was standing before him, he folded his hands
below his stomach, hung his head, inclining it a little on one
side, and did not stir a limb. He was silent; but the expression
of his face and the pose of his whole body said: 'I know, I
know, it's not the first time I have heard this. Well, beat me if
you must. I'll endure it.' He seemed to wish that his master
would stop speaking and be quick and beat him, even beat
him painfully on his plump cheeks, if having done so he would
but leave him in peace. Noticing that David did not understand him, Nekhlyúdov tried by various questions to rouse
the peasant from his submissively patient taciturnity.

'Why did you ask me for timber, and then leave it lying
about here a whole month, and that too at the time when
you have most leisure, eh?'

David remained persistently silent and did not stir.

'Come now, answer me!'

David muttered something and blinked his white eyelashes.

'You know one has to work, friend. What would there be without work? You see you have no grain now, and why? Because your land was badly ploughed, not harrowed, and sown too late—and all from laziness. You ask me for grain: well suppose I give you some, since you must not starve—but that sort of thing won't do. Whose grain am I to give you? Whose do you think? Come, answer me! Whose grain am I to give you?' Nekhlyúdov insisted.

'The proprietor's,' muttered David, raising his eyes timidly and questioningly.

'But where does the proprietor's grain come from? Think of it. Who ploughed and harrowed the land? Who sowed and reaped it? The peasants. Is that not so? Then you see if I am to give away the grain, I ought to give more to those who worked most to produce it, and you have worked least. They complain about your work on the estate too. You work least, but ask for your master's grain more than anyone. Why should I give it to you and not to others? You know if everybody lay on their backs as you do, we should all have starved long ago. One must work, friend. This sort of thing is wrong. Do you hear me, David?'

'I hear, sir,' muttered David slowly through his teeth.

CHAPTER X

Just then the head of a peasant woman carrying linen hung on a wooden yoke was seen through the window, and a moment later David's mother, a tall, very fresh-looking and active woman of about fifty, entered the hut. Her pockmarked and wrinkled face was not handsome, but her straight firm nose, her thin compressed lips and keen grey eyes, expressed intelligence and energy. The squareness of her shoulders and flatness of her bosom, the leanness of her arms and the solid muscles of her dark bare legs, bore witness to the fact that she

had long since ceased to be a woman and had become simply a labourer. She hurried into the hut, closed the door,
pulled down her skirt, and looked angrily at her son. Nekhlyúdov was about to speak to her, but she turned her back on him
and began crossing herself before a grimy icon that was visible
behind the loom. Having finished doing this, she adjusted the
dirty checked kerchief she wore on her head and bowed low to
her master.

'A pleasant Lord's day to your Excellency,' she said. 'God
bless you, our father. . . .'

When David saw his mother he evidently became confused,
and stooped and hung his head still more.

'Thanks, Arína,' replied Nekhlyúdov. 'I've just been speaking to your son about your household.'

'Arína the barge-hauler,' as the peasants had called her since
she was a girl, rested her chin on her right fist, supporting that
elbow on the palm of her left hand, and without waiting for
the master to finish began to speak in such a shrill and ringing
tone that her voice filled the whole hut, and from outside it
might have seemed as if several women were talking together.

'What's the use of talking to him, dear sir? He can't even
speak like a man. There he stands, the lout!' she continued,
contemptuously wagging her head at David's pathetic massive
figure. 'What's my household, sir, your Excellency? We're
paupers. You've got none worse than us in the whole village!
We don't do anything for ourselves or for the estate—it's a disgrace! And it's him that's brought us to it. I bore, fed, and
reared him, and could scarcely wait for him to grow up, and
now this is what we've got at last! He eats the bread, but we
get no more work out of him than from that rotten log. All he
does is to lie on the oven, or stand like that and scratch his
empty pate,' she went on, mimicking him. 'If only you would
frighten him a bit, sir! I ask it myself—punish him for God's
sake, or send him to the army. There's no other way out. I can
do nothing with him—that's how it is.'

'Now isn't it a sin for you to bring your mother to this,
David?' said Nekhlyúdov reproachfully, turning to the peasant.

David did not budge.

'If he were sickly now,' Arína continued with the same animated gestures, 'but look at him, he's as big as the mill chimney! You would think there'd be enough of him to do some work, the lubberly lout; but no, he's taking a rest on the oven, the sluggard. And if he does start on anything my eyes grow tired of looking at him before he's had time to get up, turn round, and get anything done!' she added in a drawling tone, turning her square shoulders awkwardly from side to side. 'To-day, for instance, my old man himself went to fetch brushwood from the forest and told him to dig holes for the posts: but not he, didn't so much as take the spade in his hands. . . .' She paused for a moment. 'He's done for me, lone woman that I am!' she suddenly shrieked, flourishing her arms and going up to her son with a threatening gesture. 'You fat lazy mug! God forgive me. . . .'

She turned contemptuously and yet with desperation from him, spat, and with tears in her eyes again addressed her master with the same animation, still waving her arms. 'I'm all alone, benefactor! My old man is ill, old, and there's not much good in him either, and I have always to do everything alone. It's enough to crush a stone. To die would be better, that would end it. He has worn me out, the wretch! Really, father, I'm at the end of my tether! My daughter-in-law died of overwork, and so shall I.'

CHAPTER XI

'Died of what?' Nekhlyúdov asked incredulously.

'From overwork, benefactor, as God is holy, she was used up. We took her from Babúrino the year before last,' continued Arína, and her angry expression suddenly changed to a sad and tearful one. 'She was a quiet, fresh-looking young woman, dear sir. She had lived in comfort as a girl at her father's and had not known want; but when she came to us and knew what our work was—work on the master's estate and at home and everywhere. . . . She and I alone to do it. It is nothing to me! I'm used to it. But she was with child, dear sir, and began to suffer pain, and was always working beyond her strength, and she overdid it, poor thing. A year ago, during St. Peter's Fast,[1] to her misfortune, she bore a son. We had no bread: we had to eat anything, just anything, and there was urgent work to be done—and her milk dried up. It was her first baby, we had no cow, and how can we peasants rear a baby by hand? Well, she was a woman and foolish—that made her grieve still more. And when the baby died she wept and wept for him, lamented and lamented, and there was want and the work had to be done, and things got worse and worse: she was so worn out in the summer that at the Feast of the Intercession[2] she herself died. It was he who destroyed her— the beast!' she repeated, turning with despairing anger to her son. 'What I wanted to ask of your Excellence . . .' she went on after a pause, lowering her voice and bowing.

'What is it?' Nekhlyúdov asked absent-mindedly, still agitated by her story.

'You see he is still a young man. What work can be expected from me? I'm alive to-day but shall be dead to-morrow. How is he to get on without a wife? He won't be a worker for you. . . . Think of something for us. You are as a father to us.'

'You mean you want to get him married? Well, all right.'

'Be merciful, you who are a father and mother to us!' and on her making a sign to her son, they both dropped on their knees at their master's feet.

'Why do you bow in such a way?' Nekhlyúdov said irritably, raising her by the shoulder. 'Can't you say what you want to say simply? You know I don't like grovellings. Get your son married if you like. I shall be very glad if you know of a wife for him.'

The old woman rose and began rubbing her dry eyes with her sleeve. David followed her example and having rubbed

---

[1] The feast of St. Peter and St. Paul is June 9th, o.s.
[2] October 1st, o.s.

his eyes with his puffy fist continued to stand in the same patiently meek attitude listening to what Arína said.

'There are girls—of course there are. There's Váska Mikháy's girl, she's all right, but she won't consent unless it's your wish.'

'Doesn't she agree?'

'No, benefactor, not if she's to marry by consent.'

'Then what's to be done? I can't compel her. Look for someone else—if not one of ours, one from another village. I'll buy her out if she comes willingly, but I won't force her to marry. There is no law that allows that, and it would be a great sin.'

'Eh, eh, benefactor! Is it likely, seeing what our life is and our poverty, that any girl would come of her own accord? Even the poorest soldier's wife wouldn't agree to such poverty. What peasant will give his girl into a house like this? A desperate man wouldn't do it. Why, we're paupers, beggars. They'd say that we have starved one to death and that the same would happen to their daughter. Who would give his girl?' she added, shaking her head dubiously. 'Just consider, your Excellency.'

'But what can I do?'

'Think of something for us, dear sir,' Arína repeated earnestly. 'What are we to do?'

'But what can I contrive? I can't do anything at all in such a case.'

'Who is to arrange it for us if not you?' said Arína, hanging down her head and spreading her arms out in mournful perplexity.

'As to the grain you asked for, I'll give orders that you shall have some—' said the master after a pause, during which Arína kept sighing and David echoed her. 'I can't do anything more.'

And Nekhlyúdov went out into the passage. The mother and son followed him, bowing.

CHAPTER XII

'Oh, what a life mine is!' Arína said, sighing deeply.

She stopped and looked angrily at her son. David at once turned and clumsily lifting his thick foot in its enormous and dirty bast shoe heavily over the threshold, disappeared through the door.

'What am I to do with him, master?' Arína went on. 'You see yourself what he is like. He is not a bad man, doesn't drink, is gentle, and wouldn't harm a child—it would be a sin to say otherwise. There's nothing bad in him, and God only knows what has happened to make him his own enemy. He himself is sad about it. Would you believe it, sir, my heart bleeds when I look at him and see how he suffers. Whatever he may be, I bore him and pity him—oh, how I pity him! . . . You see it's not as if he went against me, or his father, or the authorities. He's timid—like a little child, so to say. How can he live a widower? Arrange something for us, benefactor!' she said again, evidently anxious to remove the bad impression her bitter words might have produced on the master. 'Do you know, sir, your Excellence,' she went on in a confidential whisper, 'I have thought one thing and another and can't imagine why he is like that. It can only be that bad folk have bewitched him.'

She remained silent for a while.

'If I could find the right man, he might be cured.'

'What nonsense you talk, Arína. How can a man be bewitched?'

'Oh, my dear sir, a man can be so bewitched that he's never again a man! As if there were not many bad people in the world! Out of spite they'll take a handful of earth from a man's footprints . . . or something of that sort . . . and he is no longer a man. Is evil far from us? I've been thinking— shouldn't I go to old Dundúk, who lives in Vorobëvka? He knows all sorts of charms and herbs, and removes spells and makes water flow from a cross. Perhaps he would help!' said the old woman. 'Maybe he would cure him.'

'Now there is poverty and ignorance!' thought the young master as he strode with big steps through the village, sorrowfully hanging his head. 'What am I to do with him? It's impossible to leave him like that, both for my own sake and on account of the example to others, as well as for himself,' he said, counting off these different reasons on his fingers. 'I can't bear to see him in such a state, but how am I to get him out of it? He ruins all my best plans for the estate. . . . As long as there are peasants like that my dreams will never be realized,' he reflected, experiencing vexation and anger against White David for ruining his plans. 'Shall I have him sent to Siberia, as Jacob suggests, since he doesn't want to get on; or send him to be a soldier? I should at least be rid of him and should save another and better peasant from being conscripted,' he argued to himself.

He thought of this with satisfaction; but at the same time a vague consciousness told him that he was thinking with only one side of his mind and that it was not right. He stopped. 'Wait a bit, what was I thinking about?' he asked himself. 'Oh yes, into the army or to exile. But what for? He is a good man, better than many others—and besides what do I know. . . . Shall I set him free?' he thought, not now considering the question with only one side of his mind as previously. 'That would be unfair and impossible.' But suddenly a thought occurred to him which pleased him very much, and he smiled with the expression of a man who has solved a difficult problem. 'Take him into my house,' he reflected, 'observe him myself and get him used to work and reform him by kindness, persuasion, and a proper choice of occupation.'

CHAPTER XIII

'That's what I will do,' said Nekhlyúdov to himself with cheerful self-satisfaction, and remembering that he still had to see the rich peasant Dútlov he turned towards a tall roomy homestead with two chimneys, that stood in the middle of the village. As he drew near it he met at the neighbouring hut a plainly dressed woman of about forty coming to meet him.

'A pleasant holiday, sir!' said she without any sign of timidity, stopping beside him, smiling pleasantly and bowing.

'Good morning, nurse,' he replied. 'How are you? I am going to see your neighbour.'

'Yes, your Excellence, that's a good thing. But won't you please come in? My old man would be so glad!'

'Well, I'll come in and we'll have a talk, nurse. Is this your hut?'

'That's it, sir.'

The woman, who had been his wet-nurse, ran on in front. Following her into the entry Nekhlyúdov sat down on a barrel and lit a cigarette.

'It's hot in there. Let's sit out here and have a chat,' he said in answer to his nurse's invitation to enter the hut. The nurse was still a fresh-looking and handsome woman. Her features, and especially her large dark eyes, much resembled those of her master. She folded her arms under her apron and looking fearlessly at Nekhlyúdov, and continually moving her head, began to talk.

'Why are you pleased to honour Dútlov with a visit, sir?'

'I want him to rent land from me, about thirty desyatíns,[1] and start a farm, and also buy a forest jointly with me. You see he has money, so why should it lie idle? What do you think of it, nurse?'

'Well, why not? Of course, sir, everyone knows that the Dútlovs are strong people. I reckon he's the leading peasant on the whole estate,' the nurse answered, swaying her head. 'Last year they put up another building with their own timber, without troubling you. They must have at least eighteen horses apart from foals and colts, and as to cattle and sheep—when the women go out into the street to drive them in it's a sight to see how they crowd the gateway, and they must also have two hundred hives of bees if not more. Dútlov is a very strong peasant and must have money.'

---

[1] A desyatín is nearly two and three-quarter acres.

'Do you think he has much money?' asked Nekhlyúdov.

'People say—it may be their spite—that the old man has a good lot of money. Naturally he won't talk about it or tell his sons, but he must have. Why shouldn't he be interested in a forest? Unless he may be afraid of the talk spreading of his having money. Some five years back he took up meadows in a small way, in shares with Shkálik, the inn-keeper, but either Shkálik swindled him or something happened, and the old man lost some three hundred rubles and since then he has given it up. How can they help being well-to-do, your Excellence?' the nurse went on. 'They have three allotments of lands, a big family all of them workers, and the old man himself—there's no denying it—is a capital manager. He has such luck everywhere that people all wonder; what with his grain, his horses, and cattle, and bees, and his sons. He's got them all married now. He used to find wives for them among our own people, but now he's got Ilyúshka married to a free girl— he paid for her emancipation himself—and she, too, has turned out well.'

'And do they live peaceably?'

'Where there's a real head to a house there's always peace. Take the Dútlovs—of course the daughters-in-law have words behind the oven, but with their father at the head the sons live in unity all the same.'

The nurse paused a little.

'It seems that the old man wants to make his eldest son Karp head of the house now. "I am getting old," he says. "My place is to see to the bees." Well, Karp is a good peasant, a careful peasant, but all the same he won't be anything like the old man was as a manager—he hasn't the same sense.'

'Then Karp may like to take up the land and the forest. What do you think?' Nekhlyúdov asked, wishing to get from his nurse all that she knew about her neighbours.

'Scarcely, sir,' she replied. 'The old man hasn't told his son anything about his money. As long as he lives and the money is in his house, the old man will control things; besides, they go in chiefly for carting.'

'And you think the old man won't consent?'

'He will be afraid.'

'But what of?'

'But how can a serf belonging to a master let it be known what he has got, sir? In a hapless hour he might lose all his money! When he went into business with the inn-keeper and made a mistake, how could he go to law with him? So the money was lost. And with his proprietor he'd get settled at once.'

'Oh, is that it? . . .' said Nekhlyúdov flushing. 'Well, good-bye nurse.'

'Good-bye, dear sir, your Excellence. Thank you kindly.'

CHAPTER XIV

'Hadn't I better go home?' thought Nekhlyúdov as he approached Dútlov's gate, feeling an indefinite sadness and moral weariness.

But at that moment the new plank gates opened before him with a creak, and in the gateway appeared a handsome, ruddy, fire-haired lad of eighteen dressed as a stage-coach-driver and leading three strong-limbed shaggy horses, which were still perspiring. Briskly shaking back his flaxen hair he bowed to the master.

'Is your father at home, Ilyá?' asked Nekhlyúdov.

'He's in the apiary at the back of the yard,' replied the lad, leading one horse after the other out through the half-open gate.

'No, I'll keep to my intention and make him the offer, and do what depends on me,' Nekhlyúdov thought, and letting the horses pass out he entered Dútlov's large yard. He could see that the manure had recently been carted away: the earth was still dark and damp, and here and there, especially by the gateway, lay bits of reddish, fibrous manure. In the yard and under the high penthouse stood many carts, ploughs, sledges, troughs, tubs, and peasant property of all kinds, in good order. Pigeons flew about and cooed in the shade under the broad strong rafters. There was a smell of manure and tar in the place. In one corner Karp and Ignát were fixing a new transom under a large iron-bound three-horse cart. Dútlov's three sons all bore a strong family resemblance. The youngest, Ilyá, whom Nekhlyúdov had met by the gate, had no beard and was shorter, ruddier, and more smartly dressed than the others. The second, Ignát, was taller, darker, had a pointed beard, and though also wearing boots, a driver's shirt, and a felt hat, had not such a festive and carefree appearance as his younger brother. The eldest, Karp, was still taller, and was wearing bast shoes, a grey coat, and a shirt without gussets. He had a large red beard and looked not only serious but almost gloomy.

'Shall I send father to you, your Excellence?' he asked, coming up to his master and awkwardly making a slight bow.

'No, I'll go myself to the apiary and see his arrangements there . . . but I want to speak to you,' said Nekhlyúdov stepping to the opposite side of the yard so that Ignát should not hear what he was about to say to Karp.

The self-confidence of these two peasants and a certain pride in their deportment, as well as what his nurse had told him, so embarrassed the young master that he did not find it easy to speak of the business he had in mind. He had a sort of guilty feeling and it seemed to him easier to speak to one brother out of hearing of the others. Karp seemed surprised that the master should take him aside, but followed him.

'This is what it is,' Nekhlyúdov began hesitatingly. 'I wanted to ask, have you many horses?'

'We can muster five tróyka teams, and there are some foals too,' Karp answered readily, scratching his back.

'Do your brothers drive the stage-coach?'

'We drive stage-coaches with three tróykas, and Ilyá has been away carting; he's only just back.'

'And does that pay? What do you earn by it?'

'Earnings, your Excellence? At most we feed ourselves and the horses—and thank God for that.'

'Then why don't you take up something else? You might buy some forest or rent land.'

'Of course, your Excellence, we might rent land if there were any handy.'

'That is what I want to propose to you. Instead of the carting business that does no more than keep you, why not rent some thirty desyatíns of land from me? I'll let you have that whole strip beyond Sápov and you could start your own farming on a large scale.'

And Nekhlyúdov, carried away by the plan for a peasant farm which he had repeatedly thought out and considered, went on to explain his offer, no longer hesitatingly. Karp listened very attentively to his master's words.

'We are very grateful to your honour,' he said when Nekhlyúdov, having finished, looked at him inquiringly expecting an answer. 'Of course it is not a bad plan. It's better for a peasant to work on the land than to drive with a whip in his hand. Getting among strangers and seeing all sorts of people, the likes of us get spoilt. There is nothing better for a peasant than to work the land.'

'Then what do you think of it?'

'As long as father is alive what can I think, your Excellence? It is as he pleases.'

'Take me to the apiary. I'll talk to him.'

'This way, please,' said Karp, walking slowly towards the barn at the back. He opened a low door that led to the apiary, and having let his master pass, and shut the door behind him, returned to Ignát and silently resumed his interrupted work.

CHAPTER XV

Nekhlyúdov, stooping, passed from under the shade of the penthouse through the low doorway to the apiary beyond the yard. Symmetrically placed hives covered with pieces of board stood in a small space surrounded by a loosely-woven fence of straw and wattle. Golden bees circled noisily round the hives, and the place was flooded by the hot brilliant beams of the June sun. From the door a trodden path led to a wooden shrine on which stood a small tinsel-faced icon which glittered in the sunlight. Several graceful young lime trees, stretching their curly crowns above the thatch of the neighbouring building, mingled the just audible rustle of their fresh dark-green foliage with the humming of the bees. On the fine curly grass that crept in between the hives lay black and sharply defined shadows of the roofed fence, of the lime trees, and of the hives with their board roofs. At the door of a freshly-thatched wooden shed that stood among the limes could be seen the short, bent figure of an old man whose uncovered grey head, with a bald patch, shone in the sun. On hearing the creak of the door the old man turned and, wiping his perspiring sunburnt face with the skirt of his smock, came with a mild and pleasant smile to meet his master.

It was so cosy, pleasant, and quiet in the sun-lit apiary; the grey-haired old man with the fine, close wrinkles radiating from his eyes who, with large shoes on his bare feet, came waddling and smiling with good-natured self-satisfaction to welcome his master to his own private domain, was so simple-hearted and kind that Nekhlyúdov immediately forgot the unpleasant impressions he had received that morning, and his cherished dream vividly recurred to him. He saw all his peasants as well off and kindly as old Dútlov, and all smiling happily and affectionately at him because they were indebted to him alone for their wealth and happiness.

'Wouldn't you like a net, your Excellence? The bees are angry now, and sting,' said the old man, taking down from the fence a dirty linen bag attached to a bark hoop and smelling of honey, and offering it to his master. 'The bees know me and don't sting me,' he added with the mild smile that seldom left his handsome sunburnt face.

'Then I don't want it either. Are they swarming yet?' Nekhlyúdov asked, also smiling, without knowing why.

'Hardly swarming, sir, Dmítri Nikoláevich,' replied the old man, expressing a special endearment by addressing his master by his Christian name and patronymic. 'Why, they've only just begun to be active. You know what a cold spring it has been.'

'I have been reading in a book,' Nekhlyúdov began, driving off a bee which had got into his hair and buzzed just above his ear, 'that if the combs are placed straight up, fixed to little laths, the bees swarm earlier. For this purpose hives are made of boards with cross-pieces. . . .'

'Please don't wave your arm about, it makes them worse,' said the old man. 'Hadn't you better have the net?'

Nekhlyúdov was in pain; but a certain childish vanity made him reluctant to own it, and so he again declined the net and continued to tell the old man about the construction of beehives of which he had read in *Maison Rustique* and in which, he believed, there would be twice as many swarms; but a bee stung him on the neck and he grew confused and hesitated in the midst of his description.

'It's true, sir, Dmítri Nikoláevich,' said the old man, looking with fatherly condescension at his master, 'people do write in books. But it may be that it is written wrongly. Perhaps they say "he'll do as we advise, and then we'll laugh at him." That does happen! How can one teach the bees where to build their comb? They do it themselves according to the hive, sometimes across it and sometimes lengthways. There, please look in,' he added, opening one of the nearest hives and looking into the opening where buzzing bees were crawling about on the crooked combs. 'These are young ones: they have their mind on the queen bee, but they make the comb straight or to one side as best fits the hive,' continued the old man, evidently carried away by his favourite subject and not noticing his master's condition. 'See, they're coming in laden to-day. It's a warm day and everything can be seen,' he added, closing the opening and pressing a crawling bee with a rag and then with his hand brushing several from his wrinkled neck. The bees did not sting him, but Nekhlyúdov could hardly refrain from running away from the apiary: they had stung him in three places and were buzzing all round his head and neck.

"How many hives have you?" he asked, stepping back towards the door.

'As many as God has given,' replied Dútlov laughingly. 'One mustn't count them, sir. The bees don't like it. There now, your Excellence, I wanted to ask your honour something,' he continued, pointing to some narrow hives standing near the fence. It's about Ósip, your nurse's husband—if you would only speak to him. It's wrong to act so to a neighbour in one's own village.'

'What is bad? . . . Oh, but they do sting!' said the master, with his hand already on the door-handle.

'Well, you see, every year he lets his bees out among my young ones. They ought to have a chance to improve, but the strange bees enter the combs and take the wax from them,' said the old man, not noticing his master's grimaces.

'All right . . . afterwards . . . in a moment . . .' muttered Nekhlyúdov, and unable to bear the pain any longer he ran quickly through the door waving both hands.

'Rub it with earth and it will be all right,' said the old man, following the master into the yard. The master rubbed the places that had been stung with earth, flushed as he gave a quick glance at Karp and Ignát, who were not looking at him, and frowned angrily.

CHAPTER XVI

'What I wanted to ask your Excellence,' . . . said the old man, pretending not to notice or really not noticing his master's angry look.

'What?'

'Well, you see, we are well off for horses, thank God, and have a labourer, so that the owner's work will not be neglected by us.'

'Well, what about it?'

'If you would be so kind as to accept quit-rent and excuse my lads from service, Ilyá and Ignát could go carting all summer with three teams of horses, and might earn something.'

'Where would they go?'

'Well, that all depends,' interposed Ilyá who had tied the horses under the penthouse and came up to his father. 'The Kadmínski lads went to Rómen with eight tróykas and earned their keep and brought back about thirty rubles for each tróyka; or there's Odessa where they say fodder is cheap.'

'That's what I wanted to talk to you about,' said the master, turning to the old man and trying tactfully to introduce the question of farming. 'Tell me, is it more profitable to go carting than to farm at home?'

'Much more profitable, your Excellence,' Ilyá again broke in, vigorously shaking back his hair. 'At home we've no fodder for the horses.'

'And how much will you earn in a summer?'

'Well, after the spring—though fodder was dear—we carted goods to Kiev and loaded up grits for Moscow in Kursk, and kept ourselves, fed the horses well, and brought fifteen rubles home.'

'There's no harm in working at an honest job be it what it may,' said the master, again addressing the old man, 'but it seems to me that other work might be found. This carting work makes a young fellow go anywhere and see all sorts of people and he may get spoilt,' he added, repeating Karp's words.

'What are we peasants to take up, if not carting?'

'What are we peasants to take up, if not carting?' re-joined the old man, with a mild smile. 'On a good carting job a man has enough to eat himself, and the horses have enough. As to getting spoilt, it's not the first time the lads have been carting, and I used to go myself and got nothing bad from anyone—nothing but good.'

'There's plenty of work you could do at home: land, mea-dows . . .'

'How could we, your Excellency?' Ilyá interrupted with ani-mation. 'We are born to this, we know all about it, it's suitable work for us: the pleasantest work for us, your Excellence, is carting.'

'May we ask your Excellence to do us the honour to come to the hut? You have not been there since our house-warming,' said the old man, bowing low and making a sign to his son. Ilyá raced into the hut and the old man followed with Nekhlyúdov.

CHAPTER XVII

On entering the hut the old man bowed again, dusted the
front bench with the skirt of his smock, and asked with a
smile:

'What may I offer your Excellency?'

The hut was clean and roomy, with sleeping places near
the ceiling, and bunks. It also had a chimney. The fresh aspen
logs, between which the moss-caulking could be seen, had
not yet turned dark; the new benches and sleeping places
had not yet worn smooth, and the earthen floor was not yet
trodden hard. Ilyá's wife, a thin young peasant woman with a
dreamy oval face, sat on a bunk and rocked a cradle that hung
by a long pole from the ceiling. In the cradle, breathing softly,
lay an infant with eyes closed and outstretched limbs. Karp's
wife, a plump, red-cheeked woman, stood by the oven shred-
ding onions over a wooden bowl, her sleeves turned up above
her elbows, showing her hands and arms tanned to above
her wrists. A pock-marked pregnant woman stood beside the
oven hiding her face with her sleeve. It was hot in the hut,
for besides the heat of the sun there was the heat of the oven,
and there was a strong smell of freshly-baked bread. From the
sleeping places aloft two fair-haired little boys and a girl, who
had climbed up there while awaiting dinner, looked down
with curiosity on the master.

The sight of this prosperity pleased Nekhlyúdov and yet he
felt embarrassed in the presence of these women and children,
who were all looking at him. He sat down on the bench,
blushing.

'Give me a bit of hot bread, I like it,' he said, and flushed
still more.

Karp's wife cut off a big bit, and handed it to the master on
a plate. Nekhlyúdov said nothing, not knowing what to say;
the women were also silent, and the old man kept mildly smiling.

'Really now, what am I ashamed of—just as if I had done
something wrong?' thought Nekhlyúdov. 'Why shouldn't I

suggest their starting a farm? What stupidity . . . !' Yet he
still kept silent.

'Well, sir, how about the lads? What are your orders?' said
the old man.

'Well I should advise you not to let them go but to find them
work here,' Nekhlyúdov said, suddenly gaining courage. 'Do
you know what I have thought of for you? Join me in buying
a grove in the State forest, and some land too.'

'How could I, your Excellence? Where is the money to
come from?' the old man interrupted him.

'Only a small grove, you know, for about two hundred rubles,' Nekhlyúdov remarked.

The old man smiled grimly.

'If I had the money, why not buy it?' he said.

'Have you no longer that amount?' said the master reproachfully.

'Oh sir, your Excellence!' said the old man in a sorrowful
voice, looking towards the door. 'I have enough to do to keep
the family. It's not for us to buy groves.'

'But you have the money, why should it lie idle?' insisted
Nekhlyúdov.

The old man suddenly became greatly agitated; his eyes glittered and his shoulders began to twitch.

'Maybe evil persons have said it of me,' he began in a
trembling voice, 'but believe me, I say before God,' he went
on, becoming more and more excited and turning towards
the icon, 'may my eyes burst, may I fall through the ground
here, if I have anything but the fifteen rubles Ilyá brought
home and even then I have the poll-tax to pay. You know
yourself we have built the cottage . . .'

'Well, all right, all right!' said the master, rising. 'Good-bye,
friends.'

CHAPTER XVIII

'My God, my God!' thought Nekhlyúdov as he walked home
with big strides through the shady avenues of his neglected

garden, absent-mindedly plucking twigs and leaves on his way. 'Can it be that all my dreams of the aims and duties of my life are mere nonsense? When I planned this path of life I fancied that I should always experience the complete moral satisfaction I felt when the idea first occurred to me— so why do I now feel so depressed and sad and dissatisfied with myself?' And he remembered with extraordinary vividness and distinctness that happy moment a year before.

He had got up very early that May morning, before any-one else in the house, feeling painfully agitated by the secret, unformulated impulses of youth, and had gone first into the garden and then into the forest, where he wandered about alone amid the vigorous, luscious, yet peaceful works of nature, suffering from an exuberance of vague feeling and find-ing no expression for it. With all the charm of the unknown his youthful imagination pictured to him the voluptuous form of a woman, and it seemed to him that here it was—the ful-filment of that unexpressed desire. But some other, deeper feeling told him: 'Not that,' and impelled him to seek some-thing else. Then his inexperienced, ardent mind, rising higher and higher into realms of abstraction, discovered, as it seemed to him, the laws of being, and he dwelt on those thoughts with proud delight. But again a higher feeling told him: 'Not that,' and once more agitated him and forced him to continue his search. Empty of thought and feeling—a condition which al-ways follows intensive activity—he lay on his back under a tree and began to gaze at the translucent morning clouds drift-ing across the limitless blue sky above him. Suddenly without any reason tears filled his eyes and, Heaven knows why, a definite thought to which he clung with delight entered his mind, filling his whole soul—the thought that love and good-ness are truth and happiness—the only truth and the only hap-piness possible in the world. And this time his deeper feeling did not say: 'Not that,' and he rose and began to verify this new thought. 'That is it! This! So it is!' he said to himself in ecstasy, looking at all the phenomena of life in the light of this newly-discovered and as it seemed to him perfectly novel truth, which displaced his former convictions. 'What rubbish is all I knew and loved and believed in,' he said to himself. 'Love, self-denial—that is the only true happiness—a happiness independent of chance!' and he smiled and flourished his arms. Applying this thought to all sides of life and finding it confirmed by life as well as by the inner voice which told him, 'This is it,' he experienced a new sensation of joyful agitation and delight. 'And so, to be happy I must do good,' he thought, and his whole future presented itself to him no longer in the abstract, but in vivid pictures of a landed proprietor's life.

He saw before him an immense field of action for his whole life, which he would devote to well-doing and in which consequently he would be happy. There was no need to search for a sphere of activity: it lay ready before him; he had a direct duty—he owned serfs. . . . And what a joyful and grateful task lay before him! 'To influence this simple, receptive, unperverted class of people; to save them from poverty, give them a sufficiency, transmit to them an education which fortunately I possess, to reform their vices arising from ignorance and superstition, to develop their morality, to make them love the right. . . . What a brilliant, happy future! And I, who do it all for my own happiness, shall in return enjoy their gratitude, and see myself advancing day by day further towards the appointed aim. A marvellous future! How could I have failed to see it before?'

'And besides all that,' he thought at the same time, 'what prevents my being happy in the love of a woman, in the joys of family life?' And his youthful imagination painted a still more enchanting future. 'I and my wife, whom I love as no one ever before loved anyone in the world, will always live amid this peaceful poetic nature, with our children and perhaps with my old aunt. We have our mutual love, our love for our children, and we both know that our aim is to do good. We help each other to move towards that goal. I shall make general arrangements, give general and just assistance, carry on the farm, a savings-bank and workshops, while she, with her pretty little head, wearing a simple white dress which she lifts above her dainty foot, walks through the mud to the peasant school, to the infirmary, to some unfortunate peasant who strictly speaking does not deserve aid, and everywhere brings consolation and help. The children, the old men, and the old women, adore her and look on her as an angel—as Providence. Then she returns, and conceals from me the fact that she has been to see the unfortunate peasant and given him some money; but I know it all and embrace her tightly, and firmly and tenderly kiss her lovely eyes, her shyly blushing cheeks, and her smiling rosy lips.'

CHAPTER XIX

'Where are those dreams?' thought the young man now as he neared his house after his visits. 'For more than a year I have been seeking happiness in that way, and what have I found? It is true I sometimes feel that I have a right to be satisfied with myself, but it is a dry, reasoning sort of satisfaction. No, that is not true, I am simply dissatisfied with myself! I am dissatisfied because I do not find happiness here, and I long for happiness so passionately. I have not only experienced no enjoyment, I have cut myself off from all that gives it. Why? What for? Who is the better for it? My aunt was right when she wrote that it is easier to find happiness for oneself than to give it to others. Have my peasants grown richer? Are they more educated or morally more developed? Not at all! They are no better off, and it grows harder for me every day. If I saw my plans succeeding, or met with any gratitude . . . but no, I see a false routine, vice, suspicion, helplessness. I am wasting the best years of my life in vain,' he thought, and remembered that he had heard from his nurse that his neighbours called him a whipper-snapper; that he had no money left in the counting-house, that his newly-introduced threshing machine, to the general amusement of the peasants, had only whistled and had not threshed anything when for the first time it was started at the threshing-floor before a large audience; and that he had to expect officials from the Land Court any day to take an inventory of his estate because, tempted by different new undertakings, he had let the payments on his mortgage lapse. And suddenly, as vividly as the walk in the forest and the dream of a landlord's life had presented themselves to his mind before, so now did his little room in Moscow, where as a student he had sat late at night, by the light of one candle, with his beloved sixteen-year-old friend and comrade. They had read and repeated some dry notes on civic law for five hours on end, and having finished them had sent for supper and gone shares in the price of a bottle of champagne, and discussed the future awaiting them. How very different the future had appeared to the young student! Then it had been full of enjoyment, of varied activities, of brilliant success, and indubitably led them both to what then seemed the greatest blessing in the world—fame!

'He is already getting on, rapidly getting on, along that road,' thought Nekhlyúdov of his friend 'while I . . .'

But by this time he was already approaching the porch of his house, where ten or more peasant- and domestic-serfs stood awaiting him with various requests, and his dreams were replaced by realities.

There was a tattered, dishevelled, blood-stained peasant woman who complained with tears that her father-in-law wanted to kill her: there were two brothers, who for two years had been quarrelling about the division of a peasant farm between them, and now stood gazing at one another with desperate hatred: and there was an unshaven grey-headed domestic serf, with hands trembling from drunkenness, whom his son, the gardener, had brought to the master with a complaint of his depraved conduct: there was a peasant who had turned his wife out of the house because she had not worked all spring: and there was his wife, a sick woman who did not speak, but sat on the grass near the entrance, sobbing and showing an inflamed and swollen leg roughly bandaged with dirty rags. . . .

Nekhlyúdov listened to all the petitions and complaints, and having given advice to some, settled the disputes of others, and made promises to yet others, went to his room with a mixed feeling of weariness, shame, helplessness, and remorse.

CHAPTER XX

In the room occupied by Nekhlyúdov—which was not a large
one—there was an old leather couch studded with brass nails,
several armchairs of a similar kind, an old-fashioned carved
and inlaid card-table with a brass rim, which stood open and
on which were some papers, and an open, old-fashioned
English grand piano with a yellowish case and worn and
warped narrow keys. Between the windows hung a large mirror in an old gilt carved frame. On the floor beside the table
lay bundles of papers, books, and accounts. In general the
whole room had a disorderly and characterless appearance,
and this air of untidy occupancy formed a sharp contrast to
the stiff, old-fashioned aristocratic arrangement of the other
rooms of the large house.

On entering the room Nekhlyúdov angrily flung his hat on
the table and sat down on a chair before the piano, crossing his
legs and hanging his head.

'Will you have lunch, your Excellence?' asked a tall, thin,
wrinkled old woman who entered the room in a cap, a print
dress, and a large shawl.

Nekhlyúdov turned to look at her and was silent for a moment as if considering something.

'No, I don't want any, nurse,' he said, and again sank into
thought.

The old nurse shook her head at him with vexation, and
sighed.

'Eh, Dmítri Nikoláevich, why are you moping? There are
worse troubles! It will pass—be sure it will . . .'

'But I'm not moping. What has put that into your head.
Malánya Finogénovna?' replied Nekhlyúdov trying to smile.

'How can you help moping—don't I see?' the old nurse retorted warmly. 'All alone the whole day long. And you take
everything so to heart and see to everything yourself and
now you hardly eat anything. Is it reasonable? If only you
went to town or visited your neighbours, but who ever saw
the likes of this? You are young to trouble so about everything.

. . . Excuse me, master, I'll sit down,' she continued, taking a chair near the door. 'Why, you've been so indulgent with them that they're not afraid of anyone. Does a master behave like that? There is nothing good in it; you only ruin yourself and let the people get spoilt. Our people are like that: they don't understand it—really they don't. You might at least go to see your aunt. What she wrote was true . . .' she ended admonishingly.

Nekhlyúdov grew more and more dejected. He wearily touched the keys with his right hand, his elbow resting on his knee. Some sort of chord resulted, then another, and another. . . . He drew up his chair, took his other hand out of his pocket and began to play. The chords he struck were sometimes unprepared and not even quite correct; they were often trivial and commonplace, and did not indicate that he had any musical talent, but this occupation gave him a kind of indefinite, melancholy pleasure. At every change of harmony he waited with bated breath to see how it would resolve itself, and when a fresh harmony resulted his imagination vaguely supplied what was lacking. It seemed to him that he heard hundreds of melodies: a chorus and an orchestra in conformity with his harmony. What chiefly gave him pleasure was the intensified activity of his imagination which incoherently and fragmentarily, but with amazing clearness, presented him with the most varied, confused, and absurd pictures and images of the past and the future. Now it was the plump figure of White David responding to torment and privation with patience and submission: he saw his round shoulders, his immense hands covered with white hair, and his white lashes fluttering timidly at the sight of his mother's brown sinewy fist. Then he saw his self-confident wet-nurse, emboldened by residence at the master's house, and he imagined her for some reason going about the village and preaching to the serfs that they should hide their money from the landlord, and he unconsciously repeated to himself: 'Yes, one must hide one's money from the landlord.' Then suddenly the small brown head of his future wife—for some reason in tears—presented itself to him, resting on his shoulder. Then he saw Chúris's kindly blue eyes looking tenderly at his pot-bellied little son. 'Yes, he sees in him not only a son, but a helper and deliverer. That is love!' whispered Nekhlyúdov to himself. Then he remembered Epifán's mother and the patient, all-forgiving expression he had noticed on her aged face in spite of her one protruding tooth and ugly features. 'Probably I am the first person in the whole seventy years of her life to notice that,' he thought, and whispering, 'Strange!' he unconsciously continued to touch the keys and listen to the sounds they produced. Then he vividly recalled his flight from the apiary and the expression on Ignát's and Karp's faces when they obviously wanted to laugh but pretended not to see him. He blushed, and involuntarily looked round at his nurse, who was still sitting silently by the door gazing intently at him and occasionally shaking her grey head. Then suddenly he seemed to see three sweating horses, and Ilyá's fine powerful figure with his fair curls, his merrily beaming narrow blue eyes, his fresh ruddy cheeks, and the light-coloured down just beginning to appear on his lips and chin. He remembered how afraid Ilyá had been that he would not be allowed to go carting, and how warmly he had pleaded for that favourite job; and he suddenly saw a grey, misty early morning, a slippery highway and a long row of three-horsed carts, loaded high and covered by bast-matting marked with big black lettering. The strong-limbed, well-fed horses, bending their backs, tugging at the traces and jingling their bells, pull evenly uphill, tenaciously gripping the slippery road with their rough-shod hoofs. Rapidly descending the hill a mail-coach gallops towards the train of loaded carts, jingling its bells which re-echo far into the depth of the forest that extends along both sides of the road.

'Hey, hey, hey!' shouts the driver of the first cart in a boyish voice. He has a brass number-plate on his felt hat and flourishes his whip above his head.

Karp, with his red beard and gloomy looks, strides heavily in his huge boots beside the front wheel of the first cart. From the second cart Ilyá thrusts his handsome head out from under a piece of matting where he has been getting pleasantly warm in the early sunlight. Three tróykas loaded with boxes dash by with rattling wheels, jingling bells, and shouts. Ilyá again hides his handsome head under the matting and drops asleep. And now it is evening, clear and warm. The boarded gates open with a creak for the weary tróykas crowded together in the station yard, and one after another the high, mat-covered carts jolt over the board that lies in the gateway and come to rest under the roomy penthouse. Ilyá gaily exchanges greetings with the fair-faced, broad-bosomed hostess, who asks, 'Have you come far? And how many of you will want supper?' and with her bright kindly eyes looks with pleasure at the handsome lad. Now having seen to his horse he goes into the hot crowded house, crosses himself, sits down before a full wooden bowl, and chats merrily with the landlady and his comrades. And here, under the penthouse, is his place for the night, where the open starry sky is visible and where he will lie on the scented hay near the horses, which changing from foot to foot and snorting pick out the fodder from the wooden mangers. He goes up to the hay, turns to the east and, crossing his broad powerful chest some thirty times and shaking back his fair curls, repeats 'Our Father' and 'Lord have mercy!' some twenty times, covers himself head and all with his coat, and falls into the healthy careless sleep of strong young manhood. And now he dreams of the towns: Kiev with its saints and throngs of pilgrims, Rómen with its traders and merchandise, Odessa and the distant blue sea with its white sails, and Tsargrad[1] with its golden houses and white-breasted, dark-browed Turkish women— and thither he flies lifted on invisible wings. He flies freely and easily further and further, and sees below him golden cities bathed in bright radiance, and the blue sky with its many stars, and the blue sea with its white sails, and it is gladsome and gay to fly on further and further. . . .

'Splendid!' Nekhlyúdov whispered to himself, and the thought came to him: 'Why am I not Ilyá?'

---

[1] Constantinople.

FAMILY HAPPINESS

Part I

CHAPTER I

We were in mourning for my mother, who had died in the autumn, and I spent all that winter alone in the country with Kátya and Sónya.

Kátya was an old friend of the family, our governess who had brought us all up, and I had known and loved her since my earliest recollections. Sónya was my younger sister. It was a dark and sad winter which we spent in our old house of Pokróvskoe. The weather was cold and so windy that the snowdrifts came higher than the windows; the panes were almost always dimmed by frost, and we seldom walked or drove anywhere throughout the winter. Our visitors were few, and those who came brought no addition of cheerfulness or happiness to the household. They all wore sad faces and spoke low, as if they were afraid of waking someone; they never laughed, but sighed and often shed tears as they looked at me and especially at little Sónya in her black frock. The feeling of death clung to the house; the air was still filled with the grief and horror of death. My mother's room was kept locked; and whenever I passed it on my way to bed, I felt a strange uncomfortable impulse to look into that cold empty room.

I was then seventeen; and in the very year of her death my mother was intending to move to Petersburg, in order to take me into society. The loss of my mother was a great grief to me; but I must confess to another feeling behind that grief

—a feeling that though I was young and pretty (so everybody told me), I was wasting a second winter in the solitude of the country. Before the winter ended, this sense of dejection, solitude, and simple boredom increased to such an extent that I refused to leave my room or open the piano or take up a book. When Kátya urged me to find some occupation, I said that I did not feel able for it; but in my heart I said, 'What is the good of it? What is the good of doing anything, when the best part of my life is being wasted like this?' And to this question, tears were my only answer.

I was told that I was growing thin and losing my looks; but even this failed to interest me. What did it matter? For whom? I felt that my whole life was bound to go on in the same solitude and helpless dreariness, from which I had myself no strength and even no wish to escape. Towards the end of winter Kátya became anxious about me and determined to make an effort to take me abroad. But money was needed for this, and we hardly knew how our affairs stood after my mother's death. Our guardian, who was to come and clear up our position, was expected every day.

In March he arrived.

'Well, thank God!' Kátya said to me one day, when I was walking up and down the room like a shadow, without occupation, without a thought, and without a wish. 'Sergéy Mikháylych has arrived; he has sent to inquire about us and means to come here for dinner. You must rouse yourself, dear Máshechka,' she added, 'or what will he think of you? He was so fond of you all.'

Sergéy Mikháylych was our near neighbour, and, though a much younger man, had been a friend of my father's. His coming was likely to change our plans and to make it possible to leave the country; and also I had grown up in the habit of love and regard for him; and when Kátya begged me to rouse myself, she guessed rightly that it would give me especial pain to show to disadvantage before him, more than before any other of our friends. Like everyone in the house, from Kátya and his god-daughter Sónya down to the helper in the stables, I loved him from old habit; and also he had a special significance for me, owing to a remark which my mother had once made in my presence. 'I should like you to marry a man like him,' she said. At the time this seemed to me strange and even unpleasant. My ideal husband was quite different: he was to be thin, pale, and sad; and Sergéy Mikháylych was middle-aged, tall, robust, and always, as it seemed to me, in good spirits. But still my mother's words stuck in my head; and even six years before this time, when I was eleven, and he still said 'thou' to me, and played with me, and called me by the pet-name of 'violet'—even then I sometimes asked myself in a fright, 'What *shall* I do, if he suddenly wants to marry me?'

Before our dinner, to which Kátya made an addition of sweets and a dish of spinach, Sergéy Mikháylych arrived. From the window I watched him drive up to the house in a small sleigh; but as soon as it turned the corner, I hastened to the drawing-room, meaning to pretend that his visit was a complete surprise. But when I heard his tramp and loud voice and Kátya's footsteps in the hall, I lost patience and went to meet him myself. He was holding Kátya's hand, talking loud, and smiling. When he saw me, he stopped and looked at me for a time without bowing. I was uncomfortable and felt myself blushing.

'Can this be really you?' he said in his plain decisive way, walking towards me with his arms apart. 'Is so great a change possible? How grown-up you are! I used to call you "violet", but now you are a rose in full bloom!'

He took my hand in his own large hand and pressed it so hard that it almost hurt. Expecting him to kiss my hand, I bent towards him, but he only pressed it again and looked straight into my eyes with the old firmness and cheerfulness in his face.

It was six years since I had seen him last. He was much changed—older and darker in complexion; and he now wore whiskers which did not become him at all; but much remained the same—his simple manner, the large features of his honest open face, his bright intelligent eyes, his friendly, almost boy-ish, smile.

Five minutes later he had ceased to be a visitor and had become the friend of us all, even of the servants, whose visible eagerness to wait on him proved their pleasure at his arrival.

He behaved quite unlike the neighbours who had visited us after my mother's death. They had thought it necessary to be silent when they sat with us, and to shed tears. He, on the contrary, was cheerful and talkative, and said not a word about my mother, so that this indifference seemed strange to me at first and even improper on the part of so close a friend. But I understood later that what seemed indifference was sincerity, and I felt grateful for it. In the evening Kátya poured out tea, sitting in her old place in the drawing-room, where she used to sit in my mother's lifetime; Sónya and I sat near him; our old butler Grigóri had hunted out one of my father's pipes and brought it to him; and he began to walk up and down the room as he used to do in past days.

'How many terrible changes there are in this house, when one thinks of it all!' he said, stopping in his walk.

'Yes,' said Kátya with a sigh; and then she put the lid on the samovar and looked at him, quite ready to burst out crying.

'I suppose you remember your father?' he said, turning to me.

'Not clearly,' I answered.

'How happy you would have been together now!' he added in a low voice, looking thoughtfully at my face above the eyes. 'I was very fond of him,' he added in a still lower tone, and it seemed to me that his eyes were shining more than usual.

'And now God has taken her too!' said Kátya; and at once she laid her napkin on the teapot, took out her handkerchief, and began to cry.

'Yes, the changes in this house are terrible,' he repeated, turning away. 'Sónya, show me your toys,' he added after a little and went off to the parlour. When he had gone, I looked at Kátya with eyes full of tears.

'What a splendid friend he is!' she said. And, though he

was no relation, I did really feel a kind of warmth and comfort in the sympathy of this good man.

I could hear him moving about in the parlour with Sónya, and the sound of her high childish voice. I sent tea to him there; and I heard him sit down at the piano and strike the keys with Sónya's little hands.

Then his voice came—'Márya Alexándrovna, come here and play something.'

I liked his easy behaviour to me and his friendly tone of command; I got up and went to him.

'Play this,' he said, opening a book of Beethoven's music at the *adagio* of the Moonlight Sonata. 'Let me hear how you play,' he added, and went off to a corner of the room, carrying his cup with him.

I somehow felt that with him it was impossible to refuse or to say beforehand that I played badly: I sat down obedi- ently at the piano and began to play as well as I could; yet I was afraid of criticism, because I knew that he understood and enjoyed music. The *adagio* suited the remembrance of past days evoked by our conversation at tea, and I believe that I played it fairly well. But he would not let me play the *scherzo.* 'No,' he said, coming up to me; 'you don't play that right; don't go on; but the first movement was not bad; you seem to be musical.' This moderate praise pleased me so much that I even reddened. I felt it pleasant and strange that a friend of my father's, and his contemporary, should no longer treat me like a child but speak to me seriously. Kátya now went up- stairs to put Sónya to bed, and we were left alone in the par- lour.

He talked to me about my father, and about the beginning of their friendship and the happy days they had spent to- gether, while I was still busy with lesson-books and toys; and his talk put my father before me in quite a new light, as a man of simple and delightful character. He asked me too about my tastes, what I read and what I intended to do, and gave me advice. The man of mirth and jest who used to tease me and make me toys had disappeared; here was a serious, simple, and affectionate friend, for whom I could not help feeling respect and sympathy. It was easy and pleasant to talk to him; and yet I felt an involuntary strain also. I was anxious about each word I spoke: I wished so much to earn for my own sake the love which had been given me already merely because I was my father's daughter.

After putting Sónya to bed, Kátya joined us and began to complain to him of my apathy, about which I had said nothing.

'So she never told me the most important thing of all!' he said, smiling and shaking his head reproachfully at me.

'Why tell you?' I said. 'It is very tiresome to talk about, and it will pass off.' (I really felt now, not only that my dejection would pass off, but that it had already passed off, or rather had never existed.)

'It is a bad thing,' he said, 'not to be able to stand solitude. Can it be that you are a young lady?'

'Of course, I am a young lady,' I answered, laughing.

'Well, I can't praise a young lady who is alive only when people are admiring her, but as soon as she is left alone, collapses and finds nothing to her taste—one who is all for show and has no resources in herself.'

'You have a flattering opinion of me!' I said, just for the sake of saying something.

He was silent for a little. Then he said: 'Yes; your likeness to your father means something. There is something in you . . . ,' and his kind attentive look again flattered me and made me feel a pleasant embarrassment.

I noticed now for the first time that his face, which gave one at first the impression of high spirits, had also an expression peculiar to himself—bright at first and then more and more attentive and rather sad.

'You ought not to be bored and you cannot be,' he said; 'you have music, which you appreciate, books, study; your whole life lies before you, and now or never is the time to prepare for it and save yourself future regrets. A year hence it will be too late.'

He spoke to me like a father or an uncle, and I felt that he kept a constant check upon himself, in order to keep on my level. Though I was hurt that he considered me as inferior to himself, I was pleased that for me alone he thought it necessary to try to be different.

For the rest of the evening he talked about business with Kátya.

'Well, good-bye, dear friends,' he said. Then he got up, came towards me, and took my hand.

'When shall we see you again?' asked Kátya.

'In spring,' he answered, still holding my hand. 'I shall go now to Danílovka' (this was another property of ours), 'look into things there and make what arrangements I can; then I go to Moscow on business of my own; and in summer we shall meet again.'

'Must you really be away so long?' I asked, and I felt terribly grieved. I had really hoped to see him every day, and I felt a sudden shock of regret, and a fear that my depression would return. And my face and voice must have made this plain.

'You must find more to do and not get depressed,' he said; and I thought his tone too cool and unconcerned. 'I shall put you through an examination in spring,' he added, letting go my hand and not looking at me.

When we saw him off in the hall, he put on his fur coat in a hurry and still avoided looking at me. 'He is taking a deal of trouble for nothing!' I thought. 'Does he think me so anxious that he should look at me? He is a good man, a very good man; but that's all.'

That evening, however, Kátya and I sat up late, talking, not about him but about our plans for the summer, and where we should spend next winter and what we should do then. I had ceased to ask that terrible question—what is the good of it all? Now it seemed quite plain and simple: the proper object of life was happiness, and I promised myself much happiness ahead. It seemed as if our gloomy old house had suddenly become full of light and life.

CHAPTER II

Meanwhile spring arrived. My old dejection passed away and gave place to the unrest which spring brings with it, full of dreams and vague hopes and desires. Instead of living as I had done at the beginning of winter, I read and played the piano and gave lessons to Sónya; but also I often went into the garden and wandered for long alone through the avenues, or sat on a bench there; and Heaven knows what my thoughts and wishes and hopes were at such times. Sometimes at night, especially if there was a moon, I sat by my bedroom window till dawn; sometimes, when Kátya was not watching, I stole out into the garden wearing only a wrapper and ran through the dew as far as the pond; and once I went all the way to the open fields and walked right round the garden alone at night.

I find it difficult now to recall and understand the dreams which then filled my imagination. Even when I *can* recall them I find it hard to believe that my dreams were just like that: they were so strange and so remote from life.

Sergéy Mikháylych kept his promise: he returned from his travels at the end of May.

His first visit to us was in the evening and was quite unexpected. We were sitting in the veranda, preparing for tea. By this time the garden was all green, and the nightingales had taken up their quarters for the whole of St. Peter's Fast in the leafy borders. The tops of the round lilac bushes had a sprinkling of white and purple—a sign that their flowers were ready to open. The foliage of the birch avenue was all transparent in the light of the setting sun. In the veranda there was shade and freshness. The evening dew was sure to be heavy on the grass. Out of doors beyond the garden the last sounds of day were audible, and the noise of the sheep and cattle, as they were driven home. Níkon, the half-witted boy, was driving his water-cart along the path outside the veranda, and a cold stream of water from the sprinkler made dark circles on the mould round the stems and supports of the dahlias.

In our veranda the polished samovar shone and hissed on the white table-cloth; there were cracknels and biscuits and cream on the table. Kátya was busy washing the cups with her plump hands. I was too hungry after bathing to wait for tea, and was eating bread with thick fresh cream. I was wearing a gingham blouse with loose sleeves, and my hair, still wet, was covered with a kerchief. Kátya saw him first, even before he came in.

'You, Sergéy Mikháylych!' she cried. 'Why, we were just talking about you.'

I got up, meaning to go and change my dress, but he caught me just by the door.

'Why stand on such ceremony in the country?' he said, looking with a smile at the kerchief on my head. 'You don't mind the presence of your butler, and I am really the same to you as Grigóri is.' But I felt just then that he was looking at me in a way quite unlike Grigóri's way, and I was uncomfortable.

'I shall come back at once,' I said, as I left them.

'But what is wrong?' he called out after me; 'it's just the dress of a young peasant woman.'

'How strangely he looked at me!' I said to myself as I was quickly changing upstairs. 'Well, I'm glad he has come; things will be more lively.' After a look in the glass I ran gaily downstairs and into the veranda; I was out of breath and did not disguise my haste. He was sitting at the table, talking to Kátya about our affairs. He glanced at me and smiled; then he went on talking. From what he said it appeared that our affairs were in capital shape: it was now possible for us, after spending the summer in the country, to go either to Petersburg for Sónya's education, or abroad.

'If only you would go abroad with us—' said Kátya; 'without you we shall be quite lost there.'

'Oh, I should like to go round the world with you,' he said, half in jest and half in earnest.

'All right,' I said; 'let us start off and go round the world.'

He smiled and shook his head.

'What about my mother? What about my business?' he said. 'But that's not the question just now: I want to know

how you have been spending your time. Not depressed again,
I hope?'

When I told him that I had been busy and not bored during his absence, and when Kátya confirmed my report, he
praised me as if he had a right to do so, and his words and
looks were kind, as they might have been to a child. I felt
obliged to tell him, in detail and with perfect frankness, all my
good actions, and to confess, as if I were in church, all that
he might disapprove of. The evening was so fine that we
stayed in the veranda after tea was cleared away; and the
conversation interested me so much that I did not notice how
we ceased by degrees to hear any sound of the servants indoors. The scent of flowers grew stronger and came from all
sides; the grass was drenched with dew; a nightingale struck
up in a lilac bush close by and then stopped on hearing our
voices; the starry sky seemed to come down lower over our
heads.

It was growing dusk, but I did not notice it till a bat suddenly and silently flew in beneath the veranda awning and
began to flutter round my white shawl. I shrank back against
the wall and nearly cried out; but the bat as silently and
swiftly dived out from under the awning and disappeared in
the half-darkness of the garden.

'How fond I am of this place of yours!' he said, changing
the conversation; 'I wish I could spend all my life here, sitting
in this veranda.'

'Well, do then!' said Kátya.

'That's all very well,' he said, 'but life won't sit still.'

'Why don't you marry?' asked Kátya; 'you would make an
excellent husband.'

'Because I like sitting still?' and he laughed. 'No, Katerína
Kárlovna, too late for you and me to marry. People have long
ceased to think of me as a marrying man, and I am even surer
of it myself; and I declare I have felt quite comfortable since
the matter was settled.'

It seemed to me that he said this in an unnaturally persuasive way.

'Nonsense!' said Kátya; 'a man of thirty-six makes out that he is too old!'

'Too old indeed,' he went on, 'when all one wants is to sit still. For a man who is going to marry that's not enough. Just you ask her,' he added, nodding at me; 'people of her age should marry, and you and I can rejoice in their happiness.'

The sadness and constraint latent in his voice was not lost upon me. He was silent for a little, and neither Kátya nor I spoke.

'Well, just fancy,' he went on, turning a little on his seat; 'suppose that by some mischance I married a girl of seventeen, Másha, if you like—I mean, Márya Alexándrovna. The instance is good; I am glad it turned up; there could not be a better instance.'

I laughed; but I could not understand why he was glad, or what it was that had turned up.

'Just tell me honestly, with your hand on your heart,' he said, turning as if playfully to me, 'would it not be a misfortune for you to unite your life with that of an old worn-out man who only wants to sit still, whereas Heaven knows what wishes are fermenting in that heart of yours?'

I felt uncomfortable and was silent, not knowing how to answer him.

'I am not making you a proposal, you know,' he said, laughing; 'but am I really the kind of husband you dream of when walking alone in the avenue at twilight? It would be a misfortune, would it not?'

'No, not a misfortune,' I began.

'But a bad thing,' he ended my sentence.

'Perhaps; but I may be mistaken . . .' He interrupted me again.

'There, you see! She is quite right, and I am grateful to her for her frankness, and very glad to have had this conversation. And there is something else to be said'—he added: 'for me too it would be a very great misfortune.'

'How odd you are! You have not changed in the least,' said Kátya, and then left the veranda, to order supper to be served.

When she had gone, we were both silent and all was still around us, but for one exception. A nightingale, which had sung last night by fitful snatches, now flooded the garden with a steady stream of song, and was soon answered by another from the dell below, which had not sung till that evening. The nearer bird stopped and seemed to listen for a moment, and then broke out again still louder than before, pouring out his song in piercing long-drawn cadences. There was a regal calm in the birds' voices, as they floated through the realm of night which belongs to those birds and not to man. The gardener walked past to his sleeping-quarters in the greenhouse, and the noise of his heavy boots grew fainter and fainter along the path. Someone whistled twice sharply at the foot of the hill; and then all was still again. The rustling of leaves could just be heard; the veranda awning flapped; a faint perfume, floating in the air, came down on the veranda and filled it. I felt silence awkward after what had been said, but what to say I did not know. I looked at him. His eyes, bright in the half-darkness, turned towards me.

'How good life is!' he said.

I sighed, I don't know why.

'Well?' he asked.

'Life is good,' I repeated after him.

Again we were silent, and again I felt uncomfortable. I could not help fancying that I had wounded him by agreeing that he was old; and I wished to comfort him but did not know how.

'Well, I must be saying good-bye,' he said, rising; 'my mother expects me for supper; I have hardly seen her all day.'

'I meant to play you the new sonata,' I said.

'That must wait,' he replied; and I thought that he spoke coldly.

'Good-bye.'

I felt still more certain that I had wounded him, and I was sorry. Kátya and I went to the steps to see him off and stood for a while in the open, looking along the road where he had disappeared from view. When we ceased to hear the sound of his horse's hoofs, I walked round the house to the veranda, and again sat looking into the garden; and all I wished to see and hear, I still saw and heard for a long time in the dewy mist filled with the sounds of night.

He came a second time, and a third; and the awkwardness arising from that strange conversation passed away entirely, never to return. During that whole summer he came two or three times a week; and I grew so accustomed to his presence, that, when he failed to come for some time, I missed him and felt angry with him, and thought he was behaving badly in deserting me. He treated me like a boy whose company he liked, asked me questions, invited the most cordial frankness on my part, gave me advice and encouragement, or sometimes scolded and checked me. But in spite of his constant effort to keep on my level, I was aware that behind the part of him which I could understand there remained an entire region of mystery, into which he did not consider it necessary to admit me; and this fact did much to preserve my respect for him and his attraction for me. I knew from Kátya and from our neighbours that he had not only to care for his old mother with whom he lived, and to manage his own estate and our affairs, but was also responsible for some public business which was the source of serious worries; but what view he took of all this, what were his convictions, plans, and hopes, I could not in the least find out from him. Whenever I turned the conversation to his affairs, he frowned in a way peculiar to himself and seemed to imply, 'Please stop! That is no business of yours;' and then he changed the subject. This hurt me at first; but I soon grew accustomed to confining our talk to my affairs, and felt this to be quite natural.

There was another thing which displeased me at first and then became pleasant to me. This was his complete indifference and even contempt for my personal appearance. Never by word or look did he imply that I was pretty; on the contrary, he frowned and laughed, whenever the word was applied to me in his presence. He even liked to find fault with my looks and tease me about them. On special days Kátya liked to dress me out in fine clothes and to arrange my hair effectively; but my finery met only with mockery from him, which pained kind-hearted Kátya and at first disconcerted me. She had made up her mind that he admired me; and she could not understand how a man could help wishing a woman whom he admired to appear to the utmost advantage. But I soon understood what he wanted. He wished to make sure that I had not a trace of affectation. And when I understood this I was really quite free from affectation in the clothes I wore, or the arrangement of my hair, or my movements; but a very obvious form of affectation took its place—an affectation of simplicity, at a time when I could not yet be really simple. That he loved me, I knew; but I did not yet ask myself whether he loved me as a child or as a woman. I valued his love; I felt that he thought me better than all other young women in the world, and I could not help wishing him to go on being deceived about me. Without wishing to deceive him, I did deceive him, and I became better myself while deceiving him. I felt it a better and worthier course to show him the good points of my heart and mind than of my body. My hair, hands, face, ways—all these, whether good or bad, he had appraised at once and knew so well, that I could add nothing to my external appearance except the wish to deceive him. But my mind and heart he did not know, because he loved them, and because they were in the very process of growth and development; and on this point I could and did deceive him. And how easy I felt in his company, once I understood this clearly! My causeless bashfulness and awkward movements completely disappeared. Whether he saw me from in front, or in profile, sitting or standing, with my hair up or my hair down, I felt that he knew me from head to foot, and I fancied, was satisfied with me as I was. If, contrary to his habit, he had suddenly said to me as other people did, that I had a pretty face, I believe that I should not have liked it at all. But, on the other hand, how light and happy my heart was when, after I had said something, he looked hard at me and said, hiding emotion under a mask of raillery:

'Yes, there *is* something in you! you are a fine girl—that I must tell you.'

And for what did I receive such rewards, which filled my

heart with pride and joy? Merely for saying that I felt for old Grigóri in his love for his little granddaughter; or because the reading of some poem or novel moved me to tears; or because I liked Mozart better than Schulhof. And I was surprised at my own quickness in guessing what was good and worthy of love, when I certainly did not know then what *was* good and worthy to be loved. Most of my former tastes and habits did not please him; and a mere look of his, or a twitch of his eyebrow was enough to show that he did not like what I was trying to say; and I felt at once that my own standard was changed. Sometimes, when he was about to give me a piece of advice, I seemed to know beforehand what he would say. When he looked in my face and asked me a question, his very look would draw out of me the answer he wanted. All my thoughts and feelings of that time were not really mine: they were his thoughts and feelings, which had suddenly become mine and passed into my life and lighted it up. Quite unconsciously I began to look at everything with different eyes— at Kátya and the servants and Sónya and myself and my occupations. Books, which I used to read merely to escape boredom, now became one of the chief pleasures of my life, merely because he brought me the books and we read and discussed them together. The lessons I gave to Sónya had been a burdensome obligation which I forced myself to go through from a sense of duty; but, after he was present at a lesson, it became a joy to me to watch Sónya's progress. It used to seem to me an impossibility to learn a whole piece of music by heart; but now, when I knew that he would hear it and might praise it, I would play a single movement forty times over without stopping, till poor Kátya stuffed her ears with cotton-wool, while I was still not weary of it. The same old sonatas seemed quite different in their expression, and came out quite changed and much improved. Even Kátya, whom I knew and loved like a second self, became different in my eyes. I now understood for the first time that she was not in the least bound to be the mother, friend, and slave that she was to us. Now I appreciated all the self-sacrifice and devotion of this affectionate creature, and all my obligations to her; and I began to love her even better. It was he too who taught me to take quite a new view of our serfs and servants and maids. It is an absurd confession to make—but I had spent seventeen years among these people and yet knew less about them than about strangers whom I had never seen; it had never once occurred to me that they had their affections and wishes and sorrows, just as I had. Our garden and woods and fields, which I had known so long, became suddenly new and beautiful to me. He was right in saying that the only certain happiness in life is to live for others. At the time his words seemed to me strange, and I did not understand them; but by degrees this became a conviction with me, without thinking about it. He revealed to me a whole new world of joys in the present, without changing anything in my life, without adding anything except himself to each impression in my mind. All that had surrounded me from childhood without saying anything to me, suddenly came to life. The mere sight of him made everything begin to speak and press for admittance to my heart, filling it with happiness.

Often during that summer, when I went upstairs to my room and lay down on my bed, the old unhappiness of spring with its desires and hopes for the future gave place to a passionate happiness in the present. Unable to sleep, I often got up and sat on Kátya's bed, and told her how perfectly happy I was, though I now realize that this was quite unnecessary, as she could see it for herself. But she told me that she was quite content and perfectly happy, and kissed me. I believed her—it seemed to me so necessary and just that everyone should be happy. But Kátya could think of sleep too; and sometimes, pretending to be angry, she drove me from her bed and went to sleep, while I turned over and over in my mind all that made me so happy. Sometimes I got up and said my prayers over again, praying in my own words and thanking God for all the happiness he had given me.

All was quiet in the room; there was only the even breathing of Kátya in her sleep, and the ticking of the clock by her bed, while I turned from side to side and whispered words of prayer, or crossed myself and kissed the cross round my neck.

The door was shut and the windows shuttered; perhaps a fly or gnat hung buzzing in the air. I felt a wish never to leave that room—a wish that dawn might never come, that my present frame of mind might never change. I felt that my dreams and thoughts and prayers were live things, living there in the dark with me, hovering about my bed, and standing over me. And every thought was his thought, and every feeling his feeling. I did not know yet that this was love; I thought that things might go on so for ever, and that this feeling involved no consequences.

CHAPTER III

One day when the corn was being carried, I went with Kátya and Sónya to our favourite seat in the garden, in the shade of the lime-trees and above the dell, beyond which the fields and woods lay open before us. It was three days since Sergéy Mikháylych had been to see us; we were expecting him, all the more because our bailiff reported that he had promised to visit the harvest-field. At two o'clock we saw him ride on to the rye-field. With a smile and a glance at me, Kátya ordered peaches and cherries, of which he was very fond, to be brought; then she lay down on the bench and began to doze. I tore off a crooked flat lime-tree branch, which made my hand wet with its juicy leaves and juicy bark. Then I fanned Kátya with it and went on with my book, breaking off from time to time, to look at the field-path along which he must come. Sónya was making a dolls' house at the root of an old lime-tree. The day was sultry, windless, and steaming; the clouds were packing and growing blacker; all morning a thunder-storm had been gathering, and I felt restless, as I always did before thunder. But by afternoon the clouds began to part, the sun sailed out into a clear sky, and only in one quarter was there a faint rumbling. A single heavy cloud, louring above the horizon and mingling with the dust from the fields, was rent from time to time by pale zigzags of lightning which ran down to the ground. It was clear that for to-day the storm would pass off, with us at all events. The road beyond the garden was visible in places, and we could see a procession of high creaking carts slowly moving along it with their load of sheaves, while the empty carts rattled at a faster pace to meet them, with swaying legs and shirts fluttering in them. The thick dust neither blew away nor settled down—it stood still beyond the fence, and we could see it through the transparent foliage of the garden trees. A little farther off, in the stack-yard, the same voices and the same creaking of wheels were audible; and the same yellow sheaves that had moved slowly past the fence were now flying aloft, and I could see the oval stacks gradually rising higher, and their conspicuous pointed tops, and the labourers swarming upon them. On the dusty field in front more carts were moving and more yellow sheaves were visible; and the noise of the carts, with the sound of talking and singing, came to us from a distance. At one side the bare stubble, with strips of fallow covered with worm-wood, came more and more into view. Lower down, to the right, the gay dresses of the women were visible, as they bent down and swung their arms to bind the sheaves. Here the bare stubble looked untidy; but the disorder was cleared by degrees, as the pretty sheaves were ranged at close intervals. It seemed as if summer had suddenly turned to autumn before my eyes. The dust and heat were everywhere, except in our favourite nook in the garden; and everywhere, in this heat and dust and under the burning sun, the labourers carried on their heavy task with talk and noise.

Meanwhile Kátya slept so sweetly on our shady bench, beneath her white cambric handkerchief, the black juicy cherries glistened so temptingly on the plate, our dresses were so clean and fresh, the water in the jug was so bright with rainbow colours in the sun, and I felt so happy! 'How can I help it?' I thought; 'am I to blame for being happy? And how can I share my happiness? How and to whom can I surrender all myself and all my happiness?'

By this time the sun had sunk behind the tops of the birch avenue, the dust was settling on the fields, the distance be-

came clearer and brighter in the slanting light. The clouds had
dispersed altogether; I could see through the trees the thatch
of three new corn-stacks. The labourers came down off the
stacks; the carts hurried past, evidently for the last time, with
a loud noise of shouting; the women, with rakes over their
shoulders and straw-bands in their belts, walked home past us,
singing loudly; and still there was no sign of Sergéy Mikháylych, though I had seen him ride down the hill long ago.
Suddenly he appeared upon the avenue, coming from a
quarter where I was not looking for him. He had walked
round by the dell. He came quickly towards me, with his hat
off and radiant with high spirits. Seeing that Kátya was
asleep, he bit his lip, closed his eyes, and advanced on tiptoe;
I saw at once that he was in that peculiar mood of causeless
merriment which I always delighted to see in him, and which
we called 'wild ecstasy'. He was just like a schoolboy playing
truant; his whole figure, from head to foot, breathed content,
happiness, and boyish frolic.

'Well, young violet, how are you? All right?' he said in a
whisper, coming up to me and taking my hand. Then, in answer to my question, 'Oh, I'm splendid to-day, I feel like a boy
of thirteen—I want to play at horses and climb trees.'

'Is it wild ecstasy?' I asked, looking into his laughing eyes,
and feeling that the 'wild ecstasy' was infecting me.

'Yes,' he answered, winking and checking a smile. 'But I
don't see why you need hit Katerína Kárlovna on the nose.'

With my eyes on him I had gone on waving the branch,
without noticing that I had knocked the handkerchief off
Kátya's face and was now brushing her with the leaves. I
laughed.

'She will say she was awake all the time,' I whispered, as if
not to awake Kátya; but that was not my real reason—it was
only that I liked to whisper to him.

He moved his lips in imitation of me, pretending that my
voice was too low for him to hear. Catching sight of the dish
of cherries, he pretended to steal it, and carried it off to
Sónya under the lime-tree, where he sat down on her dolls.

Sónya was angry at first, but he soon made his peace with her by starting a game, to see which of them could eat cherries faster.

'If you like, I will send for more cherries,' I said; 'or let us go ourselves.'

He took the dish and set the dolls on it, and we all three started for the orchard. Sónya ran behind us, laughing and pulling at his coat, to make him surrender the dolls. He gave them up and then turned to me, speaking more seriously.

'You really are a violet,' he said, still speaking low, though there was no longer any fear of waking anybody; 'when I came to you out of all that dust and heat and toil, I positively smelt violets at once. But not the sweet violet—you know, that early dark violet that smells of melting snow and spring grass.'

'Is harvest going on well?' I asked, in order to hide the happy agitation which his words produced in me.

'First-rate! Our people are always splendid. The more you know them, the better you like them.'

'Yes,' I said; 'before you came I was watching them from the garden, and suddenly I felt ashamed to be so comfortable myself while they were hard at work, and so . . .'

He interrupted me, with a kind but grave look: 'Don't talk like that, my dear; it is too sacred a matter to talk of lightly. God forbid that you should use fine phrases about that!'

'But it is only to *you* I say this.'

'All right, I understand. But what about those cherries?'

The orchard was locked, and no gardener to be seen: he had sent them all off to help with the harvest. Sónya ran to fetch the key. But he would not wait for her: climbing up a corner of the wall, he raised the net and jumped down on the other side.

His voice came over the wall—'If you want some, give me the dish.'

'No,' I said; 'I want to pick for myself. I shall fetch the key; Sónya won't find it.'

But suddenly I felt that I must see what he was doing there and what he looked like—that I must watch his movements while he supposed that no one saw him. Besides I was simply unwilling just then to lose sight of him for a single minute. Running on tiptoe through the nettles to the other side of the orchard where the wall was lower, I mounted on an empty cask, till the top of the wall was on a level with my waist, and then leaned over into the orchard. I looked at the gnarled old trees, with their broad dented leaves and the ripe black cherries hanging straight and heavy among the foliage; then I pushed my head under the net, and from under the knotted bough of an old cherry-tree I caught sight of Sergéy Mikháylych. He evidently thought that I had gone away and that no one was watching him. With his hat off and his eyes shut, he was sitting on the fork of an old tree and carefully rolling into a ball a lump of cherry-tree gum. Suddenly he shrugged his shoulders, opened his eyes, muttered something, and smiled. Both words and smile were so unlike him that I felt ashamed of myself for eavesdropping. It seemed to me that he had said, 'Másha!' 'Impossible,' I thought. 'Darling Másha!' he said again, in a lower and more tender tone. There was no possible doubt about the two words this time. My heart beat hard, and such a passionate joy—illicit joy, as I felt —took hold of me, that I clutched at the wall, fearing to fall and betray himself. Startled by the sound of my movement, he looked round—he dropped his eyes instantly, and his face turned red, even scarlet, like a child's. He tried to speak, but in vain; again and again his face positively flamed up. Still he smiled as he looked at me, and I smiled too. Then his whole face grew radiant with happiness. He had ceased to be the old uncle who spoiled or scolded me; he was a man on my level, who loved and feared me as I loved and feared him. We looked at one another without speaking. But suddenly he frowned; the smile and light in his eyes disappeared, and he resumed his cold paternal tone, just as if we were doing something wrong and he was repenting and calling on me to repent.

'You had better get down, or you will hurt yourself,' he said; 'and do put your hair straight; just think what you look like!'

'What makes him pretend? what makes him want to give

me pain?' I thought in my vexation. And the same instant brought an irresistible desire to upset his composure again and test my power over him.

'No,' I said; 'I mean to pick for myself.' I caught hold of the nearest branch and climbed to the top of the wall; then, before he had time to catch me, I jumped down on the other side.

'What foolish things you do!' he muttered, flushing again and trying to hide his confusion under a pretence of annoyance; 'you might really have hurt yourself. But how do you mean to get out of this?'

He was even more confused than before, but this time his confusion frightened rather than pleased me. It infected me too and made me blush; avoiding his eye and not knowing what to say, I began to pick cherries though I had nothing to put them in. I reproached myself, I repented of what I had done, I was frightened; I felt that I had lost his good opinion for ever by my folly. Both of us were silent and embarrassed. From this difficult situation Sónya rescued us by running back with the key in her hand. For some time we both addressed our conversation to her and said nothing to each other. When we returned to Kátya, who assured us that she had never been asleep and was listening all the time, I calmed down, and he tried to drop into his fatherly patronizing manner again, but I was not taken in by it. A discussion which we had had some days before came back clear before me.

Kátya had been saying that it was easier for a man to be in love and declare his love than for a woman.

'A man may say that he is in love, and a woman can't,' she said.

'I disagree,' said he; 'a man has no business to say, and can't say, that he is in love.'

'Why not?' I asked.

'Because it never can be true. What sort of a revelation is that, that a man is in love? A man seems to think that whenever he says the word, something will go pop!—that some miracle will be worked, signs and wonders, with all the big guns firing at once! In my opinion,' he went on, 'whoever solemnly brings out the words "I love you" is either deceiving himself or, which is even worse, deceiving others.'

'Then how is a woman to know that a man is in love with her, unless he tells her?' asked Kátya.

'That I don't know,' he answered; 'every man has his own way of telling things. If the feeling exists, it will out somehow. But when I read novels, I always fancy the crestfallen look of Lieut. Strélsky or Alfred, when he says, "I love you, Eleanora", and expects something wonderful to happen at once, and no change at all takes place in either of them—their eyes and their noses and their whole selves remain exactly as they were.'

Even then I had felt that this banter covered something serious that had reference to myself. But Kátya resented his disrespectful treatment of the heroes in novels.

'You are never serious,' she said; 'but tell me truthfully, have you never yourself told a woman that you loved her?'

'Never, and never gone down on one knee,' he answered, laughing; 'and never will.'

This conversation I now recalled, and I reflected that there was no need for him to tell me that he loved me. 'I know that he loves me,' I thought, 'and all his endeavours to seem indifferent will not change my opinion.'

He said little to me throughout the evening, but in every word he said to Kátya and Sónya and in every look and movement of his I saw love and felt no doubt of it. I was only vexed and sorry for him, that he thought it necessary still to hide his feelings and pretend coldness, when it was all so clear, and when it would have been so simple and easy to be boundlessly happy. But my jumping down to him in the orchard weighed on me like a crime. I kept feeling that he would cease to respect me and was angry with me.

After tea I went to the piano, and he followed me.

'Play me something—it is long since I heard you,' he said, catching me up in the parlour.

'I was just going to,' I said. Then I looked straight in his face and said quickly, 'Sergéy Mikháylych, you are not angry with me, are you?'

'What for?' he asked.

'For not obeying you this afternoon,' I said, blushing.

He understood me: he shook his head and made a grimace, which implied that I deserved a scolding but that he did not feel able to give it.

'So it's all right, and we are friends again?' I said, sitting down at the piano.

'Of course!' he said.

In the drawing-room, a large lofty room, there were only two lighted candles on the piano, the rest of the room remaining in half-darkness. Outside the open windows the summer night was bright. All was silent, except when the sound of Kátya's footsteps in the unlighted parlour was heard occasionally, or when his horse, which was tied up under the window, snorted or stamped his hoof on the burdocks that grew there. He sat behind me, where I could not see him; but everywhere—in the half-darkness of the room, in every sound, in myself—I felt his presence. Every look, every movement of his, though I could not see them, found an echo in my heart. I played a sonata of Mozart's which he had brought me and which I had learnt in his presence and for him. I was not thinking at all of what I was playing, but I believe that I played it well, and I thought that he was pleased. I was conscious of his pleasure, and conscious too, though I never looked at him, of the gaze fixed on me from behind. Still moving my fingers mechanically, I turned round quite involuntarily and looked at him. The night had grown brighter, and his head stood out on a background of darkness. He was sitting with his head propped on his hands, and his eyes shone as they gazed at me. Catching his look, I smiled and stopped playing. He smiled too and shook his head reproachfully at the music, for me to go on. When I stopped, the moon had grown brighter and was riding high in the heavens; and the faint light of the candles was supplemented by a new silvery light which came in through the windows and fell on the floor. Kátya called out that it was really too bad—that I had stopped at the best part of the piece, and that I was playing badly. But he declared that I had never played so well; and then he began to walk about the rooms—through the drawing-room to the unlighted parlour and back again to the drawing-room, and each time he looked at me and smiled. I smiled too; I wanted even to laugh with no reason; I was so happy at something that had happened that very day. Kátya and I were standing by the piano; and each time that he vanished through the drawing-room door, I started kissing her in my favourite place, the soft part of her neck under the chin; and each time he came back, I made a solemn face and refrained with difficulty from laughing.

'What is the matter with her to-day?' Kátya asked him.

He only smiled at me without answering; he knew what was the matter with me.

'Just look what a night it is!' he called out from the parlour, where he had stopped by the open French window looking into the garden.

We joined him; and it really was such a night as I have never seen since. The full moon shone above the house and behind us, so that we could not see it, and half the shadow, thrown by the roof and pillars of the house and by the veranda awning, lay slanting and foreshortened on the gravel path and the strip of turf beyond. Everything else was bright and saturated with the silver of the dew and the moonlight. The broad garden-path, on one side of which the shadows of the dahlias and their supports lay aslant, all bright and cold, and shining on the inequalities of the gravel, ran on till it vanished in the mist. Through the trees the roof of the greenhouse shone bright, and a growing mist rose from the dell. The lilac-bushes, already partly leafless, were all bright to the centre. Each flower was distinguishable apart, and all were drenched with dew. In the avenues light and shade were so mingled that they looked, not like paths and trees but like transparent houses, swaying and moving. To our right, in the shadow of the house, everything was black, indistinguishable, and uncanny. But all the brighter for the surrounding darkness was the top of a poplar, with a fantastic crown of leaves, which for some strange reason remained there close to the house, towering into the bright light, instead of flying away into the dim distance, into the retreating dark-blue of the sky.

'Let us go for a walk,' I said.

Kátya agreed, but said I must put on goloshes.

'I don't want them, Kátya,' I said; 'Sergéy Mikháylych will give me his arm.'

As if that would prevent me from wetting my feet! But to us three this seemed perfectly natural at the time. Though he never used to offer me his arm, I now took it of my own accord, and he saw nothing strange in it. We all went down from the veranda together. That whole world, that sky, that garden, that air, were different from those that I knew.

We were walking along an avenue, and it seemed to me, whenever I looked ahead, that we could go no farther in the same direction, that the world of the possible ended there, and that the whole scene must remain fixed for ever in its beauty. But we still moved on, and the magic wall kept parting to let us in; and still we found the familiar garden with trees and paths and withered leaves. And we were really walking along the paths, treading on patches of light and shade; and a withered leaf was really crackling under my foot, and a live twig brushing my face. And that was really he, walking steadily and slowly at my side, and carefully supporting my arm; and that was really Kátya walking beside us with her creaking shoes. And that must be the moon in the sky, shining down on us through the motionless branches.

But at each step the magic wall closed up again behind us and in front, and I ceased to believe in the possibility of advancing farther—I ceased to believe in the reality of it all.

'Oh, there's a frog!' cried Kátya.

'Who said that? and why?' I thought. But then I realized it was Kátya, and that she was afraid of frogs. Then I looked at the ground and saw a little frog which gave a jump and then stood still in front of me, while its tiny shadow was reflected on the shining clay of the path.

'You're not afraid of frogs, are you?' he asked.

I turned and looked at him. Just where we were there was a gap of one tree in the lime-avenue, and I could see his face clearly—it was so handsome and so happy!

Though he had spoken of my fear of frogs, I knew that he

meant to say, 'I love you, my dear one!' 'I love you, I love you' was repeated by his look, by his arm; the light, the shadow, and the air all repeated the same words.

We had gone all round the garden. Kátya's short steps had kept up with us, but now she was tired and out of breath. She said it was time to go in; and I felt very sorry for her. 'Poor thing!' I thought; 'why does not she feel as we do? why are we not all young and happy, like this night and like him and me?'

We went in, but it was a long time before he went away, though the cocks had crowed, and everyone in the house was asleep, and his horse, tethered under the window, snorted continually and stamped his hoof on the burdocks. Kátya never reminded us of the hour, and we sat on talking of the merest trifles and not thinking of the time, till it was past two. The cocks were crowing for the third time and the dawn was breaking when he rode away. He said good-bye as usual and made no special allusion; but I knew that from that day he was mine, and that I should never lose him now. As soon as I had confessed to myself that I loved him, I took Kátya into my confidence. She rejoiced in the news and was touched by my telling her; but she was actually able—poor thing!—to go to bed and sleep! For me, I walked for a long, long time about the veranda; then I went down to the garden, where, recalling each word, each movement, I walked along the same avenues through which I had walked with him. I did not sleep at all that night, and saw sunrise and early dawn for the first time in my life. And never again did I see such a night and such a morning. 'Only why does he not tell me plainly that he loves me?' I thought; 'what makes him invent obstacles and call himself old, when all is so simple and so splendid? What makes him waste this golden time which may never return? Let him say "I love you"—say it in plain words; let him take my hand in his and bend over it and say "I love you". Let him blush and look down before me; and then I will tell him all. No! not tell him, but throw my arms round him and press close to him and weep.' But then a thought came to me— 'What if I am mistaken and he does not love me?'

I was startled by this fear—God knows where it might have

led me. I recalled his embarrassment and mine, when I jumped down to him in the orchard; and my heart grew very heavy. Tears gushed from my eyes, and I began to pray. A strange thought occurred to me, calming me and bringing hope with it. I resolved to begin fasting on that day, to take the Communion on my birthday, and on that same day to be betrothed to him.

How this result would come to pass I had no idea; but from that moment I believed and felt sure it would be so. The dawn had fully come and the labourers were getting up when I went back to my room.

CHAPTER IV

The fast of the Assumption falling in August, no one in the house was surprised by my intention of fasting.

During the whole of the week he never once came to see us; but, far from being surprised or vexed or made uneasy by his absence, I was glad of it—I did not expect him until my birthday. Each day during the week I got up early. While the horses were being harnessed, I walked in the garden alone, turning over in my mind the sins of the day before, and considering what I must do to-day, so as to be satisfied with my day and not spoil it by a single sin. It seemed so easy to me then to abstain from sin altogether; only a trifling effort seemed necessary. When the horses came round, I got into the carriage with Kátya or one of the maids, and we drove to the church two miles away. While entering the church, I always recalled the prayer for those who 'come unto the Temple in the fear of God', and tried to get just that frame of mind when mounting the two grass-grown steps up to the building. At that hour there were not more than a dozen worshippers— household servants or peasant women keeping the Fast. They bowed to me, and I returned their bows with studied humility. Then, with what seemed to me a great effort of courage, I went myself and got candles from the man who kept them, an old soldier and an Elder; and I placed the candles before the icons. Through the central door of the altar-screen I could see the altar-cloth which my mother had worked; on the screen were the two angels which had seemed so big to me when I was little, and the dove with a golden halo which had fascinated me long ago. Behind the choir stood the old battered font, where I had been christened myself and had stood godmother to so many of the servants' children. The old priest came out, wearing a cope made of the pall that had covered my father's coffin, and began to read in the same voice that I had heard all my life—at services held in our house, at Sónya's christening, at memorial services for my father, and at my mother's funeral. The same old quavering voice of the deacon rose in the choir; and the same old woman, whom I could remember at every service in that church, crouched by the wall, fixing her streaming eyes on an icon in the choir, pressing her folded fingers against her faded kerchief, and muttering with her toothless gums. And these objects were no longer merely curious to me, merely interesting from old recollections—each had become important and sacred in my eyes and seemed charged with profound meaning. I listened to each word of the prayers and tried to suit my feeling to it; and if I failed to understand, I prayed silently that God would enlighten me, or made up a prayer of my own in place of what I had failed to catch. When the penitential prayers were repeated, I recalled my past life, and that innocent childish past seemed to me so black when compared to the present brightness of my soul, that I wept and was horrified at myself; but I felt too that all those sins would be forgiven, and that if my sins had been even greater, my repentance would be all the sweeter. At the end of the service when the priest said, 'The blessing of the Lord be upon you!' I seemed to feel an immediate sensation of physical well-being, of a mysterious light and warmth that instantly filled my heart. The service over, the priest came and asked me whether he should come to our house to say Mass, and what hour would suit me; and I thanked him for the suggestion, intended, as I thought, to please me, but said that I would come to church instead, walking or driving.

'Is that not too much trouble?' he asked. And I was at a loss for an answer, fearing to commit a sin of pride.

After the Mass, if Kátya was not with me. I always sent the carriage home and walked back alone, bowing humbly to all who passed, and trying to find an opportunity of giving help or advice. I was eager to sacrifice myself for someone, to help in lifting a fallen cart, to rock a child's cradle, to give up the path to others by stepping into the mud. One evening I heard the bailiff report to Kátya that Simon, one of our serfs, had come to beg some boards to make a coffin for his daughter, and a ruble to pay the priest for the funeral; the bailiff had given what he asked. 'Are they as poor as that?' I asked. 'Very poor, Miss,' the bailiff answered; 'they have no salt to their food.' My heart ached to hear this, and yet I felt a kind of pleasure too. Pretending to Kátya that I was merely going for a walk, I ran upstairs, got out all my money (it was very little but it was all I had), crossed myself, and started off alone, through the veranda and the garden, on my way to Simon's hut. It stood at the end of the village, and no one saw me as I went up to the window, placed the money on the sill, and tapped on the pane. Someone came out, making the door creak, and hailed me; but I hurried home, cold and shaking with fear like a criminal. Kátya asked where I had been and what was the matter with me; but I did not answer, and did not even understand what she was saying. Everything suddenly seemed to me so petty and insignificant. I locked myself up in my own room, and walked up and down alone for a long time, unable to do anything, unable to think, unable to understand my own feelings. I thought of the joy of the whole family, and of what they would say of their benefactor; and I felt sorry that I had not given them the money myself. I thought too of what Sergéy Mikháylych would say, if he knew what I had done; and I was glad to think that no one would ever find out. I was so happy, and I felt myself and everyone else so bad, and yet was so kindly disposed to myself and to all the world, that the thought of death came to me as a dream of happiness. I smiled and prayed and wept, and felt at that

moment a burning passion of love for all the world, myself included. Between services I used to read the Gospel; and the
book became more and more intelligible to me, and the story
of that divine life simpler and more touching; and the depths
of thought and feeling I found in studying it became more
awful and impenetrable. On the other hand, how clear and
simple everything seemed to me when I rose from the study
of this book and looked again on life around me and reflected
on it! It was so difficult, I felt, to lead a bad life, and so simple
to love everyone and be loved. All were so kind and gentle to
me; even Sónya, whose lessons I had not broken off, was quite
different—trying to understand and please me and not to vex
me. Everyone treated me as I treated them. Thinking over
my enemies, of whom I must ask pardon before confession, I
could only remember one—one of our neighbours, a girl, whom
I had made fun of in company a year ago, and who had ceased
to visit us. I wrote to her, confessing my fault and asking her
forgiveness. She replied that she forgave me and wished me to
forgive her. I cried for joy over her simple words, and saw in
them, at the time, a deep and touching feeling. My old nurse
cried, when I asked her to forgive me. 'What makes them all
so kind to me? what have I done to deserve their love?' I asked
myself. Sergéy Mikháylych would come into my mind, and I
thought for long about him. I could not help it, and I did
not consider these thoughts sinful. But my thoughts of him
were quite different from what they had been on the night
when I first realized that I loved him: he seemed to me now
like a second self, and became a part of every plan for the future. The inferiority which I had always felt in his presence
had vanished entirely: I felt myself his equal, and could understand him thoroughly from the moral elevation I had
reached. What had seemed strange in him was now quite
clear to me. Now I could see what he meant by saying that to
live for others was the only true happiness, and I agreed with
him perfectly. I believed that our life together would be endlessly happy and untroubled. I looked forward, not to foreign
tours or fashionable society or display, but to a quite different

scene—a quiet family life in the country, with constant self-sacrifice, constant mutual love, and constant recognition in all things of the kind hand of Providence.

I carried out my plan of taking the Communion on my birthday. When I came back from church that day, my heart was so swelling with happiness that I was afraid of life, afraid of any feeling that might break in on that happiness. We had hardly left the carriage for the steps in front of the house, when there was a sound of wheels on the bridge, and I saw Sergéy Mikháylych drive up in his well-known trap. He congratulated me,[1] and we went together to the parlour. Never since I had known him had I been so much at my ease with him and so self-possessed as on that morning. I felt in myself a whole new world, out of his reach and beyond his comprehension. I was not conscious of the slightest embarrassment in speaking to him. He must have understood the cause of this feeling; for he was tender and gentle beyond his wont and showed a kind of reverent consideration for me. When I made for the piano, he locked it and put the key in his pocket.

'Don't spoil your present mood,' he said, 'you have the sweetest of all music in your soul just now.'

I was grateful for his words, and yet I was not quite pleased at his understanding too easily and clearly what ought to have been an exclusive secret in my heart. At dinner he said that he had come to congratulate me and also to say good-bye; for he must go to Moscow to-morrow. He looked at Kátya as he spoke; but then he stole a glance at me, and I saw that he was afraid he might detect signs of emotion on my face. But I was neither surprised nor agitated; I did not even ask whether he would be long away. I knew he would say this, and I knew that he would not go. How did I know? I cannot explain that to myself now; but on that memorable day it seemed that I knew everything that had been and that would be. It was like a delightful dream, when all that happens seems to have happened already and to be quite familiar, and it will all happen over again, and one knows that it will happen.

---

[1] It is the custom in Russia to congratulate anyone on his or her birthday, and also on receiving Communion.

He meant to go away immediately after dinner; but, as Kátya was tired after church and went to lie down for a little, he had to wait until she woke up in order to say good-bye to her. The sun shone into the drawing-room, and we went out to the veranda. When we were seated, I began at once, quite calmly, the conversation that was bound to fix the fate of my heart. I began to speak, no sooner and no later, but at the very moment when we sat down, before our talk had taken any turn or colour that might have hindered me from saying what I meant to say. I cannot tell myself where it came from—my coolness and determination and preciseness of expression. It was as if something independent of my will was speaking through my lips. He sat opposite me with his elbows resting on the rails of the veranda; he pulled a lilac-branch towards him and stripped the leaves off it. When I began to speak, he let go the branch and leaned his head on one hand. His attitude might have shown either perfect calmness or strong emotion.

'Why are you going?' I asked, significantly, deliberately, and looking straight at him.

He did not answer at once.

'Business!' he muttered at last and dropped his eyes.

I realized how difficult he found it to lie to me, and in reply to such a frank question.

'Listen,' I said; 'you know what to-day is to me, how important for many reasons. If I question you, it is not to show an interest in your doings (you know that I have become intimate with you and fond of you)—I ask you this question, because I *must* know the answer. Why are you going?'

'It is very hard for me to tell you the true reason,' he said. 'During this week I have thought much about you and about myself, and have decided that I must go. You understand why; and if you care for me, you will ask no questions.' He put up a hand to rub his forehead and cover his eyes. 'I find it very difficult . . . But you will understand.'

My heart began to beat fast.

'I cannot understand you,' I said; 'I *cannot! you* must tell me; in God's name and for the sake of this day tell me what you please, and I shall hear it with calmness,' I said.

He changed his position, glanced at me, and again drew the lilac-twig towards him.

'Well!' he said, after a short silence in a voice that tried in vain to seem steady, 'it is a foolish business and impossible to put into words, and I feel the difficulty, but I will try to explain it to you,' he added, frowning as if in bodily pain.

'Well?' I said.

'Just imagine the existence of a man—let us call him A—who has left youth far behind, and of a woman whom we may call B, who is young and happy and has seen nothing as yet of life or of the world. Family circumstances of various kinds brought them together, and he grew to love her as a daughter, and had no fear that his love would change its nature.'

He stopped, but I did not interrupt him.

'But he forgot that B was so young, that life was still all a May-game to her,' he went on with a sudden swiftness and determination and without looking at me, 'and that it was easy to fall in love with her in a different way, and that this would amuse her. He made a mistake and was suddenly aware of another feeling, as heavy as remorse, making its way into his heart, and he was afraid. He was afraid that their old friendly relations would be destroyed, and he made up his mind to go away before that happened.' As he said this, he began again to rub his eyes, with a pretence of indifference, and to close them.

'Why was he afraid to love differently?' I asked very low; but I restrained my emotion and spoke in an even voice. He evidently thought that I was not serious; for he answered as if he were hurt.

'You are young, and I am not young. You want amusement, and I want something different. Amuse yourself, if you like, but not with me. If you do, I shall take it seriously; and then I shall be unhappy, and you will repent. That is what A said,' he added; 'however, this is all nonsense; but you understand why I am going. And don't let us continue this conversation. Please not!'

'No! no!' I said, 'we must continue it,' and tears began to tremble in my voice 'Did he love her, or not?'

He did not answer.

'If he did not love her, why did he treat her as a child and pretend to her?' I asked.

'Yes, A behaved badly,' he interrupted me quickly; 'but it all came to an end and they parted friends.'

'This is horrible! Is there no other ending?' I said with a great effort, and then felt afraid of what I had said.

'Yes, there is,' he said, showing a face full of emotion and looking straight at me. 'There are two different endings. But, for God's sake, listen to me quietly and don't interrupt. Some say'—here he stood up and smiled with a smile that was heavy with pain—'some say that A went off his head, fell passionately in love with B, and told her so. But she only laughed. To her it was all a jest, but to him a matter of life and death.'

I shuddered and tried to interrupt him—tried to say that he must not dare to speak for me; but he checked me, laying his hand on mine.

'Wait!' he said, and his voice shook. 'The other story is that she took pity on him, and fancied, poor child, from her ignorance of the world, that she really could love him, and so consented to be his wife. And he, in his madness, believed it—believed that his whole life could begin anew; but she saw herself that she had deceived him and that he had deceived her. . . . But let us drop the subject finally,' he ended, clearly unable to say more; and then he began to walk up and down in silence before me.

Though he had asked that the subject should be dropped, I saw that his whole soul was hanging on my answer. I tried to speak, but the pain at my heart kept me dumb. I glanced at him—he was pale and his lower lip trembled. I felt sorry for him. With a sudden effort I broke the bonds of silence which had held me fast, and began to speak in a low inward voice, which I feared would break every moment.

'There is a third ending to the story,' I said, and then paused, but he said nothing; 'the third ending is that he did not love her, but hurt her, hurt her, and thought that he was right; and he left her and was actually proud of himself. You have been pretending, not I; I have loved you since the first day we met, loved you,' I repeated, and at the word 'loved' my low inward voice changed, without intention of mine, to a wild cry which frightened me myself.

He stood pale before me, his lip trembled more and more violently, and two tears came out upon his cheeks.

'It is wrong!' I almost screamed, feeling that I was choking with angry unshed tears. 'Why do you do it?' I cried, and got up to leave him.

But he would not let me go. His head was resting on my knees, his lips were kissing my still trembling hands, and his tears were wetting them. 'My God! if I had only known!' he whispered.

'Why? why?' I kept on repeating, but in my heart there was happiness, happiness which had now come back, after so nearly departing for ever.

Five minutes later Sónya was rushing upstairs to Kátya and proclaiming all over the house that Másha intended to marry Sergéy Mikháylych.

CHAPTER V

There were no reasons for putting off our wedding, and neither he nor I wished for delay. Kátya, it is true, thought we ought to go to Moscow, to buy and order wedding-clothes; and his mother tried to insist that, before the wedding, he must set up a new carriage, buy new furniture, and re-paper the whole house. But we two together carried our point, that all these things, if they were really indispensable, should be done afterwards, and that we should be married within a fortnight after my birthday, quietly, without wedding-clothes, without a party, without best men and supper and champagne, and all the other conventional features of a wedding. He told me how dissatisfied his mother was that there should be no band, no mountain of luggage, no renovation of the whole house—so unlike her own marriage which had cost thirty thousand rubles; and he told of the solemn and secret confabulations which she held in her store-room with her

housekeeper, Maryúshka, rummaging the chests and discussing carpets, curtains, and salvers as indispensable conditions
of our happiness. At our house Kátya did just the same with
my old nurse, Kuzmínichna. It was impossible to treat the matter lightly with Kátya. She was firmly convinced that he and I,
when discussing our future, were merely talking the sentimental nonsense natural to people in our position; and that our
real future happiness depended on the hemming of table-
cloths and napkins and the proper cutting-out and stitching of
under-clothing. Several times a day secret information passed
between the two houses, to communicate what was going forward in each; and though the external relations between
Kátya and his mother were most affectionate, yet a slightly
hostile though very subtle diplomacy was already perceptible
in their dealings. I now became more intimate with Tatyána
Semënovna, the mother of Sergéy Mikháylych, an old-fashioned
lady, strict and formal in the management of her household.
Her son loved her, and not merely because she was his mother:
he thought her the best, cleverest, kindest, and most affectionate woman in the world. She was always kind to us and
to me especially, and was glad that her son should be getting
married; but when I was with her after our engagement, I always felt that she wished me to understand that, in her opinion, her son might have looked higher, and that it would be
as well for me to keep that in mind. I understood her meaning
perfectly and thought her quite right.

During that fortnight he and I met every day. He came to
dinner regularly and stayed on till midnight. But though he
said—and I knew he was speaking the truth—that he had no
life apart from me, yet he never spent the whole day with me,
and tried to go on with his ordinary occupations. Our outward
relations remained unchanged to the very day of our marriage: we went on saying 'you' and not 'thou' to each other; he
did not even kiss my hand; he did not seek, but even avoided,
opportunities of being alone with me. It was as if he feared to
yield to the harmful excess of tenderness he felt. I don't know
which of us had changed; but I now felt myself entirely his
equal; I no longer found in him the pretence of simplicity

which had displeased me earlier; and I often delighted to see in him, not a grown man inspiring respect and awe but a loving and wildly happy child. 'How mistaken I was about him!' I often thought; 'he is just such another human being as myself!' It seemed to me now, that his whole character was before me and that I thoroughly understood it. And how simple was every feature of his character, and how congenial to my own! Even his plans for our future life together were just my plans, only more clearly and better expressed in his words.

The weather was bad just then, and we spent most of our time indoors. The corner between the piano and the window was the scene of our best intimate talks. The candle-light was reflected on the blackness of the window near us; from time to time drops struck the glistening pane and rolled down. The rain pattered on the roof; the water splashed in a puddle under the spout; it felt damp near the window; but our corner seemed all the brighter and warmer and happier for that.

'Do you know, there is something I have long wished to say to you,' he began one night when we were sitting up late in our corner; 'I was thinking of it all the time you were playing.'

'Don't say it, I know all about it,' I replied.

'All right! mum's the word!'

'No! what is it?' I asked.

'Well, it is this. You remember the story I told you about A and B?'

'I should just think I did! What a stupid story! Lucky that it ended as it did!'

'Yes, I was very near destroying my happiness by my own act. You saved me. But the main thing is that I was always telling lies then, and I'm ashamed of it, and I want to have my say out now.'

'Please don't! you really mustn't!'

'Don't be frightened,' he said, smiling. 'I only want to justify myself. When I began then, I meant to argue.'

'It is always a mistake to argue,' I said.

'Yes, I argued wrong. After all my disappointments and mistakes in life, I told myself firmly when I came to the coun-

try this year, that love was no more for me, and that all I had
to do was to grow old decently. So for a long time, I was unable to clear up my feeling towards you, or to make out
where it might lead me. I hoped, and I didn't hope: at one
time I thought you were trifling with me; at another I felt
sure of you but could not decide what to do. But after that
evening, you remember, when we walked in the garden at
night, I got alarmed: the present happiness seemed too great
to be real. What if I allowed myself to hope and then
failed? But of course I was thinking only of myself, for I am
disgustingly selfish.'

He stopped and looked at me.

'But it was not all nonsense that I said then. It was possible and right for me to have fears. I take so much from you
and can give so little. You are still a child, a bud that has yet
to open; you have never been in love before, and I . . .'

'Yes, do tell me the truth. . . ,' I began, and then stopped,
afraid of his answer. 'No, never mind,' I added.

'Have I been in love before? is that it?' he said, guessing my
thoughts at once. 'That I can tell you. No, never before—
nothing at all like what I feel now.' But a sudden painful recollection seemed to flash across his mind. 'No,' he said sadly;
'in this too I need your compassion, in order to have the right
to love you. Well, was I not bound to think twice before saying
that I loved you? What do I give you? love, no doubt.'

'And is that little?' I asked, looking him in the face.

'Yes, my dear, it is little to give *you*,' he continued; 'you
have youth and beauty. I often lie awake at night from happiness, and all the time I think of our future life together. I
have lived through much, and now I think I have found
what is needed for happiness. A quiet secluded life in the
country, with the possibility of being useful to people to whom
it is easy to do good, and who are not accustomed to have it
done to them; then work which one hopes may be of some use;
then rest, nature, books, music, love for one's neighbour—such
is my idea of happiness. And then, on the top of all that, you
for a mate, and children, perhaps—what more can the heart of
man desire?'

'It should be enough' I said.

'Enough for me whose youth is over,' he went on, 'but not for you. Life is still before you, and you will perhaps seek happiness, and perhaps find it, in something different. You think now that this is happiness, because you love me.'

'You are wrong,' I, said; 'I have always desired just that quiet domestic life and prized it. And you only say just what I have thought.'

He smiled.

'So you think, my dear; but that is not enough for you. You have youth and beauty,' he repeated thoughtfully.

But I was angry because he disbelieved me and seemed to cast my youth and beauty in my teeth.

'Why do you love me then?' I asked angrily; 'for my youth or for myself?'

'I don't know, but I love you,' he answered, looking at me with his attentive and attractive gaze.

I did not reply and involuntarily looked into his eyes. Suddenly a strange thing happened to me: first I ceased to see what was around me; then his face seemed to vanish till only the eyes were left, shining over against mine; next the eyes seemed to be in my own head, and then all became confused—I could see nothing and was forced to shut my eyes, in order to break loose from the feeling of pleasure and fear which his gaze was producing in me . . .

The day before our wedding-day, the weather cleared up towards evening. The rains which had begun in summer gave place to clear weather, and we had our first autumn evening, bright and cold. It was a wet, cold, shining world, and the garden showed for the first time the spaciousness and colour and bareness of autumn. The sky was clear, cold, and pale. I went to bed happy in the thought that to-morrow, our wedding-day, would be fine. I awoke with the sun, and the thought that this very day . . . seemed alarming and surprising. I went out into the garden. The sun had just risen and shone fitfully through the meagre yellow leaves of the lime avenue. The path was strewn with rustling leaves, clusters of mountain-ash berries hung red and wrinkled on the boughs, with a sprinkling of frost-bitten crumpled leaves; the dahlias were black and wrinkled. The first rime lay like silver on the pale green of the grass and on the broken burdock plants round the house. In the clear cold sky there was not, and could not be, a single cloud.

'Can it possibly be to-day?' I asked myself, incredulous of my own happiness. 'Is it possible that I shall wake to-morrow, not here but in that strange house with the pillars? Is it possible that I shall never again wait for his coming and meet him, and sit up late with Kátya to talk about him? Shall I never sit with him beside the piano in our drawing-room? never see him off and feel uneasy about him on dark nights?' But I remembered that he promised yesterday to pay a last visit, and that Kátya had insisted on my trying on my wedding-dress, and had said 'For to-morrow'. I believed for a moment that it was all real, and then doubted again. 'Can it be that after to-day I shall be living there with a mother-in-law, without Nadézhda or old Grigóri or Kátya? Shall I go to bed without kissing my old nurse good-night and hearing her say, while she signs me with the cross from old custom, "Good-night, Miss"? Shall I never again teach Sónya and play with her and knock through the wall to her in the morning and hear her hearty laugh? Shall I become from to-day someone that I myself do not know? and is a new world, that will realize my hopes and desires, opening before me? and will that new world last for ever?' Alone with these thoughts I was depressed and impatient for his arrival. He came early, and it required his presence to convince me that I should really be his wife that very day, and the prospect ceased to frighten me.

Before dinner we walked to our church, to attend a memorial service for my father.

'If only he were living now!' I thought as we were returning and I leant silently on the arm of him who had been the dearest friend of the object of my thoughts. During the service, while I pressed my forehead against the cold stone of the chapel floor, I called up my father so vividly; I was so convinced that he understood me and approved my choice, that I felt as if his spirit were still hovering over us and blessing me.

And my recollections and hopes, my joy and sadness, made up one solemn and satisfied feeling which was in harmony with the fresh still air, the silence, the bare fields and pale sky, from which the bright but powerless rays, trying in vain to burn my check, fell over all the landscape. My companion seemed to understand and share my feeling. He walked slowly and silently; and his face, at which I glanced from time to time, expressed the same serious mood between joy and sorrow which I shared with nature.

Suddenly he turned to me, and I saw that he intended to speak. 'Suppose he starts some other subject than that which is in my mind?' I thought. But he began to speak of my father and did not even name him.

'He once said to me in jest, "you should marry my Másha",' he began.

'He would have been happy now,' I answered, pressing closer the arm which held mine.

'You were a child then,' he went on, looking into my eyes; 'I loved those eyes then and used to kiss them only because they were like his, never thinking they would be so dear to me for their own sake. I used to call you Másha then.'

'I want you to say "thou" to me,' I said.

'I was just going to,' he answered; 'I feel for the first time that *thou* art entirely mine;' and his calm happy gaze that drew me to him rested on me.

We went on along the footpath over the beaten and trampled stubble; our voices and footsteps were the only sounds. On one side the brownish stubble stretched over a hollow to a distant leafless wood; across it at some distance a peasant was noiselessly ploughing a black strip which grew wider and wider. A drove of horses scattered under the hill seemed close to us. On the other side, as far as the garden and our house peeping through the trees, a field of winter corn, thawed by the sun, showed black with occasional patches of green. The winter sun shone over everything, and everything was covered with long gossamer spider's webs, which floated in the air round us, lay on the frost-dried stubble, and got into our eyes and hair and clothes. When we spoke, the sound of our voices hung in the motionless air above us, as if we two were alone in the whole world—alone under that azure vault, in which the beams of the winter sun played and flashed without scorching.

I too wished to say 'thou' to him, but I felt ashamed.

'Why *dost thou* walk so fast?' I said quickly and almost in a whisper; I could not help blushing.

He slackened his pace, and the gaze he turned on me was even more affectionate, gay, and happy.

At home we found that his mother and the inevitable guests had arrived already, and I was never alone with him again till we came out of church to drive to Nikólskoe.

The church was nearly empty: I just caught a glimpse of his mother standing up straight on a mat by the choir and of Kátya wearing a cap with purple ribbons and with tears on her cheeks, and of two or three of our servants looking curiously at me. I did not look at him, but felt his presence there beside me. I attended to the words of the prayers and repeated them, but they found no echo in my heart. Unable to pray, I looked listlessly at the icons, the candles, the embroidered cross on the priest's cope, the screen, and the window, and took nothing in. I only felt that something strange was being done to me. At last the priest turned to us with the cross in his hand, congratulated us, and said, 'I christened you and by God's mercy have lived to marry you.' Kátya and his mother kissed us, and Grigóri's voice was heard, calling up the carriage. But I was only frightened and disappointed: all was over, but nothing extraordinary, nothing worthy of the Sacrament I had just received, had taken place in myself. He and I exchanged kisses, but the kiss seemed strange and not expressive of our feeling. 'Is this all?' I thought. We went out of church, the sound of wheels reverberated under the vaulted roof, the fresh air blew on my face, he put on his hat and handed me into the carriage. Through the window I could see a frosty moon with a halo round it. He sat down beside me and shut the door after him. I felt a sudden pang. The assurance of his proceedings seemed to me insulting. Kátya called out that I should put something on my head; the wheels rumbled on the stone and then moved along the soft road, and we were off. Huddling in a corner, I looked out at the distant fields and the road flying past in the cold glitter of the moon. Without looking at him, I felt his presence beside me. 'Is this all I have got from the moment, of which I expected so much?' I thought; and still it seemed humiliating and insulting to be sitting alone with him, and so close. I turned to him, intending to speak; but the words would not come, as if my love had vanished, giving place to a feeling of mortification and alarm.

'Till this moment I did not believe it was possible,' he said in a low voice in answer to my look.

'But I am afraid somehow,' I said.

'Afraid of me, my dear?' he said, taking my hand and bending over it.

My hand lay lifeless in his, and the cold at my heart was painful.

'Yes,' I whispered.

But at that moment my heart began to beat faster, my hand trembled and pressed his, I grew hot, my eyes sought his in the half-darkness, and all at once I felt that I did not fear him, that this fear was love—a new love still more tender and stronger than the old. I felt that I was wholly his, and that I was happy in his power over me.

Part II

CHAPTER I

Days, weeks, two whole months, of seclusion in the country slipped by unnoticed, as we thought then; and yet those two months comprised feelings, emotions, and happiness, sufficient for a lifetime. Our plans for the regulation of our life in the country were not carried out at all in the way that we expected; but the reality was not inferior to our ideal. There was none of that hard work, performance of duty, self-sacrifice, and life for others, which I had pictured to myself before our marriage; there was, on the contrary, merely a selfish feeling of love for one another, a wish to be loved, a constant cause-less gaiety and entire oblivion of all the world. It is true that my husband sometimes went to his study to work, or drove to town on business, or walked about attending to the manage-ment of the estate; but I saw what it cost him to tear him-self away from me. He confessed later that every occupation, in my absence, seemed to him mere nonsense in which it was impossible to take any interest. It was just the same with me. If I read, or played the piano, or passed my time with his mother, or taught in the school, I did so only because each of these occupations was connected with him and won his approval; but whenever the thought of him was not asso-ciated with any duty, my hands fell by my sides and it seemed to me absurd to think that anything existed apart from him. Perhaps it was a wrong and selfish feeling, but it gave me hap-piness and lifted me high above all the world. He alone existed on earth for me, and I considered him the best and most fault-less man in the world; so that I could not live for anything else than for him, and my one object was to realize his concep-tion of me. And in his eyes I was the first and most excel-lent woman in the world, the possessor of all possible virtues; and I strove to be that woman in the opinion of the first and best of men.

He came to my room one day while I was praying. I looked round at him and went on with my prayers. Not wish-ing to interrupt me, he sat down at a table and opened a book. But I thought he was looking at me and looked round myself. He smiled, I laughed, and had to stop my prayers.

'Have you prayed already?' I asked.

'Yes. But you go on; I'll go away.'

'You do say your prayers, I hope?'

He made no answer and was about to leave the room when I stopped him.

'Darling, for my sake, please repeat the prayers with me!' He stood up beside me, dropped his arms awkwardly, and began, with a serious face and some hesitation. Occasionally he turned towards me, seeking signs of approval and aid in my face.

When he came to an end, I laughed and embraced him.

'I feel just as if I were ten! And you do it all!' he said, blushing and kissing my hands.

Our house was one of those old-fashioned country houses in which several generations have passed their lives together under one roof, respecting and loving one another. It was all redolent of good sound family traditions, which as soon as I entered it seemed to become mine too. The management of the household was carried on by Tatyána Semënovna, my mother-in-law, on old-fashioned lines. Of grace and beauty there was not much; but, from the servants down to the furniture and food, there was abundance of everything, and a general cleanliness, solidity, and order, which inspired respect. The drawing-room furniture was arranged symmetrically; there were portraits on the walls, and the floor was covered with home-made carpets and mats. In the morning-room there was an old piano, with chiffoniers of two different patterns, sofas, and little carved tables with bronze ornaments. My sitting-room, specially arranged by Tatyána Semënovna, contained the best furniture in the house, of many styles and periods, including an old pier-glass, which I was frightened to look into at first, but came to value as an old friend. Though Tatyána Semënovna's voice was never heard, the whole household went like a clock. The number of servants was far too large (they all wore soft boots with no heels, because Tatyána Semënovna had an intense dislike for stamping heels and creaking soles); but they all seemed proud of their calling, trembled before their old mistress, treated my husband and me with an affectionate air of patronage, and performed their duties, to all appearance, with extreme satisfaction. Every Saturday the floors were scoured and the carpets beaten without fail; on the first of every month there was a religious service in the house and holy water was sprinkled; on Tatyána Semënovna's name-day and on her son's (and on mine too, beginning from that autumn) an entertainment was regularly provided for the whole neighbourhood. And all this had gone on without a break ever since the beginning of Tatyána Semënovna's life.

My husband took no part in the household management, he attended only to the farm-work and the labourers, and gave much time to this. Even in winter he got up so early that I often woke to find him gone. He generally came back for early tea, which we drank alone together; and at that time, when the worries and vexations of the farm were over, he was almost always in that state of high spirits which we called 'wild ecstasy'. I often made him tell me what he had been doing in the morning, and he gave such absurd accounts that we both laughed till we cried. Sometimes I insisted on a serious account, and he gave it, restraining a smile. I watched his eyes and moving lips and took nothing in: the sight of him and the sound of his voice was pleasure enough.

'Well, what have I been saying? repeat it,' he would sometimes say. But I could repeat nothing. It seemed so absurd that *he* should talk to *me* of any other subject than ourselves. As if it mattered in the least what went on in the world outside! It was at a much later time that I began to some extent to understand and take an interest in his occupations. Tatyána Semënovna never appeared before dinner: she breakfasted alone and said good-morning to us by deputy. In our exclusive little world of frantic happiness a voice from the staid orderly region in which she dwelt was quite startling: I often lost self-control and could only laugh without speaking, when the maid stood before me with folded hands and made her formal report: 'The mistress bade me inquire how you slept after your walk yesterday evening; and about her I was to report that she had pain in her side all night, and a stupid dog barked in the village and kept her awake: and also I was to ask how you liked the bread this morning, and to tell you that it was not Tarás who baked to-day, but Nikoláshka who was trying his hand for the first time; and she says his baking is not at all bad, especially the cracknels: but the tea-rusks were over-baked.' Before dinner we saw little of each other: he wrote or went out again while I played the piano or read; but at four o'clock we all met in the drawing-room before dinner. Tatyána Seménovna sailed out of her own room, and certain poor and pious maiden ladies, of whom there were always two or three living in the house, made their appearance also. Every day without fail my husband by old habit offered his arm to his mother, to take her in to dinner; but she insisted that I should take the other, so that every day, without fail, we stuck in the doors and got in each other's way. She also presided at dinner, where the conversation, if rather solemn, was polite and sensible. The commonplace talk between my husband and me was a pleasant interruption to the formality of those entertainments. Sometimes there were squabbles between mother and son and they bantered one another; and I especially enjoyed those scenes, because they were the best proof of the strong and tender love which united the two. After dinner Tatyána Seménovna went to the parlour, where she sat in an armchair and ground her snuff or cut the leaves of new books, while we read aloud or went off to the piano in the morning-room. We read much together at this time, but music was our favourite and best enjoyment, always evoking fresh chords in our hearts and as it were revealing each afresh to the other. While I played his favourite pieces, he sat on a distant sofa where I could hardly see him. He was ashamed to betray the impression produced on him by the music; but often, when he was not expecting it, I rose from the piano, went up to him, and tried to detect on his face signs of emotion—the unnatural brightness and moistness of the eyes, which he tried in vain to conceal. Tatyána Seménovna, though she often wanted to take a look at us there, was also anxious to put no constraint upon us. So she always passed through the room with an air of indifference and a pretence of being busy; but I knew that she had no real reason for going to her room and returning so soon. In the evening I poured out tea in the large drawing-room, and all the household met again. This solemn ceremony of distributing cups and glasses before the solemnly shining samovar made me nervous for a long time. I felt myself still unworthy of such a distinction, too young and frivolous to turn the tap of such a big samovar, to put glasses on Nikíta's salver, saying 'For Peter Ivánovich', 'For Márya Mínicha', to ask 'Is it sweet enough?' and to leave out lumps of sugar for Nurse and other deserving persons. 'Capital! capital! Just like a grown-up person!' was a frequent comment from my husband, which only increased my confusion.

After tea Tatyána Semënovna played patience or listened to Márya Mínichna telling fortunes by the cards. Then she kissed us both and signed us with the cross, and we went off to our own rooms. But we generally sat up together till midnight, and that was our best and pleasantest time. He told me stories of his past life; we made plans and some-times even talked philosophy; but we tried always to speak low, for fear we should be heard upstairs and reported to Tatyána Semënovna, who insisted on our going to bed early. Sometimes we grew hungry; and then we stole off to the pantry, secured a cold supper by the good offices of Nikíta, and ate it in my sitting-room by the light of one candle. He and I lived like strangers in that big old house, where the uncompromising spirit of the past and of Tatyána Semënovna ruled supreme. Not she only, but the servants, the old ladies, the furniture, even the pictures, inspired me with respect and a little alarm, and made me feel that he and I were a little out of place in that house and must always be very careful and cautious in our doings. Thinking it over now, I see that many things—the pressure of that unvarying routine, and that crowd of idle and inquisitive servants—were uncomfortable and oppressive; but at the time that very constraint made our love for one another still keener. Not I only, but he also, never grumbled openly at anything; on the contrary he shut his eyes to what was amiss. Dmítri Sídorov, one of the footmen, was a great smoker; and regularly every day, when we two were in the morning-room after dinner, he went to my husband's study to take tobacco from the jar; and it was a sight to see Sergéy Mikháylych creeping on tiptoe to me with a face between delight and terror, and a wink and a warn-ing forefinger, while he pointed at Dmítri Sídorov, who was quite unconscious of being watched. Then, when Dmítri

Sídorov had gone away without having seen us, in his joy that all had passed off successfully, he declared (as he did on every other occasion) that I was a darling, and kissed me. At times his calm connivance and apparent indifference to everything annoyed me, and I took it for weakness, never noticing that I acted in the same way myself. 'It's like a child who dares not show his will,' I thought.

'My dear! my dear!' he said once when I told him that his weakness surprised me; 'how can a man, as happy as I am, be dissatisfied with anything? Better to give way myself than to put compulsion on others; of that I have long been convinced. There is no condition in which one cannot be happy; but our life is such bliss! I simply cannot be angry; to me now nothing seems bad, but only pitiful and amusing. Above all—*le mieux est l'ennemi du bien.*[1] Will you believe it, when I hear a ring at the bell, or receive a letter, or even wake up in the morning, I'm frightened. Life must go on, something may change; and nothing can be better than the present.'

I believed him but did not understand him. I was happy; but I took that as a matter of course, the invariable experience of people in our position, and believed that there was somewhere, I knew not where, a different happiness, not greater but different.

So two months went by and winter came with its cold and snow; and, in spite of his company, I began to feel lonely, that life was repeating itself, that there was nothing new either in him or in myself, and that we were merely going back to what had been before. He began to give more time to business which kept him away from me, and my old feeling returned, that there was a special department of his mind into which he was unwilling to admit me. His unbroken calmness provoked me. I loved him as much as ever and was as happy as ever in his love; but my love, instead of increasing, stood still; and another new and disquieting sensation began to creep into my heart. To love him was not enough for me

---

[1] The better is the enemy of the good.

after the happiness I had felt in falling in love. I wanted movement and not a calm course of existence. I wanted excitement and danger and the chance to sacrifice myself for my love. I felt in myself a superabundance of energy which found no outlet in our quiet life. I had fits of depression which I was ashamed of and tried to conceal from him, and fits of excessive tenderness and high spirits which alarmed him. He realized my state of mind before I did, and proposed a visit to Petersburg; but I begged him to give this up and not to change our manner of life or spoil our happiness. Happy indeed I was; but I was tormented by the thought that this happiness cost me no effort and no sacrifice, though I was even painfully conscious of my power to face both. I loved him and saw that I was all in all to him; but I wanted everyone to see our love; I wanted to love him in spite of obstacles. My mind, and even my senses, were fully occupied; but there was another feeling of youth and craving for movement, which found no satisfaction in our quiet life. What made him say that, whenever I liked, we could go to town? Had he not said so I might have realized that my uncomfortable feelings were my own fault and dangerous nonsense, and that the sacrifice I desired was there before me, in the task of overcoming these feelings. I was haunted by the thought that I could escape from depression by a mere change from the country; and at the same time I felt ashamed and sorry to tear him away, out of selfish motives, from all he cared for. So time went on, the snow grew deeper, and there we remained together, all alone and just the same as before, while outside I knew there was noise and glitter and excitement, and hosts of people suffering or rejoicing without one thought of us and our remote existence. I suffered most from the feeling that custom was daily petrifying our lives into one fixed shape, that our minds were losing their freedom and becoming enslaved to the steady passionless course of time. The morning always found us cheerful; we were polite at dinner, and affectionate in the evening. 'It is all right,' I thought, 'to do good to others and lead upright lives, as he says; but there is time for that later; and there are other things, for which the

time is now or never.' I wanted, not what I had got, but a
life of struggle; I wanted feeling to be the guide of life, and
not life to guide feeling. If only I could go with him to the
edge of a precipice and say, 'One step, and I shall fall over—
one movement, and I shall be lost!' then, pale with fear, he
would catch me in his strong arms and hold me over the edge
till my blood froze, and then carry me off whither he pleased.

This state of feeling even affected my health, and I began
to suffer from nerves. One morning I was worse than usual. He
had come back from the estate-office out of sorts, which was
a rare thing with him. I noticed it at once and asked what was
the matter. He would not tell me and said it was of no importance. I found out afterwards that the police-inspector, out
of spite against my husband, was summoning our peasants,
making illegal demands on them, and using threats to them.
My husband could not swallow this at once; he could not feel
it merely 'pitiful and amusing'. He was provoked, and therefore unwilling to speak of it to me. But it seemed to me that
he did not wish to speak to me about it because he considered
me a mere child, incapable of understanding his concerns. I
turned from him and said no more. I then told the servant
to ask Márya Mínichna, who was staying in the house, to join
us at breakfast. I ate my breakfast very fast and took her to
the morning-room, where I began to talk loudly to her about
some trifle which did not interest me in the least. He walked
about the room, glancing at us from time to time. This made
me more and more inclined to talk and even to laugh; all
that I said myself, and all that Márya Mínichna said, seemed
to me laughable. Without a word to me he went to his
study and shut the door behind him. When I ceased to
hear him, all my high spirits vanished at once: indeed Márya
Mínichna was surprised and asked what was the matter. I sat
down on a sofa without answering, and felt ready to cry.
'What has he got on his mind?' I wondered; 'some trifle
which he thinks important; but, if he tried to tell it me, I
should soon show him it was mere nonsense. But he must
needs think that I won't understand, must humiliate me by his
majestic composure, and always be in the right as against

me. But I too am in the right when I find things tiresome
and trivial,' I reflected; 'and I do well to want an active life
rather than to stagnate in one spot and feel life flowing past
me. I want to move forward, to have some new experience
every day and every hour, whereas he wants to stand still and
to keep me standing beside him. And how easy it would
be for him to gratify me! He need not take me to town; he
need only be like me and not put compulsion on himself and
regulate his feelings, but live simply. That is the advice he
gives me, but he is not simple himself. That is what is the
matter.'

I felt the tears rising and knew that I was irritated with him.
My irritation frightened me, and I went to his study. He was
sitting at the table, writing. Hearing my step, he looked up for
a moment and then went on writing; he seemed calm and unconcerned. His look vexed me: instead of going up to him, I
stood beside his writing-table, opened a book, and began to
look at it. He broke off his writing again and looked at me.

'Másha, are you out of sorts?' he asked.

I replied with a cold look, as much as to say, 'You are very
polite, but what is the use of asking?' He shook his head
and smiled with a tender timid air; but his smile, for the
first time, drew no answering smile from me.

'What happened to you to-day?' I asked; 'why did you not
tell me?'

'Nothing much—a trifling nuisance,' he said. 'But I might
tell you now. Two of our serfs went off to the town . . .'

But I would not let him go on.

'Why should you not tell me, when I asked you at breakfast?'

'I was angry then and should have said something foolish.'

'I wished to know then.'

'Why?'

'Why do you suppose that I can never help you in anything?'

'Not help me!' he said, dropping his pen. 'Why, I believe
that without you I could not live. You not only help me in
everything I do, but you do it yourself. You are very wide of

the mark,' he said, and laughed. 'My life depends on you. I am pleased with things, only because you are there, because I need you . . .'

'Yes, I know; I am a delightful child who must be humoured and kept quiet,' I said in a voice that astonished him, so that he looked up as if this was a new experience; 'but I don't want to be quiet and calm; that is more in your line, and too much in your line,' I added.

'Well,' he began quickly, interrupting me and evidently afraid to let me continue, 'when I tell you the facts, I should like to know your opinion.'

'I don't want to hear them now,' I answered. I did want to hear the story, but I found it so pleasant to break down his composure. 'I don't want to play at life,' I said, 'but to live, as you do yourself.'

His face, which reflected every feeling so quickly and so vividly, now expressed pain and intense attention.

'I want to share your life, to . . . ,' but I could not go on— his face showed such deep distress. He was silent for a moment.

'But what part of my life do you not share?' he asked; 'is it because I, and not you, have to bother with the inspector and with tipsy labourers?'

'That's not the only thing,' I said.

'For God's sake try to understand me, my dear!' he cried. 'I know that excitement is always painful; I have learnt that from the experience of life. I love you, and I can't but wish to save you from excitement. My life consists of my love for you; so you should not make life impossible for me.'

'You are always in the right,' I said without looking at him.

I was vexed again by his calmness and coolness while I was conscious of annoyance and some feeling akin to penitence.

'Másha, what is the matter?' he asked. 'The question is not, which of us is in the right—not at all; but rather, what grievance have you against me? Take time before you answer, and tell me all that is in your mind. You are dissatisfied with me: and you are, no doubt, right; but let me understand what I have done wrong.'

But how could I put my feeling into words? That he understood me at once, that I again stood before him like a child, that I could do nothing without his understanding and foreseeing it—all this only increased my agitation.

'I have no complaint to make of you,' I said; 'I am merely bored and want not to be bored. But you say that it can't be helped, and, as always, you are right.'

I looked at him as I spoke. I had gained my object: his calmness had disappeared, and I read fear and pain in his face.

'Másha,' he began in a low troubled voice, 'this is no mere trifle: the happiness of our lives is at stake. Please hear me out without answering. Why do you wish to torment me?'

But I interrupted him.

'Oh, I know you will turn out to be right. Words are useless; of course you are right.' I spoke coldly, as if some evil spirit were speaking with my voice.

'If you only knew what you are doing!' he said, and his voice shook.

I burst out crying and felt relieved. He sat down beside me and said nothing. I felt sorry for him, ashamed of myself, and annoyed at what I had done. I avoided looking at him. I felt that any look from him at that moment must express severity or perplexity. At last I looked up and saw his eyes: they were fixed on me with a tender gentle expression that seemed to ask for pardon. I caught his hand and said.

'Forgive me! I don't know myself what I have been saying.'

'But I do; and you spoke the truth.'

'What do you mean?' I asked.

'That we must go to Petersburg,' he said; 'there is nothing for us to do here just now.'

'As you please,' I said.

He took me in his arms and kissed me.

'You must forgive me,' he said; 'for I am to blame.'

That evening I played to him for a long time, while he walked about the room. He had a habit of muttering to himself; and when I asked him what he was muttering, he always thought for a moment and then told me exactly what it was. It was generally verse, and sometimes mere nonsense, but

I could always judge of his mood by it. When I asked him
now, he stood still, thought an instant, and then repeated
two lines from Lérmontov:

> *He in his madness prays for storms,*
> *And dreams that storms will bring him peace.*

'He is really more than human,' I thought; 'he knows everything. How can one help loving him?'

I got up, took his arm, and began to walk up and down
with him, trying to keep step.

'Well?' he asked, smiling and looking at me.

'All right,' I whispered. And then a sudden fit of merriment
came over us both: our eyes laughed, we took longer and
longer steps, and rose higher and higher on tiptoe. Prancing in
this manner, to the profound dissatisfaction of the butler and
astonishment of my mother-in-law, who was playing patience
in the parlour, we proceeded through the house till we
reached the dining-room; there we stopped, looked at one
another, and burst out laughing.

A fortnight later, before Christmas, we were in Petersburg.

CHAPTER II

The journey to Petersburg, a week in Moscow, visits to my
own relations and my husband's, settling down in our new
quarters, travel, new towns and new faces—all this passed before me like a dream. It was all so new, various, and delightful, so warmly and brightly lighted up by his presence
and his love, that our quiet life in the country seemed to me
something very remote and unimportant. I had expected to
find people in society proud and cold; but to my great surprise, I was received everywhere with unfeigned cordiality
and pleasure, not only by relations, but also by strangers. I
seemed to be the one object of their thoughts, and my arrival
the one thing they wanted, to complete their happiness. I was
surprised too to discover in what seemed to me the very best
society a number of people acquainted with my husband,

though he had never spoken of them to me; and I often felt it odd and disagreeable to hear him now speak disapprovingly of some of these people who seemed to me so kind. I could not understand his coolness towards them or his endeavours to avoid many acquaintances that seemed to me flattering. Surely, the more kind people one knows, the better; and here everyone was kind.

'This is how we must manage, you see,' he said to me before we left the country; 'here we are little Croesuses, but in town we shall not be at all rich. So we must not stay after Easter, or go into society, or we shall get into difficulties. For your sake too I should not wish it.'

'Why should we go into society?' I asked; 'we shall have a look at the theatres, see our relations, go to the opera, hear some good music, and be ready to come home before Easter.'

But these plans were forgotten the moment we got to Petersburg. I found myself at once in such a new and delightful world, surrounded by so many pleasures and confronted by such novel interests, that I instantly, though unconsciously, turned my back on my past life and its plans. 'All that was preparatory, a mere playing at life; but here is the real thing! And there is the future too!' Such were my thoughts. The restlessness and symptoms of depression which had troubled me at home vanished at once and entirely, as if by magic. My love for my husband grew calmer, and I ceased to wonder whether he loved me less. Indeed I could not doubt his love: every thought of mine was understood at once, every feeling shared, and every wish gratified by him. His composure, if it still existed, no longer provoked me. I also began to realize that he not only loved me but was proud of me. If we paid a call, or made some new acquaintance, or gave an evening party at which I, trembling inwardly from fear of disgracing myself, acted as hostess, he often said when it was over: 'Bravo, young woman! capital! you needn't be frightened; a real success!' And his praise gave me great pleasure. Soon after our arrival he wrote to his mother and asked me to add a postscript, but refused to let me see his letter; of course I insisted on reading it; and he had said: 'You would not know Másha again, I don't myself. Where does she get that charming graceful self-confidence and ease, such social gifts with such simplicity and charm and kindliness? Everybody is delighted with her. I can't admire her enough myself, and should be more in love with her than ever, if that were possible.'

'Now I know what I am like,' I thought. In my joy and pride I felt that I loved him more than before. My success with all our new acquaintances was a complete surprise to me. I heard on all sides, how this uncle had taken a special fancy for me, and that aunt was raving about me; I was told by one admirer that I had no rival among the Petersburg ladies, and assured by another, a lady, that I might, if I cared, lead the fashion in society. A cousin of my husband's, in particular, a Princess D., middle-aged and very much at home in society, fell in love with me at first sight and paid me compliments which turned my head. The first time that she invited me to a ball and spoke to my husband about it, he turned to me and asked if I wished to go; I could just detect a sly smile on his face. I nodded assent and felt that I was blushing.

'She looks like a criminal when confessing what she wishes,' he said with a good-natured laugh.

'But you said that we must not go into society, and you don't care for it yourself,' I answered, smiling and looking imploringly at him.

'Let us go, if you want to very much,' he said.

'Really, we had better not.'

'Do you want to? very badly?' he asked again.

I said nothing.

'Society in itself is no great harm,' he went on; 'but unsatisfied social aspirations are a bad and ugly business. We must certainly accept, and we will.'

'To tell you the truth,' I said, 'I never in my life longed for anything as much as I do for this ball.'

So we went, and my delight exceeded all my expectations. It seemed to me, more than ever, that I was the centre round which everything revolved, that for my sake alone this great room was lighted up and the band played, and that this crowd of people had assembled to admire me. From the hairdresser and the lady's maid to my partners and the old gentlemen promenading the ball-room, all alike seemed to make it plain that they were in love with me. The general verdict formed at the ball about me and reported by my cousin, came to this: I was quite unlike the other women and had a rural simplicity and charm of my own. I was so flattered by my success that I frankly told my husband I should like to attend two or three more balls during the season, and 'so get thoroughly sick of them', I added; but I did not mean what I said.

He agreed readily; and he went with me at first with obvious satisfaction. He took pleasure in my success, and seemed to have quite forgotten his former warning or to have changed his opinion.

But a time came when he was evidently bored and wearied by the life we were leading. I was too busy, however, to think about that. Even if I sometimes noticed his eyes fixed questioningly on me with a serious attentive gaze, I did not realize its meaning. I was utterly blinded by this sudden affection which I seemed to evoke in all our new acquaintances, and confused by the unfamiliar atmosphere of luxury, refinement, and novelty. It pleased me so much to find myself in these surroundings not merely his equal but his superior, and yet to love him better and more independently than before, that I could not understand what he could object to for me in society life. I had a new sense of pride and self-satisfaction when my entry at a ball attracted all eyes, while he, as if ashamed to confess his ownership of me in public, made haste to leave my side and efface himself in the crowd of black coats. 'Wait a little!' I often said in my heart, when I identified his obscure and sometimes woebegone figure at the end of the room—'Wait till we get home! Then you will see and understand for whose sake I try to be beautiful and brilliant, and what it is I love in all that surrounds me this evening!' I really believed that my success pleased me only because it enabled me to give it up for his sake. One danger I recognized as possible—that I might be carried away by a fancy for some new acquaintance, and that my husband might grow jealous. But he trusted me so absolutely, and seemed so undisturbed and indifferent, and all the young men were so inferior to him, that I was not alarmed by this one danger. Yet the attention of so many people in society gave me satisfaction, flattered my vanity, and made me think that there was some merit in my love for my husband. Thus I became more offhand and self-confident in my behaviour to him.

'Oh, I saw you this evening carrying on a most animated conversation with Mme N.,' I said one night on returning from a ball, shaking my finger at him. He had really been talking to this lady, who was a well-known figure in Petersburg society. He was more silent and depressed than usual, and I said this to rouse him up.

'What is the good of talking like that, for *you* especially, Másha?' he said with half-closed teeth and frowning as if in pain. 'Leave that to others; it does not suit you and me. Pretence of that sort may spoil the true relation between us, which I still hope may come back.'

I was ashamed and said nothing.

'Will it ever come back, Másha, do you think?' he asked.

'It never was spoilt and never will be,' I said; and I really believed this then.

'God grant that you are right!' he said; 'if not, we ought to be going home.'

But he only spoke like this once—in general he seemed as satisfied as I was, and I was so gay and so happy! I comforted myself too by thinking, 'If he is bored sometimes, I endured the same thing for his sake in the country. If the relation between us has become a little different, everything will be the same again in summer, when we shall be alone in our house at Nikólskoe with Tatyána Semënovna.'

So the winter slipped by, and we stayed on, in spite of our plans, over Easter in Petersburg. A week later we were preparing to start; our packing was all done; my husband, who had bought things—plants for the garden and presents for people at Nikólskoe, was in a specially cheerful and affectionate mood. Just then Princess D. came and begged us to stay till the Saturday, in order to be present at a reception to be given by Countess R. The Countess was very anxious to secure me, because a foreign prince, who was visiting Petersburg and had seen me already at a ball, wished to make my acquaintance; indeed this was his motive for attending the reception, and he declared that I was the most beautiful woman in Russia. All the world was to be there; and, in a word, it would really be too bad, if I did not go too.

My husband was talking to someone at the other end of the drawing-room.

'So you will go, won't you, Mary?' said the Princess.

'We meant to start for the country the day after tomorrow,' I answered undecidedly, glancing at my husband. Our eyes met, and he turned away at once.

'I must persuade him to stay,' she said, 'and then we can go on Saturday and turn all heads. All right?'

'It would upset our plans; and we have packed,' I answered, beginning to give way.

'She had better go this evening and make her curtsey to the Prince,' my husband called out fom the other end of the room; and he spoke in a tone of suppressed irritation which I had never heard from him before.

'I declare he's jealous, for the first time in his life,' said the lady, laughing. 'But it's not for the sake of the Prince I urge it, Sergéy Mikháylych, but for all our sakes. The Countess was so anxious to have her.'

'It rests with her entirely,' my husband said coldly, and then left the room.

I saw that he was much disturbed, and this pained me. I gave no positive promise. As soon as our visitor left, I went to my husband. He was walking up and down his room, thinking, and neither saw nor heard me when I came in on tiptoe.

Looking at him I said to myself: 'He is dreaming already of his dear Nikólskoe, our morning coffee in the bright drawing-room, the land and the labourers, our evenings in the music-room, and our secret midnight suppers.' Then I decided in my own heart: 'Not for all the balls and all the flattering

princes in the world will I give up his glad confusion and tender cares.' I was just about to say that I did not wish to go to
the ball and would refuse, when he looked round, saw me,
and frowned. His face, which had been gentle and thoughtful,
changed at once to its old expression of sagacity, penetra-
tion, and patronizing composure. He would not show himself
to me as a mere man, but had to be a demigod on a pedestal.

'Well, my dear?' he asked, turning towards me with an unconcerned air.

I said nothing. I was provoked, because he was hiding his
real self from me, and would not continue to be the man I
loved.

'Do you want to go to this reception on Saturday?' he
asked.

'I did, but you disapprove. Besides, our things are all
packed,' I said.

Never before had I heard such coldness in his tone to me,
and never before seen such coldness in his eye.

'I shall order the things to be unpacked,' he said, 'and I
shall stay till Tuesday. So you can go to the party, if you like.
I hope you will; but I shall not go.'

Without looking at me, he began to walk about the room
jerkily, as his habit was when perturbed.

'I simply can't understand you,' I said, following him with
my eyes from where I stood. 'You say that you never lose self-
control' (he had never really said so); 'then why do you talk
to me so strangely? I am ready on your account to sacrifice
this pleasure, and then you, in a sarcastic tone which is new
from you to me, insist that I should go.'

'So you make a *sacrifice!*' he threw special emphasis on the
last word. 'Well, so do I. What could be better? We compete
in generosity—what an example of family happiness!'

Such harsh and contemptuous language I had never
heard from his lips before. I was not abashed, but mortified
by his contempt; and his harshness did not frighten me but
made me harsh too. How could *he* speak thus, he who was always so frank and simple and dreaded insincerity in our
speech to one another? And what had I done that he should

speak so? I really intended to sacrifice for his sake a pleasure in which I could see no harm; and a moment ago I loved him and understood his feelings as well as ever. We had changed parts: now he avoided direct and plain words, and I desired them.

'You are much changed,' I said, with a sigh. 'How am I guilty before you? It is not this party—you have something else, some old count against me. Why this insincerity? You used to be so afraid of it yourself. Tell me plainly what you complain of.' 'What will he say?' thought I, and reflected with some complacency that I had done nothing all winter which he could find fault with.

I went into the middle of the room, so that he had to pass close to me, and looked at him. I thought, 'He will come and clasp me in his arms, and there will be an end of it.' I was even sorry that I should not have the chance of proving him wrong. But he stopped at the far end of the room and looked at me.

'Do you not understand yet?' he asked.

'No, I don't.'

'Then I must explain. What I feel, and cannot help feeling, positively sickens me for the first time in my life.' He stopped, evidently startled by the harsh sound of his own voice.

'What do you mean?' I asked, with tears of indignation in my eyes.

'It sickens me that the Prince admired you, and you therefore run to meet him, forgetting your husband and yourself and womanly dignity; and you wilfully misunderstand what your want of self-respect makes your husband feel for you: you actually come to your husband and speak of the "sacrifice" you are making, by which you mean—"To show myself to His Highness is a great pleasure to me, but I 'sacrifice' it." '

The longer he spoke, the more he was excited by the sound of his own voice, which was hard and rough and cruel. I had never seen him, had never thought of seeing him, like that. The blood rushed to my heart and I was frightened; but I felt that I had nothing to be ashamed of, and the excitement of wounded vanity made me eager to punish him.

'I have long been expecting this,' I said. 'Go on. Go on!'

'What you expected, I don't know,' he went on; 'but I might well expect the worst, when I saw you day after day sharing the dirtiness and idleness and luxury of this foolish society, and it has come at last. Never have I felt such shame and pain as now—pain for myself, when your friend thrusts her unclean fingers into my heart and speaks of my jealousy!— jealousy of a man whom neither you nor I know; and you refuse to understand me and offer to make a sacrifice for me— and what sacrifice? I am ashamed for you, for your degradation! . . . Sacrifice!' he repeated again.

'Ah, so this is a husband's power,' thought I: 'to insult and humiliate a perfectly innocent woman. Such may be a husband's rights, but I will not submit to them.' I felt the blood leave my face and a strange distension of my nostrils, as I said, 'No! I make no sacrifice on your account. I shall go to the party on Saturday without fail.'

'And I hope you may enjoy it. But all is over between us two!' he cried out in a fit of unrestrained fury. 'But you shall not torture me any longer! I was a fool, when I . . .', but his lips quivered, and he refrained with a visible effort from ending the sentence.

I feared and hated him at that moment. I wished to say a great deal to him and punish him for all his insults; but if I had opened my mouth, I should have lost my dignity by bursting into tears. I said nothing and left the room. But as soon as I ceased to hear his footsteps, I was horrified at what we had done. I feared that the tie which had made all my happiness might really be snapped for ever; and I thought of going back. But then I wondered: 'Is he calm enough now to understand me, if I mutely stretch out my hand and look at him? Will he realize my generosity? What if he calls my grief a mere pretence? Or he may feel sure that he is right and ac-cept my repentance and forgive me with unruffled pride. And why, oh why, did he whom I loved so well insult me so cruelly?'

I went not to him but to my own room, where I sat for a long time and cried. I recalled with horror each word of our conversation, and substituted different words, kind words, for those that we had spoken, and added others; and then again I remembered the reality with horror and a feeling of injury. In the evening I went down for tea and met my husband in the presence of a friend who was staying with us; and it seemed to me that a wide gulf had opened between us from that day. Our friend asked me when we were to start; and before I could speak, my husband answered:

'On Tuesday,' he said; 'we have to stay for Countess R.'s reception.' He turned to me: 'I believe you intend to go?' he asked.

His matter-of-fact tone frightened me, and I looked at him timidly. His eyes were directed straight at me with an unkind and scornful expression; his voice was cold and even.

'Yes,' I answered.

When we were alone that evening, he came up to me and held out his hand.

'Please forget what I said to you to-day,' he began.

As I took his hand, a smile quivered on my lips and the tears were ready to flow; but he took his hand away and sat down on an armchair at some distance, as if fearing a sentimental scene. 'Is it possible that he still thinks himself in the right?' I wondered; and, though I was quite ready to explain and to beg that we might not go to the party, the words died on my lips.

'I must write to my mother that we have put off our departure,' he said; 'otherwise she will be uneasy.'

'When do you think of going?' I asked.

'On Tuesday, after the reception,' he replied.

'I hope it is not on my account,' I said, looking into his eyes; but those eyes merely looked—they said nothing, and a veil seemed to cover them from me. His face seemed to me to have grown suddenly old and disagreeable.

We went to the reception, and good friendly relations between us seemed to have been restored, but these relations were quite different from what they had been.

At the party I was sitting with other ladies when the Prince came up to me, so that I had to stand up in order to speak to him. As I rose, my eyes involuntarily sought my hus-

band. He was looking at me from the other end of the room,
and now turned away. I was seized by a sudden sense of
shame and pain; in my confusion I blushed all over my face
and neck under the Prince's eye. But I was forced to stand and
listen, while he spoke, eyeing me from his superior height. Our
conversation was soon over: there was no room for him beside
me, and he, no doubt, felt that I was uncomfortable with him.
We talked of the last ball, of where I should spend the summer, and so on. As he left me, he expressed a wish to make
the acquaintance of my husband, and I saw them meet and
begin a conversation at the far end of the room. The Prince
evidently said something about me; for he smiled in the middle of their talk and looked in my direction.

My husband suddenly flushed up. He made a low bow and
turned away from the Prince without being dismissed. I
blushed too: I was ashamed of the impression which I and,
still more, my husband must have made on the Prince. Everyone, I thought, must have noticed my awkward shyness when
I was presented, and my husband's eccentric behaviour.
'Heaven knows how they will interpret such conduct? Perhaps they know already about my scene with my husband!'

Princess D. drove me home, and on the way I spoke to her
about my husband. My patience was at an end, and I told her
the whole story of what had taken place between us owing to
this unlucky party. To calm me, she said that such differences
were very common and quite unimportant, and that our quar-
rel would leave no trace behind. She explained to me her
view of my husband's character—that he had become very
stiff and unsociable. I agreed, and believed that I had learned
to judge him myself more calmly and more truly.

But when I was alone with my husband later, the thought
that I had sat in judgement upon him weighed like a crime
upon my conscience; and I felt that the gulf which divided us
had grown still greater.

CHAPTER III

From that day there was a complete change in our life and our relations to each other. We were no longer as happy when we were alone together as before. To certain subjects we gave a wide berth, and conversation flowed more easily in the presence of a third person. When the talk turned on life in the country, or on a ball, we were uneasy and shrank from looking at one another. Both of us knew where the gulf between us lay, and seemed afraid to approach it. I was convinced that he was proud and irascible, and that I must be careful not to touch him on his weak point. He was equally sure that I disliked the country and was dying for social distraction, and that he must put up with this unfortunate taste of mine. We both avoided frank conversation on these topics, and each misjudged the other. We had long ceased to think each other the most perfect people in the world; each now judged the other in secret, and measured the offender by the standard of other people. I fell ill before we left Petersburg, and we went from there to a house near town, from which my husband went on alone, to join his mother at Nikólskoe. By that time I was well enough to have gone with him, but he urged me to stay on the pretext of my health. I knew, however, that he was really afraid we should be uncomfortable together in the country; so I did not insist much, and he went off alone. I felt it dull and solitary in his absence; but when he came back, I saw that he did not add to my life what he had added formerly. In the old days every thought and experience weighed on me like a crime till I had imparted it to him; every action and word of his seemed to me a model of perfection; we often laughed for joy at the mere sight of each other. But these relations had changed, so imperceptibly that we had not even noticed their disappearance. Separate interests and cares, which we no longer tried to share, made their appearance, and even the fact of our estrangement ceased to trouble us. The idea became familiar, and, before a year had passed, each could look at the other without confusion. His fits of boyish merriment with me had quite vanished; his mood of calm indulgence to all that passed, which used to provoke me, had disappeared; there was an end of those penetrating looks which used to confuse and delight me, an end of the ecstasies and prayers which we once shared in common. We did not even meet often: he was continually absent, with no fears or regrets for leaving me alone; and I was constantly in society, where I did not need him.

There were no further scenes or quarrels between us. I tried to satisfy him, he carried out all my wishes, and we seemed to love each other.

When we were by ourselves, which we seldom were, I felt neither joy nor excitement nor embarrassment in his company: it seemed like being alone. I realized that he was my husband and no mere stranger, a good man, and as familiar to me as my own self. I was convinced that I knew just what he would say and do, and how he would look; and if anything he did surprised me, I concluded that he had made a mistake. I expected nothing from him. In a word, he was my husband— and that was all. It seemed to me that things must be so, as a matter of course, and that no other relations between us had ever existed. When he left home, especially at first, I was lonely and frightened and felt keenly my need of support; when he came back, I ran to his arms with joy, though two hours later my joy was quite forgotten, and I found nothing to say to him. Only at moments which sometimes occurred between us of quiet undemonstrative affection, I felt something wrong and some pain at my heart, and I seemed to read the same story in his eyes. I was conscious of a limit to tenderness, which he seemingly would not, and I could not, overstep. This saddened me sometimes; but I had no leisure to reflect on anything, and my regret for a change which I vaguely realized I tried to drown in the distractions which were always within my reach. Fashionable life, which had dazzled me at first by its glitter and flattery of my self-love, now took entire command of my nature, became a habit, laid its fetters upon me, and monopolized my capacity for feeling. I could not bear solitude, and was afraid to reflect on my position. My whole

day, from late in the morning till late at night, was taken up by
the claims of society; even if I stayed at home, my time was
not my own. This no longer seemed to me either gay or dull,
but it seemed that so, and not otherwise, it always had to be.

So three years passed, during which our relations to one
another remained unchanged and seemed to have taken a
fixed shape which could not become either better or worse.
Though two events of importance in our family life took place
during that time, neither of them changed my own life. These
were the birth of my first child and the death of Tatyána
Semënovna. At first the feeling of motherhood did take hold
of me with such power, and produce in me such a passion of
unanticipated joy, that I believed this would prove the beginning of a new life for me. But, in the course of two months,
when I began to go out again, my feeling grew weaker and
weaker, till it passed into mere habit and the lifeless performance of a duty. My husband, on the contrary, from the
birth of our first boy, became his old self again—gentle, composed, and home-loving, and transferred to the child his old
tenderness and gaiety. Many a night when I went, dressed
for a ball, to the nursery, to sign the child with the cross before he slept, I found my husband there and felt his eyes
fixed on me with something of reproof in their serious gaze.
Then I was ashamed and even shocked by my own callous-
ness, and asked myself if I was worse than other women. 'But
it can't be helped,' I said to myself; 'I love my child, but to sit
beside him all day long would bore me; and nothing will make
me pretend what I do not really feel.'

His mother's death was a great sorrow to my husband; he
said that he found it painful to go on living at Nikólskoe. For
myself, although I mourned for her and sympathized with my
husband's sorrow, yet I found life in that house easier and
pleasanter after her death. Most of those three years we spent
in town: I went only once to Nikólskoe for two months; and
the third year we went abroad and spent the summer at Baden.

I was then twenty-one; our financial position was, I believed, satisfactory; my domestic life gave me all that I asked

of it; everyone I knew, it seemed to me, loved me; my health was good; I was the best-dressed woman in Baden; I knew that I was good-looking; the weather was fine; I enjoyed the atmosphere of beauty and refinement; and, in short, I was in excellent spirits. They had once been even higher at Nikólskoe, when my happiness was in myself and came from the feeling that I deserved to be happy, and from the anticipation of still greater happiness to come. That was a different state of things; but I did very well this summer also. I had no special wishes or hopes or fears; it seemed to me that my life was full and my conscience easy. Among all the visitors at Baden that season there was no one man whom I preferred to the rest, or even to our old ambassador, Prince K., who was assiduous in his attentions to me. One was young, and another old; one was English and fair, another French and wore a beard—to me they were all alike, but all indispensable. Indistinguishable as they were, they together made up the atmosphere which I found so pleasant. But there was one, an Italian marquis, who stood out from the rest by reason of the boldness with which he expressed his admiration. He seized every opportunity of being with me—danced with me, rode with me, and met me at the casino; and everywhere he spoke to me of my charms. Several times I saw him from my windows loitering round our hotel, and the fixed gaze of his bright eyes often troubled me, and made me blush and turn away. He was young, handsome, and well-mannered; and, above all, by his smile and the expression of his brow, he resembled my husband, though much handsomer than he. He struck me by this likeness, though in general, in his lips, eyes, and long chin, there was something coarse and animal which contrasted with my husband's charming expression of kindness and noble serenity. I supposed him to be passionately in love with me, and thought of him sometimes with proud commiseration. When I tried at times to soothe him and change his tone to one of easy, half-friendly confidence, he resented the suggestion with vehemence, and continued to disquiet me by a smouldering passion which was ready at any moment to burst forth. Though I would not own it even to myself, I feared him and often thought of him against my will. My husband knew him, and treated him—even more than other acquaintances of ours who regarded him only as my husband—with coldness and disdain.

Towards the end of the season I fell ill and stayed indoors for a fortnight. The first evening that I went out again to hear the band, I learnt that Lady S., an Englishwoman famous for her beauty, who had long been expected, had arrived in my absence. My return was welcomed, and a group gathered round me; but a more distinguished group attended the beautiful stranger. She and her beauty were the one subject of conversation around me. When I saw her, she was really beautiful, but her self-satisfied expression struck me as disagreeable, and I said so. That day everything that had formerly seemed amusing, seemed dull. Lady S. arranged an expedition to the ruined castle for the next day; but I declined to be of the party. Almost everyone else went; and my opinion of Baden underwent a complete change. Everything and everybody seemed to me stupid and tiresome; I wanted to cry, to break off my cure, to return to Russia. There was some evil feeling in my soul, but I did not yet acknowledge it to myself. Pretending that I was not strong, I ceased to appear at crowded parties; if I went out, it was only in the morning by myself, to drink the waters; and my only companion was Mme M., a Russian lady, with whom I sometimes took drives in the surrounding country. My husband was absent: he had gone to Heidelberg for a time, intending to return to Russia when my cure was over, and only paid me occasional visits at Baden.

One day when Lady S. had carried off all the company on a hunting-expedition, Mme M. and I drove in the afternoon to the castle. While our carriage moved slowly along the winding road, bordered by ancient chestnut-trees and commanding a vista of the pretty and pleasant country round Baden, with the setting sun lighting it up, our conversation took a more serious turn than had ever happened to us before. I had known my companion for a long time; but she appeared to me now in a new light, as a well-principled and intelligent woman, to whom it was possible to speak without reserve, and whose friendship was worth having. We spoke of our private concerns, of our children, of the emptiness of life at Baden, till we felt a longing for Russia and the Russian country-side. When we entered the castle we were still under the impression of this serious feeling. Within the walls there was shade and coolness; the sunlight played from above upon the ruins. Steps and voices were audible. The landscape, charming enough but cold to a Russian eye, lay before us in the frame made by a doorway. We sat down to rest and watched the sunset in silence. The voices now sounded louder, and I thought I heard my own name. I listened and could not help overhearing every word. I recognized the voices: the speakers were the Italian marquis and a French friend of his whom I knew also. They were talking of me and of Lady S., and the Frenchman was comparing us as rival beauties. Though he said nothing insulting, his words made my pulse quicken. He explained in detail the good points of us both. I was already a mother, while Lady S. was only nineteen; though I had the advantage in hair, my rival had a better figure. 'Besides,' he added, 'Lady S. is a real *grande dame*, and the other is nothing in particular, only one of those obscure Russian princesses who turn up here nowadays in such numbers.' He ended by saying that I was wise in not attempting to compete with Lady S., and that I was completely buried as far as Baden was concerned.

'I am sorry for her—unless indeed she takes a fancy to console herself with you,' he added with a hard ringing laugh.

'If she goes away, I follow her'—the words were blurted out in an Italian accent.

'Happy man! he is still capable of a passion!' laughed the Frenchman.

'Passion!' said the other voice and then was still for a moment. 'It is a necessity to me: I cannot live without it. To make life a romance is the one thing worth doing. And with me romance never breaks off in the middle, and this affair I shall carry through to the end.'

'*Bonne chance, mon ami!*' [1] said the Frenchman.

They now turned a corner, and the voices stopped. Then we heard them coming down the steps, and a few minutes later they came out upon us by a side-door. They were much surprised to see us. I blushed when the marquis approached me, and felt afraid when we left the castle and he offered me his arm. I could not refuse, and we set off for the carriage, walking behind Mme M. and his friend. I was mortified by what the Frenchman had said of me, though I secretly admitted that he had only put in words what I felt myself; but the plain speaking of the Italian had surprised and upset me by its coarseness. I was tormented by the thought that, though I had overhead him, he showed no fear of me. It was hateful to have him so close to me; and I walked fast after the other couple, not looking at him or answering him and trying to hold his arm in such a way as not to hear him. He spoke of the fine view, of the unexpected pleasure of our meeting, and so on; but I was not listening. My thoughts were with my husband, my child, my country; I felt ashamed, distressed, anxious; I was in a hurry to get back to my solitary room in the Hôtel de Bade, there to think at leisure of the storm of feeling that had just risen in my heart. But Mme M. walked slowly, it was still a long way to the carriage, and my escort seemed to loiter on purpose as if he wished to detain me. 'None of that!' I thought, and resolutely quickened my pace. But it soon became unmistakable that he was detaining me and even pressing my arm. Mme M. turned a corner, and we were quite alone. I was afraid.

'Excuse me,' I said coldly and tried to free my arm; but the lace of my sleeve caught on a button of his coat. Bending towards me, he began to unfasten it, and his ungloved fingers touched my arm. A feeling new to me, half horror and half pleasure, sent an icy shiver down my back. I looked at him, intending by my coldness to convey all the contempt I felt for him; but my look expressed nothing but fear and excitement. His liquid blazing eyes, right up against my face, stared

---

[1] Good luck, my friend!

strangely at me, at my neck and breast; both his hands fingered my arm above the wrist; his parted lips were saying that he loved me, and that I was all the world to him; and those lips were coming nearer and nearer, and those hands were squeezing mine harder and harder and burning me. A fever ran through my veins, my sight grew dim, I trembled, and the words intended to check him died in my throat. Suddenly I felt a kiss on my cheek. Trembling all over and turning cold, I stood still and stared at him. Unable to speak or move, I stood there, horrified, expectant, even desirous. It was over in a moment, but the moment was horrible! In that short time I saw him exactly as he was—the low straight forehead (that forehead so like my husband's!) under the straw hat; the handsome regular nose and dilated nostrils; the long waxed moustache and short beard; the close-shaved cheeks and sunburnt neck. I hated and feared him; he was utterly repugnant and alien to me. And yet the excitement and passion of this hateful strange man raised a powerful echo in my own heart; I felt an irresistible longing to surrender myself to the kisses of that coarse handsome mouth, and to the pressure of those white hands with their delicate veins and jewelled fingers; I was tempted to throw myself headlong into the abyss of forbidden delights that had suddenly opened up before me.

'I am so unhappy already,' I thought; 'let more and more storms of unhappiness burst over my head!'

He put one arm round me and bent towards my face. 'Better so!' I thought: 'let sin and shame cover me ever deeper and deeper!'

'*Je vous aime!*' [2] he whispered in the voice which was so like my husband's. At once I thought of my husband and child, as creatures once precious to me who had now passed altogether out of my life. At that moment I heard Mme M.'s voice; she called to me from round the corner. I came to myself, tore my hand away without looking at him, and almost ran after her: I only looked at him after she and I were already seated in the carriage. Then I saw him raise his hat and ask some

---

[2] I love you.

commonplace question with a smile. He little knew the inex-
pressible aversion I felt for him at that moment.

My life seemed so wretched, the future so hopeless, the
past so black! When Mme M. spoke, her words meant nothing
to me. I thought that she talked only out of pity, and to hide
the contempt I aroused in her. In every word and every look
I seemed to detect this contempt and insulting pity. The shame
of that kiss burnt my cheek, and the thought of my husband
and child was more than I could bear. When I was alone in my
own room, I tried to think over my position; but I was afraid
to be alone. Without drinking the tea which was brought me,
and uncertain of my own motives, I got ready with feverish
haste to catch the evening train and join my husband at Heidelberg.

I found seats for myself and my maid in an empty carriage.
When the train started and the fresh air blew through the
window on my face, I grew more composed and pictured my
past and future to myself more clearly. The course of our married life from the time of our first visit to Petersburg now presented itself to me in a new light, and lay like a reproach on
my conscience. For the first time I clearly recalled our start at
Nikólskoe and our plans for the future; and for the first time
I asked myself what happiness had my husband had since
then. I felt that I had behaved badly to him. 'But why', I
asked myself, 'did he not stop me? Why did he make pretences? Why did he always avoid explanations? Why did he
insult me? Why did he not use the power of his love to influence me? Or did he not love me?' But whether he was to
blame or not, I still felt the kiss of that strange man upon my
cheek. The nearer we got to Heidelberg, the clearer grew my
picture of my husband, and the more I dreaded our meeting.
'I shall tell him all,' I thought, 'and wipe out everything with
tears of repentance; and he will forgive me.' But I did not
know myself what I meant by 'everything'; and I did not
believe in my heart that he would forgive me.

As soon as I entered my husband's room and saw his calm
though surprised expression, I felt at once that I had nothing
to tell him, no confession to make, and nothing to ask forgive-

ness for. I had to suppress my unspoken grief and penitence.

'What put this into your head?' he asked. 'I meant to go to Baden to-morrow.' Then he looked more closely at me and seemed to take alarm. 'What's the matter with you? What has happened?' he said.

'Nothing at all,' I replied, almost breaking down. 'I am not going back. Let us go home, to-morrow if you like, to Russia.'

For some time he said nothing but looked at me attentively. Then he said, 'But do tell me what has happened to you.'

I blushed involuntarily and looked down. There came into his eyes a flash of anger and displeasure. Afraid of what he might imagine, I said with a power of pretence that surprised myself:

'Nothing at all has happened. It was merely that I grew weary and sad by myself; and I have been thinking a great deal of our way of life and of you. I have long been to blame towards you. Why do you take me abroad, when you can't bear it yourself? I have long been to blame. Let us go back to Nikólskoe and settle there for ever.'

'Spare us these sentimental scenes, my dear,' he said coldly. 'To go back to Nikólskoe is a good idea, for our money is running short; but the notion of stopping there "for ever" is fanciful. I know you would not settle down. Have some tea, and you will feel better,' and he rose to ring for the waiter.

I imagined all he might be thinking about me; and I was offended by the horrible thoughts which I ascribed to him when I encountered the dubious and shame-faced look he directed at me. 'He will not and cannot understand me.' I said I would go and look at the child, and I left the room. I wished to be alone, and to cry and cry and cry . . .

CHAPTER IV

The house at Nikólskoe, so long unheated and uninhabited, came to life again; but much of the past was dead beyond recall. Tatyána Semënova was no more, and we were now alone together. But far from desiring such close companionship, we even found it irksome. To me that winter was the more trying because I was in bad health, from which I only recovered after the birth of my second son. My husband and I were still on the same terms as during our life in Petersburg: we were coldly friendly to each other; but in the country each room and wall and sofa recalled what he had once been to me, and what I had lost. It was as if some unforgiven grievance held us apart, as if he were punishing me and pretending not to be aware of it. But there was nothing to ask pardon for, no penalty to deprecate; my punishment was merely this, that he did not give his whole heart and mind to me as he used to do; but he did not give it to anyone or to anything; as though he had no longer a heart to give. Sometimes it occurred to me that he was only pretending to be like that, in order to hurt me, and that the old feeling was still alive in his breast; and I tried to call it forth. But I always failed: he always seemed to avoid frankness, evidently suspecting me of insincerity, and dreading the folly of any emotional display. I could read in his face and the tone of his voice, 'What is the good of talking? I know all the facts already, and I know what is on the tip of your tongue, and I know that you will say one thing and do another.' At first I was mortified by his dread of frankness, but I came later to think that it was rather the absence, on his part, of any need of frankness. It would never have occurred to me now, to tell him of a sudden that I loved him, or to ask him to repeat the prayers with me or listen while I played the piano. Our intercourse came to be regulated by a fixed code of good manners. We lived our separate lives: he had his own occupations in which I was not needed, and which I no longer wished to share, while I continued my idle life which no longer vexed or grieved him. The children were still too young to form a bond between us.

But spring came round and brought Kátya and Sónya to spend the summer with us in the country. As the house at Nikólskoe was under repair, we went to live at my old home at Pokróvskoe. The old house was unchanged—the veranda, the folding table and the piano in the sunny drawing-room, and my old bedroom with its white curtains and the dreams of my girlhood which I seemed to have left behind me there. In that room there were two beds: one had been mine, and in it now my plump little Kokósha lay sprawling, when I went at night to sign him with the cross; the other was a crib, in which the little face of my baby, Ványa, peeped out from his swaddling-clothes. Often, when I had made the sign over them and remained standing in the middle of the quiet room, suddenly there rose up from all the corners, from the walls and curtains, old forgotten visions of youth. Old voices began to sing the songs of my girlhood. Where were those visions now? where were those dear old sweet songs? All that I had hardly dared to hope for had come to pass. My vague confused dreams had become a reality, and the reality had become an oppressive, difficult, and joyless life. All remained the same —the garden visible through the window, the grass, the path, the very same bench over there above the dell, the same song of the nightingale by the pond, the same lilacs in full bloom, the same moon shining above the house; and yet, in everything such a terrible inconceivable change! Such coldness in all that might have been near and dear! Just as in old times, Kátya and I sit quietly alone together in the parlour and talk, and talk of him. But Kátya has grown wrinkled and pale; and her eyes no longer shine with joy and hope, but express only sympathy, sorrow, and regret. We do not go into raptures as we used to, we judge him coolly; we do not wonder what we have done to deserve such happiness, or long to proclaim our thoughts to all the world. No! we whisper together like conspirators and ask each other for the hundredth time why all has changed so sadly. Yet he was still the same man, save for the deeper furrow between his eyebrows and the whiter hair on his temples; but his serious attentive look was constantly veiled from me by a cloud. And I am the same woman, but without love or desire for love, with no longing for work and no content with myself. My religious ecstasies, my love for my husband, the fullness of my former life—all these now seem utterly remote and visionary. Once it seemed so plain and right that to live for others was happiness; but now it has become unintelligible. Why live for others, when life had no attraction even for oneself?

I had given up my music altogether since the time of our first visit to Petersburg; but now the old piano and the old music tempted me to begin again.

One day I was not well and stayed indoors alone. My husband had taken Kátya and Sónya to see the new buildings at Nikólskoe. Tea was laid; I went downstairs and while waiting for them sat down at the piano. I opened the 'Moonlight Sonata' and began to play. There was no one within sight or sound, the windows were open over the garden, and the familiar sounds floated through the room with a solemn sadness. At the end of the first movement I looked round instinctively to the corner where he used to sit and listen to my playing. He was not there; his chair, long unmoved, was still in its place; through the window I could see a lilac-bush against the light of the setting sun; the freshness of evening streamed in through the open windows. I rested my elbows on the piano and covered my face with both hands; and so I sat for a long time, thinking. I recalled with pain the irrevocable past, and timidly imagined the future. But for me there seemed to be no future, no desires at all and no hopes. 'Can life be over for me?' I thought with horror; then I looked up, and, trying to forget and not to think, I began playing the same movement over again. 'O God!' I prayed, 'forgive me if I have sinned, or restore to me all that once blossomed in my heart, or teach me what to do and how to live now.' There was a sound of wheels on the grass and before the steps of the house; then I heard cautious and familiar footsteps pass along the veranda and cease; but my heart no longer replied to the sound. When I stopped playing the footsteps were behind me and a hand was laid on my shoulder.

'How clever of you to think of playing that!' he said.

I said nothing.

'Have you had tea?' he asked.

I shook my head without looking at him—I was unwilling to let him see the signs of emotion on my face.

'They'll be here immediately,' he said; 'the horse gave trouble, and they got out on the high road to walk home.'

'Let us wait for them,' I said, and went out to the veranda, hoping that he would follow; but he asked about the children and went upstairs to see them. Once more his presence and simple kindly voice made me doubt if I had really lost anything. What more could I wish? 'He is kind and gentle, a good husband, a good father; I don't know myself what more I want.' I sat down under the veranda awning on the very bench on which I had sat when we became engaged. The sun had set, it was growing dark, and a little spring rain-cloud hung over the house and garden, and only behind the trees the horizon was clear, with the fading glow of twilight, in which one star had just begun to twinkle. The landscape, covered by the shadow of the cloud, seemed waiting for the light spring shower. There was not a breath of wind; not a single leaf or blade of grass stirred; the scent of lilac and bird-cherry was so strong in the garden and veranda that it seemed as if all the air was in flower; it came in wafts, now stronger and now weaker, till one longed to shut both eyes and ears and drink in that fragrance only. The dahlias and rose-bushes, not yet in flower, stood motionless on the black mould of the border, looking as if they were growing slowly upwards on their white-shaved props; beyond the dell, the frogs were making the most of their time before the rain drove them to the pond, croaking busily and loudly. Only the high continuous note of water falling at some distance rose above their croaking. From time to time the nightingales called to one another, and I could hear them flitting restlessly from bush to bush. Again this spring a nightingale had tried to build in a bush under the window, and I heard her fly off across the avenue when I went into the veranda. From there she whistled once and then stopped; she, too, was expecting the rain.

I tried in vain to calm my feelings: I had a sense of anticipation and regret.

He came downstairs again and sat down beside me.

'I am afraid they will get wet,' he said.

'Yes,' I answered; and we sat for long without speaking.

The cloud came down lower and lower with no wind. The air grew stiller and more fragrant. Suddenly a drop fell on the canvas awning and seemed to rebound from it; then another broke on the gravel path; soon there was a splash on the burdock leaves, and a fresh shower of big drops came down faster and faster. Nightingales and frogs were both dumb; only the high note of the falling water, though the rain made it seem more distant, still went on; and a bird, which must have sheltered among the dry leaves near the veranda, steadily repeated its two unvarying notes. My husband got up to go in.

'Where are you going?' I asked, trying to keep him; 'it is so pleasant here.'

'We must send them an umbrella and goloshes,' he replied.

'Don't trouble—it will soon be over.'

He thought I was right, and we remained together in the veranda. I rested one hand upon the wet slippery rail and put my head out. The fresh rain wetted my hair and neck in places. The cloud, growing lighter and thinner, was passing overhead; the steady patter of the rain gave place to occasional drops that fell from the sky or dripped from the trees. The frogs began to croak again in the dell; the nightingales woke up and began to call from the dripping bushes from one side and then from another. The whole prospect before us grew clear.

'How delightful!' he said, seating himself on the veranda rail and passing a hand over my wet hair.

This simple caress had on me the effect of a reproach: I felt inclined to cry.

'What more can a man need?' he said; 'I am so content now that I want nothing; I am perfectly happy!'

He told me a different story once, I thought. He had said that, however great his happiness might be, he always wanted more and more. Now he is calm and contented; while my heart is full of unspoken repentance and unshed tears.

'I think it delightful too,' I said; 'but I am sad just because of the beauty of it all. All is so fair and lovely outside me, while my own heart is confused and baffled and full of vague unsatisfied longing. Is it possible that there is no element of pain, no yearning for the past, in your enjoyment of nature?'

He took his hand off my head and was silent for a little.

'I used to feel that too,' he said, as though recalling it, 'especially in spring. I used to sit up all night too, with my hopes and fears for company, and good company they were! But life was all before me then. Now it is all behind me, and I am content with what I have. I find life capital,' he added with such careless confidence, that I believed, whatever pain it gave me to hear it, that it was the truth.

'But is there nothing you wish for?' I asked.

'I don't ask for impossibilities,' he said, guessing my thoughts. 'You go and get your head wet,' he added, stroking my head like a child's and again passing his hand over the wet hair; 'you envy the leaves and the grass their wetting from the rain, and you would like yourself to be the grass and the leaves and the rain. But I am content to enjoy them and everything else that is good and young and happy.'

'And do you regret nothing of the past?' I asked, while my heart grew heavier and heavier.

Again he thought for a time before replying. I saw that he wished to reply with perfect frankness.

'Nothing,' he said shortly.

'Not true! not true!' I said, turning towards him and looking into his eyes. 'Do you really not regret the past?'

'No!' he repeated; 'I am grateful for it, but I don't regret it.'

'But would you not like to have it back?' I asked.

He turned away and looked out over the garden.

'No; I might as well wish to have wings. It is impossible.'

'And would you not alter the past? do you not reproach yourself or me?'

'No, never! It was all for the best.'

'Listen to me!' I said, touching his arm to make him look round. 'Why did you never tell me that you wished me to live as you really wished me to? Why did you give me a freedom for which I was unfit? Why did you stop teaching me? If you had wished it, if you had guided me differently, none of all this would have happened!' said I in a voice that increasingly expressed cold displeasure and reproach, in place of the love of former days.

'What would not have happened?' he asked, turning to me in surprise. 'As it is, there is nothing wrong. Things are all right, quite all right,' he added with a smile.

'Does he really not understand?' I thought; 'or, still worse, does he not wish to understand?'

Then I suddenly broke out. 'Had you acted differently, I should not now be punished, for no fault at all, by your indifference and even contempt, and you would not have taken from me unjustly all that I valued in life!'

'What do you mean, my dear one?' he asked—he seemed not to understand me.

'No! don't interrupt me! You have taken from me your confidence, your love, even your respect; for I cannot believe, when I think of the past, that you still love me. No! don't speak! I must once for all say out what has long been torturing me. Is it my fault that I knew nothing of life, and that you left me to learn experience for myself? Is it my fault that now, when I have gained the knowledge and have been struggling for nearly a year to come back to you, you push me away and pretend not to understand what I want? And you always do it so that it is impossible to reproach you, while I am guilty and unhappy. Yes, you wish to drive me out again to that life which might rob us both of happiness.'

'How did I show that?' he asked in evident alarm and surprise.

'No later than yesterday you said, and you constantly say, that I can never settle down here, and that we must spend this winter too at Petersburg; and I hate Petersburg!' I went on. 'Instead of supporting me, you avoid all plain speaking, you never say a single frank affectionate word to me. And then, when I fall utterly, you will reproach me and rejoice in my fall.'

'Stop!' he said with cold severity. 'You have no right to say that. It only proves that you are ill-disposed towards me, that you don't . . .'

'That I don't love you? Don't hesitate to say it!' I cried, and the tears began to flow. I sat down on the bench and covered my face with my handkerchief.

'So that is how he understood me!' I thought, trying to restrain the sobs which choked me. 'Gone, gone is our former love!' said a voice at my heart. He did not come close or try to comfort me. He was hurt by what I had said. When he spoke, his tone was cool and dry.

'I don't know what you reproach me with,' he began. 'If you mean that I don't love you as I once did . . .'

'Did love!' I said, with my face buried in the handkerchief, while the bitter tears fell still more abundantly.

'If so, time is to blame for that, and we ourselves. Each time of life has its own kind of love.' He was silent for a moment. 'Shall I tell you the whole truth, if you really wish for frankness? In that summer when I first knew you, I used to lie awake all night, thinking about you, and I made that love myself, and it grew and grew in my heart. So again, in Petersburg and abroad, in the course of horrible sleepless nights, I strove to shatter and destroy that love, which had come to torture me. I did not destroy it, but I destroyed that part of it which gave me pain. Then I grew calm; and I feel love still, but it is a different kind of love.'

'You call it love, but I call it torture!' I said. 'Why did you allow me to go into society, if you thought so badly of it that you ceased to love me on that account?'

'No, it was not society, my dear,' he said.

'Why did you not exercise your authority?' I went on; 'why did you not lock me up or kill me? That would have been better than the loss of all that formed my happiness. I should have been happy, instead of being ashamed.'

I began to sob again and hid my face.

Just then Kátya and Sónya, wet and cheerful, came out to the veranda, laughing and talking loudly. They were silent as soon as they saw us, and went in again immediately.

We remained silent for a long time. I had had my cry out and felt relieved. I glanced at him. He was sitting with his head resting on his hand; he intended to make some reply to my glance, but only sighed deeply and resumed his former position.

I went up to him and removed his hand. His eyes turned thoughtfully to my face.

'Yes,' he began, as if continuing his thoughts aloud, 'all of us, and especially you women, must have personal experience of all the nonsense of life, in order to get back to life itself; the evidence of other people is no good. At that time you had not got near the end of that charming nonsense which I admired in you. So I let you go through it alone, feeling that I had no right to put pressure on you, though my own time for that sort of thing was long past.'

'If you loved me,' I said, 'how could you stand beside me and suffer me to go through it?'

'Because it was impossible for you to take my word for it, though you would have tried to. Personal experience was necessary, and now you have had it.'

'There was much calculation in all that,' I said, 'but little love.'

Again we were silent.

'What you said just now is severe, but it is true,' he began, rising suddenly and beginning to walk about the veranda. 'Yes, it is true. I was to blame,' he added, stopping opposite me; 'I ought either to have kept myself from loving you at all, or to have loved you in a simpler way.'

'Let us forget it all,' I said timidly.

'No,' he said; 'the past can never come back, never;' and his voice softened as he spoke.

'It is restored already,' I said, laying a hand on his shoulder.

He took my hand away and pressed it.

'I was wrong when I said that I did not regret the past. I do regret it; I weep for that past love which can never return. Who is to blame, I do not know. Love remains, but not the old love; its place remains, but it is all wasted away and has lost all strength and substance; recollections are still left, and gratitude; but . . .'

'Do not say that!' I broke in. 'Let all be as it was before!

Surely that is possible?' I asked, looking into his eyes; but their gaze was clear and calm, and did not look deeply into mine.

Even while I spoke, I knew that my wishes and my petition were impossible. He smiled calmly and gently; and I thought it the smile of an old man.

'How young you are still!' he said, 'and I am so old. What you seek in me is no longer there. Why deceive ourselves?' he added, still smiling.

I stood silent opposite to him, and my heart grew calmer.

'Don't let us try to repeat life,' he went on. 'Don't let us make pretences to ourselves. Let us be thankful that there is an end of the old emotions and excitements. The excitement of searching is over for us; our quest is done, and happiness enough has fallen to our lot. Now we must stand aside and make room—for him, if you like,' he said, pointing to the nurse who was carrying Ványa out and had stopped at the veranda door. 'That's the truth, my dear one,' he said, drawing down my head and kissing it, not a lover any longer but an old friend.

The fragrant freshness of the night rose ever stronger and sweeter from the garden; the sounds and the silence grew more solemn; star after star began to twinkle overhead. I looked at him, and suddenly my heart grew light; it seemed that the cause of my suffering had been removed like an aching nerve. Suddenly I realized clearly and calmly that the past feeling, like the past time itself, was gone beyond recall, and that it would be not only impossible but painful and uncomfortable to bring it back. And after all, was that time so good which seemed to me so happy? And it was all so long, long ago!

'Time for tea!' he said, and we went together to the parlour. At the door we met the nurse with the baby. I took him in my arms, covered his bare little red legs, pressed him to me, and kissed him with the lightest touch of my lips. Half asleep, he moved the parted fingers of one creased little hand and opened dim little eyes, as if he was looking for something or recalling something. All at once his eyes rested on me, a spark of consciousness shone in them, the little pouting lips, parted before, now met and opened in a smile. 'Mine, mine, mine!' I thought, pressing him to my breast with such an impulse of joy in every limb that I found it hard to restrain myself from hurting him. I fell to kissing the cold little feet, his stomach and hand and head with its thin covering of down. My husband came up to me, and I quickly covered the child's face and uncovered it again.

'Iván Sergéich!' said my husband, tickling him under the chin. But I made haste to cover Iván Sergéich up again. None but I had any business to look long at him. I glanced at my husband. His eyes smiled as he looked at me; and I looked into them with an ease and happiness which I had not felt for a long time.

That day ended the romance of our marriage; the old feeling became a precious irrecoverable remembrance; but a new feeling of love for my children and the father of my children laid the foundation of a new life and a quite different happiness; and that life and happiness have lasted to the present time.

POLIKÚSHKA

I

'It's for you to say, ma'am! Only it would be a pity if it's the Dútlovs. They're all good men and one of them must go if we don't send at least one of the house-serfs,' said the steward. 'As it is, everyone is hinting at them. . . . But it's just as you please, ma'am!'

And he placed his right hand over his left in front of him, inclined his head towards his right shoulder, drew in his thin lips almost with a smack, turned up his eyes, and said no more, evidently intending to keep silent for a long time and to listen without reply to all the nonsense his mistress was sure to utter.

The steward—clean-shaven and dressed in a long coat of a peculiar steward-like cut—who had come to report to his proprietress that autumn evening, was by birth a domestic serf.

The report from the lady's point of view meant listening to a statement of the business done on her estate and giving instructions for further business. From Egór Mikháylovich's (the steward's) point of view, 'reporting' was a ceremony of standing straight on both feet with out-turned toes in a corner facing the sofa, and listening to all sorts of irrelevant chatter, and by various ways and means getting the mistress into a state of mind in which she would quickly and impatiently say, 'All right, all right!' to all that Egór Mikháylovich proposed.

The business under consideration was the conscription. The Pokróvsk estate had to supply three recruits at the Feast of Pokróv.[1] Fate itself seemed to have selected two of them by a

---

[1] The Intercession of the Virgin, the 1st of October old style.

coincidence of domestic, moral, and economic circumstances. As far as they were concerned there could be no hesitation or dispute either on the part of the mistress, the commune, or of public opinion. But who the third was to be was a debatable point. The steward was anxious to save the Dútlovs (in which family there were three men of military age), and to send Polikúshka, a married house-serf with a very bad reputation, who had been caught more than once stealing sacks, harness, and hay; but the mistress, who had often petted Polikúshka's ragged children and improved his morals by exhortations from the Bible, did not wish to give him up. At the same time she did not wish to injure the Dútlovs, whom she did not know and had never even seen. But for some reason she did not seem able to grasp the fact, and the steward could not make up his mind to tell her straight out, that if Polikúshka did not go one of the Dútlovs would have to. 'But I don't wish the Dútlovs any ill!' she said feelingly. 'If you don't—then pay three hundred rubles for a substitute,' should have been the steward's reply; but that would have been bad policy.

So Egór Mikháylovich took up a comfortable position, and even leaned imperceptibly against the door-post, while keeping a servile expression on his face and watching the movements of the lady's lips and the flutter of the frills of her cap and their shadow on the wall beneath a picture. But he did not consider it at all necessary to attend to the meaning of her words. The lady spoke long and said much. A desire to yawn gave him cramp behind his ears, but he adroitly turned the spasm into a cough, and holding his hand to his mouth gave a croak. Not long ago I saw Lord Palmerston sitting with his hat over his face while a member of the Opposition was storming at the Ministry, and then suddenly rise and in a three hours' speech answer his opponent point by point. I saw it without surprise, because I had seen the same kind of thing going on between Egór Mikháylovich and his mistress a thousand times. At last—perhaps he was afraid of falling asleep or thought she was letting herself go too far—he changed the weight of his body from his left to his right foot and began, as he always did, with an unctuous preface:

'Just as you please to order, ma'am. . . . Only there is a gathering of the commune now being held in front of my office window and we must come to some decision. The order says that the recruits are to be in town before the Feast of Pokróv. Among the peasants the Dútlovs are being suggested, and no one else. The *mir*[2] does not trouble about your interests. What does it care if we ruin the Dútlovs? I know what a hard time they've been having! Ever since I first had the stewardship they have been living in want. The old man's youngest nephew has scarcely had time to grow up to be a help, and now they're to be ruined again! And I, as you well know, am as careful of your property as of my own. . . . It's a pity, ma'am, whatever you're pleased to think! . . . After all they're neither kith nor kin to me, and I've had nothing from them. . . .'

'Why, Egór, as if I ever thought of such a thing!' interrupted the lady, and at once suspected him of having been bribed by the Dútlovs.

'. . . Only theirs is the best-kept homestead in the whole of Pokróvsk. They're God-fearing, hard-working peasants. The old man has been church Elder for thirty years; he doesn't drink or swear, and he goes to church' (the steward well knew with what to bait the hook). '. . . But the chief thing that I would like to report to you is that he has only two sons—the others are nephews adopted out of charity—and so they ought to cast lots only with the two-men families. Many families have split up because of their own improvidence and their sons have separated from them, and so they are safe now—while these will have to suffer just because they have been charitable.'

Here the lady could not follow at all. She did not understand what he meant by 'two-men families' or 'charitableness'. She only heard sounds and observed the nankeen buttons on the steward's coat. The top one, which he probably did not button up so often, was firmly fixed on, the middle one was

---

[2] The village commune.

hanging loose and ought long ago to have been sewn on again. But it is a well-known fact that in a conversation, especially a business conversation, it is not at all necessary to understand what is being said, but only to remember what you yourself want to say. The lady acted accordingly.

'How is it you won't understand, Egór Mikháylovich?' she said. 'I have not the least desire that a Dútlov should go as a soldier. One would think that knowing me as you do you might credit me with the wish to do everything in my power to help my serfs, and that I don't want any harm to come to them, and would sacrifice all I possess to escape from this sad necessity and to send neither Dútlov nor Polikúshka.' (I don't know whether it occurred to the steward that to escape the sad necessity there was no need to sacrifice everything—that, in fact, three hundred rubles would suffice; but this thought might well have crossed his mind.)

'I will only tell you this: that I will not give up Polikúshka on any account. When he confessed to me of his own accord after that affair with the clock, and wept, and gave his word to amend, I talked to him for a long time and saw that he was touched and sincerely penitent.' ('There! She's off now!' thought Egór Mikháylovich, and began to scrutinize the syrup she had in a glass of water: 'Is it orange or lemon? Slightly bitter, I expect,' thought he.) 'That is seven months ago now, and he has not once been tipsy, and has behaved splendidly. His wife tells me he is a different man. How can you wish me to punish him now that he has reformed? Besides it would be inhuman to make a soldier of a man who has five children, and only he to keep them. . . . No, you'd better not say any more about it, Egór!'

And the lady took a sip from her glass.

Egór Mikháylovich watched the motion of her throat as the liquid passed down it and then replied shortly and dryly:

'Then Dútlov's decided on?'

The lady clasped her hands together.

'How is it you don't understand? Do I wish Dútlov ill? Have I anything against him? God is my witness I am pre-

pared to do anything for them. . . .' (She glanced at a picture in the corner, but remembered it was not an icon. 'Well,
never mind . . . that's not to the point,' she thought. And
again, strange to say, the idea of the three hundred rubles did
not occur to her. . . .) 'Well, what can I do? What do I know
about it? It's impossible for me to know. Well then, I rely on
you—you know my wishes. . . . Act so as to satisfy everybody and according to the law. . . . What's to be done?
They are not the only ones: everyone has times of trouble.
Only Polikúshka can't be sent. You must understand that it
would be dreadful of me to do such a thing. . . .'

She was roused and would have continued to speak for a
long time had not one of her maid-servants entered the room
at that moment.

'What is it, Dunyásha?'

'A peasant has come to ask Egór Mikháylovich if the meeting is to wait for him,' said Dunyásha, and glanced angrily at
Egór Mikháylovich. ('Oh, that steward!' she thought; 'he's
upset the mistress. Now she won't let me get a wink of sleep
till two in the morning!')

'Well then, Egór, go and do the best you can.'

'Yes, ma'am.' He did not say anything more about Dútlov.
'And who is to go to the market-gardener to fetch the
money?'

'Has not Peter returned from town?'

'No, ma'am.'

'Could not Nicholas go?'

'Father is down with backache,' remarked Dunyásha.

'Shall I go myself to-morrow, ma'am?' asked the steward.

'No, Egór, you are wanted here.' The lady pondered. 'How
much is it?'

'Four hundred and sixty-two rubles.'

'Send Polikúshka,' said the lady, with a determined glance
at Egór Mikháylovich's face.

Egór Mikháylovich stretched his lips into the semblance of
a smile but without parting his teeth, and the expression on
his face did not change.

'Yes, ma'am.'

'Send him to me.'

'Yes, ma'am;' and Egór Mikháylovich went to the counting-house.

II

Polikéy (or Polikúshka, as he was usually contemptuously called), as a man of little importance, of tarnished reputation, and not a native of the village, had no influence either with the housekeeper, the butler, the steward, or the lady's-maid. His *corner* was the very worst, though there were seven in his family. The late proprietor had had these *corners* built in the following manner: in the middle of a brick building, about twenty-three feet square, there was a large brick baking-oven surrounded by a passage, and the four corners of the building were separated from this 'colidor' (as the domestic serfs called it) by wooden partitions. So there was not much room in these *corners*, especially in Polikéy's, which was nearest to the door. The conjugal couch, with a print quilt and pillow-cases, a cradle with a baby in it, and a small three-legged table (on which the cooking and washing were done and all sorts of domestic articles placed, and at which Polikéy—who was a horse-doctor—worked), tubs, clothing, some chickens, a calf, and the seven members of the family, filled the whole *corner*—and could not have stirred in it had it not been for their quarter of the brick stove (on which both people and things could lie) and for the possibility of going out onto the steps. That, however, was hardly possible, for it is cold in October and the seven of them only possessed one sheepskin cloak between them; but on the other hand the children could keep warm by running about and the grown-ups by working, and both the one and the other could climb on the top of the stove where the temperature rose as high as 120 degrees Fahrenheit. It may seem dreadful to live in such conditions, but they did not mind—it was quite possible to live. Akulína washed and sewed her husband's and her children's clothes, spun, wove, and bleached her linen, cooked and baked in the common oven, and quarrelled and gossiped with her neighbours. The monthly rations sufficed not only for the children, but for an addition to the cow's food. Fire-wood was free, and so was fodder for the cattle, and a little hay from the stables sometimes came their way. They had a strip of kitchen garden. Their cow had calved, and they had their own fowls. Polikéy was employed in the stables to look after two stallions; he bled horses and cattle, cleaned their hoofs, lanced their sores, administered ointments of his own invention, and for this was paid in money and in kind. Also some of the proprietress's oats used to find their way into his possession, and for two measures of it a peasant in the village gave twenty pounds of mutton regularly every month. Life would have been quite bearable had there been no trouble at heart. But the family had a great trouble. Polikéy in his youth had lived at a stud-farm in another village. The groom into whose hands he happened to fall was the greatest thief in the whole district, and got exiled to Siberia. Under this man Polikéy served his apprenticeship, and in his youth be-came so used to 'these trifles' that in later life, though he would willingly have left off, he could not rid himself of the habit. He was a young man and weak; he had neither father nor mother nor anyone else to teach him. Polikéy liked drink, and did not like to see anything lying about loose. Whether it was a strap, a piece of harness, a padlock, a bolt, or a thing of greater value, Polikéy found some use for everything. There were people everywhere who would take these things and pay for them in drink or in money, by agreement. Such earn-ings, so people say, are the easiest to get: no apprenticeship is required, no labour or anything, and he who has once tried that kind of work does not care for any other. It has only one drawback: although you get things cheap and easily and live pleasantly, yet all of a sudden—through somebody's malice—things go all wrong, the trade fails, everything has to be ac-counted for at once, and you rue the day you were born.

And so it happened to Polikéy. Polikéy had married and God had given him good luck. His wife, the herdsman's daughter, turned out to be a healthy, intelligent, hard-working woman, who bore him one fine baby after another. And though Polikéy still stuck to his trade all went well till one fine day his luck forsook him and he was caught. And it was all about a trifle: he had hidden away some leather reins of a peasant's. They were found, he was beaten, the mistress was told of it, and he was watched. He was caught a second and a third time. People began to taunt him, the steward threatened to have him conscripted, the mistress gave him a scolding, and his wife wept and was broken-hearted. Everything went wrong. He was a good-natured man; not bad, but only weak. He was fond of drink and so in the habit of it that he could not leave it alone. Sometimes his wife would scold him and even beat him when he came home drunk, and he would weep, saying: 'Unfortunate man that I am, what shall I do? Blast my eyes, I'll give it up! Never again!' A month would go by, he would leave home, get drunk, and not be seen for a couple of days. And his neighbours would say: 'He must get the money somewhere to go on the spree with!' His latest trouble had been with the office clock. There was an old wall-clock there that had not been in working order for a long time. He happened to go in at the open door by himself and the clock tempted him. He took it and got rid of it in the town. As ill luck would have it the shopman to whom he sold the clock was related to one of the house-serfs, and coming to see her one holiday he spoke about the clock. People began making inquiries—especially the steward, who disliked Polikéy—just as if it was anybody else's concern! It was all found out and reported to the mistress, and she sent for Polikéy. He fell at her feet at once and pathetically confessed everything, just as his wife had told him to do. He carried out her instructions very well. The mistress began admonishing him; she talked and talked and maundered on about God and virtue and the future life and about wife and children, and at last moved him to tears. Then she said:

'I forgive you; only you must promise me never to do it again!'

'Never in all my life. May I go to perdition! May my bowels gush out!' said Polikéy, and wept touchingly.

Polikéy went home and for the rest of the day lay on the

stove blubbering like a calf. Since then nothing more had been
traced to him. But his life was no longer pleasant; he was
looked on as a thief, and when the time of the conscription
drew near everybody hinted at him.

As already mentioned, Polikéy was a horse-doctor. How he
had suddenly become one nobody knew, himself least of all.
At the stud-farm, when he worked under the head-keeper
who got exiled, his only duties were to clean out the dung
from the stables, sometimes to groom the horses, and to carry
water. He could not have learned it there. Then he became a
weaver: after that he worked in a garden, weeding the paths;
then he was condemned to break bricks for some offence; then
he took a place as yard-porter with a merchant, paying a
yearly sum to his mistress for leave to do so. So evidently he
could not have had any experience as a veterinary there either; yet somehow during his last stay at home his reputation
as a wonderfully and even a rather supernaturally clever horse-
doctor began gradually to spread. He bled a horse once or
twice, then threw it down and prodded about in its thigh,
and then demanded that it should be placed in a trave, where
he began cutting its frog till it bled, though the horse struggled and even whined, and he said this meant 'letting off the
sub-hoof blood'! Then he explained to a peasant that it was
absolutely necessary to let the blood from both veins, 'for
greater ease,' and began to strike the dull lancet with a mallet;
then he bandaged the innkeeper's horse under its belly with a
selvedge torn from his wife's shawl, and finally he began to
sprinkle all sorts of sores with vitriol, to drench them with
something out of a bottle, and sometimes to give internally
whatever came into his head. And the more horses he tormented and did to death, the more he was believed in and the
more of them were brought to him.

I feel that for us educated people it is hardly the thing to
laugh at Polikéy. The methods he employed to inspire confidence are the same that influenced our fathers, that influence
us, and will influence our children. The peasant lying prone on
the head of his only mare (which not only constitutes his
whole wealth but is almost one of his family) and gazing with

faith and horror at Políkéy's frowning look of importance and
thin arms with upturned sleeves, as, with the healing rag or a
bottle of vitriol between his teeth, he presses upon the very
spot that is sore and boldly cuts into the living flesh (with the
secret thought, 'The bow-legged brute will be sure to get over
it!'), at the same time pretending to know where is blood and
where pus, which is a tendon and which a vein—that peasant
cannot conceive that Políkéy could lift his hand to cut without
knowing where to do it. He himself could not do so. And once
the thing is done he will not reproach himself with having
given permission to cut unnecessarily. I don't know how you
feel about it, but I have gone through the same experience
with a doctor who, at my request, was tormenting those dear
to me. The lancet, the whitish bottle of sublimate, and the
words, 'the staggers—glanders—to let blood, or matter,' and so
on, do they not come to the same thing as 'neurosis, rheuma-
tism, organisms,' and so forth? *Wage du zu irren und zu
träumen*[1] refers not so much to poets as to doctors and veterinary surgeons.

III

On the evening when the village meeting, in the cold darkness
of an October night, was choosing the recruits and vociferat-
ing in front of the office, Políkéy sat on the edge of his bed
pounding some horse medicine on the table with a bottle—but
what it was he himself did not know. He had there corrosive
sublimate, sulphur, Glauber's salts, and some kind of herb
which he had gathered, having suddenly imagined it to be
good for broken wind and then considered it not amiss for
other disorders. The children were already lying down—two
on the stove, two on the bed, and one in the cradle beside
which Akulína sat spinning. The candle-end—one of the proprietress's candles which had not been put away carefully
enough—was burning in a wooden candlestick on the window-
sill and Akulína every now and then got up to snuff it with

---

[1] 'Dare to err and dream.'

her fingers, so that her husband should not have to break off his important occupation. There were some free-thinkers who regarded Polikéy as a worthless veterinary and a worthless man. Others, the majority, considered him a worthless man but a great master of his art; but Akulína, though she often scolded and even beat her husband, thought him undoubtedly the first of horse-doctors and the best of men. Polikéy sprinkled some kind of simple on the palm of his hand (he never used scales, and spoke ironically of the Germans who use them: 'This,' he used to say, 'is not an apothecary's!'). Polikéy weighed the simple on his hand and tossed it up, but there did not seem enough of it and he poured in ten times more. 'I'll put in the lot,' he said to himself. 'It will pick 'em up better.' Akulína quickly turned round at the sound of her lord and master's voice, expecting some command; but seeing that the business did not concern her she shrugged her shoulders. 'What knowledge! . . . Where does he get it?' she thought, and went on spinning. The paper which had held the simple fell to the floor. Akulína did not overlook this.

'Annie,' she cried, 'look! Father has dropped something. Pick it up!'

Annie put out her thin little bare legs from under the cloak with which she was covered, slid down under the table like a kitten, and got the paper.

'Here, daddy,' she said, and darted back into bed with her chilled little feet.

'Don't puth!' squeaked her lisping younger sister sleepily.

'I'll give it you!' muttered Akulína, and both heads disappeared again under the cloak.

'He'll give me three rubles,' said Polikéy, corking up the bottle. 'I'll cure the horse. It's even too cheap,' he added, 'brain-splitting work! . . . Akulína, go and ask Nikíta for a little 'baccy. I'll pay him back to-morrow.'

Polikéy took out of his trouser-pocket a lime-wood pipe-stem, which had once been painted, with a sealing-wax mouth-piece, and began fixing it onto the bowl.

Akulína left her spindle and went out, managing to steer clear of everything—though this was not easy. Polikéy opened the cupboard and put away the medicine, then tilted a vodka bottle into his mouth, but it was empty and he made a grimace. But when his wife brought the tobacco he sat down on the edge of the bed, after filling and lighting his pipe, and his face beamed with the content and pride of a man who has completed his day's task. Whether he was thinking how on the morrow he would catch hold of the horse's tongue and pour his wonderful mixture down its throat, or reflecting that a useful person never gets a refusal—'There, now! Hadn't Nikíta sent him the tobacco?'—anyhow he felt happy. Suddenly the door, which hung on one hinge, was thrown open and a maidservant from *up there*—not the second maid but the third, the little one that was kept to run errands—entered their *corner*. (*Up there*, as every one knows, means the master's house, even if it stands on lower ground.) Aksyútka—that was the girl's name—always flew like a bullet, and did it without bending her arms, which keeping time with the speed of her flight swung like pendulums, not at her sides but in front of her. Her cheeks were always redder than her pink dress, and her tongue moved as fast as her legs. She flew into the room, and for some reason catching hold of the stove, began to sway to and fro; then as if intent on not emitting more than two or three words at once, she suddenly addressed Akulína breathlessly as follows:

'The mistress . . . has given orders . . . that Polikéy should come this minute . . . orders to come up. . . .'

She stopped, drawing breath with difficulty.

'Egór Mikháylovich has been with the mistress . . . they talked about *rickruits* . . . they mentioned Polikéy . . . Avdótya Nikoláevna . . . has ordered him to come this minute . . . Avdótya Nikoláevna has ordered . . .' again a sigh, 'to come this minute. . . .'

For half a minute Aksyútka looked round at Polikéy and at Akulína and the children—who had put out their heads from under their coverlets—picked up a nutshell that lay on the stove and threw it at little Annie. Then she repeated: 'To come this minute! . . .' and rushed out of the room like a whirlwind, the pendulums swinging as usual across her line of flight.

Akulína again rose and got her husband his boots—abominable soldier's boots with holes in them—and took down his coat
from the stove and handed it to him without looking at him.

'Won't you change your shirt, Polikéy?'

'No,' he answered.

Akulína never once looked at his face while he put on his
boots and coat, and she did well not to look. Polikéy's face
was pale, his nether jaw twitched, and in his eyes there was
that tearful, meek, and deeply mournful look one only sees in
the eyes of kindly, weak, and guilty people.—He combed his
hair and was going out; but his wife stopped him, tucked in
the string of his shirt that hung down from under his coat, and
put his cap on for him.

'What's that, Polikéy? Has the mistress sent for you?' came
the voice of the carpenter's wife from behind the partition.

Only that very morning the carpenter's wife had had high
words with Akulína about her pot of lye[1] that Polikéy's children had upset in her *corner*, and at first she was pleased to
hear Polikéy being summoned to the mistress—most likely for
no good. She was a subtle, diplomatic lady, with a biting
tongue. Nobody knew better than she how to cut one with a
word: so at least she imagined.

'I expect you'll be sent to town to buy things,' she continued.
'I suppose a trusty person is wanted for that job so she is send-
ing you! You might buy me a quarter of a pound of tea there,
Polikéy.'

Akulína forced back her tears, and an angry expression distorted her lips. She felt as if she could have clutched 'that
vixen, the joiner's wife, by her mangy hair.' But as she looked
at her children and thought that they would be left fatherless
and she herself be a soldier's wife and as good as widowed,
she forgot the sharp-tongued carpenter's wife, hid her face in
her hands, sat down on the bed, and let her head sink in the
pillows.

'Mammy, you're cwushing me!' lisped the little girl, pulling

---

[1] Made by scalding wood-ash taken from the stove, and used for
washing clothes.

the cloak with which she was covered from under her mother's elbow.

'If only you'd die, all of you! I've brought you into the world for nothing but sorrow!' cried Akulína, and sobbed aloud, to the delight of the carpenter's wife who had not yet forgotten the lye spilt that morning.

IV

Half an hour passed. The baby began to cry. Akulína got up and gave it the breast. Weeping no longer, but resting her thin though still handsome face on her hand and fixing her eyes on the last flickerings of the candle, she sat thinking why she had married, wondering why so many soldiers were needed, and also how she could pay out the carpenter's wife.

She heard her husband's footsteps and, wiping her tears, got up to let him pass. Polikéy entered like a conqueror, threw his cap on the bed, puffed, and undid his girdle.

'Well, what did she want you for?'

'H'm! Of course! Polikúshka is the least of men . . . but when there's business to be done, who's wanted? Why, Polikúshka. . . .'

'What business?'

Polikéy was in no hurry to reply. He lit his pipe and spat.

'To go and fetch money from a merchant.'

'To fetch money?' Akulína asked.

Polikéy chuckled and wagged his head.

'Ah! Ain't she clever at words? . . . "You have been regarded," she says, "as an untrustworthy man, but I trust you more than another" ' (Polikéy spoke loud that the neighbours might hear). ' "You promised me you'd reform; here," she says, "is the first proof that I believe you. Go," she says, "to the merchant, fetch the money he owes, and bring it back to me." And I say: "We are all your serfs, ma'am," I say, "and must serve you as we serve God; so I feel that I can do anything for your honour and cannot refuse any kind of work; whatever you order I will do, because I am your slave." ' (He again smiled that peculiar, weak, kindly, guilty smile.) ' "Well,

then," she says, "you will do it faithfully? . . . You understand," she says, "that your fate depends on it?"—"How could
I fail to understand that I can do it all? If they have told tales
about me—well, anyone can tell tales about another . . . but
I never in any way, I believe, have even had a thought against
your honour . . ." In a word, I buttered her up till my lady
was quite softened. . . . "I shall think highly of you," she
says.' (He kept silent a minute, then the smile again appeared
on his face.) 'I know very well how to talk to the likes of
them! Formerly, when I used to go out to work on my own, at
times some one would come down hard on me; but only let
me get in a word or two and I'd butter him up till he'd be as
smooth as silk!'

'Is it much money?'

'Fifteen hundred rubles,' carelessly replied Polikéy.

She shook her head.

'When are you to go?'

' "To-morrow," she says. "Take any horse you like," she says,
"call at the office, and then start and God be with you!" '

'The Lord be praised!' said Akulína, rising and crossing herself. 'May God help you, Polikéy,' she added in a whisper, so
that she might not be heard beyond the partition and holding
him by his shirt-sleeve. 'Polikéy, listen to me! I beseech you
in the name of Christ our God: kiss the cross when you start,
and promise that not a drop shall pass your lips.'

'A likely thing!' he ejaculated; 'drink when carrying all that
money! . . . Ah! how somebody was playing the piano up
there! Fine! . . .' he said, after a pause, and smiled. 'I suppose it was the young lady. I was standing like this in front
of the mistress, beside the whatnot, and the young lady was
rattling away behind the door. She rattled and rattled on,
fitting it together so pat! O my! Wouldn't I like to play a tune!
I'd soon master it, I would. I'm awfully good at that sort of
thing. . . . Let me have a clean shirt to-morrow!'

And they went to bed happy.

V

Meanwhile the meeting in front of the office had been noisy. The business before them was no trifle. Almost all the peasants were present. While the steward was with the mistress they kept their caps on, more voices were heard, and they talked more loudly. The hum of deep voices, interrupted at rare intervals by breathless, husky, and shrill tones, filled the air and, entering through the windows of the mistress's house, sounded like the noise of a distant sea, making her feel a nervous agitation like that produced by a heavy thunderstorm—a sensation between fear and discomfort. She felt as if the voices might at any moment grow yet louder and faster and then something would happen. 'As if it could not all be done quietly, peaceably, without disputing and shouting,' she thought, 'according to the Christian law of brotherly love and meekness!'

Many voices were speaking at once, but Theodore Rezún, the carpenter, shouted loudest. There were two grown-up young men in his family and he was attacking the Dútlovs. Old Dútlov was defending himself: he stepped forward from the crowd behind which he had at first been standing. Now spreading out his arms, now clutching his little beard, he sputtered and snuffled in such a way that it would have been hard for him to understand what he himself was saying. His sons and nephews—splendid fellows all of them—stood huddled behind him, and the old man resembled the mother-hen in the game of Hawk and Chickens. The hawk was Rezún; and not only Rezún, but all the men who had two grown lads in family, and the fathers of only sons, and almost the whole meeting, were attacking Dútlov. The point was that Dútlov's brother had been recruited thirty years before, and that Dútlov wished therefore to be excused from taking his turn with the families in which there were three eligible young men, and wanted his brother's service in the army to be reckoned to the credit of his family, so that it should be given the same chance as those in which there were only two young men; and that these families should all draw lots equally and the third recruit be chosen from among all of them. Besides Dútlov's family there were four others in which there were three young men, but one was the village Elder's family and the mistress had exempted him. From the second a recruit had been taken the year before, and from each of the remaining families a recruit was now being taken. One of them had not even come to this meeting, but his wife stood sorrowfully behind all the others, vaguely hoping that the wheel of fortune might somehow turn her way. The red-haired Román, the father of the other recruit, in a tattered coat—though he was not poor—hung his head and silently leaned against the porch, only now and then looking up attentively at any one who raised his voice, and then hanging his head again. Misery seemed to breathe from his whole figure. Old Semën Dútlov was a man to whose keeping anyone who knew anything of him would have trusted hundreds and thousands of rubles. He was a steady, God-fearing, reliable man, and was the church Elder. Therefore the excitement he was now in was all the more striking.

Rezún the carpenter, a tall dark man, was, on the contrary, a riotous drunkard, very smart in a dispute and in arguing with workmen, tradespeople, peasants, or gentlefolk, at meetings and fairs. Now he was self-possessed and sarcastic, and from his superior height was crushing down the spluttering church Elder with the whole strength of his ringing voice and oratorical talent. The church Edler was exasperated out of his usual sober groove. Besides these, the youngish, round-faced, square-headed, curly-bearded, thick-set Garáska Kopýlov, one of the speakers of the younger generation, followed Rezún and took part in the dispute. He had already gained some weight at village meetings, having distinguished himself by his trenchant speeches. Then there was Theodore Mélnichny, a tall, thin, yellow-faced, round-shouldered man, also young, with a scanty beard and small eyes, always embittered and gloomy, seeing the dark side of everything and often bewildering the meeting by unexpected and abrupt questions and remarks. Both these speakers sided with Rezún. Besides these there were two babblers who now and then joined in:

one, called Khrapkóv, with a most good-humoured face and
flowing brown beard, who kept repeating the words, 'Oh, my
dearest friend!' the other, Zhidkóv, a little fellow with a bird-
like face who also kept remarking at every opportunity, 'That's
how it is, brothers mine!' addressing himself to everybody and
speaking fluently but never to the point. Both of these sided
first with one and then with the other party, but no one listened to them. There were others like them, but these two,
who kept moving through the crowd and shouting louder than
anybody and frightening the mistress, were listened to less
than anyone else. Intoxicated by the noise and shouting, they
gave themselves up entirely to the pleasure of letting their
tongues wag. There were many other characters among the
members of the commune, stern, respectable, indifferent, or
depressed; and there were women standing behind the men
with sticks in their hands, but, God willing, I'll speak of them
some other time. The greater part of the crowd, however, consisted of peasants who stood as if they were in church, whispering behind each other's backs about home affairs, or of
when to cut faggots in the wood, or silently awaiting the end
of the jabber. There were also rich peasants whose well-being
the meeting could not add to nor diminish. Such was Ermíl,
with his broad shiny face, whom the peasants called the 'big-
bellied', because he was rich. Such too was Stárostin, whose
face showed a self-satisfied expression of power that seemed
to say, 'You may talk away, but no one will touch me! I
have four sons, but not one of them will have to go.' Now and
then these two were attacked by some independent thinker
such as Kopýlov and Rezún, but they replied quietly and
firmly and with a consciousness of their own inviolability. If
Dútlov was like the mother-hen in the game of Hawk and
Chickens, his lads did not much resemble the chickens. They
did not flutter about and squeak, but stood quietly behind
him. His eldest son, Ignát, was already thirty; the second,
Vasíli, also was already a married man and moreover not fit for
a recruit; the third, his nephew Elijah, who had just got married—a fair, rosy young man in a smart sheepskin coat (he
was a post-chaise driver)—stood looking at the crowd, some-

times scratching his head under his hat, as if the whole matter was no concern of his, though it was just on him that the hawks wished to swoop down.

'If it comes to that, my grandfather was a soldier,' said one, 'and so I might refuse to draw lots in just the same way! . . . There's no such law, friend. Last recruiting, Mikhéchev was taken though his uncle had not even returned from service then.'

'Neither your father nor your uncle ever served the Tsar,' Dútlov was saying at the same time. 'Why, you don't even serve the mistress or the commune, but spend all your time in the pub. Your sons have separated from you because it's impossible to live with you, so you go suggesting other people's sons for recruits! But I have done police duty for ten years, and served as Elder. Twice I have been burnt out, and no one helped me over it; and now, because things are peaceable and decent in my home, am I to be ruined? . . . Give me back my brother, then! He has died in service for sure. . . . Judge honestly according to God's law, Christian commune, and don't listen to a drunkard's drivel.'

And at the same time Geráska was saying to Dútlov:

'You are making your brother an excuse; but he was not sent by the commune. He was sent by the master because of his evil ways, so he's no excuse for you.'

Geráska had not finished when the lank yellow-faced Theodore Mélnichny stepped forward and began dismally:

'Yes, that's the way! The masters send whom they please, and then the commune has to get the muddle straight. The commune has fixed on your lad, and if you don't like it, go and ask the lady. Perhaps she will order me, the one man of our family, to leave my children and go! . . . There's law for you!' he said bitterly, and waving his hand he went back to his former place.

Red-haired Román, whose son had been chosen as a recruit, raised his head and muttered: 'That's it, that's it!' and even sat down on the step in vexation.

But these were not the only ones who were speaking at

once. Besides those at the back who were talking about their
own affairs, the babblers did not forget to do their part.

'And so it is, faithful commune,' said little Zhidkóv, supporting Dútlov. 'One must judge in a Christian way. . . . Like
Christians I mean, brothers, we must judge.'

'One must judge according to one's conscience, my dear
friend,' spoke the good-humoured Khrapkóv, repeating Garáska
Kopýlov's words and pulling Dútlov by his sheepskin coat. 'It
was the master's will and not the commune's decision.'

'That's right! So it was!' said others.

'What drunkard is drivelling there?' Rezún retorted to
Dútlov. 'Did you stand me any drinks? Or is your son, whom
they pick up by the roadside, going to reproach me for drinking? . . . Friends, we must decide! If you want to spare the
Dútlovs, choose not only out of families with two men, but
even an only son, and he will have the laugh on us!'

'A Dútlov will have to go! What's the good of talking?'

'Of course the three-men families must be the first to draw
lots,' began different voices.

'We must first see what the mistress will say. Egór Mikháylovich was saying that they wished to send a house-serf,'
put in a voice.

This remark checked the dispute for a while, but soon it
flared up anew and again came to personalities.

Ignát, whom Rezún had accused of being picked up drink
by the roadside, began to make out that Rezún had stolen a
saw from some travelling carpenters, and that he had almost
beaten his wife to death when he was drunk.

Rezún replied that he beat his wife drunk or sober, and
still it was not enough, and this set everybody laughing. But
about the saw he became suddenly indignant, stepped closer
to Ignát and asked:

'Who stole? . . .'

'You did,' replied the sturdy Ignát, drawing still closer.

'Who stole? . . . Wasn't it you?' shouted Rezún.

'No, it was you,' said Ignát.

From the saw they went on to the theft of a horse, a sack of oats, some strip of communal kitchen-garden, and to a certain dead body; and the two peasants said such terrible things of one another that if a hundredth part of them had been true they would by law at the very least have deserved exile to Siberia.

In the meantime old Dútlov had chosen another way of defending himself. He did not like his son's shouting, and tried to stop him, saying: 'It's a sin. . . . Leave off, I tell you!' At the same time he argued that not only those who had three young men at home were three-men families, but also those whose sons had separated from them, and he also pointed to Stárostin.

Stárostin smiled slightly, cleared his throat, and stroking his beard with the air of a well-to-do peasant, answered that it all depended on the mistress, and that evidently his sons had deserved well, since the order was for them to be exempt.

Garáska smashed Dútlov's arguments about the families that had broken up, by the remark that they ought not to have been allowed to break up, as was the rule during the lifetime of the late master; but that no one went raspberry-picking when summer was over, and that one could not now conscript the only man left in a household.

'Did they break up their households for fun? Why should they now be quite ruined?' came the voices of the men whose families had separated; and the babblers joined in too.

'You'd better buy a substitute if you're not satisfied. You can afford it!' said Rezún to Dútlov.

Dútlov wrapped his coat round him with a despairing gesture and stepped back behind the others.

'It seems you've counted my money!' he muttered angrily. 'We shall see what Egór Mikháylovich will say when he comes from the mistress.'

VI

At that very moment Egór Mikháylovich came out of the house. One cap after another was lifted, and as the steward approached all the heads—grey, grizzled, red, brown, fair, or bald in front or on top—were uncovered, and the voices were gradually silenced till at last all was quiet. Egór Mikháylovich stepped onto the porch, evidently intending to speak. In his long coat, his hands awkwardly thrust into the front pockets, his town-made cap pulled over his forehead, he stood firmly, with feet apart, in this elevated position, towering above all these heads—mostly old, bearded, and handsome—that were turned towards him. He was now a different man from what he had been when he stood before his mistress. He was majestic.

'This is the mistress's decision, men! It is not her pleasure to give up any of the house-serfs, but from among you—whom you yourselves decide on shall go. Three are wanted this time. By rights only two and a half are wanted, but the half will be taken into account next time. It comes to the same thing: if not to-day it would have to be to-morrow.'

'Of course, that's quite right!' some voices said.

'In my opinion,' continued Egór Mikháylovich, 'Kharyúsh-kin and Váska Mityúkhin must go, that is evidently God's will.'

'Yes, that's quite right!' said the voices.

'. . . The third will have to be one of the Dútlovs, or one out of a two-men family. . . . What do you say?'

'Dútlov!' cried the voices. 'There are three of them of the right age!'

And again, little by little, the shouting increased, and some-how the question of the strip of kitchen-garden and certain sacks stolen from the mistress's yard came up again. Egór Mikháylovich had been managing the estate for the last twenty years and was a shrewd and experienced man. He stood and listened for about a quarter of an hour, then he ordered all to be silent, and the three younger Dútlovs to draw lots to see which of them was to go. The lots were prepared, shaken up in a hat, and Khrapkóv drew one out. It was Elijah's. All became silent.

'Is it mine? Let me see it!' said Elijah in a faltering voice.

All remained silent. Egór Mikháylovich ordered that every-body should bring the recruit money—seven kopeks from each household—next day, and saying that all was over, dismissed the meeting. The crowd moved off, the men covered their heads as they turned the corner, and their voices and the sound of their footsteps mingled into a hum. The steward stood on the porch watching the departing crowd, and when the young Dútlovs were round the corner he beckoned old Dútlov, who had stopped of his own accord, and they went into the office.

'I am sorry for you, old man,' said Egór Mikháylovich, sitting down in an arm-chair before the table. 'It was your turn though. Will you buy a recruit to take your nephew's place, or not?'

The old man, without speaking, gave Egór Mikháylovich a significant look.

'There's no getting out of it,' said Egór Mikháylovich in answer to that look.

'We'd be glad enough to buy a substitute, Egór Mikháylovich, but we haven't the means. Two horses went to the knacker's this summer, and there was my nephew's wedding. . . . Evidently it's our fate . . . for living honestly. It's very well for him to talk!' (He was thinking of Rezún.)

Egór Mikháylovich rubbed his face with his hand and yawned. He was evidently tired of the business and was ready for his tea.

'Eh, old fellow, don't be mean!' said he. 'Have a hunt under your floor, I dare say you'll turn up some four hundred old ruble notes, and I'll get you a substitute—a regular wonder! . . . The other day a fellow came offering himself.'

'In the *government?*' asked Dútlov, meaning the town.

'Well, will you buy him?'

'I'd be glad enough, God is my witness! . . . but . . .'

Egór Mikháylovich interrupted him sternly.

'Well then, listen to me, old man! See that Elijah does himself no mischief,[1] and as soon as I send word—whether to-day or to-morrow—he is to be taken to town at once. You will take him and you will be answerable for him, but if anything

---

[1] It sometimes happened that to escape service men mutilated themselves, for instance by cutting off the finger needed to pull the trigger.

should happen to him—which God forbid!—I'll send your eldest son instead! Do you hear?'

'But could not one be sent from a two-man family? . . . Egór Mikháylovich, this is not fair!' he said. Then after a pause he went on, almost with tears: 'When my brother has died a soldier, now they are taking my son! How have I deserved such a blow?' and he was ready to fall on his knees.

'Well, well, go away!' said Egór Mikháylovich. 'Nothing can be done. It's the law. Keep an eye on Elijah: you'll have to answer for him!'

Dútlov went home, thoughtfully tapping the ruts with his linden stick as he walked.

VII

Early next morning a big-boned bay gelding (for some reason called Drum) harnessed to a small cart (the steward himself used to drive in that cart), stood at the porch of the house-serfs' quarters. Annie, Polikéy's eldest daughter, barefoot in spite of the falling sleet and the cold wind, and evidently frightened, stood at the horse's head holding the bridle at arm's length, and with her other hand held a faded yellowy-green jacket that was thrown over her head, and which served the family as blanket, cloak, hood, carpet, overcoat for Polikéy, and many other things besides. Polikéy's *corner* was all in a bustle. The dim light of a rainy morning was just glimmering in at the window, which was broken here and there and mended with paper. Akulína had left her cooking in the oven, and left her children—of whom the younger were still in bed—shivering, because the jacket that served them as blanket had been taken away to serve as a garment and only replaced by the shawl off their mother's head. Akulína was busy getting her husband ready for his journey. His shirt was clean, but his boots, which as the saying is were 'begging for porridge', gave her much trouble. She had taken off her thick worsted stockings (her only pair) and given them to her husband, and had managed to cut out a pair of inner soles from a saddle-cloth (which had been carelessly left about in the stable and had been brought home by Polikéy two days before) in such a way as to stop up the holes in his boots and keep his feet dry. Polikéy sat, feet and all, on the bed, untwisting his girdle so that it should not look like a dirty cord. The cross, lisping little girl, wrapped in the sheepskin (which though it covered her head was trailing round her feet), had been dispatched to ask Nikíta to lend them a cap. The bustle was increased by house-serfs coming in to ask Polikéy to get different things for them in town. One wanted needles, another tea, a third some to-bacco, and another some olive oil. The carpenter's wife—who to conciliate Polikéy had already found time to make her samovar boil and bring him a mug full of liquid which she called tea—wanted some sugar. Though Nikíta refused to lend a cap and they had to mend his own—that is, to push in the protruding bits of wadding and sew them up with a veterinary needle; though at first the boots with the saddle-cloth soles would not go on his feet; though Annie, chilled through, nearly let Drum get out of hand, and Mary in the long sheepskin had to take her place, and then Mary had to take off the sheepskin and Akulína had to hold the horse her-self—it all ended by Polikéy successfully getting all the warm family garments on himself, leaving only the jacket and a pair of slippers behind. When ready, he got into the little cart, wrapped the sheepskin round him, shook up the bag of hay at the bottom of the cart, again wrapped himself up, took the reins, wrapped the coat still closer round him as very impor-tant people do, and started.

His little boy Míshka, running out onto the steps, begged to have a ride; the lisping Mary also begged that she might 'have a lide', and was 'not cold even without the theepthkin'; so Polikéy stopped Drum and smiled his weak smile while Akulína put the children into the cart and, bending towards him, begged him in a whisper to remember his oath and not drink anything on the way. Polikéy took the children through the village as far as the smithy, put them down, wrapped him-self up and put his cap straight again, and drove off at a slow, sedate trot, his cheeks quivering at every jolt and his feet knocking against the bark sides of the cart. Mary and Míshka, barefoot, rushed down the slippery hill to the house at such a rate and yelling so loudly that a stray dog from the village looked up at them and scurried home with its tail between its legs, which made Polikéy's heirs yell ten times louder.

It was abominable weather: the wind was cutting, and something between rain and snow, and now and then fine hail, beat on Polikéy's face and on his bare hands which held the reins—and over which he kept drawing the sleeves of his coat—and on the leather of the horse-collar, and on the head of old Drum, who set back his ears and half closed his eyes.

Then suddenly the rain stopped and it brightened up in a moment. The bluish snowclouds stood out clear and the sun began to come out, but uncertainly and cheerlessly like Polikéy's own smile. Notwithstanding all this, Polikéy was deep in pleasant thoughts. He whom they threatened to exile and conscript, whom only those who were too lazy did not scold and beat, who was always shoved into the worst places, *he* was driving now to fetch *a sum of money,* and a large sum too, and his mistress trusted him, and he was driving in the steward's cart behind Drum—with whom the lady herself sometimes drove out—just as if he were some proprietor with leather collar-strap and reins instead of ropes. And Polikéy sat up straighter, pushed in the bits of wadding hanging out of his cap, and again wrapped his coat closer.

If Polikéy, however, imagined that he looked just like a wealthy peasant proprietor he deluded himself. It is true, as every one knows, that tradesmen worth ten thousand rubles drive in carts with leather harness, only this was not quite the same thing. A bearded man in a blue or black coat drives past sitting alone in a cart, driving a well-fed horse, and you just glance to see if the horse is sleek and he himself well fed, and at the way he sits, at the horse's harness, and the tires on the cartwheels, and at his girdle, and you know at once whether the man does business in hundreds or in thousands of rubles. Every experienced person looking closer at Polikéy, at his hands, his face, his newly-grown beard, his girdle, at the hay carelessly thrown into the cart, at lean Drum, at the worn tires, would know at once that it was only a serf driving past, and not a merchant or a cattle-dealer or even a peasant proprietor, and that he did not deal in thousands or hundreds, or even tens of rubles. But Polikéy did not think so: he deceived himself, and deceived himself agreeably. He was going to carry home fifteen hundred rubles in the bosom of his coat. If he liked, he might turn Drum's head towards Odessa instead of homewards, and drive off where Fate might take him. But he will not do such a thing; he will bring the lady her money all in order, and will talk about having had larger sums than that on him. When they came to an inn Drum began pulling at the left rein, turning towards the inn and stopping; but Polikéy, though he had the money given him to do the shopping with, gave Drum the whip and drove on. The same thing happened at the next inn, and about noon he got out of the cart, and opening the gate of the inn-keeper's house where all his mistress's people put up, he led the horse and cart into the yard. There he unharnessed, gave the horse some hay, dined with the inn-keeper's men, not omitting to mention what important business he had come on, and then went out with the market-gardener's bill in the crown of his cap.

The market-gardener (who knew and evidently mistrusted Polikéy) having read the letter questioned him as to whether he had really been sent for the money. Polikéy tried to seem offended, but could not manage it, and only smiled his peculiar smile. The market-gardener read the letter over once more and handed him the money. Having received the money, Polikéy put it into his bosom and went back to the inn. Neither the beershop nor the tavern nor anything tempted him. He felt a pleasant agitation through his whole being, and stopped more than once in front of shops that showed tempting wares: boots, coats, caps, chintz, and foodstuffs, and went on with the pleasant feeling: 'I could buy it all, but there now, I won't do it!' He went to the bazaar for the things he had been asked to buy, got them all, and started bargaining for a lined sheepskin coat, for which he was asked twenty-five rubles. For some reason the dealer, after looking at Polikéy, seemed to doubt his ability to buy it. But Polikéy pointed to his bosom, saying that he could buy the whole shop if he liked, and insisted on trying the coat on; felt it, patted it, blew into the wool till he became permeated with the smell of it, and then took it off with a sigh. 'The price does not suit me. If you'll let it go for fifteen rubles, now!' he said. The dealer angrily threw the coat across the table, and Polikéy went out and cheerfully returned to his inn. After supper, having watered Drum and given him some oats, he climbed up on the stove, took out the envelope with the money and examined it for a long time, and then asked a porter who knew how to read to read him the address and the inscription: 'With enclosure of one thousand six hundred and seventeen assignation rubles.' [1] The envelope was made of common paper and sealed with brown sealing-wax with the impression of an anchor. There was one large seal in the middle, four at the corners, and there were some drops of sealing-wax near the edge. Polikéy examined all this, and studied it. He even felt the sharp edges of the notes. It gave him a kind of childish pleasure to know that he had such a sum in his hands. He thrust the envelope into a hole in the lining of his cap, and lay down with the cap under his head; but even in the night he kept waking and feeling the envelope. And each time he found it in its place he experienced the pleasant feeling that here was he, the disgraced, the down-trodden Polikéy, carrying such a sum and delivering it up more accurately than even the steward could have done.

VIII

About midnight the inn-keeper's men and Polikéy were awakened by a knocking at the gate and the shouting of peasants. It was the party of recruits from Pokróvsk. There were about ten people: Khoryúshkin, Mityúkin, and Elijah (Dútlov's nephew), two substitutes in case of need, the village Elder, old Dútlov, and the men who had driven them. A night-light was burning in the room, and the cook was sleeping on a bench under the icons. She jumped up and began lighting a

---

[1] Equal to 462 'silver rubles', at 3½ assignations for one silver ruble.

candle. Polikéy also awoke, and leaning over from the top of the stove looked at the peasants as they came in. They came in crossing themselves, and sat down on the benches round the room. They all seemed perfectly calm, so that one could not tell which of them were the conscripts and which their escorts. They were greeting the people of the inn, talking loudly, and asking for food. It is true that some were silent and sad; but on the other hand others were unusually merry, evidently drunk. Among these was Elijah, who had never had too much to drink before.

'Well, lads, shall we go to sleep or have some supper?' asked the Elder.

'Supper!' said Elijah, throwing open his coat and setting himself on a bench. 'Send for some vodka.'

'Enough of your vodka!' answered the Elder shortly, and turning to the others he said: 'You just cut yourselves a bit of bread, lads! Why wake people up?'

'Give me vodka!' Elijah repeated, without looking at anybody, and in a voice that showed that he would not soon stop.

The peasants took the Elders' advice, fetched some bread out of their carts, ate it, asked for a little kvas, and lay down, some on the floor and some on the stove.

Elijah kept repeating at intervals: 'Let me have some vodka, I say, let me have some.' Then, noticing Polikéy: 'Polikéy! Hi, Polikéy! You here, dear friend? Why, I am going for a soldier. . . . Have said good-bye to my mother and my missus. . . . How she howled! They've bundled me off for a soldier. . . . Stand me some vodka!'

'I haven't got any money,' answered Polikéy, and to comfort him added: 'Who knows? By God's aid you may be rejected! . . .'

'No, friend. I'm as sound as a young birch. I've never had an illness. There's no rejecting for me! What better soldier can the Tsar want?'

Polikéy began telling him how a peasant gave a doctor a five-ruble note and got rejected.

Elijah drew nearer the oven, and they talked more freely.

'No, Polikéy, it's all up now! I don't want to stay now myself. Uncle has done for me. As if he couldn't have bought a substitute! . . . No, he grudged his son, and grudges the money, so they send me. No! I don't myself want to stay.' (He spoke gently, confidingly, under the influence of quiet sorrow.) 'One thing only—I am sorry for mother, dear heart! . . . How she grieved! And the wife, too! . . . They've ruined the woman just for nothing; now she'll perish—in a word, she'll be a soldier's wife! Better not to have married. What did they marry me for? . . . They're coming here to-morrow.'

'But why have they brought you so soon?' asked Polikéy; 'nothing was heard about it, and then, all of a sudden . . .'

'Why, they're afraid I shall do myself some mischief,' answered Elijah, smiling. 'No fear! I'll do nothing of the kind. I shall not be lost even as a soldier; only I'm sorry for mother. . . . Why did they get me married?' he said gently and sadly.

The door opened and shut with a loud slam as old Dútlov came in, shaking the wet off his cap, and as usual in bast-shoes so big that they looked like boats.

'Afanásy,' he said to the porter, when he had crossed himself, 'isn't there a lantern to get some oats by?'

And without looking at Elijah he began slowly lighting a bit of candle. His mittens and whip were stuck into the girdle tied neatly round his coat, and his toil-worn face appeared as usual, simple, quiet, and full of business cares, as if he had just arrived with a train of loaded carts.

Elijah became silent when he saw his uncle, and looked dismally down at the bench again. Then, addressing the Elder, he muttered:

'Vodka, Ermíl! I want some drink!' His voice sounded wrathful and dejected.

'Drink, at this time?' answered the Elder, who was eating something out of a bowl. 'Don't you see the others have had a bite and lain down? Why are you making a row?'

The word 'row' evidently suggested to Elijah the idea of violence.

'Elder, I'll do some mischief if you don't give me vodka!'

'Couldn't you bring him to reason?' the Elder said, turning

to Dútlov, who had lit the lantern, but had stopped, evidently
to see what would happen, and was looking pityingly at his
nephew out of the corner of his eyes, as if surprised at his
childishness.

Elijah, looking down, again muttered:

'Vodka! Give . . . do mischief!'

'Leave off, Elijah!' said the Elder mildly. 'Really, now, leave
off! You'd better!'

But before the words were out Elijah had jumped up and
hit a window-pane with his fist, and shouting at the top of his
voice: 'You would not listen to me, so there you have it!'
rushed to the other window to break that too.

Polikéy in the twinkling of an eye rolled over twice and hid
in the farthest corner of the top of the stove, so quickly that he
scared all the cockroaches there. The Elder threw down his
spoon and rushed toward Elijah. Dútlov slowly put down his
lantern, untied his girdle, and shaking his head and making a
clicking noise with his tongue, went up to Elijah, who was already struggling with the Elder and the inn-keeper's man,
who were keeping him away from the window. They had
caught his arms and seemed to be holding him fast; but the
moment he saw his uncle with the girdle his strength increased tenfold and he tore himself away, and with rolling
eyes and clenched fists stepped up to Dútlov.

'I'll kill you! Keep away, you brute! . . . You have ruined
me, you and your brigands of sons, you've ruined me! . . .
Why did they get me married? . . . Keep away! I'll kill
you! . . .'

Elijah was terrible. His face was purple, his eyes rolled, the
whole of his healthy young body trembled as in a fever. He
seemed to wish and to be able to kill all the three men who
were facing him.

'You're drinking your brother's blood, you blood-sucker!'

Something flashed across Dútlov's ever-serene face. He took
a step forward.

'You won't take it peaceably!' said he suddenly. The wonder was where he got the energy; for with a quick motion he

çaught hold of his nephew, rolled to the ground with him, and with the aid of the Elder began binding his hands with the girdle. They struggled for about five minutes. At last with the help of the peasants Dútlov rose, pulling his coat out of Elijah's clutch. Then he raised Elijah, whose hands were tied behind his back, and made him sit down on a bench in a corner.

'I told you it would be the worse for you,' he said, still out of breath with the struggle, and pulling straight the narrow girdle tied over his shirt. 'Why sin? We shall all have to die! . . . Fold a coat for a pillow for him,' he said, turning to the inn-keeper's men, 'or the blood will go to his head.' And he tied the cord round his waist over his sheepskin and, taking up the lantern, went to see after the horses.

Elijah, pale, dishevelled, his shirt pulled out of place, was gazing round the room as though trying to remember where he was. The inn-keepers' men picked up the broken bits of glass and stuffed a coat into the hole in the window to keep the draught out. The Elder sat down again to his bowl.

'Ah, Elijah, Elijah! I'm sorry for you, really! What's to be done? There's Khoryúshkin . . . he, too, is married. Seems it can't be helped!'

'It's all on account of that fiend, my uncle, that I'm being ruined!' Elijah repeated, dryly and bitterly. 'He was chary of his own son! . . . Mother says the steward told him to buy me off. He won't: he says he can't afford it. As if what my brother and I have brought into his house were a trifle! . . . He is a fiend!'

Dútlov returned to the room, said a prayer in front of the icons, took off his outdoor things, and sat down beside the Elder. The cook brought more kvas and another spoon. Elijah grew silent, and closing his eyes lay down on the folded coat. The Elder pointed to him and shook his head silently. Dútlov waved his hand.

'As if one was not sorry! . . . My own brother's son! . . . And as if things were not bad enough it seems they also made me out a villain to him. . . . Whether it's his wife—she's a cunning little woman for all she's so young—that has put it into his head that we could afford to buy a substitute! . . . Anyhow, he's reproaching me. But one does pity the lad! . . .'

'Ah! he's a fine lad,' said the Elder.

'But I'm at the end of my tether with him! To-morrow I shall let Ignát come, and his wife wanted to come too.'

'All right—let them come,' said the Elder, rising and climbing onto the stove. 'What is money? Money is dross!'

'If one had the money, who would grudge it?' muttered one of the inn-keeper's men, lifting his head.

'Ah, money, money! It causes much sin,' replied Dútlov. 'Nothing in the world causes so much sin, and the Scriptures say so too.'

'Everything is said there,' the workman agreed. 'There was a man told me how a merchant had stored up a heap of money and did not want to leave any behind; he loved it so that he took it with him to the grave. As he was dying he asked to have a small pillow buried with him. No one suspected anything, and so it was done. Then his sons began looking for his money and nothing was to be found. At last one of them guessed that probably the notes were all in the pillow. The matter went to the Tsar, and he allowed the grave to be opened. And what do you think? They opened the coffin. There was nothing in the pillow, but the coffin was full of small snakes, and so it was buried again. . . . You see what money does!'

'It's a fact, it brings much sin,' said Dútlov, and he got up and began saying his prayers.

When he had finished he looked at his nephew. The lad was asleep. Dútlov came up to him, untied the girdle with which he was bound, and then lay down. Another peasant went out to sleep with the horses.

IX

As soon as all was quiet Polikéy climbed down softly, like a guilty man, and began to get ready. For some reason he felt uneasy at the thought of spending the night there among the recruits. The cocks were already crowing to one another more

often. Drum had eaten all his oats and was straining towards
the drinking-trough. Polikéy harnessed him and led him out
past the peasants' carts. His cap with its contents was safe,
and the wheels of the cart were soon rattling along the frosty
road to Pokróvsk. Polikéy felt more at ease only when he had
left the town behind. Till then he kept imagining that at any
moment he might hear himself being pursued, that he would
be stopped, and they would tie up his arms instead of Elijah's,
and he would be taken to the recruiting station next morning.
It might have been the frost, or it might have been fear, but
something made cold shivers run down his back, and again
and again he touched Drum up. The first person he met was
a priest in a tall fur cap, accompanied by a one-eyed labourer.
Taking this for an evil omen Polikéy grew still more alarmed,
but outside the town this fear gradually passed. Drum went
on at a walking pace and the road in front became more visible. Polikéy took off his cap and felt the notes. 'Shall I hide it
in my bosom?' he thought. 'No; I should have to undo my
girdle. . . . Wait a bit! When I get to the foot of the hill I'll
get down and put myself to rights. . . . The cap is sewn up
tight at the top, and it can't fall through the lining. After all,
I'd better not take the cap off till I get home.' When he had
reached the foot of the incline Drum of his own accord galloped up the next hill and Polikéy, who was as eager as Drum
to get home, did not check him. All was well—at any rate so
Polikéy imagined, and he gave himself up to dreams of his
mistress's gratitude, of the five rubles she would give him, and
of the joy of his family. He took off his cap, felt for the envelope, and, smiling, put the cap tighter on his head. The velveteen crown of the cap was very rotten, and just because
Akulína had carefully sewn up the rents in one place, it burst
open in another; and the very movement by which Polikéy in
the dusk had thought to push the envelope with the money
deeper under the wadding, tore the cap farther and pushed
out a corner of the envelope through the velveteen crown.

The dawn was appearing, and Polikéy, who had not slept
all night, began to drowse. Pulling his cap lower down and
thereby pushing the envelope still farther out, Polikéy in his

drowsiness let his head knock against the front of the cart. He woke up near home and was about to catch hold of his cap, but feeling that it sat firmly on his head he did not take it off, convinced that the envelope was inside. He gave Drum a touch, arranged the hay in the cart again, assumed once more the appearance of a well-to-do peasant, and proudly looking about him rattled homewards.

There was the kitchen, there the house-serfs' quarters. There was the carpenter's wife carrying some linen; there was the office, and there the mistress's house where in a few moments Polikéy would show that he was a trustworthy and honest man. 'One can say anything about anybody,' he would say; and the lady would reply, 'Well, thank you, Polikéy! Here are three (or perhaps five, perhaps even ten) rubles,' and she would tell them to give him some tea, or even some vodka. It would not be amiss, after being out in the cold! 'With ten rubles we would have a treat for the holiday, and buy boots, and return Nikíta his four and a half rubles (it can't be helped! . . . He has begun bothering). . . .' When he was about a hundred paces from the house, Polikéy wrapped his coat round him, pulled his girdle straight and his collar, took off his cap, smoothed his hair, and without haste thrust his hand under the lining. The hand began to fumble faster and faster inside the lining, then the other hand went in too, while his face grew paler and paler. One of the hands went right through the cap. Polikéy fell on his knees, stopped the horse, and began searching in the cart among the hay and the things he had bought, feeling inside his coat and in his trousers. The money was nowhere to be found.

'Heavens! What does it mean? . . . What will happen? . . .' He began to roar, clutching at his hair.

But recollecting that he might be seen, he turned the horse round, pulled the cap on, and drove the surprised and disgusted Drum back along the road.

'I can't bear going out with Polikéy,' Drum must have thought. 'For once in his life he has fed and watered me properly, and then only to deceive me so unpleasantly! How hard I tried, running home! I am tired, and hardly have we got within smell of our hay than he starts driving me back!'

'Now then, you devil's jade!' shouted Polikéy through his tears, standing up in the cart, pulling at Drum's mouth, and beating him with the whip.

X

All that day no one saw Polikéy in Pokróvsk. The mistress asked for him several times after dinner, and Aksyútka flew down to Akulína; but Akulína said he had not yet returned, and that evidently the market-gardener had detained him or something had happened to the horse. 'If only it has not gone lame!' she said. 'Last time, when Maxím went, he was on the road a whole day—had to walk back all the way.'

And Aksyútka turned her pendulums back to the house again, while Akulína, trying to calm her own fears, invented reasons to account for her husband's absence, but in vain! Her heart was heavy and she could not work with a will at any of the preparations for the morrow's holiday. She suffered all the more because the carpenter's wife assured her that she herself had seen 'a man just like Polikéy drive up to the avenue and then turn back again'. The children, too, were anxiously and impatiently expecting 'Daddy', but for another reason. Annie and Mary, being left without the sheepskin and the coat which made it possible to take turns out of doors, could only run out in their indoor dresses with increasing rapidity in a small circle round the house. This was not a little inconvenient to all the dwellers in the serfs' quarters who wanted to go in or out. Once Mary ran against the legs of the carpenter's wife who was carrying water, and though she began to howl in anticipation as soon as she knocked against the woman's knees, she got her curls cuffed all the same, and cried still louder. When she did not knock against anyone, she flew in at the door, and immediately climbing up by means of a tub, got onto the top of the oven. Only the mistress and Akulína were really anxious about Polikéy; the children were concerned only about what he had on.

Egór Mikháylovich reporting to his mistress, in answer to

her questions, 'Hasn't Políkéy come back yet?' and 'Where can he be?' answered: 'I can't say,' and seemed pleased that his expectations were being fulfilled. 'He ought to have been back by noon,' he added significantly.

All that day no one heard anything of Políkéy; only later on it was known that some neighbouring peasants had seen him running about on the road bareheaded, and asking everyone whether they hadn't found a letter. Another man had seen him asleep by the roadside beside a tied-up horse and cart. 'I thought he was tipsy,' the man said, 'and the horse looked as if it had not been watered or fed for two days, its sides were so fallen in.' Akulína did not sleep all night and kept listening, but Políkéy did not return. Had she been alone, or had she kept a cook or a maid, she would have felt still more unhappy; but as soon as the cocks crowed and the carpenter's wife got up, Akulína was obliged to rise and light the fire. It was a holiday. The bread had to come out of the oven before daybreak, kvas had to be made, cakes baked, the cow milked, frocks and shirts ironed, the children washed, water fetched, and her neighbour prevented from taking up the whole oven. So Akulína, still listening, set to work. It had grown light and the church bells were ringing, the children were up, but still Políkéy had not returned. There had been a first frost the day before, a little snow had fallen and lay in patches on the fields, on the road, and on the roofs; and now, as if in honour of the holiday, the day was fine, sunny, and frosty, so that one could see and hear a long way. But Akulína, standing by the brick oven, her head thrust into the opening, was so busy with her cakes that she did not hear Políkéy drive up, and only knew from the children's cries that her husband had returned.

Annie, as the eldest, had greased her hair and dressed herself without help. She wore a new but crumpled print dress—a present from the mistress. It stuck out as stiff as if it were made of bast, and was an object of envy to the neighbours; her hair glistened; she had smeared half an inch of tallow candle onto it. Her shoes, though not new, were thin ones. Mary was still wrapped in the old jacket and was covered with mud, and Annie would not let her come near her for fear of getting soiled. Mary was outside. She saw her father drive up with a sack. 'Daddy has come!' she shrieked, and rushed headlong through the door past Annie, dirtying her. Annie, no longer fearing to be soiled, went for her at once and hit her. Akulína could not leave her work, and only shouted at the children: 'Now, then . . . I'll whip you all!' and looked round at the door. Políkey came in with a sack, and at once made his way to his own corner. It seemed to Akulína that he was pale, and his face looked as if he were either smiling or crying, but she had no time to find out which it was.

'Well, Políkey, is it all right?' she called to him from the oven.

Políkey muttered something that she did not understand.

'Eh?' she cried. 'Have you been to the mistress?'

Políkey sat down on the bed in his corner looking wildly round him and smiling his guilty, intensely miserable smile. He did not answer for a long time.

'Eh, Políkey? Why have you been so long?' came Akulína's voice.

'Yes, Akulína, I have handed the lady her money. How she thanked me!' he said suddenly, and began looking round and smiling still more uneasily. Two things attracted his feverishly staring eyes: the baby, and the cords attached to the hanging cradle. He went up to where the cradle hung, and began hastily undoing the knot of the rope with his thin fingers. Then his eyes fixed themselves on the baby; but just then Akulína entered, carrying a board of cakes, and Políkey quickly hid the rope in his bosom and sat down on the bed.

'What is it, Políkey? You are not like yourself,' said Akulína.

'Haven't slept,' he answered.

Suddenly something flitted past the window, and in a moment Aksyútka, the maid from 'up there', darted in like an arrow.

'The mistress orders Políkey to come this minute,' she said—'this minute, Avdótya Nikoláevna's orders are . . . this minute!'

Políkey looked at Akulína, then at the girl.

'I'm coming. What can she want?' he said, so simply that Akulína grew quieter. 'Perhaps she wants to reward me. Tell her I'm coming.'

He rose and went out. Akulína took the washing-trough, put it on a bench, filled it with water from the pails which stood by the door and from the cauldron in the oven, rolled up her sleeves, and tried the water.

'Come, Mary, I'll wash you.'

The cross, lisping little girl began howling.

'Come, you brat! I'll give you a clean smock. Now then, don't make a fuss. Come along. . . . I've still got your brother to wash.'

Meanwhile Polikéy had not followed the maid from 'up there', but had gone to quite a different place. In the passage by the wall was a ladder leading to the loft. Polikéy, when he came out, looked round, and seeing no one, bent down and climbed that ladder almost at a run, nimbly and hurriedly.

'Why ever doesn't Polikéy come?' asked the mistress impatiently of Dunyásha, who was dressing her hair. 'Where is Polikéy? Why hasn't he come?'

Aksyútka again flew to the serfs' quarters, and again rushed into the entry, calling Polikéy to her mistress.

'Why, he went long ago,' answered Akulína, who, having washed Mary, had just put her suckling baby-boy into the wash-trough and was moistening his thin short hair, regardless of his cries. The boy screamed, puckered his face, and tried to clutch something with his helpless little hands. Akulína supported his soft, plump, dimpled little back with one large hand, while she washed him with the other.

'See if he has not fallen asleep somewhere,' said she, looking round anxiously.

Just then the carpenter's wife, unkempt and with her dress unfastened and holding up her skirts, went up into the loft to get some things she had hung there to dry. Suddenly a shriek of horror filled the loft, and the carpenter's wife, like one demented, with her eyes closed, came down the steps on all fours, backwards, sliding rather than running.

'Polikéy!' she screamed.

Akulína let go the baby.

'Has hung himself!' roared the carpenter's wife.

Akulína rushed out into the passage, paying no heed to the baby, who rolled over like a ball and fell backwards with his little legs in the air and his head under water.

'On a rafter . . . hanging!' the carpenter's wife ejaculated, but stopped when she saw Akulína.

Akulína darted up the ladder, and before anyone could stop her she was at the top, but from there with a terrible scream she fell back like a corpse, and would have been killed if the people who had come running from every corner had not been in time to catch her.

XI

For several minutes nothing could be made out amidst the general uproar. A crowd of people had collected, everyone was shouting and talking, and the children and old women were crying. Akulína lay unconscious. At last the men, the carpenter and the steward who had run to the place, went up the ladder, and the carpenter's wife began telling for the twentieth time how she, 'suspecting nothing, went to fetch a dress, and just looked round like this—and saw . . . a man; and I looked again, and a cap is lying inside out, close by. I look . . . his legs are dangling. I went cold all over! Is it pleasant? . . . To think of a man hanging himself, and that I should be the one to see him! . . . How I came clattering down I myself don't remember . . . it's a miracle how God preserved me! Truly, the Lord has had mercy on me! . . . Is it a trifle? . . . so steep and from such a height. Why, I might have been killed!'

The men who had gone up had the same tale to tell. Polikéy, in his shirt and trousers, was hanging from a rafter by the cord he had taken from the cradle. His cap, turned inside out, lay beside him, his coat and sheepskin were neatly folded and lay close by. His feet touched the ground, but he no longer showed signs of life. Akulína regained consciousness, and again made for the ladder, but was held back.

'Mamma, Sëmka is dwownded!' the lisping little girl suddenly cried from their *corner*. Akulína tore herself away and ran to the *corner*. The baby lay on his back in the trough and did not stir, and his little legs were not moving. Akulína snatched him out, but he did not breathe or move. She threw him on the bed, and with arms akimbo burst into such loud, piercing, terrible laughter that Mary, who at first laughed too, covered her ears with her hands, and ran out into the passage crying. The neighbours thronged into the *corner*, wailing and weeping. They carried out the little body and began rubbing it, but in vain. Akulína tossed about on the bed and laughed—laughed so that all who heard her were horror-stricken. Only now, seeing this motley crowd of men and women, old people and children, did one realize what a number of people and what sort of people lived in the serfs' quarters. All were bustling and talking, many wept, but nobody did anything. The carpenter's wife still found people who had not heard her tale of how her sensitive feelings were shocked by the unexpected sight, and how God had preserved her from falling down the ladder. An old man who had been a footman, with a woman's jacket thrown over his shoulders, was telling how in the days of the old master a woman had drowned herself in the pond. The steward sent messengers to the priest and to the constable, and appointed men to keep guard. Aksyútka, the maid from 'up there', kept gazing with staring eyes at the opening that led to the loft, and though she could not see anything was unable to tear herself away and go back to her mistress. Agatha Mikháylovna, who had been lady's-maid to the former proprietress, was weeping and asking for some tea to soothe her nerves. Anna the midwife was laying out the little body on the table, with her plump practised hands moistened with olive oil. Other women stood round Akulína, silently looking at her. The children, huddled together in the corner, peeped at their mother and burst into howls; and then subsiding for a moment, peeped again, and huddled still closer. Boys and men thronged round the porch, looking in at the door and the windows with frightened faces unable to see or understand anything, and asking one another what was the matter. One said the carpenter had chopped off his wife's foot with an axe. Another said that the laundress had been brought to bed of triplets; a third that the cook's cat had gone mad and bitten several people. But the truth gradually spread, and at last it reached the mistress; and it seems no one understood how to break it to her. That rough Egór blurted the facts straight out to her, and so upset the lady's nerves that it was a long time before she could recover. The crowd had already begun to quiet down, the carpenter's wife set the samovar to boil and made tea, and the outsiders, not being invited, thought it improper to stay longer. Boys had begun fighting outside the porch. Everybody now knew what had happened, and crossing themselves they began to disperse, when suddenly the cry was raised: 'The mistress! The mistress!' and everybody crowded and pressed together to make way for her, but at the same time everybody wanted to see what she was going to do. The lady, with pale and tear-stained face, entered the passage, crossed the threshold, and went into Akulína's *corner*. Dozens of heads squeezed together and gazed in at the door. One pregnant woman was squeezed so that she gave a squeal, but took advantage of that very circumstance to secure a front place for herself. And how could one help wishing to see the lady in Akulína's *corner?* For the house-serfs it was just what the coloured lights are at the end of a show. It's sure to be great when they burn the coloured fires; and it must be an important occasion when the lady in her silks and lace enters Akulína's *corner.* The lady went up and took Akulína's hand, but Akulína snatched it away. The old house-serfs shook their heads reprovingly.

'Akulína!' said the lady. 'You have your children—so take care of yourself!'

Akulína burst out laughing and got up.

'My children are all silver, all silver! I don't keep paper money,' she muttered very rapidly. 'I told Polikéy, "Take no notes," and there now, they've smeared him, smeared him with tar—tar and soap, madam! Any scabbiness you may have it will get rid of at once . . .' and she laughed still louder.

The mistress turned away, and gave orders that the doctor's

assistant should come with mustard poultices. 'Bring some
cold water!' she said, and began looking for it herself; but seeing the dead baby with Granny Anna the midwife beside it,
the lady turned away, and everybody saw how she hid her
face in her handkerchief and burst into tears; while Granny
Anna (it was a pity the lady did not see it—she would have
appreciated it, and it was all done for her benefit) covered the
baby with a piece of linen, straightened his arms with her
plump, deft hands, shook her head, pouted, drooped her eye-
lids, and sighed with so much feeling that everybody could
see how excellent a heart she had. But the lady did not see it,
she could not see anything. She burst out sobbing and went
into hysterics. Holding her up under the arms they led her out
into the porch and took her home. 'That's all there was to be
seen of her!' thought many, and again began to disperse.
Akulína went on laughing and talking nonsense. She was
taken into another room and bled, and plastered over with
mustard poultices, and ice was put on her head. Yet she did
not come to her senses, and did not weep, but laughed, and
kept doing and saying such things that the kind people who
were looking after her could not help laughing themselves.

XII

The holiday was not a cheerful one at Pokróvsk. Though
the day was beautiful the people did not go out to amuse
themselves: no girls sang songs in the street, the factory hands
who had come home from town for the day did not play on
their concertinas and balaláykas and did not play with the
girls. Everybody sat about in corners, and if they spoke did
so as softly as if an evil one were there who could hear them.
It was not quite so bad in the daytime, but when the twilight
fell and the dogs began to howl, and when, to make matters
worse, a wind sprang up and whistled down the chimneys,
such fear seized all the people of the place that those who had
tapers lit them before their icons. Anyone who happened to
be alone in his *corner* went to ask the neighbours' permission
to stay the night with them, to be less lonely, and anyone

whose business should have taken him into one of the out-houses did not go, but pitilessly left the cattle without fodder that night. And the holy water, of which everyone kept a little bottle to charm away anything evil, was all used up during the night. Many even heard something walking about with heavy steps up in the loft, and the blacksmith saw a serpent fly straight towards it. In Polikéy's *corner* there was no one; the children and the mad woman had been taken elsewhere. Only the little dead body lay there, and two old women sat and watched it, while a third, a pilgrim woman, was reading the psalms, actuated by her own zeal, not for the sake of the baby but in a vague way because of the whole calamity. The mistress had willed it so. The pilgrim woman and these old women themselves heard how, as soon as they finished read-ing a passage of the Psalter, the rafters above would tremble and someone would groan. Then they would say, 'Let God arise,' and all would be quiet again. The carpenter's wife in-vited a friend and, not sleeping all night, with her aid drank up all the tea she had laid in for the whole week. They, too, heard how the rafters creaked overhead, and a noise as if sacks were tumbling down. The presence of the peasant watchmen kept up the courage of the house-serfs somewhat, or they would have died of fear that night. The peasants lay on some hay in the passage, and afterwards de-clared that they too had heard wonderful things up in the loft, though at the time they were conversing very calmly to-gether about the conscription, munching crusts of bread, scratching themselves, and above all so filling the passage with the peculiar odour characteristic of peasants that the car-penter's wife, happening to pass by, spat and called them 'peasant-brood'. However that might be, the dead man was still dangling in the loft, and it seemed as if the evil one himself had overshadowed the serfs' quarters with his huge wings that night, showing his power and coming closer to these people than he had ever done before. So at least they all felt. I do not know if they were right; I even think they were quite mistaken. I think that if some bold fellow had taken a candle or lantern that terrible night, and crossing himself, or even

without crossing himself, had gone up into the loft—slowly dispelling before him the horror of the night with the candle,
lighting up the rafters, the sand, the cobweb-covered flue-
pipe, and the tippets left behind by the carpenter's wife—till
he came to Polikéy, and, conquering his fears, had raised the
lantern to the level of the face, he would have beheld the
familiar spare figure: the feet touching the ground (the cord
had stretched), the body bending lifelessly to one side, no
cross visible under the open shirt, the head drooping on the
breast, the good-natured face with open sightless eyes, and
the meek, guilty smile, and a solemn calmness and silence
over all. Really the carpenter's wife, crouching in a corner of
her bed with dishevelled hair and frightened eyes and telling
how she heard the sacks falling, was far more terrible and
frightful than Polikéy, though his cross was off and lay on
a rafter.

'Up there,' that is, in the mistress's house, reigned the same
horror as in the serfs' quarters. Her bedroom smelt of eau-de-
cologne and medicine. Dunyásha was melting yellow wax and
making a plaster. What the plaster was for I don't know, but
it was always made when the lady was unwell. And now she
was so upset that she was quite ill. To keep Dunyásha's courage up her aunt had come to stay the night, so there were
four of them, including the girl, sitting in the maids' room,
and talking in low voices.

'Who will go to get some oil?' asked Dunyásha.

'Nothing will induce me to go, Avdótya Pávlovna!' the
second maid said decidedly.

'Nonsense! You and Asyútka go together.'

'I'll run across alone. I'm not afraid of anything!' said
Aksyútka, and at once became frightened.

'Well then, go, dear; ask Granny Anna to give you some in
a tumbler and bring it here; don't spill any,' said Dunyásha.

Aksyútka lifted her skirt with one hand, and being
thereby prevented from swinging both arms, swung one of
them twice as violently across the line of her progression, and
darted away. She was afraid, and felt that if she should see

or hear anything, even her own living mother, she would perish with fright. She flew, with her eyes shut, along the familiar pathway.

XIII

'Is the mistress asleep or not?' suddenly asked a deep peasant-voice close to Aksyútka. She opened her eyes, which she had kept shut, and saw a figure that seemed to her taller than the house. She screeched, and flew back so fast that her skirts floated behind her. With one bound she was on the porch and with another in the maids' room, where she threw herself on her bed with a wild yell. Dunyásha, her aunt, and the second maid almost died of terror, and before they had time to recover they heard heavy, slow, hesitating steps in the passage and at their door. Dunyásha rushed to her mistress, spilling the melted wax. The second maid hid herself behind the skirts that hung on the wall; the aunt, a more determined character, was about to hold the door to the passage closed, but it opened and a peasant entered the room. It was Dútlov, with his boat-like shoes. Paying no heed to the maids' fears, he looked round for an icon, and not seeing the tiny one in the left-hand corner of the room, he crossed himself in front of a cupboard in which teacups were kept, laid his cap on the window-sill, and thrusting his arm deep into the bosom of his coat as if he were going to scratch himself under his other arm, he pulled out the letter with the five brown seals stamped with an anchor. Dunyásha's aunt held her hands to her heart and with difficulty brought out the words:

'Well, you did give me a fright, Naúmych! I can't utter a wo . . . ord! I thought my last moment had come!'

'Is that the way to behave?' said the second maid, appearing from under the skirts.

'The mistress herself is upset,' said Dunyásha, coming out of her mistress's door. 'What do you mean, shoving yourself in through the maid's entrance without leave? . . . Just like a peasant lout!'

Dútlov, without excusing himself, explained that he wanted to see the lady.

'She is not well,' said Dunyásha.

At this moment Aksyútka burst into such loud and unseemly laughter that she was obliged to hide her face in the pillow on the bed, from which for a whole hour, in spite of Dunyásha's and the aunt's threats, she could not for long lift it without going off again as if something were bursting in her pink print bosom and rosy cheeks. It seemed to her so funny that everybody should have been so scared, that she again hid her head in the pillows and scraped the floor with her shoe and jerked her whole body as if in convulsions.

Dútlov stopped and looked at her attentively, as if to ascertain what was happening to her, but turned away again without having discovered what it was all about, and continued:

'You see, it's just this—it's a very important matter,' he said. 'You just go and say that a peasant has found the letter with the money.'

'What money?'

Dunyásha, before going to report, read the address and questioned Dútlov as to when and how he had found this money which Polikéy was to have brought back from town. Having heard all the details and pushed the little errand-girl, who was still convulsed with laughter, out into the vestibule, Dunyásha went to her mistress; but to Dútlov's surprise the mistress would not see him and did not say anything intelligible to Dunyásha.

'I know nothing about it and don't want to know anything!' the lady said. 'What peasant? What money? . . . I can't and won't see anyone! He must leave me in peace.'

'What am I to do?' said Dútlov, turning the envelope over; 'it's not a small sum. What is written on it?' he asked Dunyásha, who again read the address to him.

Dútlov seemed in doubt. He was still hoping that perhaps the money was not the mistress's and that the address had not been read to him right, but Dunyásha confirmed it, and he put the envelope back into his bosom with a sigh, and was about to go.

'I suppose I shall have to hand it over to the police-constable,' he said.

'Wait a bit! I'll try again,' said Dunyásha, stopping him, after attentively following the disappearance of the envelope into the bosom of the peasant's coat. 'Let me have the letter.'

Dútlov took it out again, but did not at once put it into Dunyásha's outstretched hand.

'Say that Semën Dútlov found it on the road . . .'

'Well, let me have it!'

'I did think it was just nothing—only a letter; but a soldier read out to me that there was money inside . . .'

'Well then, let me have it.'

'I dared not even go home first to . . .' Dútlov continued, still not parting with the precious envelope. 'Tell the lady so.'

Dunyásha took it from him and went again to her mistress.

'O my God, Dunyásha, don't speak to me of that money!' said the lady in a reproachful tone. 'Only to think of that little baby . . .'

'The peasant does not know to whom you wish it to be given, madam,' Dunyásha again said.

The lady opened the envelope, shuddering at the sight of the money, and pondered.

'Dreadful money! How much evil it does!' she said.

'It is Dútlov, madam. Do you order him to go, or will you please come out and see him—and is the money all safe?' asked Dunyásha.

'I don't want this money. It is terrible money! What it has done! Tell him to take it himself if he likes,' said the lady suddenly, feeling for Dunyásha's hand. 'Yes, yes, yes!' she repeated to the astonished Dunyásha; 'let him take it altogether and do what he likes with it.'

'Fifteen hundred rubles,' remarked Dunyásha, smiling as if at a child.

'Let him take it all!' the lady repeated impatiently. 'How is it you don't understand me? It is unlucky money. Never speak of it to me again! Let the peasant who found it take it. Go, go along!'

Dunyásha went out into the maids' room.

'Is it all there?' asked Dútlov.

'You'd better count it yourself,' said Dunyásha, handing him the envelope. 'My orders are to give it to you.'

Dútlov put his cap under his arm, and, bending forward, began to count the money.

'Have you got a counting-frame?' [1]

Dútlov had an idea that the lady was stupid and could not count, and that that was why she ordered him to do so.

'You can count it at home—the money is yours . . . !' Dunyásha said crossly. ' "I don't want to see it," she says; "give it to the man who brought it." '

Dútlov, without unbending his back, stared at Dunyásha. Dunyásha's aunt flung up her hands.

'O holy Mother! What luck the Lord has sent him! O holy Mother!'

The second maid would not believe it.

'You don't mean it, Avdótya Pávlovna; you're joking!'

'Joking, indeed! She told me to give it to the peasant. . . . There, take your money and go!' said Dunyásha, without hiding her vexation. 'One man's sorrow is another man's luck!'

'It's not a joke . . . fifteen hundred rubles!' said the aunt.

'It's even more,' stated Dunyásha. 'Well, you'll have to give a ten-kopek candle to St. Nicholas,' she added sarcastically. 'Why don't you come to your senses? If it had come to a poor man, now! . . . But this man has plenty of his own.'

Dútlov at last grasped that it was not a joke, and began gathering together the notes he had spread out to count and putting them back into the envelope. But his hands trembled, and he kept glancing at the maids to assure himself that it was not a joke.

'See! He can't come to his senses he's so pleased,' said Dunyásha, implying that she despised both the peasant and the money. 'Come, I'll put it up for you.'

She was going to take the notes, but Dútlov would not let her. He crumpled them together, pushed them in deeper, and took his cap.

---

[1] The abacus, with wires and beads to count on, was much used in Russia.

'Are you glad?'

'I hardly know what to say! It's really . . .'

He did not finish, but waved his hand, smiled, and went out almost crying.

The mistress rang.

'Well, have you given it to him?'

'I have.'

'Well, was he very glad?'

'He was just like a madman.'

'Ah! call him back. I want to ask him how he found it. Call him in here; I can't come out.'

Dunyásha ran out and found the peasant in the entry. He was still bareheaded, but had drawn out his purse and was stooping, untying its strings, while he held the money between his teeth. Perhaps he imagined that as long as the money was not in his purse it was not his. When Dunyásha called him he grew frightened.

'What is it, Avdótya . . . Avdótya Pávlovna? Does she want to take it back? Couldn't you say a word for me? . . . Now really, and I'd bring you some nice honey.'

'Indeed! Much you ever brought!'

Again the door was opened, and the peasant was brought in to the lady. He felt anything but cheerful. 'Oh dear, she'll want it back!' he thought on his way through the rooms, lifting his feet for some reason as if he were walking through high grass, and trying not to stamp with his bast shoes. He could make nothing of his surroundings. Passing by a mirror he saw flowers of some sort and a peasant in bast shoes lifting his feet high, a gentleman with an eyeglass painted on the wall, some kind of green tub, and something white. . . . There, now! The something white began to speak. It was his mistress. He did not understand anything but only stared. He did not know where he was, and everything appeared as in a fog.

'Is that you, Dútlov?'

'Yes, lady. . . . Just as it was, so I left it . . .' he said. 'I was not glad so help me God! How I've tired out my horse! . . .'

'Well, it's your luck!' she remarked contemptuously, though with a kindly smile. 'Take it, take it for yourself.'

He only rolled his eyes.

'I am glad that you got it. God grant that it may be of use. Well, are you glad?'

'How could I help being glad? I'm so glad, ma'am, so glad! I will pray for you always! . . . So glad that, thank Heaven, our lady is alive! It was not my fault.'

'How did you find it?'

'Well, I mean, we can always do our best for our lady, quite honourably, and not anyhow . . .'

'He is in a regular muddle, madam,' said Dunyásha.

'I had taken my nephew, the conscript, and as I was driving back along the road I found it. Polikéy must have dropped it.'

'Well, then, go—go, my good man! I am glad you found it!'

'I am so glad, lady!' said the peasant.

Then he remembered that he had not thanked her properly, and did not know how to behave. The lady and Dunyásha smiled, and then he again began stepping as if he were walking in very high grass, and could hardly refrain from running so afraid was he that he might be stopped and the money taken from him.

XIV

When he got out into the fresh air Dútlov stepped aside from the road to the lindens, even undoing his belt to get at his purse more easily, and began putting away the money. His lips were twitching, stretching and drawing together again, though he uttered no sound. Having put away his money and fastened his belt, he crossed himself and went staggering along the road as though he were drunk, so full was he of the thoughts that came rushing to his mind. Suddenly he saw the figure of a man coming towards him. He called out; it was Efím, with a cudgel in his hand, on watch at the serfs' quarters.

'Ah, Daddy Semën!' said Efím cheerfully, drawing nearer (Efím felt it uncanny to be alone). 'Have you got the conscripts off, daddy?'

'We have. What are you after?'

'Why, I've been put here to watch over Polikéy who's hanged himself.'

'And where is he?'

'Up there, hanging in the loft, so they say,' answered Efím, pointing with his cudgel through the darkness to the roof of the serfs' quarters.

Dútlov looked in the direction of the arm, and though he could see nothing he puckered his brows, screwed up his eyes, and shook his head.

'The police-constable has come,' said Efím, 'so the coachman said. He'll be taken down at once. Isn't it horrible at night, daddy? Nothing would make me go up at night even if they ordered me to. If Egór Mikháylovich were to kill me outright I wouldn't go . . .'

'What a sin, oh, what a sin!' Dútlov kept repeating, evidently for propriety's sake and not even thinking what he was saying. He was about to go on his way, but the voice of Egór Mikháylovich stopped him.

'Hi! watchman! Come here!' shouted Egór Mikháylovich from the porch of the office.

Efím replied to him.

'Who was that other peasant standing with you?'

'Dútlov.'

'Ah! and you too, Semën! Come here!'

Having drawn near, Dútlov, by the light of a lantern the coachman was carrying, recognized Egór Mikháylovich and a short man with a cockade on his cap, dressed in a long uniform overcoat. This was the police-constable.

'Here, this old man will come with us too,' said Egór Mikháylovich on seeing him.

The old man felt a bit uncomfortable, but there was no getting out of it.

'And you, Efím—you're a bold lad! Run up into the loft

where he's hanged himself, and set the ladder straight for his honour to mount.'

Efím, who had declared that he would not go near the loft for anything in the world, now ran towards it, clattering with his bast shoes as if they were logs.

The police-officer struck a light and lit a pipe. He lived about a mile and a half off, and having just been severely reprimanded for drunkenness by his superior, was in a zealous mood. Having arrived at ten o'clock at night, he wished to view the corpse at once. Egór Mikháylovich asked Dútlov how he came to be there. On the way Dútlov told the steward about the money he had found and what the lady had done, and said he was coming to ask Egór Mikháylovich's sanction. To Dútlov's horror the steward asked for the envelope and examined it. The police-constable even took the envelope in his hand and briefly and dryly asked the details.

'Oh dear, the money is gone!' thought Dútlov, and began justifying himself. But the police-constable handed him back the money.

'What a piece of luck for the clodhopper!' he said.

'It comes handy for him,' said Egór Mikháylovich. 'He's just been taking his nephew to be conscripted, and now he'll buy him out.'

'Ah!' said the policeman, and went on in front.

'Will you buy him off—Elijah, I mean?' asked Egór Mikháylovich.

'How am to buy him off? Will there be money enough? And perhaps it's too late . . .'

'Well, you know best,' said the steward, and they both followed the police-constable.

They approached the serfs' house, where the ill-smelling watchmen stood waiting in the passage with a lantern. Dútlov followed them. The watchmen looked guilty, perhaps because of the smell they were spreading, for they had done nothing wrong. All were silent.

'Where is he?' asked the police-constable.

'Here,' said Egór Mikháylovich in a whisper. 'Efím,' he

added, 'you're a bold lad, go on in front with the lantern.'

Efím had already put a plank straight at the top of the ladder, and seemed to have lost all fear. Taking two or three steps at a time, he clambered up with a cheerful look, only turning round to light the way for the police-constable. The constable was followed by Egór Mikháylovich. When they had disappeared above, Dútlov, with one foot on the bottom step, sighed and stopped. Two or three minutes passed. The footsteps in the loft were no longer heard; they had no doubt reached the body.

'Daddy, they want you,' Efím called down through the opening.

Dútlov began going up. The light of the lantern showed only the upper part of the bodies of the police-constable and of Egór Mikháylovich beyond the rafters. Beyond them again someone else was standing with his back turned. It was Polikéy. Dútlov climbed over a rafter and stopped, crossing himself.

'Turn him round, lads!' said the police-constable.

No one stirred.

'Efím, you're a bold lad,' said Egó Mikháylovich.

The 'bold lad' stepped across a rafter, turned Polikéy round, and stood beside him, looking with a most cheerful face now at Polikéy now at the constable, as a showman exhibiting an albino or Julia Pastrana[1] looks now at the public and now at what he is exhibiting, ready to do anything the spectators may wish.

'Turn him round again.'

Polikéy was turned round, his arms slightly swaying and his feet dragging in the sand on the floor.

'Catch hold, and take him down.'

'Shall we cut the rope through, your honour?' asked Egór Mikháylovich. 'Hand us an axe, lads!'

The watchmen and Dútlov had to be told twice before they set to, but the 'bold lad' handled Polikéy as he would have

---

[1] Julia Pastrana was exhibited as being half-woman half-monkey, and created a considerable sensation.

handled a sheep's carcass. At last the rope was cut through and the body taken down and covered up. The police constable said that the doctor would come next day, and dis missed them all.

XV

Dútlov went homeward, still moving his lips. At first he had an uncanny feeling, but it passed as he drew nearer home, and a feeling of gladness gradually penetrated his heart. In the village he heard songs and drunken voices. Dútlov never drank, and this time too he went straight home. It was late when he entered his hut. His old wife was asleep. His eldest son and grandsons were asleep on the stove, and his second son in the store-room. Elijah's wife alone was awake, and sat on the bench bareheaded, in a dirty, working-day smock, wailing. She did not come out to meet her uncle, but only sobbed louder, lamenting her fate, when he entered. According-ing to the old woman, she 'lamented' very fluently and well, taking into consideration the fact that at her age she could not have had much practice.

The old woman rose and got supper for her husband. Dútlov turned Elijah's wife away from the table, saying: 'That's enough, that's enough!' Aksínya went away, and lying down on a bench continued to lament. The old woman put the supper on the table and afterwards silently cleared it away again. The old man did not speak either. When he had said grace he hiccupped, washed his hands, took the counting-frame from a nail in the wall, and went into the storeroom. There he and the old woman spoke in whispers for a little while, and then, after she had gone away, he began counting on the frame, making the beads click. Finally he banged the lid of the chest standing there, and clambered into the space under the floor. For a long time he went on bustling about in the room and in the space below. When he came back to the living-room it was dark in the hut. The wooden splint that served for a candle had gone out. His old woman, quiet and silent in the daytime, had rolled herself up on the sleeping-

bunk and filled the hut with her snoring. Elijah's noisy young
wife was also asleep, breathing quietly. She lay on the bench
dressed just as she had been, and with nothing under her
head for a pillow. Dútlov began to pray, then looked at Elijah's wife, shook his head, put out the light, hiccupped
again, and climbed up on the stove, where he lay down beside
his little grandson. He threw down his plaited bast shoes from
the stove in the dark, and lay on his back looking up at the
rafter which was hardly discernible just over his head above
the stove, and listening to the sounds of the cockroaches
swarming along the walls, and to the sighs, the snoring, the
rubbing of one foot against another, and the noise made by
the cattle outside. It was a long time before he could sleep.
The moon rose. It grew lighter in the hut. He could see
Aksínya in her corner and something he could not make out:
was it a coat his son had forgotten, or a tub the women had
put there, or a man standing there? Perhaps he was drowsing,
perhaps not: anyhow he began to peer into the darkness. Evidently that evil spirit who had led Polikéy to commit his awful
deed and whose presence was felt that night by all the house-
serfs, had stretched out his wing and reached across the village to the house in which lay the money that *he* had used to
ruin Polikéy. At least, Dútlov felt *his* presence and was ill at
ease. He could neither sleep nor get up. After noticing the
something he could not make out, he remembered Elijah with
his arms bound, and Aksínya's face and her eloquent lamentations; and he recalled Polikéy with his swaying hands. Suddenly it seemed to the old man that someone passed by the
window. 'Who was that? Could it be the village elder coming so early with a notice?' thought he. 'How did he open the
door?' thought the old man, hearing a step in the passage.
'Had the old woman not put up the bar when she went out
into the passage?' The dog began to howl in the yard and *he*
came stepping along the passage, so the old man related
afterwards, as though he were trying to find the door, then
passed on and began groping along the wall, stumbled over a
tub and made it clatter, and again began groping as if feeling
for the latch. Now *he* had hold of the latch. A shiver ran

down the old man's body. Now *he* pulled the latch and entered in the shape of a man. Dútlov knew it was *he*. He
wished to cross himself, but could not. *He* went up to the
table which was covered with a cloth, and, pulling it off,
threw it on the floor and began climbing onto the stove. The
old man knew that *he* had taken the shape of Polikéy. *He* was
showing his teeth and his hands were swinging about. *He*
climbed up, fell on the old man's chest, and began to strangle
him.

'The money's mine!' muttered Polikéy.

'Let me go! I won't do it!' Semën tried to say, but could not.

Polikéy was pressing down on him with the weight of a
mountain of stone. Dútlov knew that if he said a prayer *he*
would let him go, and he knew which prayer he ought to re-
cite, but could not utter it. His grandson sleeping beside him
uttered a shrill scream and began to cry. His grandfather had
pressed him against the wall. The child's cry loosened the old
man's lips. 'Let God arise! . . .' he said. *He* pressed less hard.
'And let his enemies be scattered . . .' spluttered Dútlov. *He*
got off the stove. Dútlov heard his two feet strike the floor.
Dútlov went on repeating in turn all the prayers he knew. *He*
went towards the door, passed the table, and slammed the
door so that the whole hut shook. Everybody but the grandfather and grandson continued to sleep however. The grandfather, trembling all over, muttered prayers, while the grandson was crying himself to sleep and pressing close to his
grandfather. All became quiet once more. The old man lay
still. A cock crowed behind the wall close to Dútlov's ear. He
heard the hens stirring, and a cockerel unsuccessfully trying to
crow in answer to the old cock. Something moved over the
old man's legs. It was the cat; she jumped on her soft pads
from the stove to the floor, and stood mewing by the door.
The old man got up and opened the window. It was dark
and muddy in the street. The front of the cart was standing
there close to the window. Crossing himself he went out barefoot into the yard to the horses. One could see that *he* had
been there too. The mare, standing under the lean-to beside a
tub of chaff, had got her foot into the cord of her halter and

had spilt the chaff, and now, lifting her foot, turned her head and waited for her master. Her foal had tumbled over a heap of manure. The old man raised him to his feet, disentangled the mare's foot and fed her, and went back to the hut. The old woman got up and lit the splint. 'Wake the lads, I'm going to the town!' And taking a wax taper from before the icon Dútlov lit it and went down with it into the opening under the floor. When he came up again lights were burning not only in this hut but in all the neighbouring houses. The young fellows were up and preparing to start. The women were coming in and out with pails of milk. Ignát was harnessing the horse to one cart and the second son was greasing the wheels of another. The young wife was no longer wailing. She had made herself neat and had bound a shawl over her head, and now sat waiting till it would be time to go to town to say good-bye to her husband.

The old man seemed particularly stern. He did not say a word to anyone, put on his best coat, tied his belt round him, and with all Polikéy's money in the bosom of his coat, went to Egór Mikháylovich.

'Don't dawdle,' he called to his son, who was turning the wheels round on the raised and newly greased axle. 'I'll be back in a minute; see that everything is ready.'

The steward had only just got up and was drinking tea. He himself was preparing to go to town to deliver up the recruits.

'What is it?' he asked.

'Egór Mikháylovich, I want to buy the lad off. Do be so good! You said t'other day that you knew one in the town that was willing. . . . Explain to me how to do it; we are ignorant people.'

'Why, have you reconsidered it?'

'I have, Egór Mikháylovich. I'm sorry for him. My brother's child after all, whatever he may be. I'm sorry for him! It's the cause of much sin, money is. Do be good enough to explain it to me!' he said, bowing to his waist.

Egór Mikháylovich, as was his wont on such occasions, stood for a long time thoughtfully smacking his lips. Then,

having considered the matter, he wrote two notes and told
him what to do in town and how to do it.

When Dútlov got home, the young wife had already set off
with Ignát. The fat roan mare stood ready harnessed at the
gate. Dútlov broke a stick out of the hedge and, lapping his
coat over, got into the cart and whipped up the horse. He
made the mare run so fast that her fat sides quickly shrank,
and Dútlov did not look at her so as not to feel sorry for her.
He was tormented by the thought that he might come too
late for the recruiting, that Elijah would go as a soldier
and the devil's money would be left on his hands.

I will not describe all Dútlov's proceedings that morning. I
will only say that he was specially lucky. The man to whom
Egór Mikháylovich had given him a note had a volunteer
quite ready who was already twenty-three silver rubles in
debt and had been passed by the recruiting-board. His
master wanted four hundred silver rubles for him and a
buyer in the town had for the last three weeks been offering
him three hundred. Dútlov settled the matter in a couple of
words. 'Will you take three twenty-five?' he said, holding out
his hand, but with a look that showed that he was prepared to
give more. The master held back his hand and went on asking
four hundred. 'You won't take three and a quarter?' Dútlov
said, catching hold with his left hand of the man's right and
preparing to slap his own right hand down on it. 'You won't
take it? Well, God be with you!' he said suddenly, smacking
the master's hand with the full swing of his other hand and
turning away with his whole body. 'It seems it has to be so
. . . take three and a half hundred! Get out the discharge
and bring the fellow along. And now here are two ten-ruble
notes on account. Is it enough?'

And Dútlov unfastened his girdle and got out the money.

The man, though he did not withdraw his hand, yet did
not seem quite to agree and, not accepting the deposit money,
went on stipulating that Dútlov should wet the bargain and
stand treat to the volunteer.

'Don't commit a sin,' Dútlov kept repeating as he held out
the money. 'We shall all have to die some day,' he went on,

in such a mild, persuasive and assured tone that the master said:

'So be it, then!' and again clapped Dútlov's hand and began praying for God's blessing. 'God grant you luck,' he said.

They woke the volunteer, who was still sleeping after yesterday's carouse, examined him for some reason, and went with him to the offices of the Administration. The recruit was merry. He demanded rum as a refresher, for which Dútlov gave him some money, and only when they came into the vestibule of the recruiting-board did his courage fail him. For a long time they stood in the entrance-hall, the old master in his full blue cloak and the recruit in a short sheepskin, his eyebrows raised and his eyes staring. For a long time they whispered, tried to get somewhere, looked for somebody, and for some reason took off their caps and bowed to every copying-clerk they met, and meditatively listened to the decision which a scribe whom the master knew brought out to them. All hope of getting the business done that day began to vanish, and the recruit was growing more cheerful and unconstrained again, when Dútlov saw Egór Mikháylovich, seized on him at once, and began to beg and bow to him. Egór Mikháylovich helped him so efficiently that by about three o'clock the recruit, to his great dissatisfaction and surprise, was taken into the hall and placed for examination, and amid general merriment (in which for some reason everybody joined, from the watchmen to the President), he was undressed, dressed again, shaved, and led out at the door; and five minutes later Dútlov counted out the money, received the discharge and, having taken leave of the volunteer and his master, went to the lodging-house where the Pokróvsk recruits were staying. Elijah and his young wife were sitting in a corner of the kitchen, and as soon as the old man came in they stopped talking and looked at him with a resigned expression, but not with goodwill. As was his wont the old man said a prayer, and he then unfastened his belt, got out a paper, and called into the room his eldest son Ignát and Elijah's mother, who were in the yard.

'Don't sin, Elijah,' he said, coming up to his nephew. 'Last night you said a word to me. . . . Don't I pity you? I remember how my brother left you to me. If it had been in my power would I have let you go? God has sent me luck, and I am not grudging it you. Here it is, the paper'; and he put the discharge on the table and carefully smoothed it out with his stiff, unbending fingers.

All the Pokróvsk peasants, the inn-keeper's men, and even some outsiders, came in from the yard. All guessed what was happening, but no one interrupted the old man's solemn discourse.

'Here it is, the paper! Four hundred silver rubles I've given for it. Don't reproach your uncle.'

Elijah rose, but remained silent not knowing what to say. His lips quivered with emotion. His old mother came up and would have thrown herself sobbing on his neck; but the old man motioned her away slowly and authoritatively and continued speaking.

'You said a word to me yesterday,' the old man again repeated. 'You stabbed me to the heart with that word as with a knife! Your dying father left you to me and you have been as my own son to me, and if I have wronged you in any way, well, we all live in sin! Is it not so, good Christian folk?' he said, turning to the peasants who stood round. 'Here is your own mother and your young wife, and here is the discharge for you. I don't regret the money, but forgive me for Christ's sake!'

And, turning up the skirts of his coat, he deliberately sank to his knees and bowed down to the ground before Elijah and his wife. The young people tried in vain to restrain him, but not till his forehead had touched the floor did he get up. Then, after giving his skirts a shake, he sat down on a bench. Elijah's mother and wife howled with joy, and words of approval were heard among the crowd. 'That is just, that's the godly way,' said one. 'What's money? You can't buy a fellow for money,' said another. 'What happiness!' said a third; 'no two ways about it, he's a just man!' Only the peasants who were to

go as recruits said nothing, and went quickly out into the
yard.

Two hours later Dútlov's two carts were driving through
the outskirts of the town. In the first, to which was harnessed
the roan mare, her sides fallen in and her neck moist with
sweat, sat the old man and Ignát. Behind them jerked strings
of ring-shaped fancy-bread. In the second cart, in which nobody held the reins, the young wife and her mother-in-law,
with shawls over their heads, were sitting, sedate and happy.
The former held a bottle of vodka under her apron. Elijah, very
red in the face, sat all in a heap with his back to the horse,
jolting against the front of the cart, biting into a roll and talking incessantly. The voices, the rumbling of the cart-wheels on
the stony road, and the snorting of the horses, blent into one
note of merriment. The horses, swishing their tails, increased
their speed more and more, feeling themselves on the homeward road. The passers-by, whether driving or on foot, involuntarily turned round to look at the happy family party.

Just as they left the town the Dútlovs overtook a party of
recruits. A group of them were standing in a ring outside a
tavern. One of the recruits, with that unnatural expression on
his face which comes of having the front of the head shaved,[1]
his grey cap pushed back, was vigorously strumming a balaláyka; another, bareheaded and with a bottle of vodka in his
hand, was dancing in the middle of the ring. Ignát stopped
his horse and got down to tighten the traces. All the Dútlovs looked with curiosity, approval, and amusement at the
dancer. The recruit seemed not to see anyone, but felt that
the public admiring him had grown larger, and this added to
his strength and agility. He danced briskly. His brows were
knitted, his flushed face was set, and his lips were fixed in a
grin that had long since lost all meaning. It seemed as if all
the strength of his soul was concentrated on placing one foot
as quickly as possible after the other, now on the heel and

---

[1] On being conscripted a man's head was partially shaved to make
desertion more difficult.

now on the toe. Sometimes he stopped suddenly and winked
to the balaláyka-player, who began playing still more briskly,
strumming on all the strings and even striking the case with
his knuckles. The recruit would stop, but even when he stood
still he still seemed to be dancing all over. Then he began
slowly jerking his shoulders, and suddenly twirling round,
leaped in the air with a wild cry, and descending, crouched
down, throwing out first one leg and then the other. The little
boys laughed, the women shook their heads, the men smiled
approvingly. An old sergeant stood quietly by, with a look that
seemed to say: 'You think it wonderful, but we have long been
familiar with it.' The balaláyka-player seemed tired; he
looked lazily round, struck a false chord, and suddenly
knocked on the case with his knuckles, and the dance came to
an end.

'Eh, Alëkha,' he said to the dancer, pointing at Dútlov,
'there's your sponsor!'

'Where? You, my dearest friend!' shouted Alëkha, the very
recruit whom Dútlov had bought; and staggering forward on
his weary legs and holding the bottle of vodka above his
head he moved towards the cart. 'Míshka, a glass!' he cried
to the player. 'Master! My dearest friend! What a pleasure,
really!' he shouted, drooping his tipsy head over the cart, and
he began to treat the men and women to vodka. The men
drank, but the women refused. 'My dear friends, what can I
offer you?' exclaimed Alëkha, embracing the old women.

A woman selling eatables was standing among the crowd.
Alëkha noticed her, seized her tray, and poured its contents
into the cart.

'I'll pay, no fear, you devil!' he howled tearfully, pulling a
purse from his pocket and throwing it to Míshka.

He stood leaning with his elbows on the cart and looking
with moist eyes at those who sat in it.

'Which is the mother . . . you?' he asked. 'I must treat
you too.'

He stood thinking for a moment, then he put his hand
in his pocket and drew out a new folded handkerchief, hurriedly took off a sash which was tied round his waist under

his coat, and also a red scarf he was wearing round his neck, and, crumpling them all together, thrust them into the old woman's lap.

'There! I'm sacrificing them for you,' he said in a voice that was growing more and more subdued.

'What for? Thank you, sonny! Just see what a simple lad it is!' said the old woman, addressing Dútlov, who had come up to their cart.

Alëkha was now quite quiet, quite stupefied, and looked as if he were falling asleep. He drooped his head lower and lower.

'It's for you I am going, for you I am perishing!' he muttered; 'that's why I am giving you gifts.'

'I dare say he, too, has a mother,' said someone in the crowd. 'What a simple fellow! What a pity!'

Alëkha lifted his head.

'I have a mother,' said he; 'I have a father too. All have given me up. Listen to me, old woman,' he went on, taking Elijah's mother by the hand. 'I have given you presents. Listen to me for Christ's sake! Go to Vódnoe village, ask for the old woman Nikónovna—she's my own mother, see? Say to this same old woman, Nikónovna, the third hut from the end, by the new well. Tell her that Alëkha—her son, you see. . . . Eh! musician! strike up!' he shouted.

And muttering something he immediately began dancing again, and hurled the bottle with the remaining vodka to the ground.

Ignát got into the cart and was about to start.

'Good-bye! May God bless you!' said the old woman, wrapping her cloak closer round her.

Alëkha suddenly stopped.

'Go to the devil!' he shouted, clenching his fists threateningly. 'May your mother be . . .'

'O Lord!' exclaimed Elijah's mother, crossing herself.

Ignát touched the reins, and the carts rattled on again. Alëkha, the recruit, stood in the middle of the road with clenched fists and with a look of fury on his face, and abused the peasants with all his might.

'What are you stopping for? Go on, devils! cannibals!' he cried. 'You won't escape me! . . . Devil's clodhoppers!'

At these words his voice broke, and he fell full length to the ground just where he stood.

Soon the Dútlovs reached the open fields, and looking back could no longer see the crowd of recruits. Having gone some four miles at a walking pace Ignát got down from his father's cart, in which the old man lay asleep, and walked beside Elijah's cart.

Between them they emptied the bottle they had brought from town. After a while Elijah began a song, the women joined in, and Ignát shouted merrily in time with the song. A post-chaise drove merrily towards them. The driver called lustily to his horses as he passed the two festive carts, and the post-boy turned round and winked at the men and women who with flushed faces sat jolting inside singing their jovial song.

THE COSSACKS

CHAPTER I

All is quiet in Moscow. The squeak of wheels is seldom heard in the snow-covered street. There are no lights left in the windows and the street lamps have been extinguished. Only the sound of bells, borne over the city from the church towers, suggests the approach of morning. The streets are deserted. At rare intervals a night-cabman's sledge kneads up the snow and sand in the street as the driver makes his way to another corner where he falls asleep while waiting for a fare. An old woman passes by on her way to church, where a few wax candles burn with a red light reflected on the gilt mountings of the icons. Workmen are already getting up after the long winter night and going to their work—but for the gentlefolk it is still evening.

From a window in Chevalier's Restaurant a light—illegal at that hour—is still to be seen through a chink in the shutter. At the entrance a carriage, a sledge, and a cabman's sledge, stand close together with their backs to the curbstone. A three-horse sledge from the post-station is there also.[1] A yardporter muffled up and pinched with cold is sheltering behind the corner of the house.

'And what's the good of all this jawing?' thinks the footman who sits in the hall weary and haggard. 'This always happens when I'm on duty.' From the adjoining room are heard the voices of three young men, sitting there at a table on

---

[1] In those pre-rail days travellers usually relied on vehicles hired at the posting-stations.

which are wine and the remains of supper. One, a rather plain, thin, neat little man, sits looking with tired kindly eyes at his friend, who is about to start on a journey. Another, a tall man, lies on a sofa beside a table on which are empty bottles, and plays with his watch-key. A third, wearing a short, fur-lined coat, is pacing up and down the room stopping now and then to crack an almond between his strong, rather thick, but well-tended fingers. He keeps smiling at something and his face and eyes are all aglow. He speaks warmly and gesticulates, but evidently does not find the words he wants and those that occur to him seem to him inadequate to express what has risen to his heart.

'Now I can speak out fully,' said the traveller. 'I don't want to defend myself, but I should like you at least to understand me as I understand myself, and not look at the matter superficially. You say I have treated her badly,' he continued, addressing the man with the kindly eyes who was watching him.

'Yes, you are to blame,' said the latter, and his look seemed to express still more kindliness and weariness.

'I know why you say that,' rejoined the one who was leaving. 'To be loved is in your opinion as great a happiness as to love, and if a man obtains it, it is enough for his whole life.'

'Yes, quite enough, my dear fellow, more than enough!' confirmed the plain little man, opening and shutting his eyes.

'But why shouldn't the man love too?' said the traveller thoughtfully, looking at his friend with something like pity. 'Why shouldn't one love? Because love doesn't come. . . . No, to be beloved is a misfortune. It is a misfortune to feel guilty because you do not give something you cannot give. O my God!' he added, with a gesture of his arm. 'If it all happened reasonably, and not all topsy-turvy—not in our way but in a way of its own! Why, it's as if I had stolen that love! You think so too, don't deny it. You must think so. But will you believe it, of all the horrid and stupid things I have found time to do in my life—and there are many—this is one I do not and cannot repent of. Neither at the beginning nor afterwards did I lie to myself or to her. It seemed to me that

I had at last fallen in love, but then I saw that it was an involuntary falsehood, and that that was not the way to love,
and I could not go on, but she did. Am I to blame that I
couldn't? What was I to do?'

'Well, it's ended now!' said his friend, lighting a cigar to
master his sleepiness. 'The fact is that you have not yet loved
and do not know what love is.'

The man in the fur-lined coat was going to speak again,
and put his hands to his head, but could not express what he
wanted to say.

'Never loved! . . . Yes, quite true, I never have! But after
all, I have within me a desire to love, and nothing could be
stronger than that desire! But then, again, does such love exist?
There always remains something incomplete. Ah well! What's
the use of talking? I've made an awful mess of life! But anyhow it's all over now; you are quite right. And I feel that I
am beginning a new life.'

'Which you will again make a mess of,' said the man who
lay on the sofa playing with his watch-key. But the traveller
did not listen to him.

'I am sad and yet glad to go,' he continued. 'Why I am sad
I don't know.'

And the traveller went on talking about himself, without
noticing that this did not interest the others as much as it did
him. A man is never such an egotist as at moments of spiritual
ecstasy. At such times it seems to him that there is nothing on
earth more splendid and interesting than himself.

'Dmítri Andréich! The coachman won't wait any longer!'
said a young serf, entering the room in a sheepskin coat, with
a scarf tied round his head. 'The horses have been standing
since twelve, and it's now four o'clock!'

Dmítri Andréich looked at his serf, Vanyúsha. The scarf
round Vanyúsha's head, his felt boots and sleepy face, seemed
to be calling his master to a new life of labour, hardship, and
activity.

'True enough! Good-bye!' said he, feeling for the unfastened hook and eye on his coat.

In spite of advice to mollify the coachman by another tip,

he put on his cap and stood in the middle of the room. The friends kissed once, then again, and after a pause, a third time. The man in the fur-lined coat approached the table and emptied a champagne glass, then took the plain little man's hand and blushed.

'Ah well, I will speak out all the same. . . . I must and will be frank with you because I am fond of you. . . . Of course you love her—I always thought so—don't you?'

'Yes,' answered his friend, smiling still more gently.

'And perhaps . . .'

'Please sir, I have orders to put out the candles,' said the sleepy attendant, who had been listening to the last part of the conversation and wondering why gentlefolk always talk about one and the same thing. 'To whom shall I make out the bill? To you, sir?' he added, knowing whom to address and turning to the tall man.

'To me,' replied the tall man. 'How much?'

'Twenty-six rubles.'

The tall man considered for a moment, but said nothing and put the bill in his pocket.

The other two continued their talk.

'Good-bye, you are a capital fellow!' said the short plain man with the mild eyes.

Tears filled the eyes of both. They stepped into the porch.

'Oh, by the by,' said the traveller, turning with a blush to the tall man, 'will you settle Chevalier's bill and write and let me know?'

'All right, all right!' said the tall man, pulling on his gloves. 'How I envy you!' he added quite unexpectedly when they were out in the porch.

The traveller got into his sledge, wrapped his coat about him, and said: 'Well then, come along!' He even moved a little to make room in the sledge for the man who said he envied him—his voice trembled.

'Good-bye, Mítya! I hope that with God's help you . . .' said the tall one. But his wish was that the other would go away quickly, and so he could not finish the sentence.

They were silent a moment. Then someone again said,

'Good-bye,' and a voice cried, 'Ready,' and the coachman touched up the horses.

'Hy, Elisár!' one of the friends called out, and the other coachman and the sledge-drivers began moving, clicking their tongues and pulling at the reins. Then the stiffened carriage-wheels rolled squeaking over the frozen snow.

'A fine fellow, that Olénin!' said one of the friends. 'But what an idea to go to the Caucasus—as a cadet, too! I wouldn't do it for anything. . . . Are you dining at the club to-morrow?'

'Yes.'

They separated.

The traveller felt warm, his fur coat seemed too hot. He sat on the bottom of the sledge and unfastened his coat, and the three shaggy post-horses dragged themselves out of one dark street into another, past houses he had never before seen. It seemed to Oénin that only travellers starting on a long journey went through those streets. All was dark and silent and dull around him, but his soul was full of memories, love, regrets, and a pleasant tearful feeling.

CHAPTER II

'I'm fond of them, very fond! . . . First-rate fellows! . . . Fine!' he kept repeating, and felt ready to cry. But why he wanted to cry, who were the first-rate fellows he was so fond of—was more than he quite knew. Now and then he looked round at some house and wondered why it was so curiously built; sometimes he began wondering why the post-boy and Vanyúsha, who were so different from himself, sat so near, and together with him were being jerked about and swayed by the tugs the side-horses gave at the frozen traces, and again he repeated: 'First rate . . . very fond!' and once he even said: 'And how it seizes one . . . excellent!' and wondered what made him say it. 'Dear me, am I drunk?' he asked himself. He had had a couple of bottles of wine, but it was not the wine alone that was having this effect on Olénin. He remembered all the words of friendship heartily, bashfully, spontaneously (as he believed) addressed to him on his departure. He remembered the clasp of hands, glances, the moments of silence, and the sound of a voice saying, *'Good-bye, Mítya!'* when he was already in the sledge. He remembered his own deliberate frankness. And all this had a touching significance for him. Not only friends and relatives, not only people who had been indifferent to him, but even those who did not like him, seemed to have agreed to become fonder of him, or to forgive him, before his departure, as people do before confession or death. 'Perhaps I shall not return from the Caucasus,' he thought. And he felt that he loved his friends and some one besides. He was sorry for himself. But it was not love for his friends that so stirred and uplifted his heart that he could not repress the meaningless words that seemed to rise of themselves to his lips; nor was it love for a woman (he had never yet been in love) that had brought on this mood. Love for himself, love full of hope—warm young love for all that was good in his own soul (and at that moment it seemed to him that there was nothing but good in it)—compelled him to weep and to mutter incoherent words.

Olénin was a youth who had never completed his university course, never served anywhere (having only a nominal post in some government office or other), who had squandered half his fortune and had reached the age of twenty-four without having done anything or even chosen a career. He was what in Moscow society is termed *un jeune homme*.

At the age of eighteen he was free—as only rich young Russians in the 'forties who had lost their parents at an early age could be. Neither physical nor moral fetters of any kind existed for him; he could do as he liked, lacking nothing and bound by nothing. Neither relatives, nor fatherland, nor religion, nor wants, existed for him. He believed in nothing and admitted nothing. But although he believed in nothing he was not a morose or blasé young man, nor self-opinionated, but on the contrary continually let himself be carried away. He had come to the conclusion that there is no such thing as love, yet his heart always overflowed in the presence of any young and attractive woman. He had long been aware that honours and position were nonsense, yet involuntarily he felt pleased when at a ball Prince Sergius came up and spoke to him affably. But he yielded to his impulses only in so far as they did not limit his freedom. As soon as he had yielded to any influence and became conscious of its leading on to labour and struggle, he instinctively hastened to free himself from the feeling or activity into which he was being drawn and to regain his freedom. In this way he experimented with society-life, the civil service, farming, music—to which at one time he intended to devote his life—and even with the love of women in which he did not believe. He meditated on the use to which he should devote that power of youth which is granted to man only once in a lifetime: that force which gives a man the power of making himself, or even—as it seemed to him—of making the universe, into anything he wishes: should it be to art, to science, to love of woman, or to practical activities? It is true that some people are devoid of this impulse, and on entering life at once place their necks under the first yoke that offers itself and honestly labour under it for the rest of their lives. But Olénin was too strongly conscious of the presence of that all-powerful God of Youth—of that capacity to be entirely transformed into an aspiration or idea—the capacity to wish and to do—to throw oneself headlong into a bottomless abyss without knowing why or wherefore. He bore this consciousness within himself, was proud of it and, without knowing it, was happy in that consciousness. Up to that time he had loved only himself, and could not help loving himself, for he expected nothing but good of himself and had not yet had time to be disillusioned. On leaving Moscow he was in that happy state of mind in which a young man, conscious of past mistakes, suddenly says to himself, 'That was not the real thing.' All that had gone before was accidental and unimportant. Till then he had not really tried to live, but now with his departure from Moscow a new life was beginning—a life in which there would be no mistakes, no remorse, and certainly nothing but happiness.

It is always the case on a long journey that till the first two or three stages have been passed imagination continues to dwell on the place left behind, but with the first morning on the road it leaps to the end of the journey and there begins building castles in the air. So it happened to Olénin.

After leaving the town behind, he gazed at the snowy fields and felt glad to be alone in their midst. Wrapping himself in his fur coat, he lay at the bottom of the sledge, became tranquil, and fell into a doze. The parting with his friends had touched him deeply, and memories of that last winter spent in Moscow and images of the past, mingled with vague thoughts and regrets, rose unbidden in his imagination.

He remembered the friend who had seen him off and his relations with the girl they had talked about. The girl was rich. 'How could he love her knowing that she loved me?' thought he, and evil suspicions crossed his mind. 'There is much dishonesty in men when one comes to reflect.' Then he was confronted by the question: 'But really, how is it I have never been in love? Every one tells me that I never have. Can it be that I am a moral monstrosity?' And he began to recall all his infatuations. He recalled his entry into society, and a friend's sister with whom he spent several evenings at a table with a lamp on it which lit up her slender fingers busy with needlework, and the lower part of her pretty delicate face. He recalled their conversations that dragged on like the game in which one passes on a stick which one keeps alight as long as possible, and the general awkwardness and restraint and his continual feeling of rebellion at all that conventionality. Some voice had always whispered: 'That's not it, that's not it,' and so it had proved. Then he remembered a ball and the mazurka he danced with the beautiful D——. 'How much in love I was that night and how happy! And how hurt and vexed I was next morning when I woke and felt myself still free! Why does not love come and bind me hand and foot?' thought he. 'No, there is no such thing as love! That neighbour who used to tell me, as she told Dubróvin and the Marshal, that she loved the stars, was not *it* either.' And now his farming and work in the country recurred to his mind, and in those recollections also there was nothing to dwell on with pleasure. 'Will they talk long of my departure?' came into his head; but who 'they' were he did not quite know. Next came a thought that made him wince and mutter incoherently. It was the recollection of M. Cappele the tailor, and the six hundred and seventy-eight rubles he still owed him, and he recalled the words in which he had begged him to wait another year, and the look of perplexity and resignation which had appeared on the tailor's face. 'Oh, my God, my God!' he repeated, wincing and trying to drive away the intolerable thought. 'All the same and in spite of everything she loved me,' thought he of the girl they had talked about at the farewell supper. 'Yes, had I married her I should not now be owing anything, and as it is I am in debt to Vasílyev.' Then he remembered the last night he had played with Vasílyev at the club (just after leaving her), and he recalled his humiliating requests for another game and the other's cold refusal. 'A year's economizing and they will all be paid, and the devil take them! . . . But despite this assurance he again began calculating his outstanding debts, their dates, and when he could hope to pay them off. 'And, I owe something to Morell as well as to Chevalier,' thought he, recalling the night when he had run up so large a debt. It was at a carousal at the gipsies' arranged by some fellows from Petersburg: Sáshka B——, an aide-de-camp to the Tsar, Prince D——, and that pompous old ——. 'How is it those gentlemen are so self-satisfied?' thought he, 'and by what right do they form a clique to which they think others must be highly flattered to be admitted? Can it be because they are on the Emperor's staff? Why, it's awful what fools and scoundrels they consider other people to be! But I showed them that I at any rate, on the contrary, do not at all want their intimacy. All the same, I fancy Andrew, the steward, would be amazed to know that I am on familiar terms with a man like Sáshka B——, a colonel and an aide-de-camp to the Tsar! Yes, and no one drank more than I d'd that evening, and I taught the gipsies a new song and everyone listened to it. Though I have done many foolish things, all the same I am a very good fellow,' thought he.

Morning found him at the third post-stage. He drank tea, and himself helped Vanyúsha to move his bundles and trunks and sat down among them, sensible, erect, and precise, knowing where all his belongings were, how much money he had and where it was, where he had put his passport and the post-horse requisition and toll-gate papers, and it all seemed to him so well arranged that he grew quite cheerful and the long journey before him seemed an extended pleasure-trip.

All that morning and noon he was deep in calculations of how many versts he had travelled, how many remained to the next stage, how many to the next town, to the place where he would dine, to the place where he would drink tea, and to Stavrópol, and what fraction of the whole journey was already accomplished. He also calculated how much money he had with him, how much would be left over, how much would pay off all his debts, and what proportion of his income he would spend each month. Towards evening, after tea, he calculated that to Stavrópol there still remained seven-elevenths of the whole journey, that his debts would require seven months' economy and one-eighth of his whole fortune; and then, tranquillized, he wrapped himself up, lay down in the sledge, and again dozed off. His imagination was now turned to the future: to the Caucasus. All his dreams of the future were mingled with pictures of Amalat-Beks,[1] Circassian women, mountains, precipices, terrible torrents, and perils. All these things were vague and dim, but the love of fame and the danger of death furnished the interest of that future. Now, with unprecedented courage and a strength that amazed everyone, he slew and subdued an innumerable host of hills-men; now he was himself a hillsman and with them was maintaining their independence against the Russians. As soon as he pictured anything definite, familiar Moscow figures always appeared on the scene. Sáshka B—— fights with the Russians or the hillsmen against him. Even the tailor Cappele in some strange way takes part in the conqueror's triumph. Amid all this he remembered his former humiliations, weaknesses, and mistakes, and the recollection was not disagreeable. It was clear that there among the mountains, waterfalls, fair Circas-

---

[1] Amalet-Bek, a character in a Russian novel of the Caucasus by Bestúzhev-Marlínsky.

sians, and dangers, such mistakes could not recur. Having
once made full confession to himself there was an end of it all.
One other vision, the sweetest of them all, mingled with the
young man's every thought of the future—the vision of a
woman. And there, among the mountains, she appeared to his
imagination as a Circassian slave, a fine figure with a long plait
of hair and deep submissive eyes. He pictured a lonely hut in
the mountains, and on the threshold *she* stands awaiting him
when, tired and covered with dust, blood, and fame, he returns to her. He is conscious of her kisses, her shoulders, her
sweet voice, and her submissiveness. She is enchanting, but
uneducated, wild, and rough. In the long winter evenings he
begins her education. She is clever and gifted and quickly ac-
quires all the knowledge essential. Why not? She can quite
easily learn foreign languages, read the French masterpieces
and understands them: *Notre Dame de Paris,* for instance, is
sure to please her. She can also speak French. In a drawing-
room she can show more innate dignity than a lady of the
highest society. She can sing, simply, powerfully, and passionately. . . . 'Oh, what nonsense!' said he to himself. But here
they reached a post-station and he had to change into another sledge and give some tips. But his fancy again began
searching for the 'nonsense' he had relinquished, and again
fair Circassians, glory, and his return to Russia with an ap-
pointment as aide-de-camp and a lovely wife rose before his
imagination. 'But there's no such thing as love,' said he to himself. 'Fame is all rubbish. But the six hundred and seventy-
eight rubles? . . . And the conquered land that will bring me
more wealth than I need for a lifetime? It will not be right
though to keep all that wealth for myself. I shall have to distribute it. But to whom? Well, six hundred and seventy-eight
rubles to Cappele and then we'll see.' . . . Quite vague visions now cloud his mind, and only Vanyúsha's voice and
the interrupted motion of the sledge break his healthy youthful slumber. Scarcely conscious, he changes into another
sledge at the next stage and continues his journey.

Next morning everything goes on just the same: the same
kind of post-stations and tea-drinking, the same moving horses'

cruppers, the same short talks with Vanyúsha, the same
vague dreams and drowsiness, and the same tired, healthy,
youthful sleep at night.

CHAPTER III

The farther Olénin travelled from Central Russia the farther
he left his memories behind, and the nearer he drew to the
Caucasus the lighter his heart became. 'I'll stay away for
good and never return to show myself in society,' was a
thought that sometimes occurred to him. 'These people whom
I see here are *not* people. None of them knows me and none of
them can ever enter the Moscow society I was in or find out
about my past. And no one in that society will ever know
what I am doing, living among these people.' And quite a new
feeling of freedom from his whole past came over him among
the rough beings he met on the road whom he did not consider to be *people* in the sense that his Moscow acquaintances
were. The rougher the people and the fewer the signs of
civilization the freer he felt. Stavrópol, through which he had
to pass, irked him. The signboards, some of them even in
French, ladies in carriages, cabs in the market-place, and a
gentleman wearing a fur cloak and tall hat who was walking
along the boulevard and staring at the passers-by, quite upset
him. 'Perhaps these people know some of my acquaintances,'
he thought; and the club, his tailor, cards, society . . . came
back to his mind. But after Stavrópol everything was satisfactory—wild and also beautiful and warlike, and Olénin felt happier and happier. All the Cossacks, post-boys, and post-station
masters seemed to him simple folk with whom he could jest
and converse simply, without having to consider to what class
they belonged. They all belonged to the human race which,
without his thinking about it, all appeared dear to Olénin,
and they all treated him in a friendly way.

Already in the province of the Don Cossacks his sledge had
been exchanged for a cart, and beyond Stavrópol it became
so warm that Olénin travelled without wearing his fur coat. It

was already Spring—an unexpected joyous Spring for Olénin. At night he was no longer allowed to leave the Cossack villages, and they said it was dangerous to travel in the evening. Vanyúsha began to be uneasy, and they carried a loaded gun in the cart. Olénin became still happier. At one of the post-stations the post-master told of a terrible murder that had been committed recently on the high road. They began to meet armed men. 'So this is where it begins!' thought Olénin, and kept expecting to see the snowy mountains of which mention was so often made. Once, towards evening, the Nogáy driver pointed with his whip to the mountains shrouded in clouds. Olénin looked eagerly, but it was dull and the mountains were almost hidden by the clouds. Olénin made out something grey and white and fleecy, but try as he would he could find nothing beautiful in the mountains of which he had so often read and heard. The mountains and the clouds appeared to him quite alike, and he thought the special beauty of the snow peaks, of which he had so often been told, was as much an invention as Bach's music and the love of women, in which he did not believe. So he gave up looking forward to seeing the mountains. But early next morning, being awakened in his cart by the freshness of the air, he glanced carelessly to the right. The morning was perfectly clear. Suddenly he saw, about twenty paces away as it seemed to him at first glance, pure white gigantic masses with delicate contours, the distinct fantastic outlines of their summits showing sharply against the far-off sky. When he had realized the distance between himself and them and the sky and the whole immensity of the mountains, and felt the infinitude of all that beauty, he became afraid that it was but a phantasm or a dream. He gave himself a shake to rouse himself, but the mountains were still the same.

'What's that! What is it?' he said to the driver.

'Why, the mountains,' answered the Nogáy driver with indifference.

'And I too have been looking at them for a long while,' said Vanyúsha. 'Aren't they fine? They won't believe it at home.'

The quick progress of the three-horsed cart along the

smooth road caused the mountains to appear to be running
along the horizon, while their rosy crests glittered in the light
of the rising sun. At first Olénin was only astonished at the
sight, then gladdened by it; but later on, gazing more and
more intently at that snow-peaked chain that seemed to rise
not from among other black mountains, but straight out of the
plain, and to glide away into the distance, he began by slow
degrees to be penetrated by their beauty and at length to
feel the mountains. From that moment all he saw, all he
thought, and all he felt, acquired for him a new character,
sternly majestic like the mountains! All his Moscow reminiscences, shame, and repentance, and his trivial dreams about
the Caucasus, vanished and did not return. 'Now it has begun,' a solemn voice seemed to say to him. The road and the
Térek, just becoming visible in the distance, and the Cossack
villages and the people, all no longer appeared to him as a
joke. He looked at himself or Vanyúsha, and again thought of
the mountains. . . . Two Cossacks ride by, their guns in
their cases swinging rhythmically behind their backs, the
white and bay legs of their horses mingling confusedly . . .
and the mountains! Beyond the Térek rises the smoke from a
Tartar village . . . and the mountains! The sun has risen and
glitters on the Térek, now visible beyond the reeds . . . and
the mountains! From the village comes a Tartar wagon, and
women, beautiful young women, pass by . . . and the mountains! '*Abreks*[1] canter about the plain, and here am I driving
along and do not fear them! I have a gun, and strength, and
youth . . . and the mountains!'

CHAPTER IV

That whole part of the Térek line (about fifty miles) along
which lie the villages of the Grebénsk Cossacks is uniform in
character both as to country and inhabitants. The Térek,

---

[1] Hostile Chéchens who cross over to the Russian bank of the Térek
to thieve and plunder.

which separates the Cossacks from the mountaineers, still flows turbid and rapid though already broad and smooth, always depositing greyish sand on its low reedy right bank and washing away the steep, though not high, left bank, with its roots of century-old oaks, its rotting plane trees, and young brushwood. On the right bank lie the villages of pro-Russian, though still somewhat restless, Tartars. Along the left bank, back half a mile from the river and standing five or six miles apart from one another, are Cossack villages. In olden times most of these villages were situated on the banks of the river; but the Térek, shifting northward from the mountains year by year, washed away those banks, and now there remain only the ruins of the old villages and of the gardens of pear and plum trees and poplars, all overgrown with blackberry bushes and wild vines. No one lives there now, and one only sees the tracks of the deer, the wolves, the hares, and the pheasants, who have learned to love these places. From village to village runs a road cut through the forest as a cannon-shot might fly. Along the roads are cordons of Cossacks and watch-towers with sentinels in them. Only a narrow strip about seven hundred yards wide of fertile wooded soil belongs to the Cossacks. To the north of it begin the sand-drifts of the Nogáy or Mozdók steppes, which stretch far to the north and run, Heaven knows where, into the Trukhmén, Astrakhán, and Kirghíz-Kaisátsk steppes. To the south, beyond the Térek, are the Great Chéchnya river, the Kochkálov range, the Black Mountains, yet another range, and at last the snowy mountains, which can just be seen but have never yet been scaled. In this fertile wooded strip, rich in vegetation, has dwelt as far back as memory runs the fine warlike and prosperous Russian tribe belonging to the sect of Old Believers,[1] and called the Grebénsk Cossacks.

Long long ago their Old Believer ancestors fled from Russia and settled beyond the Térek among the Chéchens on the Grében, the first range of wooded mountains of Chéchnya.

---

[1] Old Believer is a general name for the sects that separated from the Russo-Greek Church in the seventeenth century. Tobacco is one of the things prohibited by their rules.

Living among the Chéchens the Cossacks intermarried with
them and adopted the manners and customs of the hill tribes,
though they still retained the Russian language in all its purity,
as well as their Old Faith. A tradition, still fresh among them,
declares that Tsar Iván the Terrible came to the Térek, sent
for their Elders, and gave them the land on this side of the
river, exhorting them to remain friendly to Russia and promising not to enforce his rule upon them nor oblige them to
change their faith. Even now the Cossack families claim relationship with the Chéchens, and the love of freedom, of leisure,
of plunder and of war, still form their chief characteristics.
Only the harmful side of Russian influence shows itself—by
interference at elections, by confiscation of church bells, and
by the troops who are quartered in the country or march
through it. A Cossack is inclined to hate less the *dzhigit*[2]
hillsman who maybe has killed his brother, than the soldier
quartered on him to defend his village, but who has defiled
his hut with tobacco-smoke. He respects his enemy the hillsman and despises the soldier, who is in his eyes an alien and
an oppressor. In reality, from a Cossack's point of view a Russian peasant is a foreign, savage, despicable creature, of whom
he sees a sample in the hawkers who come to the country and
in the Ukraínian immigrants whom the Cossack contemptuously calls 'wool-beaters'. For him, to be smartly dressed
means to be dressed like a Circassian. The best weapons are
obtained from the hillsmen and the best horses are bought, or
stolen, from them. A dashing young Cossack likes to show off
his knowledge of Tartar, and when carousing talks Tartar
even to his fellow Cossack. In spite of all these things this small
Christian clan stranded in a tiny corner of the earth, surrounded by half-savage Mohammedan tribes and by soldiers,
considers itself highly advanced, acknowledges none but Cossacks as human beings, and despises everybody else. The Cossack spends most of his time in the cordon, in action, or in
hunting and fishing. He hardly ever works at home. When he

---

[2] Among the Chéchens a *dzhigit* is much the same as a *brave*
among the Indians, but the word is inseparably connected with the
idea of skilful horsemanship.

stays in the village it is an exception to the general rule and then he is holiday-making. All Cossacks make their own wine, and drunkenness is not so much a general tendency as a rite, the non-fulfilment of which would be considered apostasy. The Cossack looks upon a woman as an instrument for his welfare; only the unmarried girls are allowed to amuse themselves. A married woman has to work for her husband from youth to very old age: his demands on her are the Oriental ones of submission and labour. In consequence of this outlook women are strongly developed both physically and mentally, and though they are—as everywhere in the East—nominally in subjection, they possess far greater influence and importance in family-life than Western women. Their exclusion from public life and inurement to heavy male labour give the women all the more power and importance in the household. A Cossack, who before strangers considers it improper to speak affectionately or needlessly to his wife, when alone with her is involuntarily conscious of her superiority. His house and all his property, in fact the entire homestead, has been acquired and is kept together solely by her labour and care. Though firmly convinced that labour is degrading to a Cossack and is only proper for a Nogáy labourer or a woman, he is vaguely aware of the fact that all he makes use of and calls his own is the result of that toil, and that it is in the power of the woman (his mother or his wife) whom he considers his slave, to deprive him of all he possesses. Besides, the continuous performance of man's heavy work and the responsibilities entrusted to her have endowed the Grebénsk women with a peculiarly independent masculine character and have remarkably developed their physical powers, common sense, resolution, and stability. The women are in most cases stronger, more intelligent, more developed, and handsomer than the men. A striking feature of a Grebénsk woman's beauty is the combination of the purest Circassian type of face with the broad and powerful build of Northern women. Cossack women wear the Circassian dress—a Tartar smock, *beshmet*,[3] and soft slippers—but they tie their kerchiefs

---

[3] *Beshmet,* a Tartar garment with sleeves.

round their heads in the Russian fashion. Smartness, cleanliness and elegance in dress and in the arrangement of their huts, are with them a custom and a necessity. In their relations with men the women, and especially the unmarried girls, enjoy perfect freedom.

Novomlínsk village was considered the very heart of Grebénsk Cossackdom. In it more than elsewhere the customs of the old Grebénsk population have been preserved, and its women have from time immemorial been renowned all over the Caucasus for their beauty. A Cossack's livelihood is derived from vineyards, fruit-gardens, water-melon and pumpkin plantations, from fishing, hunting, maize and millet growing, and from war plunder. Novomlínsk village lies about two and a half miles away from the Térek, from which it is separated by a dense forest. On one side of the road which runs through the village is the river; on the other, green vineyards and orchards, beyond which are seen the driftsands of the Nogáy Steppe. The village is surrounded by earth-banks and prickly bramble hedges, and is entered by tall gates hung between posts and covered with little reed-thatched roofs. Beside them on a wooden gun-carriage stands an unwieldy cannon captured by the Cossacks at some time or other, and which has not been fired for a hundred years. A uniformed Cossack sentinel with dagger and gun sometimes stands, and sometimes does not stand, on guard beside the gates, and sometimes presents arm to a passing officer and sometimes does not. Below the roof of the gateway is written in black letters on a white board: 'Houses 266: male inhabitants 897: female 1012.' The Cossacks' houses are all raised on pillars two and a half feet from the ground. They are carefully thatched with reeds and have large carved gables. If not new they are at least all straight and clean, with high porches of different shapes; and they are not built close together but have ample space around them, and are all picturesquely placed along broad streets and lanes. In front of the large bright windows of many of the houses, beyond the kitchen gardens, dark green poplars and acacias with their delicate pale verdure and scented white blossoms overtop the houses, and beside them grow flaunting yellow sunflowers, creepers, and grape vines. In the broad open square are three shops where drapery, sunflower and pumpkin seeds, locust beans and gingerbreads are sold; and surrounded by a tall fence, loftier and larger than the other houses, stands the Regimental Commander's dwelling with its casement windows, behind a row of tall poplars. Few people are to be seen in the streets of the village on week-days, especially in summer. The young men are on duty in the cordons or on military expeditions; the old ones are fishing or helping the women in the orchards and gardens. Only the very old, the sick, and the children, remain at home.

CHAPTER V

It was one of those wonderful evenings that occur only in the Caucasus. The sun had sunk behind the mountains but it was still light. The evening glow had spread over a third of the sky, and against its brilliancy the dull white immensity of the mountains was sharply defined. The air was rarefied, motionless, and full of sound. The shadow of the mountains reached for several miles over the steppe. The steppe, the opposite side of the river, and the roads, were all deserted. If very occasionally mounted men appeared, the Cossacks in the cordon and the Chéchens in their *aouls* (villages) watched them with surprised curiosity and tried to guess who those questionable men could be. At nightfall people from fear of one another flock to their dwellings, and only birds and beasts fearless of man prowl in those deserted spaces. Talking merrily, the women who have been tying up the vines hurry away from the gardens before sunset. The vineyards, like all the surrounding district, are deserted, but the villages become very animated at that time of the evening. From all sides, walking, riding, or driving in their creaking carts, people move towards the village. Girls with their smocks tucked up and twigs in their hands run chatting merrily to the village gates to meet the cattle that are crowding together in a cloud of dust and mosquitoes which they bring with them from the steppe. The

well-fed cows and buffaloes disperse at a run all over the
streets and Cossack women in coloured *beshmets* go to and fro
among them. You can hear their merry laughter and shrieks
mingling with the lowing of the cattle. There an armed and
mounted Cossack, on leave from the cordon, rides up to a hut
and, leaning towards the window, knocks. In answer to the
knock the handsome head of a young woman appears at the
window and you can hear caressing, laughing voices. There
a tattered Nogáy labourer, with prominent cheek-bones, brings
a load of reeds from the steppes, turns his creaking cart into
the Cossack captain's broad and clean courtyard, and lifts the
yoke off the oxen that stand tossing their heads while he and
his master shout to one another in Tartar. Past a puddle that
reaches nearly across the street, a barefooted Cossack woman
with a bundle of firewood on her back makes her laborious
way by clinging to the fences, holding her smock high and
exposing her white legs. A Cossack returning from shooting
calls out in jest: 'Lift it higher, shameless thing!' and points
his gun at her. The woman lets down her smock and drops the
wood. An old Cossack, returning home from fishing with his
trousers tucked up and his hairy grey chest uncovered, has a
net across his shoulder containing silvery fish that are still struggling; and to take a short cut climbs over his neighbour's
broken fence and gives a tug to his coat which has caught on
the fence. There a woman is dragging a dry branch along and
from round the corner comes the sound of an axe. Cossack
children, spinning their tops wherever there is a smooth place
in the street, are shrieking; women are climbing over fences to
avoid going round. From every chimney rises the odorous
kisyak[1] smoke. From every homestead comes the sound of increased bustle, precursor to the stillness of night.

Granny Ulítka, the wife of the Cossack cornet who is also
teacher in the regimental school, goes out to the gates of her
yard like the other women, and waits for the cattle which her
daughter Maryánka is driving along the street. Before she has
had time fully to open the wattle gate in the fence, an enor-

---

[1] *Kisyak,* fuel made of straw and manure.

mous buffalo cow surrounded by mosquitoes rushes up bellow-
ing and squeezes in. Several well-fed cows slowly follow her,
their large eyes gazing with recognition at their mistress as
they swish their sides with their tails. The beautiful and
shapely Maryánka enters at the gate and throwing away her
switch quickly slams the gate to and rushes with all the speed
of her nimble feet to separate and drive the cattle into their
sheds. 'Take off your slippers, you devil's wench!' shouts her
mother, 'you've worn them into holes!' Maryánka is not at all
offended at being called a 'devil's wench', but accepting it as
a term of endearment cheerfully goes on with her task. Her
face is covered with a kerchief tied round her head. She is
wearing a pink smock and a green *beshmet*. She disappears
inside the lean-to-shed in the yard, following the big fat cattle; and from the shed comes her voice as she speaks gently
and persuasively to the buffalo: 'Won't she stand still? What a
creature! Come now, come old dear!' Soon the girl and the
old woman pass from the shed to the dairy carrying two large
pots of milk, the day's yield. From the dairy chimney rises a
thin cloud of *kisyak* smoke: the milk is being used to make
clotted cream. The girl makes up the fire while her mother
goes to the gate. Twilight has fallen on the village. The air is
full of the smell of vegetables, cattle, and scented *kisyak*
smoke. From the gates and along the streets Cossack women
come running, carrying lighted rags. From the yards one hears
the snorting and quiet chewing of the cattle eased of their
milk, while in the street only the voices of women and children
sound as they call to one another. It is rare on a week-day to
hear the drunken voice of a man.

One of the Cossack wives, a tall, masculine old woman, approaches Granny Ulítka from the homestead opposite and asks
her for a light. In her hand she holds a rag.

'Have you cleared up, Granny?'

'The girl is lighting the fire. Is it fire you want?' says Granny
Ulítka, proud of being able to oblige her neighbour.

Both women enter the hut, and coarse hands unused to
dealing with small articles tremblingly lift the lid of a match-
box which is a rarity in the Caucasus. The masculine-looking

new-comer sits down on the doorstep with the evident intention of having a chat.

'And is your man at the school, Mother?' she asked.

'He's always teaching the youngsters, Mother. But he writes that he'll come home for the holidays,' said the cornet's wife.

'Yes, he's a clever man, one sees; it all comes useful.'

'Of course it does.'

'And my Lukáshka is at the cordon; they won't let him come home,' said the visitor, though the cornet's wife had known all this long ago. She wanted to talk about her Lukáshka whom she had lately fitted out for service in the Cossack regiment, and whom she wished to marry to the cornet's daughter, Maryánka.

'So he's at the cordon?'

'He is, Mother. He's not been home since last holidays. The other day I sent him some shirts by Fómushkin. He says he's all right, and that his superiors are satisfied. He says they are looking out for *abreks* again. Lukáshka is quite happy, he says.'

'Ah well, thank God,' said the cornet's wife. ' "Snatcher" is certainly the only word for him.' Lukáshka was surnamed 'the Snatcher' because of his bravery in snatching a boy from a watery grave, and the cornet's wife alluded to this, wishing in her turn to say something agreeable to Lukáshka's mother.

'I thank God, Mother, that he's a good son! He's a fine fellow, everyone praises him,' says Lukáshka's mother. 'All I wish is to get him married; then I could die in peace.'

'Well, aren't there plenty of young women in the village?' answered the cornet's wife slyly as she carefully replaced the lid of the match-box with her horny hands.

'Plenty, Mother, plenty,' remarked Lukáshka's mother, shaking her head. 'There's your girl now, your Maryánka—that's the sort of girl! You'd have to search through the whole place to find such another!'

The cornet's wife knows what Lukáshka's mother is after, but though she believes him to be a good Cossack she hangs back: first because she is a cornet's wife and rich, while Lukáshka is the son of a simple Cossack and fatherless, secondly because she does not want to part with her daughter yet, but chiefly because propriety demands it.

'Well when Maryánka grows up she'll be marriageable too,' she answers soberly and modestly.

'I'll send the matchmakers to you—I'll send them! Only let me get the vineyard done and then we'll come and make our bows to you,' says Lukáshka's mother. 'And we'll make our bows to Elias Vasílich too.'

'Elias, indeed!' says the cornet's wife proudly. 'It's to me you must speak! All in its own good time.'

Lukáshka's mother sees by the stern face of the cornet's wife that it is not the time to say anything more just now, so she lights her rag with the match and says, rising; 'Don't refuse us, think of my words. I'll go, it is time to light the fire.'

As she crosses the road swinging the burning rag, she meets Maryánka, who bows.

'Ah, she's a regular queen, a splendid worker, that girl!' she thinks, looking at the beautiful maiden. 'What need for her to grow any more? It's time she was married and to a good home; married to Lukáshka!'

But Granny Ulítka had her own cares and she remained sitting on the threshold thinking hard about something, till the girl called her.

CHAPTER VI

The male population of the village spend their time on military expeditions and in the cordon—or 'at their posts', as the Cossacks say. Towards evening, that same Lukáshka the Snatcher, about whom the old women had been talking, was standing on a watch-tower of the Nízhni-Protótsk post situated on the very banks of the Térek. Leaning on the railing of the tower and screwing up his eyes, he looked now far into the distance beyond the Térek, now down at his fellow Cossacks, and occasionally he addressed the latter. The sun was already approaching the snowy range that gleamed white above the fleecy clouds. The clouds undulating at the base of the mountains grew darker and darker. The clearness of evening was noticeable in the air. A sense of freshness came from the woods, though round the post it was still hot. The voices of the talking Cossacks vibrated more sonorously than before. The moving mass of the Térek's rapid brown waters contrasted more vividly with its motionless banks. The waters were beginning to subside and here and there the wet sands gleamed drab on the banks and in the shallows. The other side of the river, just opposite the cordon, was deserted; only an immense waste of low-growing reeds stretched far away to the very foot of the mountains. On the low bank, a little to one side, could be seen the flat-roofed clay houses and the funnel-shaped chimneys of a Chéchen village. The sharp eyes of the Cossack who stood on the watch-tower followed, through the evening smoke of the pro-Russian village, the tiny moving figures of the Chéchen women visible in the distance in their red and blue garments.

Although the Cossacks expected *abreks* to cross over and attack them from the Tartar side at any moment, especially as it was May when the woods by the Térek are so dense that it is difficult to pass through them on foot and the river is shallow enough in places for a horseman to ford it, and despite the fact that a couple of days before a Cossack had arrived with a circular from the commander of the regiment announcing that spies had reported the intention of a party of some eight men to cross the Térek, and ordering special vigilance—no special vigilance was being observed in the cordon. The Cossacks, unarmed and with their horses unsaddled just as if they were at home, spent their time some in fishing, some in drinking, and some in hunting. Only the horse of the man on duty was saddled, and with its feet hobbled was moving about by the brambles near the wood, and only the sentinel had his Circassian coat on and carried a gun and sword. The corporal, a tall thin Cossack with an exceptionally long back and small hands and feet, was sitting on the earth-bank of a hut with his *beshmet* unbuttoned. On his face was the lazy, bored expression of a superior, and having shut his eyes he dropped his head upon the palm first of one hand and then of the other.

An elderly Cossack with a broad greyish-black beard was lying in his shirt, girdled with a black strap, close to the river and gazing lazily at the waves of the Térek as they monotonously foamed and swirled. Others, also overcome by the heat and half naked, were rinsing clothes in the Térek, plaiting a fishing line, or humming tunes as they lay on the hot sand of the river bank. One Cossack, with a thin face much burnt by the sun, lay near the hut evidently dead drunk, by a wall which though it had been in shadow some two hours previously was now exposed to the sun's fierce slanting rays.

Lukáshka, who stood on the watch-tower, was a tall handsome lad about twenty years old and very like his mother. His face and whole build, in spite of the angularity of youth, indicated great strength, both physical and moral. Though he had only lately joined the Cossacks at the front, it was evident from the expression of his face and the calm assurance of his attitude that he had already acquired the somewhat proud and warlike bearing peculiar to Cossacks and to men generally who continually carry arms, and that he felt he was a Cossack and fully knew his own value. His ample Circassian coat was torn in some places, his cap was on the back of his head Chéchen fashion, and his leggings had slipped below his knees. His clothing was not rich, but he wore it with that peculiar Cossack foppishness which consists in imitating the Chéchen brave. Everything on a real brave is ample, ragged, and neglected, only his weapons are costly. But these ragged clothes and these weapons are belted and worn with a certain air and matched in a certain manner, neither of which can be acquired by everybody and which at once strike the eye of a Cossack or a hillsman. Lukáshka had this resemblance to a brave. With his hands folded under his sword, and his eyes nearly closed, he kept looking at the distant Tartar village. Taken separately his features were not beautiful, but anyone who saw his stately carriage and his dark-browed intelligent face would involuntarily say 'What a fine fellow!'

'Look at the women, what a lot of them are walking about in the village,' said he in a sharp voice, languidly showing his brilliant white teeth and not addressing anyone in particular.

Nazárka who was lying below immediately lifted his head and remarked:

'They must be going for water.'

'Supposing one scared them with a gun?' said Lukáshka, laughing. 'Wouldn't they be frightened?'

'It wouldn't reach.'

'What! Mine would carry beyond. Just wait a bit, and when their feast comes round I'll go and visit Giréy Khan and drink *buza*[1] there,' said Lukáshka, angrily swishing away the mosquitoes which attached themselves to him.

A rustling in the thicket drew the Cossack's attention. A pied mongrel half-setter, searching for a scent and violently wagging its scantily furred tail, came running to the cordon. Lukáshka recognized the dog as one belonging to his neighbour, Uncle Eróshka, a hunter, and saw, following it through the thicket, the approaching figure of the hunter himself.

Uncle Eróshka was a gigantic Cossack with a broad, snow-white beard and such broad shoulders and chest that in the wood, where there was no one to compare him with, he did not look particularly tall, so well proportioned were his powerful limbs. He wore a tattered coat and, over the bands with which his legs were swathed, sandals made of undressed deer's hide tied on with strings; while on his head he had a rough little white cap. He carried over one shoulder a screen to hide behind when shooting pheasants, and a bag containing a hen for luring hawks, and a small falcon; over the other shoulder, attached by a strap, was a wild cat he had killed; and stuck in his belt behind were some little bags containing bullets, gunpowder, and bread, a horse's tail to swish away the mosquitoes, a large dagger in a torn scabbard smeared with old bloodstains, and two dead pheasants. Having glanced at the cordon he stopped.

'Hi, Lyam!' he called to the dog in such a ringing bass that it awoke an echo far away in the wood; and throwing over his

---

[1] Tartar beer made of millet.

shoulder his big gun, of the kind the Cossacks call a 'flint', he raised his cap.

'Had a good day, good people, eh?' he said, addressing the Cossacks in the same strong and cheerful voice, quite without effort, but as loudly as if he were shouting to someone on the other bank of the river.

'Yes, yes, Uncle!' answered from all sides the voices of the young Cossacks.

'What have you seen? Tell us!' shouted Uncle Eróshka, wiping the sweat from his broad red face with the sleeve of his coat.

'Ah, there's a vulture living in the plane tree here, Uncle. As soon as night comes he begins hovering round,' said Nazárka, winking and jerking his shoulder and leg.

'Come, come!' said the old man incredulously.

'Really, Uncle! You must keep watch,' replied Nazárka with a laugh.

The other Cossacks began laughing.

The wag had not seen any vulture at all, but it had long been the custom of the young Cossacks in the cordon to tease and mislead Uncle Eróshka every time he came to them.

'Eh, you fool, always lying!' exclaimed Lukáshka from the tower to Nazárka.

Nazárka was immediately silenced.

'It must be watched. I'll watch,' answered the old man to the great delight of all the Cossacks. 'But have you seen any boars?'

'Watching for boars, are you?' said the corporal, bending forward and scratching his back with both hands, very pleased at the chance of some distraction. 'It's *abreks* one has to hunt here and not boars! You've not heard anything, Uncle, have you?' he added, needlessly screwing up his eyes and showing his close-set white teeth.

'*Abreks*,' said the old man. 'No, I haven't, I say, have you any *chikhir*?[2] Let me have a drink, there's a good man. I'm

---

[2] Home-made Caucasian wine.

really quite done up. When the time comes I'll bring you some fresh meat, I really will. Give me a drink!' he added.

'Well, and are you going to watch?' inquired the corporal, as though he had not heard what the other said.

'I did mean to watch to-night,' replied Uncle Eróshka. 'Maybe, with God's help, I shall kill something for the holiday. Then you shall have a share, you shall indeed!'

'Uncle! Hallo, Uncle!' called out Lukáshka sharply from above, attracting everybody's attention. All the Cossacks looked up at him. 'Just go to the upper water-course, there's a fine herd of boars there. I'm not inventing, really! The other day one of our Cossacks shot one there. I'm telling you the truth,' added he, readjusting the musket at his back and in a tone that showed he was not joking.

'Ah! Lukáshka the Snatcher is here!' said the old man, looking up. 'Where has he been shooting?'

'Haven't you seen? I suppose you're too young!' said Lukáshka. 'Close by the ditch,' he went on seriously with a shake of the head. 'We were just going along the ditch when all at once we heard something crackling, but my gun was in its case. Elias fired suddenly. . . . But I'll show you the place, it's not far. You just wait a bit. I know every one of their footpaths. . . . Daddy Mósev,' said he, turning resolutely and almost commandingly to the corporal, 'it's time to relieve guard!' and holding aloft his gun he began to descend from the watch-tower without waiting for the order.

'Come down!' said the corporal, after Lukáshka had started, and glanced round. 'Is it your turn, Gúrka? Then go. . . . True enough your Lukáshka has become very skilful,' he went on, addressing the old man. 'He keeps going about just like you, he doesn't stay at home. The other day he killed a boar.'

CHAPTER VII

The sun had already set and the shades of night were rapidly spreading from the edge of the wood. The Cossacks finished their task round the cordon and gathered in the hut for supper. Only the old man still stayed under the plane tree watching for the vulture and pulling the string tied to the falcon's leg, but though a vulture was really perching on the plane tree it declined to swoop down on the lure. Lukashka, singing one song after another, was leisurely placing nets among the very thickest brambles to trap pheasants. In spite of his tall stature and big hands every kind of work, both rough and delicate, prospered under Lukáshka's fingers.

'Hallo, Luke!' came Nazárka's shrill, sharp voice calling him from the thicket close by. 'The Cossacks have gone in to supper.'

Nazárka, with a live pheasant under his arm, forced his way through the brambles and emerged on the footpath.

'Oh!' said Lukáshka, breaking off in his song, 'where did you get that cock pheasant? I suppose it was in my trap?'

Nazárka was of the same age as Lukáshka and had also only been at the front since the previous spring.

He was plain, thin and puny, with a shrill voice that rang in one's ears. They were neighbours and comrades. Lukáshka was sitting on the grass cross-legged like a Tartar, adjusting his nets.

'I don't know whose it was—yours, I expect.'

'Was it beyond the pit by the plane tree? Then it is mine! I set the nets last night.'

Lukáshka rose and examined the captured pheasant. After stroking the dark burnished head of the bird, which rolled its eyes and stretched out its neck in terror, Lukáshka took the pheasant in his hands.

'We'll have it in a pilau[1] to-night. You go and kill and pluck it.'

'And shall we eat it ourselves or give it to the corporal?'

'He has plenty!'

'I don't like killing them,' said Nazárka.

'Give it here!'

Lukáshka drew a little knife from under his dagger and

---

[1] A kind of stew, made with boiled rice.

gave it a swift jerk. The bird fluttered, but before it could spread its wings the bleeding head bent and quivered.

'That's how one should do it!' said Lukáshka, throwing down the pheasant. 'It will make a fat pilau.'

Nazárka shuddered as he looked at the bird.

'I say, Lukáshka, that fiend will be sending us to the ambush again to-night,' he said, taking up the bird. (He was alluding to the corporal.) 'He has sent Fómushkin to get wine, and it ought to be his turn. He always puts it on us.'

Luskáshka went whistling along the cordon.

'Take the string with you,' he shouted.

Nazárka obeyed.

'I'll give him a bit of my mind to-day, I really will,' continued Nazárka. 'Let's say we won't go; we're tired out and there's an end of it! No, really, you tell him, he'll listen to you. It's too bad!'

'Get along with you! What a thing to make a fuss about!' said Lukáshka, evidently thinking of something else. 'What bosh! If he made us turn out of the village at night now, that would be annoying: there one can have some fun, but here what is there? It's all one whether we're in the cordon or in ambush. What a fellow you are!'

'And are you going to the village?'

'I'll go for the holidays.'

'Gúrka says your Dunáyka is carrying on with Fómushkin,' said Nazárka suddenly.

'Well, let her go to the devil,' said Lukáshka, showing his regular white teeth, though he did not laugh. 'As if I couldn't find another!'

'Gúrka says he went to her house. Her husband was out and there was Fómushkin sitting and eating pie. Gúrka stopped awhile and then went away, and passing by the window he heard her say, "He's gone, the fiend. . . . Why don't you eat your pie, my own? You needn't go home for the night," she says. And Gúrka under the window says to himself, "That's fine!" '

'You're making it up.'

'No, quite true, by Heaven!'

'Well, if she's found another let her go to the devil,' said Lukáshka, after a pause. 'There's no lack of girls and I was sick of her anyway.'

'Well, see what a devil you are!' said Nazárka. 'You should make up to the cornet's girl, Maryánka. Why doesn't she walk out with any one?'

Lukáshka frowned. 'What of Maryánka? They're all alike,' said he.

'Well, you just try . . .'

'What do you think? Are girls so scarce in the village?'

And Lukáshka recommenced whistling, and went along the cordon pulling leaves and branches from the bushes as he went. Suddenly, catching sight of a smooth sapling, he drew the knife from the handle of his dagger and cut it down. 'What a ramrod it will make,' he said, swinging the sapling till it whistled through the air.

The Cossacks were sitting round a low Tartar table on the earthen floor of the clay-plastered outer room of the hut, when the question of whose turn it was to lie in ambush was raised. 'Who is to go to-night?' shouted one of the Cossacks through the open door to the corporal in the next room.

'Who is to go?' the corporal shouted back. 'Uncle Burlák has been and Fómushkin too,' said he, not quite confidently. 'You two had better go, you and Nazárka,' he went on, addressing Lukáshka. 'And Ergushóv must go too; surely he has slept it off?'

'You don't sleep it off yourself so why should he?' said Nazárka in a subdued voice.

The Cossacks laughed.

Ergushóv was the Cossack who had been lying drunk and asleep near the hut. He had only that moment staggered into the room rubbing his eyes.

Lukáshka had already risen and was getting his gun ready.

'Be quick and go! Finish your supper and go!' said the corporal; and without waiting for an expression of consent he shut the door, evidently not expecting the Cossack to obey. 'Of course,' thought he, 'if I hadn't been ordered to I wouldn't send anyone, but an officer might turn up at any moment. As it is, they say eight *abreks* have crossed over.'

'Well, I suppose I must go,' remarked Ergushóv, 'it's the regulation. Can't be helped! The times are such. I say, we must go.'

Meanwhile Lukáshka, holding a big piece of pheasant to his mouth with both hands and glancing now at Nazárka now at Ergushóv, seemed quite indifferent to what passed and only laughed at them both. Before the Cossacks were ready to go into ambush, Uncle Eróshka, who had been vainly waiting under the plane tree till night fell, entered the dark outer room.

'Well, lads,' his loud bass resounded through the low-roofed room drowning all the other voices, 'I'm going with you. You'll watch for Chéchens and I for boars!'

CHAPTER VIII

It was quite dark when Uncle Eróshka and the three Cossacks, in their cloaks and shouldering their guns, left the cordon and went towards the place on the Térek where they were to lie in ambush. Nazárka did not want to go at all, but Lukáshka shouted at him and they soon started. After they had gone a few steps in silence the Cossacks turned aside from the ditch and went along a path almost hidden by reeds till they reached the river. On its bank lay a thick black log cast up by the water. The reeds around it had been recently beaten down.

'Shall we lie here?' asked Nazárka.

'Why not?' answered Lukáshka. 'Sit down here and I'll be back in a minute. I'll only show Daddy where to go.'

'This is the best place; here we can see and not be seen,' said Ergushóv, 'so it's here we'll lie. It's a first-rate place!'

Nazárka and Ergushóv spread out their cloaks and settled down behind the log, while Lukáshka went on with Uncle Eróshka.

'It's not far from here, Daddy,' said Lukáshka, stepping softly in front of the old man; 'I'll show you where they've been—I'm the only one that knows, Daddy.'

'Show me! You're a fine fellow, a regular Snatcher!' replied the old man, also whispering.

Having gone a few steps Lukáshka stopped, stooped down over a puddle, and whistled. 'That's where they come to drink, d'you see?' He spoke in a scarcely audible voice, pointing to fresh hoof-prints.

'Christ bless you,' answered the old man. 'The boar will be in the hollow beyond the ditch,' he added. 'I'll watch, and you can go.'

Lukáshka pulled his cloak up higher and walked back alone, throwing swift glances now to the left at the wall of reeds, now to the Térek rushing by below the bank. 'I daresay he's watching or creeping along somewhere,' thought he of a possible Chéchen hillsman. Suddenly a loud rustling and a splash in the water made him start and seize his musket. From under the bank a boar leapt up—his dark outline showing for a moment against the glassy surface of the water and then disappearing among the reeds. Lukáshka pulled out his gun and aimed, but before he could fire the boar had disappeared in the thicket. Lukáshka spat with vexation and went on. On approaching the ambuscade he halted again and whistled softly. His whistle was answered and he stepped up to his comrades.

Nazárka, all curled up, was already asleep. Ergushóv sat with his legs crossed and moved slightly to make room for Lukáshka.

'How jolly it is to sit here! It's really a good place,' said he. 'Did you take him there?'

'Showed him where,' answered Lukáshka, spreading out his cloak. 'But what a big boar I roused just now close to the water! I expect it was the very one! You must have heard the crash?'

'I did hear a beast crashing through. I knew at once it was a beast. I thought to myself: "Lukáshka has roused a beast," ' Ergushóv said, wrapping himself up in his cloak. 'Now I'll go to sleep,' he added. 'Wake me when the cocks crow. We must have discipline. I'll lie down and have a nap, and then you will have a nap and I'll watch—that's the way.'

'Luckily I don't want to sleep,' answered Lukáshka.

The night was dark, warm, and still. Only on one side of the sky the stars were shining, the other and greater part was overcast by one huge cloud stretching from the mountain-tops. The black cloud, blending in the absence of any wind with the mountains, moved slowly onwards, its curved edges sharply defined against the deep starry sky. Only in front of him could the Cossack discern the Térek and the distance beyond. Behind and on both sides he was surrounded by a wall of reeds. Occasionally the reeds would sway and rustle against one another apparently without cause. Seen from down below, against the clear part of the sky, their waving tufts looked like the feathery branches of trees. Close in front at his very feet was the bank, and at its base the rushing torrent. A little farther on was the moving mass of glassy brown water which eddied rhythmically along the bank and round the shallows. Farther still, water, banks, and cloud all merged together in impenetrable gloom. Along the surface of the water floated black shadows, in which the experienced eyes of the Cossack detected trees carried down by the current. Only very rarely sheet-lightning, mirrored in the water as in a black glass, disclosed the sloping bank opposite. The rhythmic sounds of night—the rustling of the reeds, the snoring of the Cossacks, the hum of mosquitoes, and the rushing water, were every now and then broken by a shot fired in the distance, or by the gurgling of water when a piece of bank slipped down, the splash of a big fish, or the crashing of an animal breaking through the thick undergrowth in the wood. Once an owl flew past along the Térek, flapping one wing against the other rhythmically at every second beat. Just above the Cossack's head it turned towards the wood and then, striking its wings no longer after every other flap but at every flap, it flew to an old plane tree where it rustled about for a long time before settling down among the branches. At every one of these unexpected sounds the watching Cossack listened intently, straining his hearing, and screwing up his eyes while he deliberately felt for his musket.

The greater part of the night was past. The black cloud that had moved westward revealed the clear starry sky from under its torn edge, and the golden upturned crescent of the moon shone above the mountains with a reddish light. The cold began to be penetrating. Nazárka awoke, spoke a little, and fell asleep again. Lukáshka feeling bored got up, drew the knife from his dagger-handle and began to fashion his stick into a ramrod. His head was full of the Chéchens who lived over there in the mountains, and of how their brave lads came across and were not afraid of the Cossacks, and might even now be crossing the river at some other spot. He thrust himself out of his hiding-place and looked along the river but could see nothing. And as he continued looking out at intervals upon the river and at the opposite bank, now dimly distinguishable from the water in the faint moonlight, he no longer thought about the Chéchens but only of when it would be time to wake his comrades, and of going home to the village. In the village he imagined Dunáyka, his 'little soul', as the Cossacks call a man's mistress, and thought of her with vexation. Silvery mists, a sign of coming morning, glittered white above the water, and not far from him young eagles were whistling and flapping their wings. At last the crowing of a cock reached him from the distant village, followed by the long-sustained note of another, which was again answered by yet other voices.

'Time to wake them,' thought Lukáshka, who had finished his ramrod and felt his eyes growing heavy. Turning to his comrades he managed to make out which pair of legs belonged to whom, when it suddenly seemed to him that he heard something splash on the other side of the Térek. He turned again towards the horizon beyond the hills, where day was breaking under the upturned crescent, glanced at the outline of the opposite bank, at the Térek, and at the now distinctly visible driftwood upon it. For one instant it seemed to him that he was moving and that the Térek with the drifting wood remained stationary. Again he peered out. One large black log with a branch particularly attracted his attention. The tree was floating in a strange way right down the middle of the stream, neither rocking nor whirling. It even appeared not to be floating altogether with the current, but to be cross-

ing it in the direction of the shallows. Lukáshka stretching out
his neck watched it intently. The tree floated to the shallows,
stopped, and shifted in a peculiar manner. Lukáshka thought
he saw an arm stretched out from beneath the tree. 'Supposing
I killed an *abrek* all by myself!' he thought, and seized his gun
with a swift, unhurried movement, putting up his gun-rest,
placing the gun upon it, and holding it noiselessly in position.
Cocking the trigger, with bated breath he took aim, still peering out intently. 'I won't wake them,' he thought. But his heart
began beating so fast that he remained motionless, listening.
Suddenly the trunk gave a plunge and again began to float
across the stream towards our bank. 'Only not to miss . . .'
thought he, and now by the faint light of the moon he caught
a glimpse of a Tartar's head in front of the floating wood. He
aimed straight at the head which appeared to be quite near—
just at the end of his rifle's barrel. He glanced across. 'Right
enough it is an *abrek!*' he thought joyfully, and suddenly rising to his knees he again took aim. Having found the sight,
barely visible at the end of the long gun, he said: 'In the
name of the Father and of the Son', in the Cossack way learnt
in his childhood, and pulled the trigger. A flash of lightning
lit up for an instant the reeds and the water, and the sharp,
abrupt report of the shot was carried across the river, changing
into a prolonged roll somewhere in the far distance. The piece
of driftwood now floated not across, but with the current, rocking and whirling.

'Stop, I say!' exclaimed Ergushóv, seizing his musket and
raising himself behind the log near which he was lying.

'Shut up, you devil!' whispered Lukáshka, grinding his
teeth. '*Abreks!*'

'Whom have you shot?' asked Nazárka. 'Who was it, Lukáshka?'

Lukáshka did not answer. He was reloading his gun and
watching the floating wood. A little way off it stopped on a
sand-bank, and from behind it something large that rocked in
the water came into view.

'What did you shoot? Why don't you speak?' insisted the
Cossacks.

'*Abreks,* I tell you!' said Lukáshka.

'Don't humbug! Did the gun go off? . . .'

'I've killed an *abrek,* that's what I fired at,' muttered Lukáshka in a voice choked by emotion, as he jumped to his feet. 'A man was swimming . . .' he said, pointing to the sandbank. 'I killed him. Just look there.'

'Have done with your humbugging!' said Ergushóv again, rubbing his eyes.

'Have done with what? Look there,' said Lukáshka, seizing him by the shoulders and pulling him with such force that Ergushóv groaned.

He looked in the direction in which Lukáshka pointed, and discerning a body immediately changed his tone.

'O Lord! But I say, more will come! I tell you the truth,' said he softly, and began examining his musket. 'That was a scout swimming across: either the others are here already or are not far off on the other side—I tell you for sure!'

Lukáshka was unfastening his belt and taking off his Circassian coat.

'What are you up to, you idiot?' exclaimed Ergushóv. 'Only show yourself and you're lost all for nothing, I tell you true! If you've killed him he won't escape. Let me have a little powder for my musket-pan—you have some? Nazárka, you go back to the cordon and look alive; but don't go along the bank or you'll be killed,—I tell you true.'

'Catch me going alone! Go yourself!' said Nazárka angrily.

Having taken off his coat, Lukáshka went down to the bank.

'Don't go in, I tell you!' said Ergushóv, putting some powder on the pan. 'Look, he's not moving. I can see. It's nearly morning; wait till they come from the cordon. You go, Nazárka. You're afraid! Don't be afraid, I tell you.'

'Luke, I say, Lukáshka! Tell us how you did it!' said Nazárka.

Lukáshka changed his mind about going into the water just then. 'Go quick to the cordon and I will watch. Tell the Cossacks to send out the patrol. If the *abreks* are on this side they must be caught,' said he.

'That's what I say. They'll get off,' said Ergushóv, rising. 'True they must be caught!'

Ergushóv and Nazárka rose and, crossing themselves, started off for the cordon—not along the river bank but breaking their way through the brambles to reach a path in the wood.

'Now mind, Lukáshka—they may cut you down here, so you'd best keep a sharp look-out, I tell you!'

'Go along; I know,' muttered Lukáshka; and having examined his gun again he sat down behind the log.

He remained alone and sat gazing at the shallows and listening for the Cossacks; but it was some distance to the cordon and he was tormented by impatience. He kept thinking that the other *abreks* who were with the one he had killed would escape. He was vexed with the *abreks* who were going to escape just as he had been with the boar that had escaped the evening before. He glanced round and at the opposite bank, expecting every moment to see a man, and having arranged his gun-rest he was ready to fire. The idea that he might himself be killed never entered his head.

CHAPTER IX

It was growing light. The Chéchen's body which was gently rocking in the shallow water was now clearly visible. Suddenly the reeds rustled not far from Luke and he heard steps and saw the feathery tops of the reeds moving. He set his gun at full cock and muttered: 'In the name of the Father and of the Son,' but when the cock clicked the sound of steps ceased.

'Hullo, Cossacks! Don't kill your Daddy!' said a deep bass voice calmly; and moving the reeds apart Daddy Eróshka came up close to Luke.

'I very nearly killed you, by God I did!' said Lukáshka.

'What have you shot?' asked the old man.

His sonorous voice resounded through the wood and downward along the river, suddenly dispelling the mysterious quiet of night around the Cossack. It was as if everything had suddenly become lighter and more distinct.

'There now, Uncle, you have not seen anything, but I've killed a beast,' said Lukáshka, uncocking his gun and getting up with unnatural calmness.

The old man was staring intently at the white back, now clearly visible, against which the Térek rippled.

'He was swimming with a log on his back. I spied him out! . . . Look there. There! He's got blue trousers, and a gun I think. . . . Do you see?' inquired Luke.

'How can one help seeing?' said the old man angrily, and a serious and stern expression appeared on his face. 'You've killed a brave,' he said, apparently with regret.

'Well, I sat here and suddenly saw something dark on the other side. I spied him when he was still over there. It was as if a man had come there and fallen in. Strange! And a piece of driftwood, a good-sized piece, comes floating, not with the stream but across it; and what do I see but a head appearing from under it! Strange! I stretched out of the reeds but could see nothing; then I rose and he must have heard, the beast, and crept out into the shallow and looked about. "No, you don't!" I said, as soon as he landed and looked round, "you won't get away!" Oh, there was something choking me! I got my gun ready but did not stir, and looked out. He waited a little and then swam out again; and when he came into the moonlight I could see his whole back. "In the name of the Father and of the Son and of the Holy Ghost" . . . and through the smoke I see him struggling. He moaned, or so it seemed to me. "Ah," I thought, "the Lord be thanked, I've killed him!" And when he drifted on to the sand-bank I could see him distinctly: he tried to get up but couldn't. He struggled a bit and then lay down. Everything could be seen. Look, he does not move—he must be dead! The Cossacks have gone back to the cordon in case there should be any more of them.'

'And so you got him!' said the old man. 'He is far away now, my lad! . . .' And again he shook his head sadly.

Just then the sound reached them of breaking bushes and the loud voices of Cossacks approaching along the bank on horseback and on foot. 'Are you bringing the skiff?' shouted Lukáshka.

'You're a trump, Luke! Lug it to the bank!' shouted one of the Cossacks.

Without waiting for the skiff Lukáshka began to undress, keeping an eye all the while on his prey.

'Wait a bit, Nazárka is bringing the skiff,' shouted the corporal.

'You fool! Maybe he is alive and only pretending! Take your dagger with you!' shouted another Cossack.

'Get along,' cried Luke, pulling off his trousers. He quickly undressed and, crossing himself, jumped, plunging with a splash into the river. Then with long strokes of his white arms, lifting his back high out of the water and breathing deeply, he swam across the current of the Térek towards the shallows. A crowd of Cossacks stood on the bank talking loudly. Three horsemen rode off to patrol. The skiff appeared round a bend. Lukáshka stood up on the sand-bank, leaned over the body, and gave it a couple of shakes. 'Quite dead!' he shouted in a shrill voice.

The Chéchen had been shot in the head. He had on a pair of blue trousers, a shirt, and a Circassian coat, and a gun and dagger were tied to his back. Above all these a large branch was tied, and it was this which at first had misled Lukáshka.

'What a carp you've landed!' cried one of the Cossacks who had assembled in a circle, as the body, lifted out of the skiff, was laid on the bank, pressing down the grass.

'How yellow he is!' said another.

'Where have our fellows gone to search? I expect the rest of them are on the other bank. If this one had not been a scout he would not have swum that way. Why else should he swim alone?' said a third.

'Must have been a smart one to offer himself before the others; a regular brave!' said Lukáshka mockingly, shivering as he wrung out his clothes that had got wet on the bank.

'His beard is dyed and cropped.'

'And he has tied a bag with a coat in it to his back.'

'That would make it easier for him to swim,' said some-one.

'I say, Lukáshka,' said the corporal, who was holding the dagger and gun taken from the dead man. 'Keep the dagger for yourself and the coat too; but I'll give you three rubles for the gun. You see it has a hole in it,' said he, blowing into the muzzle. 'I want it just for a souvenir.'

Lukáshka did not answer. Evidently this sort of begging vexed him but he knew it could not be avoided.

'See, what a devil!' said he, frowning and throwing down the Chéchen's coat. 'If at least it were a good coat, but it's a mere rag.'

'It'll do to fetch firewood in,' said one of the Cossacks.

'Mósev, I'll go home,' said Lukáshka, evidently forgetting his vexation and wishing to get some advantage out of having to give a present to his superior.

'All right, you may go!'

'Take the body beyond the cordon, lads,' said the corporal, still examining the gun, 'and put a shelter over him from the sun. Perhaps they'll send from the mountains to ransom it.'

'It isn't hot yet,' said someone.

'And supposing a jackal tears him? Would that be well?' remarked another Cossack.

'We'll set a watch; if they should come to ransom him it won't do for him to have been torn.'

'Well, Lukáshka, whatever you do you must stand a pail of vodka for the lads,' said the corporal gaily.

'Of course! That's the custom,' chimed in the Cossacks. 'See what luck God has sent you! Without ever having seen anything of the kind before, you've killed a brave!'

'Buy the dagger and coat and don't be stingy, and I'll let you have the trousers too,' said Lukáshka. 'They're too tight for me; he was a thin devil.'

One Cossack bought the coat for a ruble and another gave the price of two pails of vodka for the dagger.

'Drink, lads! I'll stand you a pail!' said Luke. 'I'll bring it myself from the village.'

'And cut up the trousers into kerchiefs for the girls!' said Nazárka.

The Cossacks burst out laughing.

'Have done laughing!' said the corporal. 'And take the body away. Why have you put the nasty thing by the hut?'

'What are you standing there for? Haul him along, lads!' shouted Lukáshka in a commanding voice to the Cossacks, who reluctantly took hold of the body, obeying him as though he were their chief. After dragging the body along for a few steps the Cossacks let fall the legs, which dropped with a life-less jerk, and stepping apart they then stood silent for a few moments. Nazárka came up and straightened the head, which was turned to one side so that the round wound above the temple and the whole of the dead man's face were visible. 'See what a mark he has made right in the brain,' he said. 'He won't get lost. His owners will always know him!' No one answered, and again the Angel of Silence flew over the Cossacks.

The sun had risen high and its diverging beams were lighting up the dewy grass. Near by, the Térek murmured in the awakened wood and, greeting the morning, the pheasants called to one another. The Cossacks stood still and silent around the dead man, gazing at him. The brown body, with nothing on but the wet blue trousers held by a girdle over the sunken stomach, was well shaped and handsome. The muscular arms lay stretched straight out by his sides; the blue, freshly shaven, round head with the clotted wound on one side of it was thrown back. The smooth tanned forehead contrasted sharply with the shaven part of the head. The open glassy eyes with lowered pupils stared upwards, seeming to gaze past everything. Under the red trimmed moustache the fine lips, drawn at the corners, seemed stiffened into a smile of good-natured subtle raillery. The fingers of the small hands covered with red hairs were bent inward, and the nails were dyed red.

Lukáshka had not yet dressed. He was wet. His neck was redder and his eyes brighter than usual, his broad jaws twitched, and from his healthy body a hardly perceptible steam rose in the fresh morning air.

'He too was a man!' he muttered, evidently admiring the corpse.

'Yes, if you had fallen into his hands you would have had short shrift,' said one of the Cossacks.

The Angel of Silence had taken wing. The Cossacks began bustling about and talking. Two of them went to cut brushwood for a shelter, others strolled towards the cordon. Luke and Nazárka ran to get ready to go to the village.

Half an hour later they were both on their way homewards, talking incessantly and almost running through the dense woods which separated the Térek from the village.

'Mind, don't tell her I sent you, but just go and find out if her husband is at home,' Luke was saying in his shrill voice.

'And I'll go round to Yámka too,' said the devoted Nazárka. 'We'll have a spree, shall we?'

'When should we have one if not to-day?' replied Luke.

When they reached the village the two Cossacks drank, and lay down to sleep till evening.

CHAPTER X

On the third day after the events above described, two companies of a Caucasian infantry regiment arrived at the Cossack village of Novomlínsk. The horses had been unharnessed and the companies' wagons were standing in the square. The cooks had dug a pit, and with logs gathered from various yards (where they had not been sufficiently securely stored) were now cooking the food; the pay-sergeants were settling accounts with the soldiers. The Service Corps men were driving piles in the ground to which to tie the horses, and the quartermasters were going about the streets just as if they were at home, showing officers and men to their quarters. Here were green ammunition boxes in a line, the company's carts, horses, and cauldrons in which buckwheat porridge was being cooked. Here were the captain and the lieutenant and the sergeant-major, Onísim Mikháylovich, and all this was in the Cossack village where it was reported that the companies were ordered to take up their quarters: therefore they were at home here. But why they were stationed there, who the Cossacks were, and whether they wanted the troops to be there, and whether they were Old Believers[1] or not—was all quite immaterial. Having received their pay and been dismissed, tired out and covered with dust, the soldiers noisily and in disorder, like a swarm of bees about to settle, spread over the squares and streets: quite regardless of the Cossacks' ill will, chattering merrily and with their muskets clinking, by twos and threes they entered the huts and hung up their accoutrements, unpacked their bags, and bantered the women. At their favourite spot, round the porridge-cauldrons, a large group of soldiers assembled and with little pipes between their teeth they gazed, now at the smoke which rose into the hot sky, becoming visible when it thickened into white clouds as it rose, and now at the camp fires which were quivering in the pure air like molten glass, and bantered and made fun of the Cossack men and women because they do not live at all like Russians. In all the yards one could see soldiers and hear their laughter and the exasperated and shrill cries of Cossack women defending their houses and refusing to give the soldiers water or cooking utensils. Little boys and girls, clinging to their mothers and to each other, followed all the movements of the troopers (never before seen by them) with frightened curiosity, or ran after them at a respectful distance. The old Cossacks came out silently and dismally and sat on the earthen embankments of their huts, and watched the soldiers' activity with an air of leaving it all to the will of God without understanding what would come of it.

Olénin, who had joined the Caucasian Army as a cadet three

---

[1] As already mentioned, the Old Believers, among other peculiarities, had a strong religious disapproval of the use of tobacco ('Not that which goeth into the mouth defileth a man; but that which cometh out of the mouth, this defileth a man.' Matt. xv. 11). This made the presence of Russian soldiers, who smoke, particularly objectionable to Old Believers.

months before, was quartered in one of the best houses in the village, the house of the cornet, Elias Vasílich—that is to say at Granny Ulítka's.

'Goodness knows what it will be like, Dmítri Andréich,' said the panting Vanyúsha to Olénin, who, dressed in a Circassian coat and mounted on a Kabardá[2] horse which he had bought in Gróznoe, was after a five-hours' march gaily entering the yard of the quarters assigned to him.

'Why, what's the matter?' he asked, caressing his horse and looking merrily at the perspiring, dishevelled, and worried Vanyúsha, who had arrived with the baggage wagons and was unpacking.

Olénin looked quite a different man. In place of his clean-shaven lips and chin he had a youthful moustache and a small beard. Instead of a sallow complexion, the result of nights turned into day, his cheeks, his forehead, and the skin behind his ears were now red with healthy sunburn. In place of a clean new black suit he wore a dirty white Circassian coat with a deeply pleated skirt, and he bore arms. Instead of a freshly starched collar, his neck was tightly clasped by the red band of his silk *beshmet.* He wore Circassian dress but did not wear it well, and anyone would have known him for a Russian and not a Tartar brave. It was the thing—but not the real thing. But for all that, his whole person breathed health, joy, and satisfaction.

'Yes, it seems funny to you,' said Vanyúsha, 'but just try to talk to these people yourself: they set themselves against one and there's an end of it. You can't get as much as a word out of them.' Vanyúsha angrily threw down a pail on the threshold. 'Somehow they don't seem like Russians.'

'You should speak to the Chief of the Village!'

'But I don't know where he lives,' said Vanyúsha in an offended tone.

'Who has upset you so?' asked Olénin, looking round.

'The devil only knows. Faugh! There is no real master here.

---

[2] Kabardá is a district in the Terék Territory of the Caucasus, and the Kabardá horses are famous for their powers of endurance.

They say he has gone to some kind of *kriga*,[3] and the old woman is a real devil. God preserve us!' answered Vanyúsha, putting his hands to his head. 'How we shall live here I don't know. They are worse than Tartars, I do declare—though they consider themselves Christians! A Tartar is bad enough, but all the same he is more noble. Gone to the *kriga* indeed! What this *kriga* they have invented is, I don't know!' concluded Vanyúsha, and turned aside.

'It's not as it is in the serfs' quarters at home, eh?' chaffed Olénin without dismounting.

'Please sir, may I have your horse?' said Vanyúsha, evidently perplexed by this new order of things but resigning himself to his fate.

'So a Tartar is more noble, eh, Vanyúsha?' repeated Olénin, dismounting and slapping the saddle.

'Yes, you're laughing! You think it funny,' muttered Vanyúsha angrily.

'Come, don't be angry, Vanyúsha,' replied Olénin, still smiling. 'Wait a minute, I'll go and speak to the people of the house; you'll see I shall arrange everything. You don't know what a jolly life we shall have here. Only don't get upset.'

Vanyúsha did not answer. Screwing up his eyes he looked contemptuously after his master, and shook his head. Vanyúsha regarded Olénin as only his master, and Olénin regarded Vanyúsha as only his servant; and they would both have been much surprised if anyone had told them that they were friends, as they really were without knowing it themselves. Vanyúsha had been taken into his proprietor's house when he was only eleven and when Olénin was the same age. When Olénin was fifteen he gave Vanyúsha lessons for a time and taught him to read French, of which the latter was inordinately proud; and when in specially good spirits he still let off French words, always laughing stupidly when he did so.

Olénin ran up the steps of the porch and pushed open the door of the hut. Maryánka, wearing nothing but a pink

---

[3] A *kriga* is a place on the river-bank fenced in for fishing.

smock, as all Cossack women do in the house, jumped away
from the door, frightened, and pressing herself against the wall
covered the lower part of her face with the broad sleeve of her
Tartar smock. Having opened the door wider, Olénin in the
semi-darkness of the passage saw the whole tall, shapely figure of the young Cossack girl. With the quick and eager curiosity of youth he involuntarily noticed the firm maidenly
form revealed by the fine print smock, and the beautiful black
eyes fixed on him with childlike terror and wild curiosity. 'This
is *she*,' thought Olénin. 'But there will be many others like her'
came at once into his head, and he opened the inner door. Old
Granny Ulítka, also dressed only in a smock, was stooping with
her back turned to him, sweeping the floor.

'Good-day to you, Mother! I've come about my lodgings,'
he began.

The Cossack woman, without unbending, turned her severe but still handsome face towards him.

'What have you come here for? Want to mock at us, eh? I'll
teach you to mock; may the black plague seize you!' she
shouted, looking askance from under her frowning brow at the
new-comer.

Olénin had at first imagined that the way-worn, gallant
Caucasian Army (of which he was a member) would be
everywhere received joyfully, and especially by the Cossacks,
our comrades in the war; and he therefore felt perplexed
by this reception. Without losing presence of mind however
he tried to explain that he meant to pay for his lodgings, but
the old woman would not give him a hearing.

'What have you come for? Who wants a pest like you, with
your scraped face? You just wait a bit; when the master returns he'll show you your place. I don't want your dirty
money! A likely thing—just as if we had never seen any! You'll
stink the house out with your beastly tobacco and want to put
it right with money! Think we've never seen a pest! May you
be shot in your bowels and your heart!' shrieked the old
woman in a piercing voice, interrupting Olénin.

'It seems Vanyúsha was right!' thought Olénin. ' "A Tartar
would be nobler",' and followed by Granny Ulítka's abuse he

went out of the hut. As he was leaving, Maryánka, still wearing only her pink smock, but with her forehead covered down to her eyes by a white kerchief, suddenly slipped out from the passage past him. Pattering rapidly down the steps with her bare feet she ran from the porch, stopped, and looking round hastily with laughing eyes at the young man, vanished round the corner of the hut.

Her firm youthful step, the untamed look of the eyes glistening from under the white kerchief, and the firm stately build of the young beauty, struck Olénin even more powerfully than before. 'Yes, it must be *she*,' he thought, and troubling his head still less about the lodgings, he kept looking round at Maryánka as he approached Vanyúsha.

'There you see, the girl too is quite savage, just like a wild filly!' said Vanyúsha, who though still busy with the luggage wagon had now cheered up a bit. '*La fame!*' he added in a loud triumphant voice and burst out laughing.

CHAPTER XI

Towards evening the master of the house returned from his fishing, and having learnt that the cadet would pay for the lodging, pacified the old woman and satisfied Vanyúsha's demands.

Everything was arranged in the new quarters. Their hosts moved into the winter hut and let their summer hut to the cadet for three rubles a month. Olénin had something to eat and went to sleep. Towards evening he woke up, washed and made himself tidy, dined, and having lit a cigarette sat down by the window that looked onto the street. It was cooler. The slanting shadow of the hut with its ornamental gables fell across the dusty road and even bent upwards at the base of the wall of the house opposite. The steep reed-thatched roof of that house shone in the rays of the setting sun. The air grew fresher. Everything was peaceful in the village. The soldiers had settled down and become quiet. The herds had not yet

been driven home and the people had not returned from their
work.

Olénin's lodging was situated almost at the end of the village.
At rare intervals, from somewhere far beyond the Térek in
those parts whence Olénin had just come (the Chéchen or the
Kumýtsk plain), came muffled sounds of firing. Olénin was feeling very well contented after three months of bivouac life.
His newly washed face was fresh and his powerful body clean
(an unaccustomed sensation after the campaign) and in all
his rested limbs he was conscious of a feeling of tranquillity
and strength. His mind, too, felt fresh and clear. He thought
of the campaign and of past dangers. He remembered that he
had faced them no worse than other men, and that he was
accepted as a comrade among valiant Caucasians. His Moscow
recollections were left behind Heaven knows how far! The
old life was wiped out and a quite new life had begun in
which there were as yet no mistakes. Here as a new man
among new men he could gain a new and good reputation. He
was conscious of a youthful and unreasoning joy of life. Looking now out of the window at the boys spinning their tops in
the shadow of the house, now round his neat new lodging, he
thought how pleasantly he would settle down to this new
Cossack village life. Now and then he glanced at the mountains and the blue sky, and an appreciation of the solemn
grandeur of nature mingled with his reminiscences and
dreams. His new life had begun, not as he imagined it would
when he left Moscow, but unexpectedly well. 'The mountains,
the mountains, the mountains!' they permeated all his thoughts
and feelings.

'He's kissed his dog and licked the jug! . . . Daddy
Eróshka has kissed his dog!' suddenly the little Cossacks who
had been spinning their tops under the window shouted, looking towards the side street. 'He's drunk his bitch, and his dagger!' shouted the boys, crowding together and stepping backwards.

These shouts were addressed to Daddy Eróshka, who with
his gun on his shoulder and some pheasants hanging at his
girdle was returning from his shooting expedition.

'I have done wrong, lads, I have!' he said, vigorously swinging his arms and looking up at the windows on both sides of
the street. 'I have drunk the bitch; it was wrong,' he repeated,
evidently vexed but pretending not to care.

Olénin was surprised by the boys' behaviour towards the
old hunter, but was still more struck by the expressive, intelligent face and the powerful build of the man whom they
called Daddy Eróshka.

'Here Daddy, here Cossack!' he called. 'Come here!'

The old man looked into the window and stopped.

'Good evening, good man,' he said, lifting his little cap off
his cropped head.

'Good evening, good man,' replied Olénin. 'What is it the
youngsters are shouting at you?'

Daddy Eróshka came up to the window. 'Why they're
teasing the old man. No matter, I like it. Let them joke about
their old daddy,' he said with those firm musical intona-
tions with which old and venerable people speak. 'Are you
an army commander?' he added.

'No, I am a cadet. But where did you kill those pheasants?'
asked Olénin.

'I dispatched these three hens in the forest,' answered the
old man, turning his broad back towards the window to show
the hen pheasants which were hanging with their heads
tucked into his belt and staining his coat with blood. 'Haven't
you seen any?' he asked. 'Take a brace if you like! Here you
are,' and he handed two of the pheasants in at the window.
'Are you a sportsman yourself?' he asked.

'I am. During the campaign I killed four myself.'

'Four? What a lot!' said the old man sarcastically. 'And are
you a drinker? Do you drink *chikhir?*"

'Why not? I like a drink.'

'Ah, I see you are a tramp! We shall be *kunaks,*[1] you and
I,' said Daddy Eróshka.

'Step in,' said Olénin. 'We'll have a drop of *chikhir.*'

'I might as well,' said the old man, 'but take the pheasants.'

---

[1] *Kunak,* a sworn friend for whose sake no sacrifice is too great.

The old man's face showed that he liked the cadet. He had
seen at once that he could get free drinks from him, and that
therefore it would be all right to give him a brace of pheasants.

Soon Daddy Eróshka's figure appeared in the doorway of
the hut, and it was only then that Olénin became fully conscious of the enormous size and sturdy build of this man,
whose red-brown face with its perfectly white broad beard
was all furrowed by deep lines produced by age and toil. For
an old man, the muscles of his legs, arms, and shoulders were
quite exceptionally large and prominent. There were deep
scars on his head under the short-cropped hair. His thick
sinewy neck was covered with deep intersecting folds like a
bull's. His horny hands were bruised and scratched. He
stepped lightly and easily over the threshold, unslung his gun
and placed it in a corner, and casting a rapid glance round
the room noted the value of the goods and chattels deposited
in the hut, and with out-turned toes stepped softly, in his sandals of raw hide, into the middle of the room. He brought
with him a penetrating but not unpleasant smell of *chikhír*
wine, vodka, gunpowder, and congealed blood.

Daddy Eróshka bowed down before the icons, smoothed
his beard, and approaching Olénin held out his thick brown
hand. '*Koshkíldy,*' said he; 'That is Tartar for "Good-day"—
"Peace be unto you," it means in their tongue.'

'*Koshkíldy*, I know,' answered Olénin, shaking hands.

'Eh, but you don't, you won't know the right order! Fool!'
said Daddy Eróshka, shaking his head reproachfully. 'If anyone says "*Koshkíldy*" to you, you must say "*Allah rasi bo sun*,"
that is, "God save you." That's the way, my dear fellow, and
not "*Koshkíldy*." But I'll teach you all about it. We had a fellow here, Elias Mosévich, one of your Russians, he and I were
kunaks. He was a trump, a drunkard, a thief, a sportsman—
and what a sportsman! I taught him everything.'

'And what will you teach me?' asked Olénin, who was becoming more and more interested in the old man.

'I'll take you hunting and teach you to fish. I'll show you
Chéchens and find a girl for you, if you like—even that!

That's the sort I am! I'm a wag!'—and the old man laughed. 'I'll sit down. I'm tired. *Karga?*' he added inquiringly.

'And what does *"Karga"* mean?' asked Olénin.

'Why, that means "All right" in Georgian. But I say it just so. It is a way I have, it's my favourite word. *Karga, Karga.* I say it just so; in fun I mean. Well, lad, won't you order the *chikhir?* You've got an orderly, haven't you? Hey, Iván!' shouted the old man. 'All your soldiers are Iváns. Is yours Iván?'

'True enough, his name is Iván—Vanyúsha.[2] Here Vanyúsha! Please get some *chikhir* from our landlady and bring it here.'

'Iván or Vanyúsha, that's all one. Why are all your soldiers Iváns? Iván, old fellow,' said the old man, 'you tell them to give you some from the barrel they have begun. They have the best *chikhir* in the village. But don't give more than thirty kopeks for the quart, mind, because that witch would be only too glad. . . . Our people are anathema people; stupid people,' Daddy Eróshka continued in a confidential tone after Vanyúsha had gone out. 'They do not look upon you as on men, you are worse than a Tartar in their eyes. "Worldly Russians" they say. But as for me, though you are a soldier you are still a man, and have a soul in you. Isn't that right? Elias Mosévich was a soldier, yet what a treasure of a man he was! Isn't that so, my dear fellow? That's why our people don't like me; but I don't care! I'm a merry fellow, and I like everybody. I'm Eróshka; yes, my dear fellow.'

And the old Cossack patted the young man affectionately on the shoulder.

CHAPTER XII

Vanyúsha, who meanwhile had finished his housekeeping arrangements and had even been shaved by the company's barber and had pulled his trousers out of his high boots as a sign that the company was stationed in comfortable quarters,

---

[2] Vanyúsha is a diminutive form of 'Iván'.

was in excellent spirits. He looked attentively but not benev-
olently at Eróshka, as at a wild beast he had never seen before, shook his head at the floor which the old man had
dirtied and, having taken two bottles from under a bench,
went to the landlady.

'Good evening, kind people,' he said, having made up his
mind to be very gentle. 'My master has sent me to get some
chikhir, will you draw some for me, good folk?'

The old woman gave no answer. The girl, who was arranging the kerchief on her head before a little Tartar mirror,
looked round at Vanyúsha in silence.

'I'll pay money for it, honoured people,' said Vanyúsha,
jingling the coppers in his pocket. 'Be kind to us and we
too will be kind to you,' he added.

'How much?' asked the old woman abruptly.

'A quart.'

'Go, my own, draw some for them,' said Granny Ulítka to
her daughter. 'Take it from the cask that's begun, my precious.'

The girl took the keys and a decanter and went out of the
hut with Vanyúsha.

'Tell me, who is that young woman?' asked Olénin, pointing to Maryánka, who was passing the window. The old man
winked and nudged the young man with his elbow.

'Wait a bit,' said he and reached out of the window.
'Khm,' he coughed, and bellowed 'Maryánka dear. Hallo,
Maryánka, my girlie, won't you love me, darling? I'm a wag,'
he added in a whisper to Olénin. The girl, not turning her
head and swinging her arms regularly and vigorously, passed
the window with the peculiarly smart and bold gait of a Cossack woman and only turned her dark shaded eyes slowly towards the old man.

'Love me and you'll be happy,' shouted Eróshka, winking,
and he looked questioningly at the cadet.

'I'm a fine fellow, I'm a wag!' he added. 'She's a regular
queen, that girl. Eh?'

'She is lovely,' said Olénin. 'Call her here!'

'No, no,' said the old man. 'For that one a match is being
arranged with Lukáshka, Luke, a fine Cossack, a brave, who

killed an *abrek* the other day. I'll find you a better one. I'll find you one that will be all dressed up in silk and silver. Once I've said it I'll do it. I'll get you a regular beauty!'

'You, an old man—and say such things,' replied Olénin. 'Why, it's a sin!'

'A sin? Where's the sin?' said the old man emphatically. 'A sin to look at a nice girl? A sin to have some fun with her? Or is it a sin to love her? Is that so in your parts? . . . No, my dear fellow, it's not a sin, it's salvation! God made you and God made the girl too. He made it all; so it is no sin to look at a nice girl. That's what she was made for; to be loved and to give joy. That's how I judge it, my good fellow.'

Having crossed the yard and entered a cool dark store-room filled with barrels, Maryánka went up to one of them and re-peating the usual prayer plunged a dipper into it. Vanyúsha standing in the doorway smiled as he looked at her. He thought it very funny that she had only a smock on, close-fitting behind and tucked up in front, and still funnier that she wore a necklace of silver coins. He thought this quite un-Russian and that they would all laugh in the serfs' quarters at home if they saw a girl like that. '*La fille comme c'est tres bien*, for a change,' he thought. 'I'll tell that to my master.'

'What are you standing in the light for, you devil!' the girl suddenly shouted. 'Why don't you pass me the decanter!'

Having filled the decanter with cool red wine, Maryánka handed it to Vanyúsha.

'Give the money to Mother,' she said, pushing away the hand in which he held the money.

Vanyúsha laughed.

'Why are you so cross, little dear?' he said good-naturedly irresolutely shuffling with his feet while the girl was covering the barrel.

She began to laugh.

'And you! Are you kind?'

'We, my master and I, are very kind,' Vanyúsha answered decidedly. 'We are so kind that wherever we have stayed our hosts were always very grateful. It's because he's generous.'

The girl stood listening.

'And is your master married?' she asked.

'No. The master is young and unmarried, because noble gentlemen can never marry young,' said Vanyúsha didactically.

'A likely thing! See what a fed-up buffalo he is—and too young to marry! Is he the chief of you all?' she asked.

'My master is a cadet; that means he's not yet an officer, but he's more important than a general—he's an important man! Because not only our colonel, but the Tsar himself, knows him,' proudly explained Vanyúsha. 'We are not like those other beggars in the line regiment, and our papa himself was a Senator. He had more than a thousand serfs, all his own, and they send us a thousand rubles at a time. That's why everyone likes us. Another may be a captain but have no money. What's the use of that?'

"Go away. I'll lock up,' said the girl, interrupting him.

Vanyúsha brought Olénin the wine and announced that *'La fille c'est tres joulie,'* and, laughing stupidly, at once went out.

CHAPTER XIII

Meanwhile the tattoo had sounded in the village square. The people had returned from their work. The herd lowed as in clouds of golden dust it crowded at the village gate. The girls and the women hurried through the streets and yards, turning in their cattle. The sun had quite hidden itself behind the distant snowy peaks. One pale bluish shadow spread over land and sky. Above the darkened gardens stars just discernible were kindling, and the sounds were gradually hushed in the village. The cattle having been attended to and left for the night, the women came out and gathered at the corners of the streets and, cracking sunflower seeds with their teeth, settled down on the earthen embankments of the houses. Later on Maryánka, having finished milking the buffalo and the other two cows, also joined one of these groups.

The group consisted of several women and girls and one old Cossack man.

They were talking about the *abrek* who had been killed. The Cossack was narrating and the women questioning him.

'I expect he'll get a handsome reward,' said one of the women.

'Of course. It's said that they'll send him a cross.'

'Mósev did try to wrong him. Took the gun away from him, but the authorities at Kizlyár heard of it.'

'A mean creature that Mósev is!'

'They say Lukáshka has come home,' remarked one of the girls.

'He and Nazárka are merry-making at Yámka's.' (Yámka was an unmarried, disreputable Cossack woman who kept an illicit pot-house.) 'I heard say they had drunk half a pailful.'

'What luck the Snatcher has,' somebody remarked. 'A real snatcher. But there's no denying he's a fine lad, smart enough for anything, a right-minded lad! His father was just such another, Daddy Kiryák was: he takes after his father. When he was killed the whole village howled. Look, there they are,' added the speaker, pointing to the Cossacks who were coming down the street towards them. 'And Ergushóv has managed to come along with them too! The drunkard!'

Lukáshka, Nazárka, and Ergushóv, having emptied half a pail of vodka, were coming towards the girls. The faces of all three, but especially that of the old Cossack, were redder than usual. Ergushóv was reeling and kept laughing and nudging Nazárka in the ribs.

'Why are you not singing?' he shouted to the girls. 'Sing to our merry-making. I tell you!'

They were welcomed with the words, 'Had a good day? Had a good day?'

'Why sing? It's not a holiday,' said one of the women. 'You're tight, so you go and sing.'

Ergushóv roared with laughter and nudged Nazárka. 'You'd better sing. And I'll begin too. I'm clever, I tell you.'

'Are you asleep, fair ones?' said Nazárka. 'We've come from the cordon to drink your health. We've already drunk Lukáshka's health.'

Lukáshka, when he reached the group, slowly raised his

cap and stopped in front of the girls. His broad cheek-bones and neck were red. He stood and spoke softly and sedately, but in his tranquillity and sedateness there was more of animation and strength than in all Nazárka's loquacity and bustle. He reminded one of a playful colt that with a snort and a flourish of its tail suddenly stops short and stands as though nailed to the ground with all four feet. Lukáshka stood quietly in front of the girls, his eyes laughed, and he spoke but little as he glanced now at his drunken companions and now at the girls. When Maryánka joined the group he raised his cap with a firm deliberate movement, moved out of her way and then stepped in front of her with one foot a little forward and with his thumbs in his belt, fingering his dagger. Maryánka answered his greeting with a leisurely bow of her head, settled down on the earth-bank, and took some seeds out of the bosom of her smock. Lukáshka, keeping his eyes fixed on Maryánka, slowly cracked seeds and spat out the shells. All were quiet when Maryánka joined the group.

'Have you come for long?' asked a woman, breaking the silence.

'Till to-morrow morning,' quietly replied Lukáshka.

'Well, God grant you get something good,' said the Cossack; 'I'm glad of it, as I've just been saying.'

'And I say so too,' put in the tipsy Ergushóv, laughing. 'What a lot of visitors have come,' he added, pointing to a soldier who was passing by. 'The soldiers' vodka is good—I like it.'

'They've sent three of the devils to us,' said one of the women. 'Grandad went to the village Elders, but they say nothing can be done.'

'Ah, ha! Have you met with trouble?' said Ergushóv.

'I expect they have smoked you out with their tobacco?' asked another woman. 'Smoke as much as you like in the yard, I say, but we won't allow it inside the hut. Not if the Elder himself comes, I won't allow it. Besides, they may rob you. He's not quartered any of them on himself, no fear, that devil's son of an Elder.'

'You don't like it?' Ergushóv began again.

'And I've also heard say that the girls will have to make the soldiers' beds and offer them *chikhir* and honey,' said Nazárka, putting one foot forward and tilting his cap like Lukáshka.

Ergushóv burst into a roar of laughter, and seizing the girl nearest to him, he embraced her. 'I tell you true.'

'Now then, you black pitch!' squealed the girl, 'I'll tell your old woman.'

'Tell her,' shouted he. 'That's quite right what Nazárka says; a circular has been sent round. He can read, you know. Quite true!' And he began embracing the next girl.

'What are you up to, you beast?' squealed the rosy, round-faced Ústenka, laughing and lifting her arm to hit him.

The Cossack stepped aside and nearly fell.

'There, they say girls have no strength, and you nearly killed me.'

'Get away, you black pitch, what devil has brought you from the cordon?' said Ústenka, and turning away from him she again burst out laughing. 'You were asleep and missed the *abrek*, didn't you? Suppose he had done for you it would have been all the better.'

'You'd have howled I expect,' said Nazárka, laughing.

'Howled! A likely thing.'

'Just look, she doesn't care. She'd howl, Nazárka, eh? Would she?' said Ergushóv.

Lukáshka all this time had stood silently looking at Maryánka. His gaze evidently confused the girl.

'Well, Maryánka! I hear they've quartered one of the chiefs on you?' he said, drawing nearer.

Maryánka, as was her wont, waited before she replied, and slowly raising her eyes looked at the Cossack. Lukáshka's eyes were laughing as if something special, apart from what was said, was taking place between himself and the girl.

'Yes, it's all right for them as they have two huts,' replied an old woman on Maryánka's behalf, 'but at Fómushkin's now they also have one of the chiefs quartered on them and they say one whole corner is packed full with his things, and the family have no room left. Was such a thing ever heard of

as that they should turn a whole horde loose in the village?'
she said. 'And what the plague are they going to do here?'

'I've heard say they'll build a bridge across the Térek,' said
one of the girls.

'And I've been told that they will dig a pit to put the girls
in because they don't love the lads,' said Nazárka, approaching Ústenka; and he again made a whimsical gesture which
set everybody laughing, and Ergushóv, passing by Maryánka,
who was next in turn, began to embrace an old woman.

'Why don't you hug Maryánka? You should do it to each
in turn,' said Nazárka.

'No, my old one is sweeter,' shouted the Cossack, kissing
the struggling old woman.

'You'll throttle me,' she screamed, laughing.

The tramp of regular footsteps at the other end of the street
interrupted their laughter. Three soldiers in their cloaks, with
their muskets on their shoulders, were marching in step to
relieve the guard by the ammunition wagon.

The corporal, an old cavalry man, looked angrily at the Cossacks and led his men straight along the road where Lukáshka
and Nazárka were standing, so that they should have to get
out of the way. Nazárka moved, but Lukáshka only screwed
up his eyes and turned his broad back without moving from
his place.

'People are standing here, so you go round,' he muttered,
half turning his head and tossing it contemptuously in the direction of the soldiers.

The soldiers passed by in silence, keeping step regularly
along the dusty road.

Maryánka began laughing and all the other girls chimed in.

'What swells!' said Nazárka, 'Just like long-skirted choris-
ters,' and he walked a few steps down the road imitating the
soldiers.

Again everyone broke into peals of laughter.

Lukáshka came slowly up to Maryánka.

'And where have you put up the chief?' he asked.

Maryánka thought for a moment.

'We've let him have the new hut,' she said.

'And is he old or young?' asked Lukáshka, sitting down beside her.

'Do you think I've asked?' answered the girl. 'I went to get him some *chikhir* and saw him sitting at the window with Daddy Eróshka. Red-headed he seemed. They've brought a whole cartload of things.'

And she dropped her eyes.

'Oh, how glad I am that I got leave from the cordon!' said Lukáshka, moving closer to the girl and looking straight in her eyes all the time.

'And have you come for long?' asked Maryánka, smiling slightly.

'Till morning. Give me some sunflower seeds,' he said, holding out his hand.

Maryánka now smiled outright and unfastened the neckband of her smock.

'Don't take them all,' she said.

'Really I felt so dull all the time without you, I swear I did,' he said in a calm, restrained whisper, helping himself to some seeds out of the bosom of the girl's smock, and stooping still closer over her he continued with laughing eyes to talk to her in low tones.

'I won't come, I tell you,' Maryánka suddenly said aloud, leaning away from him.

'No really . . . what I wanted to say to you,' . . . whispered Lukáshka. 'By the Heavens! Do come!'

Maryánka shook her head, but did so with a smile.

'Nursey Maryánka! Hallo Nursey! Mammy is calling! Supper time!' shouted Maryánka's little brother, running towards the group.

'I'm coming,' replied the girl, 'Go, my dear, go alone—I'll come in a minute.'

Lukáshka rose and raised his cap.

'I expect I had better go home too, that will be best,' he said, trying to appear unconcerned but hardly able to repress a smile, and he disappeared behind the corner of the house.

Meanwhile night had entirely enveloped the village. Bright stars were scattered over the dark sky. The streets became dark and empty. Nazárka remained with the women on the earth-bank and their laughter was still heard, but Lukáshka, having slowly moved away from the girls, crouched down like a cat and then suddenly started running lightly, holding his dagger to steady it: not homeward, however, but towards the cornet's house. Having passed two streets he turned into a lane and lifting the skirt of his coat sat down on the ground in the shadow of a fence. 'A regular cornet's daughter!' he thought about Maryánka. 'Won't even have a lark—the devil! But just wait a bit.'

The approaching footsteps of a woman attracted his attention. He began listening, and laughed all by himself. Maryánka with bowed head, striking the pales of the fences with a switch, was walking with rapid regular strides straight towards him. Lukáshka rose. Maryánka started and stopped.

'What an accursed devil! You frightened me! So you have not gone home?' she said, and laughed aloud.

Lukáshka put one arm round her and with the other hand raised her face. 'What I wanted to tell you, by Heaven!' his voice trembled and broke.

'What are you talking of, at night time!' answered Maryánka. 'Mother is waiting for me, and you'd better go to your sweetheart.'

And freeing herself from his arms she ran away a few steps. When she had reached the wattle fence of her home she stopped and turned to the Cossack who was running beside her and still trying to persuade her to stay a while with him.

'Well, what do you want to say, midnight-gadabout?' and she again began laughing.

'Don't laugh at me, Maryánka! By the Heaven! Well, what if I have a sweetheart? May the devil take her! Only say the word and now I'll love *you*—I'll do anything you wish. Here they are!' and he jingled the money in his pocket. 'Now we can live splendidly. Others have pleasures, and I? I get no pleasure from you, Maryánka dear!'

The girl did not answer. She stood before him breaking her switch into little bits with a rapid movement of her fingers.

Lukáshka suddenly clenched his teeth and fists.

'And why keep waiting and waiting? Don't I love you, darling? You can do what you like with me,' said he suddenly,
frowning angrily and seizing both her hands.

The calm expression of Maryánka's face and voice did not
change.

'Don't bluster, Lukáshka, but listen to me,' she answered,
not pulling away her hands but holding the Cossack at
arm's length. 'It's true I am a girl, but you listen to me! It
does not depend on me, but if you love me I'll tell you this. Let
go my hands, I'll tell you without.——I'll marry you, but you'll
never get any nonsense from me,' said Maryánka without
turning her face.

'What, you'll marry me? Marriage does not depend on us.
Love me yourself, Maryánka dear,' said Lukáshka, from sullen
and furious becoming again gentle, submissive, and tender,
and smiling as he looked closely into her eyes.

Maryánka clung to him and kissed him firmly on the lips.

'Brother dear!' she whispered, pressing him convulsively to
her. Then, suddenly tearing herself away, she ran into the
gate of her house without looking round.

In spite of the Cossack's entreaties to wait another minute
to hear what he had to say, Maryánka did not stop.

'Go,' she cried, 'you'll be seen! I do believe that devil, our
lodger, is walking about the yard.'

'Cornet's daughter,' thought Lukáshka. 'She will marry
me. Marriage is all very well, but you just love me!'

He found Nazárka at Yámka's house, and after having a
spree with him went to Dunáyka's house, where, in spite of
her not being faithful to him, he spent the night.

CHAPTER XIV

It was quite true that Olénin had been walking about the yard
when Maryánka entered the gate, and had heard her say,
'That devil, our lodger, is walking about.' He had spent that
evening with Daddy Eróshka in the porch of his new lodging.

He had had a table, a samovar, wine, and a candle brought out, and over a cup of tea and a cigar he listened to the tales the old man told seated on the threshold at his feet. Though the air was still, the candle dripped and flickered: now lighting up the post of the porch, now the table and crockery, now the cropped white head of the old man. Moths circled round the flame and, shedding the dust of their wings, fluttered on the table and in the glasses, flew into the candle flame, and disappeared in the black space beyond. Olénin and Eróshka had emptied five bottles of *chikhir*. Eróshka filled the glasses every time, offering one to Olénin, drinking his health, and talking untiringly. He told of Cossack life in the old days: of his father, 'The Broad', who alone had carried on his back a boar's carcass weighing three hundredweight, and drank two pails of *chikhir* at one sitting. He told of his own days and his chum Gírchik, with whom during the plague he used to smuggle felt cloaks across the Térek. He told how one morning he had killed two deer, and about his 'little soul' who used to run to him at the cordon at night. He told all this so eloquently and picturesquely that Olénin did not notice how time passed. 'Ah yes, my dear fellow, you did not know me in my golden days; then I'd have shown you things. To-day it's "Eróshka licks the jug", but then Eróshka was famous in the whole regiment. Whose was the finest horse? Who had a Gurda[1] sword? To whom should one go to get a drink? With whom go on the spree? Who should be sent to the mountains to kill Ahmet Khan? Why, always Eróshka! Whom did the girls love? Always Eróshka had to answer for it. Because I was a real brave: a drinker, a thief (I used to seize herds of horses in the mountains), a singer; I was a master of every art! There are no Cossacks like that nowadays. It's disgusting to look at them. When they're that high (Eróshka held his hand three feet from the ground) they put on idiotic boots and keep looking at them—that's all the pleasure they know. Or

---

[1] The swords and daggers most highly valued in the Caucasus are called by the name of the maker—Gurda.

they'll drink themselves foolish, not like men but all wrong. And who was I? I was Eróshka, the thief; they knew me not only in this village but up in the mountains. Tartar princes, my *kunaks,* used to come to see me! I used to be everybody's *kunak.* If he was a Tartar—with a Tartar; an Armenian— with an Armenian; a soldier—with a soldier; an officer—with an officer! I didn't care as long as he was a drinker. He says you should cleanse yourself from intercourse with the world, not drink with soldiers, not eat with a Tartar.'

'Who says all that?' asked Olénin.

'Why, our teacher! But listen to a Mullah or a Tartar Cadi. He says, "You unbelieving Giaours, why do you eat pig?" That shows that everyone has his own law. But I think it's all one. God has made everything for the joy of man. There is no sin in any of it. Take example from an animal. It lives in the Tartar's reeds or in ours. Wherever it happens to go, there is its home! Whatever God gives it, that it eats! But our people say we have to lick red-hot plates in hell for that. And I think it's all a fraud,' he added after a pause.

'What is a fraud?' asked Olénin.

'Why, what the preachers say. We had an army captain in Chervlëna who was my *kunak:* a fine fellow just like me. He was killed in Chéchnya. Well, he used to say that the preachers invent all that out of their own heads. "When you die the grass will grow on your grave and that's all!" ' The old man laughed. 'He was a desperate fellow.'

'And how old are you?' asked Olénin.

'The Lord only knows! I must be about seventy. When a Tsaritsa reigned in Russia[2] I was no longer very small. So you can reckon it out. I must be seventy.'

'Yes you must, but you are still a fine fellow.'

'Well, thank Heaven I am healthy, quite healthy, except that a woman, a witch, has harmed me. . . .'

'How?'

'Oh, just harmed me.'

'And so when you die the grass will grow?' repeated Olénin.

---

[2] Catherine the Great died in 1799.

Eróshka evidently did not wish to express his thought clearly. He was silent for a while.

'And what did you think? Drink!' he shouted suddenly, smiling and handing Olénin some wine.

CHAPTER XV

'Well, what was I saying?' he continued, trying to remember. 'Yes, that's the sort of man I am. I am a hunter. There is no hunter to equal me in the whole army. I will find and show you any animal and any bird, and what and where. I know it all! I have dogs, and two guns, and nets, and a screen and a hawk. I have everything, thank the Lord! If you are not bragging but are a real sportsman, I'll show you everything. Do you know what a man I am? When I have found a track—I know the animal. I know where he will lie down and where he'll drink or wallow. I make myself a perch and sit there all night watching. What's the good of staying at home? One only gets into mischief, gets drunk. And here women come and chatter, and boys shout at me—enough to drive one mad. It's a different matter when you go out at nightfall, choose yourself a place, press down the reeds and sit there and stay waiting, like a jolly fellow. One knows everything that goes on in the woods. One looks up at the sky: the stars move, you look at them and find out from them how the time goes. One looks round—the wood is rustling; one goes on waiting, now there comes a crackling—a boar comes to rub himself; one listens to hear the young eaglets screech and then the cocks give voice in the village, or the geese. When you hear the geese you know it is not yet midnight. And I know all about it! Or when a gun is fired somewhere far away, thoughts come to me. One thinks, who is that firing? Is it another Cossack like myself who has been watching for some animal? And has he killed it? Or only wounded it so that now the poor thing goes through the reeds smearing them with its blood all for nothing? I don't like that! Oh, how I dislike it! Why injure a beast? You fool, you fool! Or one thinks, "Maybe an *abrek* has killed some silly little Cossack." All this passes through one's mind. And once as I sat watching by the river I saw a cradle floating down. It was sound except for one corner which was broken off. Thoughts did come that time! I thought some of your soldiers, the devils, must have got into a Tartar village and seized the Chéchen women, and one of the devils has killed the little one: taken it by its legs, and hit its head against a wall. Don't they do such things? Sh! Men have no souls! And thoughts came to me that filled me with pity. I thought: they've thrown away the cradle and driven the wife out, and her brave has taken his gun and come across to our side to rob us. One watches and thinks. And when one hears a litter breaking through the thicket, something begins to knock inside one. Dear one, come this way! "They'll scent me," one thinks; and one sits and does not stir while one's heart goes dun! dun! dun! and simply lifts you. Once this spring a fine litter came near me, I saw something black. "In the name of the Father and of the Son," and I was just about to fire when she grunts to her pigs: "Danger, children," she says, "there's a man here," and off they all ran, breaking through the bushes. And she had been so close I could almost have bitten her.'

'How could a sow tell her brood that a man was there?' asked Olénin.

'What do you think? You think the beast's a fool? No, he is wiser than a man though you do call him a pig! He knows everything. Take this for instance. A man will pass along your track and not notice it; but a pig as soon as it gets onto your track turns and runs at once: that shows there is wisdom in him, since he scents your smell and you don't. And there is this to be said too: you wish to kill it and it wishes to go about the woods alive. You have one law and it has another. It is a pig, but it is no worse than you—it too is God's creature. Ah, dear! Man is foolish, foolish, foolish!' The old man repeated this several times and then, letting his head drop, he sat thinking.

Olénin also became thoughtful, and descending from the porch with his hands behind his back began pacing up and down the yard.

Eróshka, rousing himself, raised his head and began gazing intently at the moths circling round the flickering flame of the candle and burning themselves in it.

'Fool, fool!' he said. 'Where are you flying to? Fool, fool!' He rose and with his thick fingers began to drive away the moths.

'You'll burn, little fool! Fly this way, there's plenty of room.' He spoke tenderly, trying to catch them delicately by their wings with his thick fingers and then letting them fly again. 'You are killing yourself and I am sorry for you!'

He sat a long time chattering and sipping out of the bottle. Olénin paced up and down the yard. Suddenly he was struck by the sound of whispering outside the gate. Involuntarily holding his breath, he heard a woman's laughter, a man's voice, and the sound of a kiss. Intentionally rustling the grass under his feet he crossed to the opposite side of the yard, but after a while the wattle fence creaked. A Cossack in a dark Circassian coat and a white sheepskin cap passed along the other side of the fence (it was Luke), and a tall woman with a white kerchief on her head went past Olénin. 'You and I have nothing to do with one another' was what Maryánka's firm step gave him to understand. He followed her with his eyes to the porch of the hut, and he even saw her through the window take off her kerchief and sit down. And suddenly a feeling of lonely depression and some vague longings and hopes, and envy of someone or other, overcame the young man's soul.

The last lights had been put out in the huts. The last sounds had died away in the village. The wattle fences and the cattle gleaming white in the yards, the roofs of the houses and the stately poplars, all seemed to be sleeping the labourers' healthy peaceful sleep. Only the incessant ringing voices of frogs from the damp distance reached the young man. In the east the stars were growing fewer and fewer and seemed to be melting in the increasing light, but overhead they were denser and deeper than before. The old man was dozing with his head on his hand. A cock crowed in the yard opposite, but Olénin still paced up and down thinking of something. The sound of a song sung by several voices reached him and he stepped up to the fence and listened. The voices of several young Cossacks carolled a merry song, and one voice was distinguishable among them all by its firm strength.

'Do you know who is singing there?' said the old man, rousing himself. 'It is the Brave, Lukáshka. He has killed a Chéchen and now he rejoices. And what is there to rejoice at? . . . The fool, the fool!'

'And have you ever killed people?' asked Olénin.

'You devil!' shouted the old man. 'What are you asking? One must not talk so. It is a serious thing to destroy a human being. . . . Ah, a very serious thing! Good-bye, my dear fellow. I've eaten my fill and am drunk,' he said rising. 'Shall I come to-morrow to go shooting?'

'Yes, come!'

'Mind, get up early; if you oversleep you will be fined!'

'Never fear, I'll be up before you,' answered Olénin.

The old man left. The song ceased, but one could hear footsteps and merry talk. A little later the singing broke out again but farther away, and Eróshka's loud voice chimed in with the other. 'What people, what a life!' thought Olénin with a sigh he returned along to his hut.

CHAPTER XVI

Daddy Eróshka was a superannuated and solitary Cossack: twenty years ago his wife had gone over to the Orthodox Church and run away from him and married a Russian sergeant-major, and he had no children. He was not bragging when he spoke of himself as having been the boldest daredevil in the village when he was young. Everybody in the regiment knew of his old-time prowess. The death of more than one Russian, as well as Chéchen, lay on his conscience. He used to go plundering in the mountains, and robbed the Russians too; and he had twice been in prison. The greater part of his life was spent in the forests, hunting. There he lived for days on a crust of bread and drank nothing but water. But on the other hand, when he was in the village he made merry from morning to night. After leaving Olénin he slept for a couple of hours and awoke before it was light. He lay on his bed thinking of the man he had become acquainted with the evening before. Olénin's 'simplicity' (simplicity in the sense of not grudging him a drink) pleased him very much, and so did Olénin himself. He wondered why the Russians were all 'simple' and so rich, and why they were educated, and yet knew nothing. He pondered on these questions and also considered what he might get out of Olénin.

Daddy Eróshka's hut was of a good size and not old, but the absence of a woman was very noticeable in it. Contrary to the usual cleanliness of the Cossacks, the whole of this hut was filthy and exceedingly untidy. A blood-stained coat had been thrown on the table, half a dough-cake lay beside a plucked and mangled crow with which to feed the hawk. Sandals of raw hide, a gun, a dagger, a little bag, wet clothes, and sundry rags lay scattered on the benches. In a corner stood a tub with stinking water, in which another pair of sandals were being steeped, and near by was a gun and a hunting-screen. On the floor a net had been thrown down and several dead pheasants lay there, while a hen tied by its legs was walking about near the table pecking among the dirt. In the unheated oven stood a broken pot with some kind of milky liquid. On the top of the oven a falcon was screeching and trying to break the cord by which it was tied, and a moulting hawk sat quietly on the edge of the oven, looking askance at the hen and occasionally bowing its head to right and left. Daddy Eróshka himself, in his shirt, lay on his back on a short bed rigged up between the wall and the oven, with his strong legs raised and his feet on the oven. He was picking with his thick fingers at the scratches left on his hands by the hawk, which he was accustomed to carry without wearing gloves. The whole room, especially near the old man, was filled with that strong but not unpleasant mixture of smells that he always carried about with him.

'*Uyde-ma*, Daddy?' (Is Daddy in?) came through the window a sharp voice, which he at once recognized as Lukáshka's.

'*Uyde, Uyde, Uyde.* I am in!' shouted the old man. 'Come in, neighbour Mark, Luke Mark. Come to see Daddy? On your way to the cordon?'

At the sound of his master's shout the hawk flapped his wings and pulled at his cord.

The old man was fond of Lukáshka, who was the only man he excepted from his general contempt for the younger generation of Cossacks. Besides that, Lukáshka and his mother, as near neighbours, often gave the old man wine, clotted cream, and other home produce which Eróshka did not possess. Daddy Eróshka, who all his life had allowed himself to get carried away, always explained his infatuations from a practical point of view. 'Well, why not?' he used to say to himself. 'I'll give them some fresh meat, or a bird, and they won't forget Daddy: they'll sometimes bring a cake or a piece of pie.'

'Good morning, Mark! I am glad to see you,' shouted the old man cheerfully, and quickly putting down his bare feet he jumped off his bed and walked a step or two along the creaking floor, looked down at his out-turned toes, and suddenly, amused by the appearance of his feet, smiled, stamped with his bare heel on the ground, stamped again, and then performed a funny dance-step. 'That's clever, eh?' he asked, his small eyes glistening. Lukáshka smiled faintly. 'Going back to the cordon?' asked the old man.

'I have brought the *chikhir* I promised you when we were at the cordon.'

'May Christ save you!' said the old man, and he took up the extremely wide trousers that were lying on the floor, and his *beshmet*, put them on, fastened a strap round his waist, poured some water from an earthenware pot over his hands, wiped them on the old trousers, smoothed his beard with a bit of comb, and stopped in front of Lukáshka. 'Ready,' he said.

Lukáshka fetched a cup, wiped it and filled it with wine, and then handed it to the old man.

'Your health! To the Father and the Son!' said the old man,

accepting the wine with solemnity. 'May you have what you desire, may you always be a hero, and obtain a cross.'

Lukáshka also drank a little after repeating a prayer, and then put the wine on the table. The old man rose and brought out some dried fish which he laid on the threshold, where he beat it with a stick to make it tender; then, having put it with his horny hands on a blue plate (his only one), he placed it on the table.

'I have all I want. I have victuals, thank God!' he said proudly. 'Well and what of Mósev?' he added.

Lukáshka, evidently wishing to know the old man's opinion, told him how the officer had taken the gun from him.

'Never mind the gun,' said the old man. 'If you don't give the gun you will get no reward.'

'But they say, Daddy, it's little reward a fellow gets when he is not yet a mounted Cossack; and the gun is a fine one, a Crimean, worth eighty rubles.'

'Eh, let it go! I had a dispute like that with an officer, he wanted my horse. "Give it me and you'll be made a cornet," says he. I wouldn't, and I got nothing!'

'Yes, Daddy, but you see I have to buy a horse; and they say you can't get one the other side of the river under fifty rubles, and mother has not yet sold our wine.'

'Eh, we didn't bother,' said the old man; 'when Daddy Eróshka was your age he already stole herds of horses from the Nogáy folk and drove them across the Térek. Sometimes we'd give a fine horse for a quart of vodka or a cloak.'

'Why so cheap?' asked Lukáshka.

'You're a fool, a fool, Mark,' said the old man contemptuously. 'Why, that's what one steals for, so as not to be stingy! As for you, I suppose you haven't so much as seen how one drives off a herd of horses? Why don't you speak?'

'What's one to say, Daddy?' replied Lukáshka. 'It seems we are not the same sort of men as you were.'

'You're a fool, Mark, a fool! "Not the same sort of men!" ' retorted the old man, mimicking the Cossack lad. 'I was not that sort of Cossack at your age.'

'How's that?' asked Lukáshka.

The old man shook his head contemptuously.

'Daddy Eróshka was *simple;* he did not grudge anything! That's why I was *kunak* with all Chéchnya. A *kunak* would come to visit me and I'd make him drunk with vodka and make him happy and put him to sleep with me, and when I went to see him I'd take him a present—a dagger! That's the way it is done, and not as you do nowadays: the only amusement lads have now is to crack seeds and spit out the shells!' the old man finished contemptuously, imitating the present-day Cossacks cracking seeds and spitting out the shells.

'Yes, I know,' said Lukáshka; 'that's so!'

'If you wish to be a fellow of the right sort, be a brave and not a peasant! Because even a peasant can buy a horse— pay the money and take the horse.'

They were silent for a while.

'Well of course it's dull both in the village and the cordon, Daddy: but there's nowhere one can go for a bit of sport. All our fellows are so timid. Take Nazárka. The other day when we went to the Tartar village, Giréy Khan asked us to come to Nogáy to take some horses, but no one went, and how was I to go alone?'

'And what of Daddy? Do you think I am quite dried up? . . . No, I'm not dried up. Let me have a horse and I'll be off to Nogáy at once.'

'What's the good of talking nonsense!' said Luke. 'You'd better tell me what to do about Giréy Khan. He says, "Only bring horses to the Térek, and then even if you bring a whole stud I'll find a place for them." You see he's also a shaven-headed Tartar—how's one to believe him?'

'You may trust Giréy Khan, all his kin were good people. His father too was a faithful *kunak.* But listen to Daddy and I won't teach you wrong: make him take an oath, then it will be all right. And if you go with him, have your pistol ready all the same, especially when it comes to dividing up the horses. I was nearly killed that way once by a Chéchen. I wanted ten rubles from him for a horse. Trusting is all right, but don't go to sleep without a gun.'

Lukáshka listened attentively to the old man.

'I say, Daddy, have you any stone-break grass?' he asked after a pause.

'No, I haven't any, but I'll teach you how to get it. You're a good lad and won't forget the old man. . . . Shall I tell you?'

'Tell me, Daddy.'

'You know a tortoise? She's a devil, the tortoise is!'

'Of course I know!'

'Find her nest and fence it round so that she can't get in. Well, she'll come, go round it, and then will go off to find the stone-break grass and will bring some along and destroy the fence. Anyhow next morning come in good time, and where the fence is broken there you'll find the stone-break grass lying. Take it wherever you like. No lock and no bar will be able to stop you.'

'Have you tried it yourself, Daddy?'

'As for trying, I have not tried it, but I was told of it by good people. I used only one charm: that was to repeat the Pilgrim rhyme when mounting my horse; and no one ever killed me!'

'What is the Pilgrim rhyme, Daddy?'

'What, don't you know it? Oh, what people! You're right to ask Daddy. Well, listen, and repeat after me:

'Hail! Ye, living in Sion,
This is your King,
Our steeds we shall sit on,
Sophonius is weeping.
Zacharias is speaking,
Father Pilgrim,
Mankind ever loving.

'Kind ever loving,' the old man repeated. 'Do you know it now? Try it.'

Lukáshka laughed.

'Come, Daddy, was it that that hindered their killing you? Maybe it just happened so!'

'You've grown too clever! You learn it all, and say it. It will do you no harm. Well, suppose you have sung "Pilgrim" it's all right,' and the old man himself began laughing. 'But just one thing, Luke, don't you go to Nogáy!'

'Why?'

'Times have changed. You are not the same men. You've become rubbishy Cossacks! And see how many Russians have come down on us! You'd get to prison. Really, give it up! Just as if you could! Now Gírchik and I, we used . . .'

And the old man was about to begin one of his endless tales, but Lukáshka glanced at the window and interrupted him.

'It's quite light, Daddy. It's time to be off. Look us up some day.'

'May Christ save you! I'll go to the officer; I promised to take him out shooting. He seems a good fellow.'

CHAPTER XVII

From Eróshka's hut Lukáshka went home. As he returned, the dewy mists were rising from the ground and enveloped the village. In various places the cattle, though out of sight, could be heard beginning to stir. The cocks called to one another with increasing frequency and insistence. The air was becoming more transparent, and the villagers were getting up. Not till he was close to it could Lukáshka discern the fence of his yard, all wet with dew, the porch of the hut, and the open shed. From the misty yard he heard the sound of an axe chopping wood. Lukáshka entered the hut. His mother was up, and stood at the oven throwing wood into it. His little sister was still lying in bed asleep.

'Well, Lukáshka, had enough holiday-making?' asked his mother softly. 'Where did you spend the night?'

'I was in the village,' replied her son reluctantly, reaching for his musket, which he drew from its cover and examined carefully.

His mother swayed her head.

Lukáshka poured a little gunpowder onto the pan, took out a little bag from which he drew some empty cartridge cases which he began filling, carefully plugging each one with a ball wrapped in a rag. Then, having tested the loaded cartridges with his teeth and examined them, he put down the bag.

'I say, Mother, I told you the bags wanted mending; have they been done?' he asked.

'Oh yes, our dumb girl was mending something last night. Why, is it time for you to be going back to the cordon? I haven't seen anything of you!'

'Yes, as soon as I have got ready I shall have to go,' answered Lukáshka, tying up the gunpowder. 'And where is our dumb one? Outside?'

'Chopping wood, I expect. She kept fretting for you. "I shall not see him at all!" she said. She puts her hand to her face like this, and clicks her tongue and presses her hands to her heart as much as to say—"sorry." Shall I call her in? She understood all about the *abrek.*'

'Call her,' said Lukáshka. 'And I had some tallow there; bring it: I must grease my sword.'

The old woman went out, and a few minutes later Lukáshka's dumb sister came up the creaking steps and entered the hut. She was six years older than her brother and would have been extremely like him had it not been for the dull and coarsely changeable expression (common to all deaf and dumb people) of her face. She wore a coarse smock all patched; her feet were bare and muddy, and on her head she had an old blue kerchief. Her neck, arms, and face were sinewy like a peasant's. Her clothing and her whole appearance indicated that she always did the hard work of a man. She brought in a heap of logs which she threw down by the oven. Then she went up to her brother, and with a joyful smile which made her whole face pucker up, touched him on the shoulder and began making rapid signs to him with her hands, her face, and whole body.

'That's right, that's right, Stëpka is a trump!' answered the brother, nodding. 'She's fetched everything and mended everything, she's a trump! Here, take this for it!' He brought out two pieces of gingerbread from his pocket and gave them to her.

The dumb woman's face flushed with pleasure, and she began making a weird noise for joy. Having seized the gingerbread she began to gesticulate still more rapidly, frequently
pointing in one direction and passing her thick finger over her
eyebrows and her face. Lukáshka understood her and kept
nodding, while he smiled slightly. She was telling him to give
the girls dainties, and that the girls liked him, and that one
girl, Maryánka—the best of them all—loved him. She indicated
Maryánka by rapidly pointing in the direction of Maryánka's
home and to her own eyebrows and face, and by smacking
her lips and swaying her head. 'Loves' she expressed by pressing her hands to her breast, kissing her hand, and pretending
to embrace someone. Their mother returned to the hut, and
seeing what the dumb daughter was saying, smiled and shook
her head. Her daughter showed her the gingerbread and
again made the noise which expressed joy.

'I told Ulítka the other day that I'd send a matchmaker
to them,' said the mother. 'She took my words well.'

Lukáshka looked silently at his mother.

'But how about selling the wine, mother? I need a horse.'

'I'll cart it when I have time. I must get the barrels ready,'
said the mother, evidently not wishing her son to meddle in
domestic matters. 'When you go out you'll find a bag in the
passage. I borrowed from the neighbours and got something
for you to take back to the cordon; or shall I put it in your
saddle-bag?'

'All right,' answered Lukáshka. 'And if Giréy Khan should
come across the river send him to me at the cordon, for I
shan't get leave again for a long time now; I have some business with him.'

He began to get ready to start.

'I will send him on,' said the old woman. 'It seems you have
been spreeing at Yámka's all the time. I went out in the night
to see the cattle, and I think it was your voice I heard singing
songs.'

Lukáshka did not reply, but went out into the passage,
threw the bags over his shoulder, tucked up the skirts of his

coat, took his musket, and then stopped for a moment on the threshold.

'Good-bye, mother!' he said as he closed the gate behind him. 'Send me a small barrel with Nazárka. I promised it to the lads, and he'll call for it.'

'May Christ keep you, Lukáshka. God be with you! I'll send you some, some from the new barrel,' said the old woman, going to the fence: 'But listen,' she added, leaning over the fence.

The Cossack stopped.

'You've been making merry here; well, that's all right. Why should not a young man amuse himself? God has sent you luck and that's good. But now look out and mind, my son. Don't you go and get into mischief. Above all, satisfy your superiors: one has to! And I will sell the wine and find money for a horse and will arrange a match with the girl for you.'

'All right, all right!' answered her son, frowning.

His deaf sister shouted to attract his attention. She pointed to her head and the palm of her hand, to indicate the shaved head of a Chéchen. Then she frowned, and pretending to aim with a gun, she shrieked and began rapidly humming and shaking her head. This meant that Lukáshka should kill another Chéchen.

Lukáshka understood. He smiled, and shifting the gun at his back under his cloak stepped lightly and rapidly, and soon disappeared in the thick mist.

The old woman, having stood a little while at the gate, returned silently to the hut and immediately began working.

CHAPTER XVIII

Lukáshka returned to the cordon and at the same time Daddy Eróshka whistled to his dogs and, climbing over his wattle fence, went to Olénin's lodging, passing by the back of the houses (he disliked meeting women before going out hunting or shooting). He found Olénin still asleep, and even Vanyúsha, though awake, was still in bed and looking round the room considering whether it was not time to get up, when Daddy Eróshka, gun on shoulder and in full hunter's trappings, opened the door.

'A cudgel!' he shouted in his deep voice, 'An alarm! The Chéchens are upon us! Iván! Get the samovar ready for your master, and get up yourself—quick:' cried the old man. 'That's our way, my good man! Why even the girls are already up! Look out of the window. See, she's going for water and you're still sleeping!'

Olénin awoke and jumped up, feeling fresh and light-hearted at the sight of the old man and at the sound of his voice.

'Quick, Vanyúsha, quick!' he cried.

'Is that the way you go hunting?' said the old man. 'Others are having their breakfast and you are asleep! Lyam! Here!' he called to his dog. 'Is your gun ready?' he shouted, as loud as if a whole crowd were in the hut.

'Well, it's true I'm guilty, but it can't be helped! The powder, Vanyúsha, and the wads!' said Olénin.

'A fine!' shouted the old man.

'*Du tay voulay vou?*' asked Vanyúsha, grinning.

'You're not one of us—your gabble is not like our speech, you devil!' the old man shouted at Vanyúsha, showing the stumps of his teeth.

'A first offence must be forgiven,' said Olénin playfully, drawing on his high boots.

'The first offence shall be forgiven,' answered Eróshka, 'but if you oversleep another time you'll be fined a pail of *chikhir*. When it gets warmer you won't find the deer.'

'And even if we do find him he is wiser than we are,' said Olénin, repeating the words spoken by the old man the evening before, 'and you can't deceive him!'

'Yes, laugh away! You kill one first, and then you may talk. Now then, hurry up! Look, there's the master himself coming to see you,' added Eróshka, looking out of the window. 'Just see how he's got himself up. He's put on a new coat so that you should see that he's an officer. Ah, these people, these people!'

Sure enough, Vanyúsha came in and announced that the master of the house wished to see Olénin.

'*L'arjan!*' he remarked profoundly, to forewarn his master of the meaning of this visitation. Following him, the master of the house in a new Circassian coat with an officer's stripes on the shoulders and with polished boots (quite exceptional among Cossacks) entered the room, swaying from side to side and congratulated his lodger on his safe arrival.

The cornet, Elias Vasílich, was an *educated* Cossack. He had been to Russia proper, was a regimental school-teacher, and above all he was noble. He wished to appear noble, but one could not help feeling that beneath his grotesque pretence of polish, his affectation, his self-confidence, and his absurd way of speaking, he was just the same as Daddy Eróshka. This could also be clearly seen by his sunburnt face and his hands and his red nose. Olénin asked him to sit down.

'Good morning, Father Elias Vasílich,' said Eróshka, rising with (or so it seemed to Olénin) an ironically low bow.

'Good morning, Daddy. So you're here already,' said the cornet, with a careless nod.

The cornet was a man of about forty, with a grey pointed beard, skinny and lean, but handsome and very fresh-looking for his age. Having come to see Olénin he was evidently afraid of being taken for an ordinary Cossack, and wanted to let Olénin feel his importance from the first.

'That's our Egyptian Nimrod,' he remarked, addressing Olénin and pointing to the old man with a self-satisfied smile. 'A mighty hunter before the Lord! He's our foremost man on every hand. You've already been pleased to get acquainted with him.'

Daddy Eróshka gazed at his feet in their shoes of wet raw hide and shook his head thoughtfully at the cornet's ability and learning, and muttered to himself: 'Gyptian Nimvrod! What things he invents!'

'Yes, you see we mean to go hunting,' answered Olénin.

'Yes, sir, exactly,' said the cornet, 'but I have a small business with you.'

'What do you want?'

'Seeing that you are a gentleman,' began the cornet, 'and as I may understand myself to be in the rank of an officer too, and therefore we may always progressively negotiate, as gentlemen do' (he stopped and looked with a smile at Olénin and at the old man). 'But if you have the desire with my consent, then, as my wife is a foolish woman of our class, she could not quite comprehend your words of yesterday's date. Therefore my quarters might be let for six rubles to the Regimental Adjutant, without the stables; but I can always avert that from myself free of charge. But, as you desire, therefore I, being myself of an officer's rank, can come to an agreement with you in everything personally, as an inhabitant of this district, not according to our customs, but can maintain the conditions in every way. . . .'

'Speaks clearly!' muttered the old man.

The cornet continued in the same strain for a long time. At last, not without difficulty, Olénin gathered that the cornet wished to let his rooms to him, Olénin, for six rubles a month. The latter gladly agreed to this, and offered his visitor a glass of tea. The cornet declined it.

'According to our silly custom we consider it a sort of sin to drink out of a "wordly" tumbler,' he said. 'Though, of course, with my education I may understand, but my wife from her human weakness . . .'

'Well then, will you have some tea?'

'If you will permit me, I will bring my own particular glass,' answered the cornet, and stepped out into the porch. 'Bring me my glass!' he cried.

In a few minutes the door opened and a young sunburnt arm in a print sleeve thrust itself in, holding a tumbler in the hand. The cornet went up, took it, and whispered something to his daughter. Olénin poured tea for the cornet into the latter's own 'particular' glass, and for Eróshka into a 'worldly' glass.

'However, I do not desire to detain you,' said the cornet, scalding his lips and emptying his tumbler. 'I too have a great liking for fishing, and I am here, so to say, only on leave of absence for recreation from my duties. I too have the desire to tempt fortune and see whether some *Gifts of the Térek*[1] may not fall to my share. I hope you too will come and see us and have a drink of our wine, according to the custom of our village,' he added.

The cornet bowed, shook hands with Olénin, and went out. While Olénin was getting ready, he heard the cornet giving orders to his family in an authoritative and sensible tone, and a few minutes later he saw him pass by the window in a tattered coat with his trousers rolled up to his knees and a fishing net over his shoulder.

'A rascal!' said Daddy Eróshka, emptying his 'worldly' tumbler. 'And will you really pay him six rubles? Was such a thing ever heard of? They would let you the best hut in the village for two rubles. What a beast! Why, I'd let you have mine for three!'

'No, I'll remain here,' said Olénin.

'Six rubles! . . . Clearly it's a fool's money. Eh, eh, eh!' answered the old man. 'Let's have some *chikhir*, Iván!'

Having had a snack and a drink of vodka to prepare themselves for the road, Olénin and the old man went out together before eight o'clock.

At the gate they came up against a wagon to which a pair of oxen were harnessed. With a white kerchief tied round her head down to her eyes, a coat over her smock, and wearing high boots, Maryánka with a long switch in her hand was dragging the oxen by a cord tied to their horns.

'Mammy,' said the old man, pretending that he was going to seize her.

Maryánka flourished her switch at him and glanced merrily at them both with her beautiful eyes.

Olénin felt still more light-hearted.

'Now then, come on, come on,' he said, throwing his gun on his shoulder and conscious of the girl's eyes upon him.

'Gee up!' sounded Maryánka's voice behind them, followed by the creak of the moving wagon.

---

[1] The name of a poem by Lérmontov.

As long as their road lay through the pastures at the back of the village Eróshka went on talking. He could not forget the cornet and kept on abusing him.

'Why are you so angry with him?' asked Olénin.

'He's stingy. I don't like it,' answered the old man. 'He'll leave it all behind when he dies! Then who's he saving up for? He's built two houses, and he's got a second garden from his brother by a law-suit. And in the matter of papers what a dog he is! They come to him from other villages to fill up documents. As he writes it out, exactly so it happens. He gets it quite exact. But who is he saving for? He's only got one boy and the girl; when she's married who'll be left?'

'Well then, he's saving up for her dowry,' said Olénin.

'What dowry? The girl is sought after, she's a fine girl. But he's such a devil that he must yet marry her to a rich fellow. He wants to get a big price for her. There's Luke, a Cossack, a neighbour and a nephew of mine, a fine lad. It's he who killed the Chéchen—he has been wooing her for a long time, but he hasn't let him have her. He's given one excuse, and another, and a third. "The girl's too young," he says. But I know what he is thinking. He wants to keep them bowing to him. He's been acting shamefully about that girl. Still, they will get her for Lukáshka, because he is the best Cossack in the village, a brave, who has killed an *abrek* and will be rewarded with a cross.'

'But how about this? When I was walking up and down the yard last night, I saw my landlord's daughter and some Cossack kissing,' said Olénin.

'You're pretending!' cried the old man, stopping.

'On my word,' said Olénin.

'Women are the devil,' said Eróshka pondering. 'But what Cossack was it?'

'I couldn't see.'

'Well, what sort of a cap had he, a white one?'

'Yes.'

'And a red coat? About your height?'

'No, a bit taller.'

'It's he!' and Eróshka burst out laughing. 'It's himself, it's

Mark. He is Luke, but I call him Mark for a joke. His very self! I love him. I was just such a one myself. What's the good of minding them? My sweetheart used to sleep with her mother and her sister-in-law, but I managed to get in. She used to sleep upstairs; that witch her mother was a regular demon; it's awful how she hated me. Well, I used to come with a chum, Gírchik his name was. We'd come under her window and I'd climb on his shoulders, push up the window and begin groping about. She used to sleep just there on a bench. Once I woke her up and she nearly called out. She hadn't recognized me. "Who is there?" she said and I could not answer. Her mother was even beginning to stir, but I took off my cap and shoved it over her mouth; and she at once knew it by a seam in it, and ran out to me. I used not to want anything then. She'd bring along clotted cream and grapes and everything,' added Eróshka (who always explained things practically), 'and she wasn't the only one. It was a life!'

'And what now?'

'Now we'll follow the dog, get a pheasant to settle on a tree, and then you may fire.'

'Would you have made up to Maryánka?'

'Attend to the dogs. I'll tell you to-night,' said the old man, pointing to his favourite dog, Lyam.

After a pause they continued talking, while they went about a hundred paces. Then the old man stopped again and pointed to a twig that lay across the path.

'What do you think of that?' he said. 'You think it's nothing? It's bad that this stick is lying so.'

'Why is it bad?'

He smiled.

'Ah, you don't know anything. Just listen to me. When a stick lies like that don't you step across it, but go round it or throw it off the path this way, and say "Father and Son and Holy Ghost," and then go on with God's blessing. Nothing will happen to you. That's what the old men used to teach me.'

'Come, what rubbish!' said Olénin. 'You'd better tell me more about Maryánka. Does she carry on with Lukáshka?'

'Hush, . . . be quiet now!' the old man again interrupted

in a whisper: 'just listen, we'll go round through the forest.'

And the old man, stepping quietly in his soft shoes, led the way by a narrow path leading into the dense, wild, overgrown forest. Now and again with a frown he turned to look at Olénin, who rustled and clattered with his heavy boots and, carrying his gun carelessly, several times caught the twigs of trees that grew across the path.

'Don't make a noise. Step softly, soldier!' the old man whispered angrily.

There was a feeling in the air that the sun had risen. The mist was dissolving but it still enveloped the tops of the trees. The forest looked terribly high. At every step the aspect changed: what had appeared like a tree proved to be a bush, and a reed looked like a tree.

CHAPTER XIX

The mist had partly lifted, showing the wet reed thatches, and was now turning into dew that moistened the road and the grass beside the fence. Smoke rose everywhere in clouds from the chimneys. The people were going out of the village, some to their work, some to the river, and some to the cordon. The hunters walked together along the damp, grass-grown path. The dogs, wagging their tails and looking at their masters, ran on both sides of them. Myriads of gnats hovered in the air and pursued the hunters, covering their backs, eyes, and hands. The air was fragrant with the grass and with the dampness of the forest. Olénin continually looked round at the ox-cart in which Maryanka sat urging on the oxen with a long switch.

It was calm. The sounds from the village, audible at first, now no longer reached the sportsmen. Only the brambles cracked as the dogs ran under them, and now and then birds called to one another. Olénin knew that danger lurked in the forest, that *abreks* always hid in such places. But he knew too that in the forest, for a man on foot, a gun is a great protection. Not that he was afraid, but he felt that another in his place might be; and looking into the damp misty forest and listening to the rare and faint sounds with strained attention, he changed his hold on his gun and experienced a pleasant feeling that was new to him. Daddy Eróshka went in front, stopping and carefully scanning every puddle where an animal had left a double track, and pointing it out to Olénin. He hardly spoke at all and only occasionally made remarks in a whisper. The track they were following had once been made by wagons, but the grass had long overgrown it. The elm and plane tree forest on both sides of them was so dense and overgrown with creepers that it was impossible to see anything through it. Nearly every tree was enveloped from top to bottom with wild grape vines, and dark bramble bushes covered the ground thickly. Every little glade was overgrown with blackberry bushes and grey feathery reeds. In places, large hoof-prints and small funnel-shaped pheasant-trails led from the path into the thicket. The vigour of the growth of this forest, untrampled by cattle, struck Olénin at every turn, for he had never seen anything like it. This forest, the danger, the old man and his mysterious whispering, Maryánka with her virile upright bearing, and the mountains—all this seemed to him like a dream.

'A pheasant has settled,' whispered the old man, looking round and pulling his cap over his face—'Cover your mug! A pheasant!' he waved his arm angrily at Olénin and pushed forward almost on all fours. 'He don't like a man's mug.'

Olénin was still behind him when the old man stopped and began examining a tree. A cock-pheasant on the tree clucked at the dog that was barking at it, and Olénin saw the pheasant; but at that moment a report, as of a cannon, came from Eróshka's enormous gun, the bird fluttered up and, losing some feathers, fell to the ground. Coming up to the old man Olénin disturbed another, and raising his gun he aimed and fired. The pheasant flew swiftly up and then, catching at the branches as he fell, dropped like a stone to the ground.

'Good man!' the old man (who could not hit a flying bird) shouted laughing.

Having picked up the pheasants they went on. Olénin, ex-

cited by the exercise and the praise, kept addressing remarks
to the old man.

'Stop! Come this way,' the old man interrupted. 'I noticed
the track of deer here yesterday.'

After they had turned into the thicket and gone some three
hundred paces they scrambled through into a glade overgrown with reeds and partly under water. Olénin failed to keep
up with the old huntsman and presently Daddy Eróshka,
some twenty paces in front, stooped down, nodding and beck-
oning with his arm. On coming up with him Olénin saw a
man's footprint to which the old man was pointing.

'D'you see?'

'Yes, well?' said Olénin, trying to speak as calmly as he
could. 'A man's footstep!'

Involuntarily a thought of Cooper's *Pathfinder* and of *abreks*
flashed through Olénin's mind, but noticing the mysterious
manner with which the old man moved on, he hesitated to
question him and remained in doubt whether this mysterious-
ness was caused by fear of danger or by the sport.

'No, it's my own footprint,' the old man said quietly, and
pointed to some grass under which the track of an animal
was just perceptible.

The old man went on, and Olénin kept up with him. Descending to lower ground some twenty paces farther on they
came upon a spreading pear-tree, under which, on the black
earth, lay the fresh dung of some animal.

The spot, all covered with wild vines, was like a cosy arbour,
dark and cool.

'He's been here this morning,' said the old man with a sigh;
'the lair is still damp, quite fresh.'

Suddenly they heard a terrible crash in the forest some ten
paces from where they stood. They both started and seized
their guns, but they could see nothing and only heard the
branches breaking. The rhythmical rapid thud of galloping
was heard for a moment and then changed into a hollow
rumble which resounded farther and farther off, re-echoing
in wider and wider circles through the forest. Olénin felt as
though something had snapped in his heart. He peered care-

fully but vainly into the green thicket and then turned to the old man. Daddy Eróshka with his gun pressed to his breast stood motionless; his cap was thrust backwards, his eyes gleamed with an unwonted glow, and his open mouth, with its worn yellow teeth, seemed to have stiffened in that position.

'A horned stag!' he muttered, and throwing down his gun in despair he began pulling at his grey beard. 'Here it stood. We should have come round by the path. . . . Fool! fool!' and he gave his beard an angry tug. 'Fool! Pig!' he repeated, pulling painfully at his own beard. Through the forest something seemed to fly away in the mist, and ever farther and farther off was heard the sound of the flight of the stag.

It was already dusk when, hungry, tired, but full of vigour, Olénin returned with the old man. Dinner was ready. He ate and drank with the old man till he felt warm and merry. Olénin then went out into the porch. Again, to the west, the mountains rose before his eyes. Again the old man told his endless stories of hunting, of *abreks*, of sweethearts, and of all that free and reckless life. Again the fair Maryánka went in and out and across the yard, her beautiful powerful form outlined by her smock.

CHAPTER XX

The next day Olénin went alone to the spot where he and the old man had startled the stag. Instead of passing round through the gate he climbed over the prickly hedge, as everybody else did, and before he had had time to pull out the thorns that had caught in his coat, his dog, which had run on in front, started two pheasants. He had hardly stepped among the briers when the pheasants began to rise at every step (the old man had not shown him that place the day before as he meant to keep it for shooting from behind the screen). Olénin fired twelve times and killed five pheasants, but clambering after them through the briers he got so fatigued that he was drenched with perspiration. He called off his dog, uncocked his gun, put in a bullet above the small shot, and brushing away the mosquitoes with the wide sleeve of his Circassian coat he went slowly to the spot where they had been the day before. It was however impossible to keep back the dog, who found trails on the very path, and Olénin killed two more pheasants, so that after being detained by this it was getting towards noon before he began to find the place he was looking for.

The day was perfectly clear, calm, and hot. The morning moisture had dried up even in the forest, and myriads of mosquitoes literally covered his face, his back, and his arms. His dog had turned from black to grey, its back being covered with mosquitoes, and so had Olénin's coat through which the insects thrust their stings. Olénin was ready to run away from them and it seemed to him that it was impossible to live in this country in the summer. He was about to go home, but remembering that other people managed to endure such pain he resolved to bear it and gave himself up to be devoured. And strange to say, by noontime the feeling became actually pleasant. He even felt that without this mosquito-filled atmosphere around him, and that mosquito-paste mingled with perspiration which his hand smeared over his face, and that unceasing irritation all over his body, the forest would lose for him some of its character and charm. These myriads of insects were so well suited to that monstrously lavish wild vegetation, these multitudes of birds and beasts which filled the forest, this dark foliage, this hot scented air, these runlets filled with turbid water which everywhere soaked through from the Térek and gurgled here and there under the overhanging leaves, that the very thing which had at first seemed to him dreadful and intolerable now seemed pleasant. After going round the place where yesterday they had found the animal and not finding anything, he felt inclined to rest. The sun stood right above the forest and poured its perpendicular rays down on his back and head whenever he came out into a glade or onto the road. The seven heavy pheasants dragged painfully at his waist. Having found the traces of yesterday's stag he crept under a bush into the thicket just where the stag

had lain, and lay down in its lair. He examined the dark foliage around him, the place marked by the stag's perspiration
and yesterday's dung, the imprint of the stag's knees, the bit
of black earth it had kicked up, and his own footprints of the
day before. He felt cool and comfortable and did not think of
or wish for anything. And suddenly he was overcome by such
a strange feeling of causeless joy and of love for everything,
that from an old habit of his childhood he began crossing himself and thanking someone. Suddenly, with extraordinary
clearness, he thought: 'Here am I, Dmítri Olénin, a being quite
distinct from every other being, now lying all alone Heaven
only knows where—where a stag used to live—an old stag, a
beautiful stag who perhaps had never seen a man, and in a
place where no human being has ever sat or thought these
thoughts. Here I sit, and around me stand old and young
trees, one of them festooned with wild grape vines, and pheasants are fluttering, driving one another about and perhaps
scenting their murdered brothers.' He felt his pheasants, examined, them, and wiped the warm blood off his hand onto his
coat. 'Perhaps the jackals scent them and with dissatisfied
faces go off in another direction: above me, flying in among
the leaves which to them seem enormous islands, mosquitoes hang in the air and buzz: one, two, three, four, a hundred, a thousand, a million mosquitoes, and all of them buzz
something or other and each one of them is separate from all
else and is just such a separate Dmítri Olénin as I am myself.'
He vividly imagined what the mosquitoes buzzed: 'This way,
this way, lads! Here's someone we can eat!' They buzzed and
stuck to him. And it was clear to him that he was not a Russian nobleman, a member of Moscow society, the friend and
relation of so-and-so and so-and-so, but just such a mosquito,
or pheasant, or deer, as those that were now living all around
him. 'Just as they, just as Daddy Eróshka, I shall live awhile
and die, and as he says truly: "grass will grow and nothing
more".'

'But what though the grass does grow?' he continued thinking, 'Still I must live and be happy, because happiness is all I
desire. Never mind what I am—an animal like all the rest,

above whom the grass will grow and nothing more; or a frame in which a bit of the one God has been set,—still I must live in the very best way. How then must I live to be happy, and why was I not happy before?' And he began to recall his former life and he felt disgusted with himself. He appeared to himself to have been terribly exacting and selfish, though he now saw that all the while he really needed nothing for himself. And he looked round at the foliage with the light shining through it, at the setting sun and the clear sky, and he felt just as happy as before. 'Why am I happy, and what used I to live for?' thought he. 'How much I exacted for myself; how I schemed and did not manage to gain anything but shame and sorrow! and, there now, I require nothing to be happy'; and suddenly a new light seemed to reveal itself to him. 'Happiness is this!' he said to himself. 'Happiness lies in living for others. That is evident. The desire for happiness is innate in every man; therefore it is legitimate. When trying to satisfy it selfishly—that is, by seeking for oneself riches, fame, comforts, or love—it may happen that circumstances arise which make it impossible to satisfy these desires. It follows that it is these desires that are illegitimate, but not the need for happiness. But what desires can always be satisfied despite external circumstances? What are they? Love, self-sacrifice.' He was so glad and excited when he had discovered this, as it seemed to him, new truth, that he jumped up and began impatiently seeking some one to sacrifice himself for, to do good to and to love. 'Since one wants nothing for oneself,' he kept thinking, 'why not live for others?' He took up his gun with the intention of returning home quickly to think this out and to find an opportunity of doing good. He made his way out of the thicket. When he had come out into the glade he looked around him; the sun was no longer visible above the tree-tops. It had grown cooler and the place seemed to him quite strange and not like the country round the village. Everything seemed changed—the weather and the character of the forest; the sky was wrapped in clouds, the wind was rustling in the tree-tops, and all around nothing was visible but reeds and dying broken-down trees. He called to his dog who had run away to follow some animal, and his voice came back as in a desert. And suddenly he was seized with a terrible sense of weirdness. He grew frightened. He remembered the *abreks* and the murders he had been told about, and he expected every moment that an *abrek* would spring from behind every bush and he would have to defend his life and die, or be a coward. He thought of God and of the future life as for long he had not thought about them. And all around was that same gloomy stern wild nature. 'And is it worth while living for oneself,' thought he, 'when at any moment you may die, and die without having done any good, and so that no one will know of it?' He went in the direction where he fancied the village lay. Of his shooting he had no further thought; but he felt tired to death and peered round at every bush and tree with particular attention and almost with terror, expecting every moment to be called to account for his life. After having wandered about for a considerable time he came upon a ditch down which was flowing cold sandy water from the Térek, and, not to go astray any longer, he decided to follow it. He went on without knowing where the ditch would lead him. Suddenly the reeds behind him crackled. He shuddered and seized his gun, and then felt ashamed of himself: the over-excited dog, panting hard, had thrown itself into the cold water of the ditch and was lapping it!

He too had a drink, and then followed the dog in the direction it wished to go, thinking it would lead him to the village. But despite the dog's company everything around him seemed still more dreary. The forest grew darker and the wind grew stronger and stronger in the tops of the broken old trees. Some large birds circled screeching round their nests in those trees. The vegetation grew poorer and he came oftener and oftener upon rustling reeds and bare sandy spaces covered with animal footprints. To the howling of the wind was added another kind of cheerless monotonous roar. Altogether his spirits became gloomy. Putting his hand behind him he felt his pheasants, and found one missing. It had broken off and was lost, and only the bleeding head and beak remained sticking in his belt. He felt more frightened than he had ever done before. He began to pray to God, and feared above all that he might die without having done anything good or kind; and he so wanted to live, and to live so as to perform a feat of self-sacrifice.

CHAPTER XXI

Suddenly it was as though the sun had shone into his soul. He heard Russian being spoken, and also heard the rapid smooth flow of the Térek, and a few steps farther in front of him saw the brown moving surface of the river, with the dim-coloured wet sand of its banks and shallows, the distant steppe, the cordon watch-tower outlined above the water, a saddled and hobbled horse among the brambles, and then the mountains opening out before him. The red sun appeared for an instant from under a cloud and its last rays glittered brightly along the river over the reeds, on the watch-tower, and on a group of Cossacks, among whom Lukáshka's vigorous figure attracted Olénin's involuntary attention.

Olénin felt that he was again, without any apparent cause, perfectly happy. He had come upon the Nízhni-Protótsk post on the Térek, opposite a pro-Russian Tartar village on the other side of the river. He accosted the Cossacks, but not finding as yet any excuse for doing anyone a kindness, he entered the hut; nor in the hut did he find any such opportunity. The Cossacks received him coldly. On entering the mud hut he lit a cigarette. The Cossacks paid little attention to him, first because he was smoking a cigarette, and secondly because they had something else to divert them that evening. Some hostile Chéchens, relatives of the *abrek* who had been killed, had come from the hills with a scout to ransom the body; and the Cossacks were waiting for their Commanding Officer's arrival from the village. The dead man's brother, tall and well shaped with a short cropped beard which was dyed red, despite his very tattered coat and cap was calm and majestic as a king. His face was very like that of the dead *abrek*. He did not deign to look at anyone and never once glanced at the dead body, but sitting on his heels in the shade he spat as he smoked his short pipe, and occasionally uttered some few guttural sounds of command, which were respectfully listened to by his companion. He was evidently a brave who had met Russians more than once before in quite other circumstances, and nothing about them could astonish or even interest him. Olénin was about to approach the dead body and had begun to look at it when the brother, looking up at him from under his brows with calm contempt, said something sharply and angrily. The scout hastened to cover the dead man's face with his coat. Olénin was struck by the dignified and stern expression of the brave's face. He began to speak to him, asking from what village he came, but the Chéchen, scarcely giving him a glance, spat contemptuously and turned away. Olénin was so surprised at the Chéchen not being interested in him that he could only put it down to the man's stupidity or ignorance of Russian; so he turned to the scout, who also acted as interpreter. The scout was as ragged as the other, but instead of being red haired he was black haired, restless, with extremely white gleaming teeth and sparkling black eyes. The scout willingly entered into conversation and asked for a cigarette.

'There were five brothers,' began the scout in his broken Russian. 'This is the third brother the Russians have killed, only two are left. He is a brave, a great brave!' he said, pointing to the Chéchen. 'When they killed Ahmet Khan (the dead brave) this one was sitting on the opposite bank among the reeds. He saw it all. Saw him laid in the skiff and brought to the bank. He sat there till the night and wished to kill the old man, but the others would not let him.'

Lukáshka went up to the speaker, and sat down.

'Of what village?' asked he.

'From there in the hills,' replied the scout, pointing to the misty bluish gorge beyond the Térek. 'Do you know Suuk-su? It is about eight miles beyond that.'

'Do you know Giréy Khan in Suuk-su?' asked Lukáshka, evidently proud of the acquaintance. 'He is my *kunak*.'

'He is my neighbour,' answered the scout.

'He's a trump!' and Lukáshka, evidently much interested, began talking to the scout in Tartar.

Presently a Cossack captain, with the head of the village, arrived on horseback with a suite of two Cossacks. The captain—one of the new type of Cossack officers—wished the Cossacks 'Good health,' but no one shouted in reply, 'Hail! Good health to your honour,' as is customary in the Russian Army, and only a few replied with a bow. Some, and among them Lukáshka, rose and stood erect. The corporal replied that all was well at the outposts. All this seemed ridiculous: it was as if these Cossacks were playing at being soldiers. But these formalities soon gave place to ordinary ways of behaviour, and the captain, who was a smart Cossack just like the others, began speaking fluently in Tartar to the interpreter. They filled in some document, gave it to the scout, and received from him some money. Then they approached the body.

'Which of you is Luke Gavrílov?' asked the captain.

Lukáshka took off his cap and came forward.

'I have reported your exploit to the Commander. I don't know what will come of it. I have recommended you for a cross; you're too young to be made a sergeant. Can you read?'

'I can't.'

'But what a fine fellow to look at!' said the captain, again playing the commander. 'Put on your cap. Which of the Gavrílovs does he come of? . . . the Broad, eh?'

'His nephew,' replied the corporal.

'I know, I know. Well, lend a hand, help them,' he said, turning to the Cossacks.

Lukáshka's face shone with joy and seemed handsomer than usual. He moved away from the corporal, and having put on his cap sat down beside Olénin.

When the body had been carried to the skiff the brother Chéchen descended to the bank. The Cossacks involuntarily stepped aside to let him pass. He jumped into the boat and pushed off from the bank with his powerful leg, and now, as Olénin noticed, for the first time threw a rapid glance at all the Cossacks and then abruptly asked his companion a question. The latter answered something and pointed to Lukáshka. The Chéchen looked at him and, turning slowly away, gazed at the opposite bank. That look expressed not hatred but cold contempt. He again made some remark.

'What is he saying?' Olénin asked of the fidgety scout.

'Yours kill ours, ours slay yours. It's always the same,' replied the scout, evidently inventing, and he smiled, showing his white teeth, as he jumped into the skiff.

The dead man's brother sat motionless, gazing at the opposite bank. He was so full of hatred and contempt that there was nothing on this side of the river that moved his curiosity. The scout, standing up at one end of the skiff and dipping his paddle now on one side now on the other, steered skilfully while talking incessantly. The skiff became smaller and smaller as it moved obliquely across the stream, the voices became scarcely audible, and at last, still within sight, they landed on the opposite bank where their horses stood waiting. There they lifted out the corpse and (though the horse shied) laid it across one of the saddles, mounted, and rode at a foot-pace along the road past a Tartar village from which a crowd came out to look at them. The Cossacks on the Russian side of the river were highly satisfied and jovial. Laughter and jokes were heard on all sides. The captain and the head of the village entered the mud hut to regale themselves. Lukáshka, vainly striving to impart a sedate expression to his merry face, sat down with his elbows on his knees beside Olénin and whittled away at a stick.

'Why do you smoke?' he said with assumed curiosity. 'Is it good?'

He evidently spoke because he noticed Olénin felt ill at ease and isolated among the Cossacks.

'It's just a habit,' answered Olénin. 'Why?'

'H'm, if one of us were to smoke there would be a row! Look there now, the mountains are not far off,' continued Lukáshka, 'yet you can't get there! How will you get back alone? It's getting dark. I'll take you, if you like. You ask the corporal to give me leave.'

'What a fine fellow!' thought Olénin, looking at the Cossack's bright face. He remembered Maryánka and the kiss he had heard by the gate, and he was sorry for Lukáshka and his want of culture. 'What confusion it is,' he thought. 'A man kills another and is happy and satisfied with himself as if he had done something excellent. Can it be that nothing tells him that it is not a reason for any rejoicing, and that happiness lies not in killing, but in sacrificing oneself?'

'Well, you had better not meet him again now, mate!' said one of the Cossacks who had seen the skiff off, addressing Lukáshka. 'Did you hear him asking about you?'

Lukáshka raised his head.

'My godson?' said Lukáshka, meaning by that word the dead Chéchen.

'Your godson won't rise, but the red one is the godson's brother!'

'Let him thank God that he got off whole himself,' replied Lukáshka.

'What are you glad about?' asked Olénin. 'Supposing your brother had been killed would you be glad?'

The Cossack looked at Olénin with laughing eyes. He seemed to have understood all that Olénin wished to say to him, but to be above such considerations.

'Well, that happens too! Don't our fellows get killed sometimes?'

CHAPTER XXII

The captain and the head of the village rode away, and Olénin, to please Lukáshka as well as to avoid going back alone through the dark forest, asked the corporal to give Lukáshka leave, and the corporal did so. Olénin thought that Lukáshka wanted to see Maryánka and he was also glad of the companionship of such a pleasant-looking and sociable Cossack. Lukáshka and Maryánka he involuntarily united in his mind, and he found pleasure in thinking about them. 'He loves Maryánka,' thought Olénin, 'and I could love her,' and a new and powerful emotion of tenderness overcame him as they walked homewards together through the dark forest. Lukáshka too felt happy; something akin to love made itself felt between these two very different young men. Every time they glanced at one another they wanted to laugh.

'By which gate do you enter?' asked Olénin.

'By the middle one. But I'll see you as far as the marsh. After that you have nothing to fear.'

Olénin laughed.

'Do you think I am afraid? Go back, and thank you. I can get on alone.'

'It's all right! What have I to do? And how can you help being afraid? Even we are afraid,' said Lukáshka to set Olénin's self-esteem at rest, and he laughed too.

'Then come in with me. We'll have a talk and a drink and in the morning you can go back.'

'Couldn't I find a place to spend the night?' laughed Lukáshka. 'But the corporal asked me to go back.'

'I heard you singing last night, and also saw you.'

'Every one . . .' and Luke swayed his head.

'Is it true you are getting married?' asked Olénin.

'Mother wants me to marry. But I have not got a horse yet.'

'Aren't you in the regular service?'

'Oh dear no! I've only just joined, and have not got a horse yet, and don't know how to get one. That's why the marriage does not come off.'

'And what would a horse cost?'

'We were bargaining for one beyond the river the other day and they would not take sixty rubles for it, though it is a Nogáy horse.'

'Will you come and be my drabánt?' (A drabánt was a kind of orderly attached to an officer when campaigning.) 'I'll get it arranged and will give you a horse,' said Olénin suddenly. 'Really now, I have two and I don't want both.'

'How—don't want it?' Lukáshka said, laughing. 'Why should you make me a present? We'll get on by ourselves by God's help.'

'No, really! Or don't you want to be a drabánt?' said Olénin, glad that it had entered his head to give a horse to Lukáshka, though, without knowing why, he felt uncomforta-

ble and confused and did not know what to say when he tried
to speak.

Lukáshka was the first to break the silence.

'Have you a house of your own in Russia?' he asked.

Olénin could not refrain from replying that he had not only
one, but several houses.

'A good house? Bigger than ours?' asked Lukáshka good-
naturedly.

'Much bigger; ten times as big and three stories high,' replied Olénin.

'And have you horses such as ours?'

'I have a hundred horses, worth three or four hundred
rubles each, but they are not like yours. They are trotters, you
know. . . . But still, I like the horses here best.'

'Well and did you come here of your own free will, or were
you sent?' said Lukáshka, laughing at him. 'Look! that's where
you lost your way,' he added, 'you should have turned to
the right.'

'I came by my own wish,' replied Olénin. 'I wanted to see
your parts and to join some expeditions.'

'I would go on an expedition any day,' said Lukáshka.
'D'you hear the jackals howling?' he added, listening.

'I say, don't you feel any horror at having killed a man?'
asked Olénin.

'What's there to be frightened about? But I should like to
join an expediiton,' Lukáshka repeated. 'How I want to! How I
want to!'

'Perhaps we may be going together. Our company is going
before the holidays, and your "hundred" too.'

'And what did you want to come here for? You've a house
and horses and serfs. In your place I'd do nothing but make
merry! And what is your rank?'

'I am a cadet, but have been recommended for a commission.'

'Well, if you're not bragging about your home, if I were
you I'd never have left it! Yes, I'd never have gone away anywhere. Do you find it pleasant living among us?'

'Yes, very pleasant,' answered Olénin.

It had grown quite dark before, talking in this way, they approached the village. They were still surrounded by the deep gloom of the forest. The wind howled through the tree-tops. The jackals suddenly seemed to be crying close beside them, howling, chuckling, and sobbing; but ahead of them in the village the sounds of women's voices and the barking of dogs could already be heard; the outlines of the huts were clearly to be seen; lights gleamed and the air was filled with the peculiar smell of *kizyak* smoke. Olénin felt keenly, that night especially, that here in this village was his home, his family, all his happiness, and that he never had and never would live so happily anywhere as he did in this Cossack village. He was so fond of everybody and especially of Lukáshka that night. On reaching home, to Lukáshka's great surprise, Olénin with his own hands led out of the shed a horse he had bought in Gróznoe—it was not the one he usually rode but another—not a bad horse though no longer young, and gave it to Lukáshka.

'Why should you give me a present?' said Lukáshka. 'I have not yet done anything for you.'

'Really it is nothing,' answered Olénin. 'Take it, and you will give me a present, and we'll go on an expedition against the enemy together.'

Lukáshka became confused.

'But what d'you mean by it? As if a horse were of little value,' he said without looking at the horse.

'Take it, take it! If you don't you will offend me. Vanyúsha! Take the grey horse to his house.'

Lukáshka took hold of the halter.

'Well then, thank you! This is something unexpected, undreamt of.'

Olénin was as happy as a boy of twelve.

'Tie it up here. It's a good horse. I bought it in Gróznoe; it gallops splendidly! Vanyúsha, bring us some *chikhir*. Come into the hut.'

The wine was brought. Lukáshka sat down and took the wine-bowl.

'God willing I'll find a way to repay you,' he said, finishing his wine. 'How are you called?'

'Dmítri Andréich.'

'Well, 'Mítry Andréich, God bless you. We will be *kunaks*. Now you must come to see us. Though we are not rich people still we can treat a *kunak*, and I will tell mother in case you need anything—clotted cream or grapes—and if you come to the cordon I'm your servant to go hunting or to go across the river, anywhere you like! There now, only the other day, what a boar I killed, and I divided it among the Cossacks, but if I had only known I'd have given it to you.'

'That's all right, thank you! But don't harness the horse, it has never been in harness.'

'Why harness the horse? And there is something else I'll tell you if you like,' said Lukáshka, bending his head. 'I have a *kunak*, Giréy Khan. He asked me to lie in ambush by the road where they come down from the mountains. Shall we go together? I'll not betray you. I'll be your *murid*.' [1]

'Yes, we'll go; we'll go some day.'

Lukáshka seemed quite to have quieted down and to have understood Olénin's attitude towards him. His calmness and the ease of his behaviour surprised Olénin, and he did not even quite like it. They talked long, and it was late when Lukáshka, not tipsy (he never was tipsy) but having drunk a good deal, left Olénin after shaking hands.

Olénin looked out of the window to see what he would do. Lukáshka went out, hanging his head. Then, having led the horse out of the gate, he suddenly shook his head, threw the reins of the halter over its head, sprang onto its back like a cat, gave a wild shout, and galloped down the street. Olénin expected that Lukáshka would go to share his joy with Maryánka, but though he did not do so Olénin still felt his soul more at ease than ever before in his life. He was as delighted as a boy, and could not refrain from telling Vanyúsha not only that he had given Lukáshka the horse, but also why he had

---

[1] In the religious and racial revival led by Shamyl, a *murid* was a follower or disciple attached to a *murshid* or teacher.

done it, as well as his new theory of happiness. Vanyúsha did not approve of his theory, and announced that '*l'argent il n'y a pas!*' and that therefore it was all nonsense.

Lukáshka rode home, jumped off the horse, and handed it over to his mother, telling her to let it out with the communal Cossack herd. He himself had to return to the cordon that same night. His deaf sister undertook to take the horse, and explained by signs that when she saw the man who had given the horse, she would bow down at his feet. The old woman only shook her head at her son's story, and decided in her own mind that he had stolen it. She therefore told the deaf girl to take it to the herd before daybreak.

Lukáshka went back alone to the cordon pondering over Olénin's action. Though he did not consider the horse a good one, yet it was worth at least forty rubles and Lukáshka was very glad to have the present. But why it had been given him he could not at all understand, and therefore he did not experience the least feeling of gratitude. On the contrary, vague suspicions that the cadet had some evil intentions filled his mind. What those intentions were he could not decide, but neither could he admit the idea that a stranger would give him a horse worth forty rubles for nothing, just out of kindness; it seemed impossible. Had he been drunk one might understand it! He might have wished to show off. But the cadet had been sober, and therefore must have wished to bribe him to do something wrong. 'Eh, humbug!' thought Lukáshka. 'Haven't I got the horse and we'll see later on. I'm not a fool myself and we shall see who'll get the better of the other,' he thought, feeling the necessity of being on his guard, and therefore arousing in himself unfriendly feelings towards Olénin. He told no one how he had got the horse. To some he said he had bought it, to others he replied evasively. However, the truth soon got about in the village, and Lukáshka's mother and Maryánka, as well as Elias Vasílich and other Cossacks, when they heard of Olénin's unnecessary gift, were perplexed, and began to be on their guard against the cadet. But despite their fears his action aroused in them a great respect for his simplicity and wealth.

'Have you heard,' said one, 'that the cadet quartered on Elias Vasílich has thrown a fifty-ruble horse at Lukáshka? He's rich! . . .'

'Yes, I heard of it,' replied another profoundly; 'he must have done him some great service. We shall see what will come of this cadet. Eh! what luck that Snatcher has!'

'Those cadets are crafty, awfully crafty,' said a third. 'See if he don't go setting fire to a building, or doing something!'

CHAPTER XXIII

Olénin's life went on with monotonous regularity. He had little intercourse with the commanding officers or with his equals. The position of a rich cadet in the Caucasus was peculiarly advantageous in this respect. He was not sent out to work, or for training. As a reward for going on an expedition he was recommended for a commission, and meanwhile he was left in peace. The officers regarded him as an aristocrat and behaved towards him with dignity. Card-playing and the officers' carousals accompanied by the soldier-singers, of which he had had experience when he was with the detachment, did not seem to him attractive, and he also avoided the society and life of the officers in the village. The life of officers stationed in a Cossack village has long had its own definite form. Just as every cadet or officer when in a fort regularly drinks porter, plays cards, and discusses the rewards given for taking part in the expeditions, so in the Cossack villages he regularly drinks *chikhir* with his hosts, treats the girls to sweetmeats and honey, dangles after the Cossack women, and falls in love, and occasionally marries there. Olénin always took his own path and had an unconscious objection to the beaten tracks. And here, too, he did not follow the ruts of a Caucasian officer's life.

It came quite naturally to him to wake up at daybreak. After drinking tea and admiring from his porch the mountains, the morning, and Maryánka, he would put on a tattered ox-hide coat, sandals of soaked raw hide, buckle on a dagger,

take a gun, put cigarettes and some lunch in a little bag, call
his dog, and soon after five o'clock would start for the forest
beyond the village. Towards seven in the evening he would return tired and hungry with five or six pheasants hanging
from his belt (sometimes with some other animal) and with
his bag of food and cigarettes untouched. If the thoughts
in his head had lain like the lunch and cigarettes in the bag,
one might have seen that during all those fourteen hours not
a single thought had moved in it. He returned morally fresh,
strong, and perfectly happy, and he could not tell what he
had been thinking about all the time. Were they ideas, memories, or dreams that had been flitting through his mind? They
were frequently all three. He would rouse himself and ask
what he had been thinking about; and would see himself as a
Cossack working in a vineyard with his Cossack wife, or an
abrek in the mountains, or a boar running away from himself.
And all the time he kept peering and watching for a pheasant, a boar, or a deer.

In the evening Daddy Eróshka would be sure to be sitting
with him. Vanyúsha would bring a jug of *chikhir*, and they
would converse quietly, drink, and separate to go quite contentedly to bed. The next day he would again go shooting,
again be healthily weary, again they would sit conversing and
drink their fill, and again be happy. Sometimes on a holiday
or day of rest Olénin spent the whole day at home. Then his
chief occupation was watching Maryánka, whose every movement, without realizing it himself, he followed greedily from
his window or his porch. He regarded Maryánka and loved her
(so he thought) just as he loved the beauty of the mountains
and the sky, and he had no thought of entering into any relations with her. It seemed to him that between him and her
such relations as there were between her and the Cossack
Lukáshka could not exist, and still less such as often existed
between rich officers and other Cossack girls. It seemed to him
that if he tried to do as his fellow officers did, he would exchange his complete enjoyment of contemplation for an abyss
of suffering, disillusionment, and remorse. Besides, he had already achieved a triumph of self-sacrifice in connexion with

her which had given him great pleasure, and above all he
was in a way afraid of Maryánka and would not for anything
have ventured to utter a word of love to her lightly.

Once during the summer, when Olénin had not gone out
shooting but was sitting at home, quite unexpectedly a Moscow acquaintance, a very young man whom he had met in society, came in.

'Ah, *mon cher,* my dear fellow, how glad I was when I
heard that you were here!' he began in his Moscow French,
and he went on intermingling French words in his remarks.
'They said, "Olénin". What Olénin? and I was so pleased. . . .
Fancy fate bringing us together here! Well and how are you?
How? Why?' and Prince Belétski told his whole story: how he
had temporarily entered the regiment, how the Commander-
in-Chief had offered to take him as an adjutant, and how he
would take up the post after this campaign although personally he felt quite indifferent about it.

'Living here in this hole one must at least make a career—
get a cross—or a rank—be transferred to the Guards. That is
quite indispensable, not for myself but for the sake of my relations and friends. The prince received me very well; he is a
very decent fellow,' said Belétski, and went on unceasingly. 'I
have been recommended for the St. Anna Cross for the expedition. Now I shall stay here a bit until we start on the campaign. It's capital here. What women! Well and how are you
getting on? I was told by our captain, Stártsev you know, a
kind-hearted stupid creature. . . . Well, he said you were
living like an awful savage, seeing no one! I quite understand
you don't want to be mixed up with the set of officers we have
here. I am so glad now you and I will be able to see something of one another. I have put up at the Cossack corporal's
house. There is such a girl there, Ústenka! I tell you she's
just charming.'

And more and more French and Russian words came pouring forth from that world which Olénin thought he had left
for ever. The general opinion about Belétski was that he was
a nice, good-natured fellow. Perhaps he really was; but in
spite of his pretty, good-natured face, Olénin thought him ex-

tremely unpleasant. He seemed just to exhale that filthiness which Olénin had forsworn. What vexed him most was that he could not—had not the strength—abruptly to repulse this man who came from that world: as if that old world he used to belong to had an irresistible claim on him. Olénin felt angry with Belétski and with himself, yet against his wish he introduced French phrases into his own conversation, was interested in the Commander-in-Chief and in their Moscow acquaintances, and because in this Cossack village he and Belétski both spoke French, he spoke contemptuously of their fellow officers and of the Cossacks, and was friendly with Belétski, promising to visit him and inviting him to drop in to see him. Olénin however did not himself go to see Belétski.

Vanyúsha for his part approved of Belétski, remarking that he was a real gentleman.

Belétski at once adopted the customary life of a rich officer in a Cossack village. Before Olénin's eyes, in one month he came to be like an old resident of the village; he made the old men drunk, arranged evening parties, and himself went to parties arranged by the girls—bragged of his conquests, and even got so far that, for some unknown reason, the women and girls began calling him 'Grandad', and the Cossacks, to whom a man who loved wine and women was clearly understandable, got used to him and even liked him better than they did Olénin, who was a puzzle to them.

CHAPTER XXIV

It was five in the morning. Vanyúsha was in the porch heating the samovar, and using the leg of a long boot instead of bellows.[1] Olénin, had already ridden off to bathe in the Térek. (He had recently invented a new amusement: to swim his horse in the river.) His landlady was in her outhouse, and the dense smoke of the kindling fire rose from the chimney. The

---

[1] These boots have concertina-like sides, and can be used instead of bellows to make the charcoal in the samovar burn up.

girl was milking the buffalo-cow in the shed. 'Can't keep quiet,
the damned thing!' came her impatient voice, followed by
the rhythmical sound of milking.

From the street in front of the house horses' hoofs were
heard clattering briskly, and Olénin, riding bareback on a
handsome dark-grey horse which was still wet and shining,
rode up to the gate. Maryánka's handsome head, tied round
with a red kerchief, appeared from the shed and again disappeared. Olénin was wearing a red silk shirt, a white Circassian
coat girdled with a strap which carried a dagger, and a tall
cap. He sat his well-fed wet horse with a slightly conscious
elegance and, holding his gun at his back, stooped to open the
gate. His hair was still wet, and his face shone with youth
and health. He thought himself handsome, agile, and like a
brave; but he was mistaken. To any experienced Caucasian he
was still only a soldier. When he noticed that the girl had put
out her head he stopped with particular smartness, threw open
the gate and, tightening the reins, swished his whip and entered the yard. 'Is tea ready, Vanyúsha?' he cried gaily, not
looking at the door of the shed. He felt with pleasure how
his fine horse, pressing down its flanks, pulling at the bridle
and with every muscle quivering and with each foot ready
to leap over the fence, pranced on the hard clay of the yard.
'C'est prê,' answered Vanyúsha. Olénin felt as if Maryánka's
beautiful head was still looking out of the shed but he did
not turn to look at her. As he jumped down from his horse
he made an awkward movement and caught his gun against
the porch, and turned a frightened look towards the shed,
where there was no one to be seen and whence the sound of
milking could still be heard.

Soon after he had entered the hut he came out again and
sat down with his pipe and a book on the side of the porch
which was not yet exposed to the rays of the sun. He meant
not to go anywhere before dinner that day, and to write some
long-postponed letters; but somehow he felt disinclined to
leave his place in the porch, and he was as reluctant to go back
into the hut as if it had been a prison. The housewife had

heated her oven, and the girl, having driven the cattle, had come back and was collecting *kisyak* and heaping it up along the fence. Olénin went on reading, but did not understand a word of what was written in the book that lay open before him. He kept lifting his eyes from it and looking at the powerful young woman who was moving about. Whether she stepped into the moist morning shadow thrown by the house, or went out into the middle of the yard lit up by the joyous young light, so that the whole of her stately figure in its bright coloured garment gleamed in the sunshine and cast a black shadow—he always feared to lose any one of her movements. It delighted him to see how freely and gracefully her figure bent: into what folds her only garment, a pink smock, draped itself on her bosom and along her shapely legs; how she drew herself up and her tight-drawn smock showed the outline of her heaving bosom, how the soles of her narrow feet in her worn red slippers rested on the ground without altering their shape; how her strong arms with the sleeves rolled up, exerting the muscles, used the spade almost as if in anger, and how her deep dark eyes sometimes glanced at him. Though the delicate brows frowned, yet her eyes expressed pleasure and a knowledge of her own beauty.

'I say, Olénin, have you been up long?' said Belétski as he entered the yard dressed in the coat of a Caucasian officer.

'Ah, Belétski,' replied Olénin, holding out his hand. 'How is it you are out so early?'

'I had to. I was driven out; we are having a ball to-night. Maryánka, of course you'll come to Ústenka's?' he added, turning to the girl.

Olénin felt surprised that Belétski could address this woman so easily. But Maryánka, as though she had not heard him, bent her head, and throwing the spade across her shoulder went with her firm masculine tread towards the outhouse.

'She's shy, the wench is shy,' Belétski called after her. 'Shy of you,' he added as, smiling gaily, he ran up the steps of the porch.

'How is it you are having a ball and have been driven out?'

'It's at Ústenka's, at my landlady's, that the ball is, and you two are invited. A ball consists of a pie and a gathering of girls.'

'What should we do there?'

Belétski smiled knowingly and winked, jerking his head in the direction of the outhouse into which Maryánka had disappeared.

Olénin shrugged his shoulders and blushed.

'Well, really you are a strange fellow!' said he.

'Come now, don't pretend!'

Olénin frowned, and Belétski noticing this smiled insinuatingly. 'Oh, come, what do you mean?' he said. 'Living in the same house—and such a fine girl, a splendid girl, a perfect beauty——'

'Wonderfully beautiful! I never saw such a woman before,' replied Olénin.

'Well then?' said Belétski, quite unable to understand the situation.

'It may be strange,' replied Olénin, 'but why should I not say what is true? Since I have lived here women don't seem to exist for me. And it is so good, really! Now what can there be in common between us and women like these? Eróshka—that's a different matter! He and I have a passion in common—sport.'

'There now! In common! And what have I in common with Amália Ivánovna? It's the same thing! You may say they're not very clean—that's another matter . . . À la guerre, comme à la guerre! . . .'

'But I have never known any Amália Ivánovnas, and have never known how to behave with women of that sort,' replied Olénin. 'One cannot respect them, but these I do respect.'

'Well go on respecting them! Who wants to prevent you?'

Olénin did not reply. He evidently wanted to complete what he had begun to say. It was very near his heart.

'I know I am an exception . . .' He was visibly confused. 'But my life has so shaped itself that I not only see no necessity to renounce my rules, but I could not live here, let alone live as happily as I am doing, were I to live as you do. Therefore

I look for something quite different from what you look for.'

Belétski raised his eyebrows incredulously. 'Anyhow, come to me this evening; Maryánka will be there and I will make you acquainted. Do come, please! If you feel dull you can go away. Will you come?'

'I would come, but to speak frankly I am afraid of being seriously carried away.'

'Oh, oh, oh!' shouted Belétski. 'Only come, and I'll see that you aren't. Will you? On your word?'

'I would come, but really I don't understand what we shall do; what part we shall play!'

'Please, I beg of you. You will come?'

'Yes, perhaps I'll come,' said Olénin.

'Really now! Charming women such as one sees nowhere else, and to live like a monk! What an idea! Why spoil your life and not make use of what is at hand? Have you heard that our company is ordered to Vozdvízhensk?'

'Hardly. I was told the 8th Company would be sent there,' said Olénin.

'No. I have had a letter from the adjutant there. He writes that the Prince himself will take part in the campaign. I am very glad I shall see something of him. I'm beginning to get tired of this place.'

'I hear we shall start on a raid soon.'

'I have not heard of it; but I have heard that Krinovítsin has received the Order of St. Anna for a raid. He expected a lieutenancy,' said Belétski laughing. 'He was let in! He has set off for headquarters.'

It was growing dusk and Olénin began thinking about the party. The invitation he had received worried him. He felt inclined to go, but what might take place there seemed strange, absurd, and even rather alarming. He knew that neither Cossack men nor older women, nor anyone besides the girls, were to be there. What was going to happen? How was he to behave? What would they talk about? What connexion was there between him and those wild Cossack girls? Belétski had told him of such curious, cynical, and yet rigid relations. It seemed strange to think that he would be there in the same hut with Maryánka and perhaps might have to talk to her. It seemed to him impossible when he remembered her majestic bearing. But Belétski spoke of it as if it were all perfectly simple. 'Is it possible that Belétski will treat Maryánka in the same way? That is interesting,' thought he. 'No, better not go. It's all so horrid, so vulgar, and above all—it leads to nothing!' But again he was worried by the question of what would take place; and besides he felt as if bound by a promise. He went out without having made up his mind one way or the other, but he walked as far as Belétski's, and went in there.

The hut in which Belétski lived was like Olénin's. It was raised nearly five feet from the ground on wooden piles, and had two rooms. In the first (which Olénin entered by the steep flight of steps) feather beds, rugs, blankets, and cushions were tastefully and handsomely arranged, Cossack fashion, along the main wall. On the side wall hung brass basins and weapons, while on the floor, under a bench, lay water-melons and pumpkins. In the second room there was a big brick oven, a table, and sectarian icons. It was here that Belétski was quartered, with his camp-bed and his pack and trunks. His weapons hung on the wall with a little rug behind them, and on the table were his toilet appliances and some portraits. A silk dressing-gown had been thrown on the bench. Belétski himself, clean and good looking, lay on the bed in his underclothing, reading *Les Trois Mousquetaires*.

He jumped up.

'There, you see how I have arranged things. Fine! Well, it's good that you have come. They are working furiously. Do you know what the pie is made of? Dough with a stuffing of pork and grapes. But that's not the point. You just look at the commotion out there!'

And really, on looking out of the window they saw an unusual bustle going on in the hut. Girls ran in and out, now for one thing and now for another.

'Will it soon be ready?' cried Belétski.

'Very soon! Why? Is Grandad hungry?' and from the hut came the sound of ringing laughter.

Ústenka, plump, small, rosy, and pretty, with her sleeves turned up, ran into Belétski's hut to fetch some plates.

'Get away or I shall smash the plates!' she squeaked, escaping from Belétski. 'You'd better come and help,' she shouted to Olénin, laughing. 'And don't forget to get some refreshments for the girls.' ('Refreshments' meaning spice-bread and sweets.)

'And has Maryánka come?'

'Of course! She brought some dough.'

'Do you know,' said Belétski, 'if one were to dress Ústenka up and clean and polish her up a bit, she'd be better than all our beauties. Have you ever seen that Cossack woman who married a colonel; she was charming! Bórsheva? What dignity! Where do they get it . . .'

'I have not seen Bórsheva, but I think nothing could be better than the costume they wear here.'

'Ah, I'm first rate at fitting into any kind of life,' said Belétski with a sigh of pleasure. 'I'll go and see what they are up to.'

He threw his dressing-gown over his shoulders and ran out, shouting, 'And you look after the "refreshments".'

Olénin sent Belétski's orderly to buy spice-bread and honey; but it suddenly seemed to him so disgusting to give money (as if he were bribing someone) that he gave no definite reply to the orderly's question: 'How much spice-bread with peppermint, and how much with honey?'

'Just as you please.'

'Shall I spend all the money,' asked the old soldier impressively. 'The peppermint is dearer. It's sixteen kopeks.'

'Yes, yes, spend it all,' answered Olénin and sat down by the window, surprised that his heart was thumping as if he were preparing himself for something serious and wicked.

He heard screaming and shrieking in the girls' hut when Belétski went there, and a few moments later saw how he jumped out and ran down the steps, accompanied by shrieks, bustle, and laughter.

'Turned out,' he said.

A little later Ústenka entered and solemnly invited her visitors to come in: announcing that all was ready.

When they came into the room they saw that everything
was really ready. Ústenka was rearranging the cushions along
the wall. On the table, which was covered by a disproportion-
ately small cloth, was a decanter of *chikhir* and some dried
fish. The room smelt of dough and grapes. Some half
dozen girls in smart tunics, with their heads not covered as
usual with kerchiefs, were huddled together in a corner behind the oven, whispering, giggling, and spluttering with
laughter.

'I humbly beg you to do honour to my patron saint,' said
Ústenka, inviting her guests to the table.

Olénin noticed Maryánka among the group of girls, who
without exception were all handsome, and he felt vexed and
hurt that he met her in such vulgar and awkward circumstances. He felt stupid and awkward, and made up his mind
to do what Belétski did. Belétski stepped to the table somewhat solemnly yet with confidence and ease, drank a glass of
wine to Ústenka's health, and invited the others to do the
same. Ústenka announced that girls don't drink.

'We might with a little honey,' exclaimed a voice from
among the group of girls.

The orderly, who had just returned with the honey and
spice-cakes, was called in. He looked askance (whether with
envy or with contempt) at the gentlemen, who in his opinion were on the spree; and carefully and conscientiously
handed over to them a piece of honeycomb and the cakes
wrapped up in a piece of greyish paper, and began explaining circumstantially all about the price and the change, but
Belétski sent him away.

Having mixed honey with wine in the glasses, and having
lavishly scattered the three pounds of spice-cakes on the table, Belétski dragged the girls from their corners by force,
made them sit down at the table, and began distributing the
cakes among them. Olénin involuntarily noticed how Maryánka's sunburnt but small hand closed on two round peppermint nuts and one brown one, and that she did not know what
to do with them. The conversation was halting and con-
strained, in spite of Ústenka's and Belétski's free and easy

manner and their wish to enliven the company. Olénin faltered and tried to think of something to say, feeling that he was exciting curiosity and perhaps provoking ridicule and infecting the others with his shyness. He blushed, and it seemed to him that Maryánka in particular was feeling uncomfortable. 'Most likely they are expecting us to give them some money,' thought he. 'How are we to do it? And how can we manage quickest to give it and get away?'

CHAPTER XXV

'How is it you don't know your own lodger?' said Belétski, addressing Maryánka.

'How is one to know him if he never comes to see us?' answered Maryánka, with a look at Olénin.

Olénin felt frightened, he did not know of what. He flushed and, hardly knowing what he was saying, remarked; 'I'm afraid of your mother. She gave me such a scolding the first time I went in.'

Maryánka burst out laughing.

'And so you were frightened?' she said, and glanced at him and turned away.

It was the first time Olénin had seen the whole of her beautiful face. Till then he had seen her and her kerchief covering her to the eyes. It was not for nothing that she was reckoned the beauty of the village. Ústenka was a pretty girl, small, plump, rosy, with merry brown eyes, and red lips which were perpetually smiling and chattering. Maryánka on the contrary was certainly not pretty but beautiful. Her features might have been considered too masculine and almost harsh had it not been for her tall stately figure, her powerful chest and shoulders, and especially the severe yet tender expression of her long dark eyes which were darkly shadowed beneath their black brows, and for the gentle expression of her mouth and smile. She rarely smiled, but her smile was always striking. She seemed to radiate virginal strength and health. All the girls were good-looking, but they themselves and Belétski,

and the orderly when he brought in the spice-cakes, all involuntarily gazed at Maryánka, and anyone addressing the
girls was sure to address her. She seemed a proud and happy
queen among them.

Belétski, trying to keep up the spirit of the party, chattered incessantly, made the girls hand round *chikhir*, fooled
about with them, and kept making improper remarks in French
about Maryánka's beauty to Olénin, calling her 'yours' (*la
vôtre*), and advising him to behave as he did himself. Olénin
felt more and more uncomfortable. He was devising an excuse to get out and run away when Belétski announced that
Ústenka, whose saint's day it was, must offer *chikhir* to everybody with a kiss. She consented on condition that they should
put money on her plate, as is the custom at weddings. 'What
fiend brought me to this disgusting feast?' thought Olénin,
rising to go away.

'Where are you off to?'

'I'll fetch some tobacco,' he said, meaning to escape, but
Belétski seized his hand.

'I have some money,' he said to him in French.

'One can't go away, one has to pay here,' thought Olénin
bitterly, vexed at his own awkwardness. 'Can't I really behave like Belétski? I ought not to have come, but once I am
here I must not spoil their fun. I must drink like a Cossack,'
and taking the wooden bowl (holding about eight tumblers)
he almost filled it with *chikhir* and drank it almost all. The
girls looked at him, surprised and almost frightened, as he
drank. It seemed to them strange and not right. Ústenka
brought them another glass each, and kissed them both.
'There girls, now we'll have some fun,' she said, clinking on
the plate the four rubles the men had put there.

Olénin no longer felt awkward, but became talkative.

'Now, Maryánka, it's your turn to offer us wine and a kiss,'
said Belétski, seizing her hand.

'Yes, I'll give you such a kiss!' she said playfully, preparing
to strike at him.

'One can kiss Grandad without payment,' said another girl.

'There's a sensible girl,' said Belétski, kissing the struggling girl. 'No, you must offer it,' he insisted, addressing Maryánka. 'Offer a glass to your lodger.'

And taking her by the hand he led her to the bench and sat her down beside Olénin.

'What a beauty,' he said, turning her head to see it in profile.

Maryánka did not resist but proudly smiling turned her long eyes towards Olénin.

'A beautiful girl,' repeated Belétski.

'Yes, see what a beauty I am,' Maryánka's look seemed to endorse. Without considering what he was doing Olénin embraced Maryánka and was going to kiss her, but she suddenly extricated herself, upsetting Belétski and pushing the top off the table, and sprang away towards the oven. There was much shouting and laughter. Then Belétski whispered something to the girls and suddenly they all ran out into the passage and locked the door behind them.

'Why did you kiss Belétski and won't kiss me?' asked Olénin.

'Oh, just so. I don't want to, that's all!' she answered, pouting and frowning. 'He's Grandad,' she added with a smile. She went to the door and began to bang at it. 'Why have you locked the door, you devils?'

'Well, let them be there and us here,' said Olénin, drawing closer to her.

She frowned, and sternly pushed him away with her hand. And again she appeared so majestically handsome to Olénin that he came to his senses and felt ashamed of what he was doing. He went to the door and began pulling at it himself.

'Belétski! Open the door! What a stupid joke!'

Maryánka again gave a bright happy laugh. 'Ah, you're afraid of me?' she said.

'Yes, you know you're as cross as your mother.'

'Spend more of your time with Eróshka; that will make the girls love you!' And she smiled, looking straight and close into his eyes.

He did not know what to reply. 'And if I were to come to see you——' he let fall.

'That would be a different matter,' she replied, tossing her head.

At that moment Belétski pushed the door open, and Maryánka sprang away from Olénin and in doing so her thigh struck his leg.

'It's all nonsense what I have been thinking about—love and self-sacrifice and Lukáshka. Happiness is the one thing. He who is happy is right,' flashed through Olénin's mind, and with a strength unexpected to himself he seized and kissed the beautiful Maryánka on her temple and her cheek. Maryánka was not angry, but only burst into a loud laugh and ran out to the other girls.

That was the end of the party. Ústenka's mother, returned from her work, gave all the girls a scolding, and turned them all out.

CHAPTER XXVI

'Yes,' thought Olénin, as he walked home. 'I need only slacken the reins a bit and I might fall desperately in love with this Cossack girl.' He went to bed with these thoughts, but expected it all to blow over and that he would continue to live as before.

But the old life did not return. His relations to Maryánka were changed. The wall that had separated them was broken down. Olénin now greeted her every time they met.

The master of the house having returned to collect the rent, on hearing of Olénin's wealth and generosity invited him to his hut. The old woman received him kindly, and from the day of the party onwards Olénin often went in of an evening and sat with them till late at night. He seemed to be living in the village just as he used to, but within him everything had changed. He spent his days in the forest, and towards eight o'clock, when it began to grow dusk, he would go to see his hosts, alone or with Daddy Eróshka. They grew so used to him that they were surprised when he stayed away. He paid well for his wine and was a quiet fellow. Vanyúsha would bring him his tea and he would sit down in a corner near the oven. The old woman did not mind him but went on with her work, and over their tea or their *chikhir* they talked about Cossack affairs, about the neighbours, or about Russia: Olénin relating and the others inquiring. Sometimes he brought a book and read to himself. Maryánka crouched like a wild goat with her feet drawn up under her, sometimes on the top of the oven,[1] sometimes in a dark corner. She did not take part in the conversations, but Olénin saw her eyes and face and heard her moving or cracking sunflower seeds, and he felt that she listened with her whole being when he spoke, and was aware of his presence while he silently read to himself. Sometimes he thought her eyes were fixed on him, and meeting their radiance he involuntarily became silent and gazed at her. Then she would instantly hide her face and he would pretend to be deep in converstion with the old woman, while he listened all the time to her breathing and to her every movement and waited for her to look at him again. In the presence of others she was generally bright and friendly with him, but when they were alone together she was shy and rough. Sometimes he came in before Maryánka had returned home. Suddenly he would hear her firm footsteps and catch a glimmer of her blue cotton smock at the open door. Then she would step into the middle of the hut, catch sight of him, and her eyes would give a scarcely perceptible kindly smile, and he would feel happy and frightened.

He neither sought for nor wished for anything from her, but every day her presence became more and more necessary to him.

Olénin had entered into the life of the Cossack village so fully that his past seemed quite foreign to him. As to the future, especially a future outside the world in which he was now living, it did not interest him at all. When he received letters from home, from relatives and friends, he was offended by the evident distress with which they regarded him as a lost man, while he in his village considered those as lost who did not live as he was living. He felt sure he would never repent of

---

[1] The stove or oven was large, with a flat top on which anyone could sit or lie.

having broken away from his former surroundings and of having settled down in this village to such a solitary and original life. When out on expeditions, and when quartered at one of the forts, he felt happy too; but it was here, from under Daddy Eróshka's wing, from the forest and from his hut at the end of the village, and especially when he thought of Maryánka and Lukáshka, that he seemed to see the falseness of his former life. That falseness used to rouse his indignation even before, but now it seemed inexpressibly vile and ridiculous. Here he felt freer and freer every day and more and more of a man. The Caucasus now appeared entirely different to what his imagination had painted it. He had found nothing at all like his dreams, nor like the descriptions of the Caucasus he had heard and read. 'There are none of all those chestnut steeds, precipices, Amalet Beks, heroes or villains,' thought he. 'The people live as nature lives: they die, are born, unite, and more are born—they fight, eat and drink, rejoice and die, without any restrictions but those that nature imposes on sun and grass, on animal and tree. They have no other laws.' Therefore these people, compared to himself, appeared to him beautiful, strong, and free, and the sight of them made him feel ashamed and sorry for himself. Often it seriously occurred to him to throw up everything, to get registered as a Cossack, to buy a hut and cattle and marry a Cossack woman (only not Maryánka, whom he conceded to Lukáshka), and to live with Daddy Eróshka and go shooting and fishing with him, and go with the Cossacks on their expeditions. 'Why ever don't I do it? What am I waiting for?' he asked himself, and he egged himself on and shamed himself. 'Am I afraid of doing what I hold to be reasonable and right? Is the wish to be a simple Cossack, to live close to nature, not to injure anyone but even to do good to others, more stupid than my former dreams, such as those of becoming a minister of state or a colonel?' But a voice seemed to say that he should wait, and not take any decision. He was held back by a dim consciousness that he could not live altogether like Eróshka and Lukáshka because he had a different idea of happiness—he was held back by the thought that happiness lies in self-sacrifice. What he

had done for Lukáshka continued to give him joy. He kept
looking for occasions to sacrifice himself for others, but did
not meet with them. Sometimes he forgot this newly discovered recipe for happiness and considered himself capable of
identifying his life with Daddy Eróshka's, but then he quickly
bethought himself and promptly clutched at the idea of conscious self-sacrifice, and from that basis looked calmly and
proudly at all men and at their happiness.

CHAPTER XXVII

Just before the vintage Lukáshka came on horseback to see
Olénin. He looked more dashing then ever.

'Well? Are you getting married?' asked Olénin, greeting
him merrily.

Lukáshka gave no direct reply.

'There, I've exchanged your horse across the river. This *is* a
horse! A Kabardá horse from the Lov[1] stud. I know horses.'

They examined the new horse and made him caracole about
the yard. The horse really was an exceptionally fine one, a
broad and long gelding, with glossy coat, thick silky tail,
and the soft fine mane and crest of a thoroughbred. He was
so well fed that 'you might go to sleep on his back' as Lukáshka
expressed it. His hoofs, eyes, teeth, were exquisitely shaped
and sharply outlined, as one only finds them in very pure-
bred horses. Olénin could not help admiring the horse, he had
not yet met with such a beauty in the Caucasus.

'And how it goes!' said Lukáshka, patting its neck. 'What a
step! And so clever—he simply runs after his master.'

'Did you have to add much to make the exchange?' asked
Olénin.

'I did not count it,' answered Lukáshka with a smile. 'I got
him from a *kunak*.'

---

[1] The Lov Stud Farm was considered one of the best in the Caucasus.

'A wonderfully beautiful horse! What would you take for it?' asked Olénin.

'I have been offered a hundred and fifty rubles for it, but I'll give it you for nothing,' said Lukáshka, merrily. 'Only say the word and it's yours. I'll unsaddle it and you may take it. Only give me some sort of a horse for my duties.'

'No, on no account.'

'Well then, here is a dagger I've brought you,' said Lukáshka, unfastening his girdle and taking out one of the two daggers which hung from it. 'I got it from across the river.'

'Oh, thank you!'

'And mother has promised to bring you some grapes herself.'

'That's quite unnecessary. We'll balance up some day. You see I don't offer you any money for the dagger!'

'How could you? We are *kunaks*. It's just the same as when Giréy Khan across the river took me into his home and said, "Choose what you like!" So I took this sword. It's our custom.'

They went into the hut and had a drink.

'Are you staying here awhile?' asked Olénin.

'No, I have come to say good-bye. They are sending me from the cordon to a company beyond the Térek. I am going to-night with my comrade Nazárka.'

'And when is the wedding to be?'

'I shall be coming back for the betrothal, and then I shall return to the company again,' Lukáshka replied reluctantly.

'What, and see nothing of your betrothed?'

'Just so—what is the good of looking at her? When you go on campaign ask in our company for Lukáshka the Broad. But what a lot of boars there are in our parts! I've killed two. I'll take you.'

'Well, good-bye! Christ save you.'

Lukáshka mounted his horse, and without calling on Maryánka, rode caracoling down the street, where Nazárka was already awaiting him.

'I say, shan't we call round?' asked Nazárka, winking in the direction of Yámka's house.

'That's a good one!' said Lukáshka. 'Here, take my horse to her and if I don't come soon give him some hay. I shall reach the company by the morning any way.'

'Hasn't the cadet given you anything more?'

'I am thankful to have paid him back with a dagger—he was going to ask for the horse,' said Lukáshka, dismounting and handing over the horse to Nazárka.

He darted into the yard past Olénin's very window, and came up to the window of the cornet's hut. It was already quite dark. Maryánka, wearing only her smock, was combing her hair preparing for bed.

'It's I——' whispered the Cossack.

Maryánka's look was severely indifferent, but her face suddenly brightened up when she heard her name. She opened the window and leant out, frightened and joyous.

'What—what do you want?' she said.

'Open!' uttered Lukáshka. 'Let me in for a minute. I am so sick of waiting! It's awful!'

He took hold of her head through the window and kissed her.

'Really, do open!'

'Why do you talk nonsense? I've told you I won't! Have you come for long?'

He did not answer but went on kissing her, and she did not ask again.

'There, through the window one can't even hug you properly,' said Lukáshka.

'Maryánka dear!' came the voice of her mother, 'who is that with you?'

Lukáshka took off his cap, which might have been seen, and crouched down by the window.

'Go, be quick!' whispered Maryánka.

'Lukáshka called round,' she answered; 'he was asking for Daddy.'

'Well then send him here!'

'He's gone; said he was in a hurry.'

In fact, Lukáshka, stooping as with big strides he passed under the windows, ran out through the yard and towards Yámka's house unseen by anyone but Olénin. After drinking two bowls of *chikhir* he and Nazárka rode away to the outpost. The night was warm, dark, and calm. They rode in silence, only the footfall of their horses was heard. Lukáshka started a song about the Cossack, Mingál, but stopped before he had finished the first verse, and after a pause, turning to Nazárka, said:

'I say, she wouldn't let me in!'

'Oh?' rejoined Nazárka. 'I knew she wouldn't. D'you know what Yámka told me? The cadet has begun going to their house. Daddy Eróshka brags that he got a gun from the cadet for getting him Maryánka.'

'He lies, the old devil!' said Lukáshka, angrily. 'She's not such a girl. If he does not look out I'll wallop that old devil's sides,' and he began his favourite song:

> 'From the village of Izmáylov,
>> From the master's favourite garden,
>> Once escaped a keen-eyed falcon.
> Soon after him a huntsman came a-riding,
>> And he beckoned to the falcon that had strayed,
>> But the bright-eyed bird thus answered:
> "In gold cage you could not keep me,
>> On your hand you could not hold me,
>> So now I fly to blue seas far away.
> There a white swan I will kill,
> Of sweet swan-flesh have my fill." '

CHAPTER XXVIII

The betrothal was taking place in the cornet's hut. Lukáshka had returned to the village, but had not been to see Olénin, and Olénin had not gone to the betrothal though he had been invited. He was sad as he had never been since he settled in this Cossack village. He had seen Lukáshka earlier in the evening and was worried by the question why Lukáshka was so cold towards him. Olénin shut himself up in his hut and began writing in his diary as follows:

'Many things have I pondered over lately and much have I changed,' wrote he, 'and I have come back to the copybook maxim: The one way to be happy is to love, to love self-denyingly, to love everybody and everything; to spread a web of love on all sides and to take all who come into it. In this way I caught Vanyúsha, Daddy Eróshka, Lukáshka, and Maryánka.'

As Olénin was finishing this sentence Daddy Eróshka entered the room.

Eróshka was in the happiest frame of mind. A few evenings before this, Olénin had gone to see him and had found him with a proud and happy face deftly skinning the carcass of a boar with a small knife in the yard. The dogs (Lyam his pet among them) were lying close by watching what he was doing and gently wagging their tails. The little boys were respectfully looking at him through the fence and not even teasing him as was their wont. His women neighbours, who were as a rule not too gracious towards him, greeted him and brought him, one a jug of *chikhir,* another some clotted cream, and a third a little flour. The next day Eróshka sat in his store-room all covered with blood, and distributed pounds of boar-flesh, taking in payment money from some and wine from others. His face clearly expressed, 'God has sent me luck. I have killed a boar, so now I am wanted.' Consequently he naturally began to drink, and had gone on for four days never leaving the village. Besides which he had had something to drink at the betrothal.

He came to Olénin quite drunk: his face red, his beard tangled, but wearing a new *beshmet* trimmed with gold braid; and he brought with him a *balaláyka*[1] which he had obtained beyond the river. He had long promised Olénin this treat, and felt in the mood for it, so that he was sorry to find Olénin writing.

---

[1] A three-stringed guitar, corresponding to the banjo.

'Write on, write on, my lad,' he whispered, as if he thought
that a spirit sat between him and the paper and must not be
frightened away, and he softly and silently sat down on the
floor. When Daddy Eróshka was drunk his favourite position was on the floor. Olénin looked round, ordered some wine
to be brought, and continued to write. Eróshka found it dull
to drink by himself and he wished to talk.

'I've been to the betrothal at the cornet's. But there! They're
shwine!—Don't want them!—Have come to you.'

'And where did you get your *balaláyka?*' asked Olénin,
still writing.

'I've been beyond the river and got it there, brother mine,'
he answered, also very quietly. 'I'm a master at it. Tartar or
Cossack, squire or soldiers' songs, any kind you please.'

Olénin looked at him again, smiled, and went on writing.

That smile emboldened the old man.

'Come, leave off my lad, leave off!' he said with sudden
firmness.

'Well, perhaps I will.'

'Come, people have injured you but leave them alone, spit
at them! Come, what's the use of writing and writing, what's
the good?'

And he tried to mimic Olénin by tapping the floor with his
thick fingers, and then twisted his big face to express contempt.

'What's the good of writing quibbles. Better have a spree
and show you're a man!'

No other conception of writing found place in his head except that of legal chicanery.

Olénin burst out laughing and so did Eróshka. Then, jumping up from the floor, the latter began to show off his skill on
the *balaláyka* and to sing Tartar songs.

'Why write, my good fellow! You'd better listen to what I'll
sing to you. When you're dead you won't hear any more
songs. Make merry now!'

First he sang a song of his own composing accompanied
by a dance:

> 'Ah, dee, dee, dee, dee, dee, dim,
> Say where did they last see him?
> In a booth, at the fair,
> He was selling pins, there.'

Then he sang a song he had learnt from his former sergeant-major:

> 'Deep I fell in love on Monday,
> Tuesday nothing did but sigh,
> Wednesday I popped the question,
> Thursday waited her reply.
> Friday, late, it came at last,
> Then all hope for me was past!
> Saturday my life to take
> I determined like a man,
> But for my salvation's sake
> Sunday morning changed my plan!'

Then he sang again:

> 'Oh dee, dee, dee, dee, dee, dim,
> Say where did they last see him.'

And after that, winking, twitching his shoulders, and footing it to the tune, he sang:

> 'I will kiss you and embrace,
> Ribbons red twine round you;
> And I'll call you little Grace.
> Oh! you little Grace now do
> Tell me, do you love me true?'

And he became so excited that with a sudden dashing movement he started dancing around the room accompanying himself the while.

Songs like 'Dee, dee, dee'—'gentlemen's songs'—he sang for Olénin's benefit, but after drinking three more tumblers of *chikhir* he remembered old times and began singing real Cossack and Tartar songs. In the midst of one of his favourite songs his voice suddenly trembled and he ceased singing, and only continued strumming on the *balaláyka*.

'Oh, my dear friend!' he said.

The peculiar sound of his voice made Olénin look round.
The old man was weeping. Tears stood in his eyes and one
tear was running down his cheek.

'You are gone, my young days, and will never come back!'
he said, blubbering and halting. 'Drink, why don't you drink!'
he suddenly shouted with a deafening roar, without wiping
away his tears.

There was one Tartar song that specially moved him. It had
few words, but its charm lay in the sad refrain. 'Ay day,
dalalay!' Eróshka translated the words of the song: 'A youth
drove his sheep from the *aoul* to the mountains: the Russians
came and burnt the *aoul*, they killed all the men and took all
the women into bondage. The youth returned from the mountains. Where the *aoul* had stood was an empty space; his
mother not there, nor his brothers, nor his house; one tree
alone was left standing. The youth sat beneath the tree and
wept. "Alone like thee, alone am I left," ' and Eróshka began
singing: 'Ay day, dalalay!' and the old man repeated several
times this wailing, heart-rending refrain.

When he had finished the refrain Eróshka suddenly seized
a gun that hung on the wall, rushed hurriedly out into the
yard and fired off both barrels into the air. Then again he began, more dolefully, his 'Ay day, dalalay—ah, ah,' and ceased.

Olénin followed him into the porch and looked up into the
starry sky in the direction where the shots had flashed. In the
cornet's house there were lights and the sound of voices. In
the yard girls were crowding round the porch and the windows, and running backwards and forwards between the hut
and the outhouse. Some Cossacks rushed out of the hut and
could not refrain from shouting, re-echoing the refrain of
Daddy Eróshka's song and his shots.

'Why are you not at the betrothal?' asked Olénin.

'Never mind them! Never mind them!' muttered the old
man, who had evidently been offended by something there.
'Don't like them, I don't. Oh, those people! Come back into
the hut! Let them make merry by themselves and we'll make
merry by ourselves.'

Olénin went in.

'And Lukáshka, is he happy? Won't he come to see me?' he asked.

'What, Lukáshka? They've lied to him and said I am getting his girl for you,' whispered the old man. 'But what's the girl? She will be ours if we want her. Give enough money—and she's ours. I'll fix it up for you. Really!'

'No, Daddy, money can do nothing if she does not love me. You'd better not talk like that!'

'We are not loved, you and I. We are forlorn,' said Daddy Eróshka suddenly, and again he began to cry.

Listening to the old man's talk Olénin had drunk more than usual. 'So now my Lukáshka is happy,' thought he; yet he felt sad. The old man had drunk so much that evening that he fell down on the floor and Vanyúsha had to call soldiers in to help, and spat as they dragged the old man out. He was so angry with the old man for his bad behaviour that he did not even say a single French word.

CHAPTER XXIX

It was August. For days the sky had been cloudless, the sun scorched unbearably and from early morning the warm wind raised a whirl of hot sand from the sand-drifts and from the road, and bore it in the air through the reeds, the trees, and the village. The grass and the leaves on the trees were covered with dust, the roads and dried-up salt marshes were baked so hard that they rang when trodden on. The water had long since subsided in the Térek and rapidly vanished and dried up in the ditches. The slimy banks of the pond near the village were trodden bare by the cattle and all day long you could hear the splashing of water and the shouting of girls and boys bathing. The sand-drifts and the reeds were already drying up in the steppes, and the cattle, lowing, ran into the fields in the day-time. The boars migrated into the distant reed-beds and to the hills beyond the Térek. Mosquitoes and gnats swarmed in thick clouds over the low lands

and villages. The snow-peaks were hidden in grey mist. The
air was rarefied and smoky. It was said that *abreks* had
crossed the now shallow river and were prowling on this side
of it. Every night the sun set in a glowing red blaze. It was
the busiest time of the year. The villagers all swarmed in the
melon-fields and the vineyards. The vineyards thickly overgrown with twining verdure lay in cool, deep shade. Everywhere between the broad translucent leaves, ripe, heavy,
black clusters peeped out. Along the dusty road from the
vineyards the creaking carts moved slowly, heaped up with
black grapes. Clusters of them, crushed by the wheels, lay in
the dirt. Boys and girls in smocks stained with grape-juice,
with grapes in their hands and mouths, ran after their mothers.
On the road you continually came across tattered labourers
with baskets of grapes on their powerful shoulders; Cossack
maidens, veiled with kerchiefs to their eyes, drove bullocks
harnessed to carts laden high with grapes. Soldiers who happened to meet these carts asked for grapes, and the maidens,
clambering up without stopping their carts, would take an
armful of grapes and drop them into the skirts of the soldiers'
coats. In some homesteads they had already begun pressing
the grapes; and the smell of the emptied skins filled the air.
One saw the blood-red troughs in the penthouses in the yards
and Nogáy labourers with their trousers rolled up and their
legs stained with the juice. Grunting pigs gorged themselves
with the empty skins and rolled about in them. The flat roofs
of the outhouses were all spread over with the dark amber
clusters drying in the sun. Daws and magpies crowded round
the roofs, picking the seeds and fluttering from one place to
another.

The fruits of the year's labour were being merrily gathered
in, and this year the fruit was unusually fine and plentiful.

In the shady green vineyards amid a sea of vines, laughter,
songs, merriment, and the voices of women were to be heard
on all sides, and glimpses of their bright-coloured garments
could be seen.

Just at noon Maryánka was sitting in their vineyard in the
shade of a peach-tree, getting out the family dinner from un-

der an unharnessed cart. Opposite her, on a spread-out-horse-
cloth, sat the cornet (who had returned from the school)
washing his hands by pouring water on them from a little jug.
Her little brother, who had just come straight out of the pond,
stood wiping his face with his wide sleeves, and gazed anxiously at his sister and his mother and breathed deeply, awaiting his dinner. The old mother, with her sleeves rolled up over
her strong sunburnt arms, was arranging grapes, dried fish,
and clotted cream on a little low, circular Tartar table. The
cornet wiped his hands, took off his cap, crossed himself,
and moved nearer to the table. The boy seized the jug and
eagerly began to drink. The mother and daughter crossed
their legs under them and sat down by the table. Even in the
shade it was intolerably hot. The air above the vineyard smelt
unpleasant: the strong warm wind passing amid the branches
brought no coolness, but only monotonously bent the tops of
the pear, peach, and mulberry trees with which the vineyard
was sprinkled. The cornet, having crossed himself once more,
took a little jug of *chikhir* that stood behind him covered with
a vine-leaf, and having had a drink from the mouth of the jug
passed it to the old woman. He had nothing on over his shirt,
which was unfastened at the neck and showed his shaggy
muscular chest. His fine-featured cunning face looked cheerful; neither in his attitude nor in his words was his usual wili-
ness to be seen, he was cheerful and natural.

'Shall we finish the bit beyond the shed to-night?' he asked,
wiping his wet beard.

'We'll manage it,' replied his wife, 'if only the weather does
not hinder us. The Dëmkins have not half finished yet,' she
added. 'Only Ústenka is at work there, wearing herself out.'

'What can you expect of them?' said the old man proudly.

'Here, have a drink, Maryánka dear!' said the old woman,
passing the jug to the girl. 'God willing we'll have enough to
pay for the wedding feast,' she added.

'That's not yet awhile,' said the cornet with a slight frown.

The girl hung her head.

'Why shouldn't we mention it?' said the old woman. 'The
affair is settled, and the time is drawing near too.'

'Don't make plans beforehand,' said the cornet. 'Now we have the harvest to get in.'

'Have you seen Lukáshka's new horse?' asked the old woman. 'That which Dmítri Andréich Olénin gave him is gone —he's exchanged it.'

'No, I have not; but I spoke with the servant to-day,' said the cornet, 'and he said his master has again received a thousand rubles.'

'Rolling in riches, in short,' said the old woman.

The whole family felt cheerful and contented.

The work was progressing successfully. The grapes were more abundant and finer than they had expected.

After dinner Maryánka threw some grass to the oxen, folded her *beshmet* for a pillow, and lay down under the wagon on the juicy down-trodden grass. She had on only a red kerchief over her head and a faded blue print smock, yet she felt unbearably hot. Her face was burning, and she did not know where to put her feet, her eyes were moist with sleepiness and weariness, her lips parted involuntarily, and her chest heaved heavily and deeply.

The busy time of year had begun a fortnight ago and the continuous heavy labour had filled the girl's life. At dawn she jumped up, washed her face with cold water, wrapped herself in a shawl, and ran out barefoot to see to the cattle. Then she hurriedly put on her shoes and her *beshmet* and, taking a small bundle of bread, she harnessed the bullocks and drove away to the vineyards for the whole day. There she cut the grapes and carried the baskets with only an hour's interval for rest, and in the evening she returned to the village, bright and not tired, dragging the bullocks by a rope or driving them with a long stick. After attending to the cattle, she took some sunflower seeds in the wide sleeve of her smock and went to the corner of the street to crack them and have some fun with the other girls. But as soon as it was dusk she returned home, and after having supper with her parents and her brother in the dark outhouse, she went into the hut, healthy and free from care, and climbed onto the oven, where half drowsing she listened to their lodger's conversation. As soon as he went away she would throw herself down on her bed and sleep soundly and quietly till morning. And so it went on day after day. She had not seen Lukáshka since the day of their betrothal, but calmly awaited the wedding. She had got used to their lodger and felt his intent looks with pleasure.

CHAPTER XXX

Although there was no escape from the heat and the mosquitoes swarmed in the cool shadow of the wagons, and her little brother tossing about beside her kept pushing her, Maryánka having drawn her kerchief over her head was just falling asleep, when suddenly their neighbour Ústenka came running towards her and, diving under the wagon, lay down beside her.

'Sleep, girls, sleep!' said Ústenka, making herself comfortable under the wagon. 'Wait a bit,' she exclaimed, 'this won't do!'

She jumped up, plucked some green branches, and stuck them through the wheels on both sides of the wagon and hung her *beshmet* over them.

'Let me in,' she shouted to the little boy as she again crept under the wagon. 'Is this the place for a Cossack—with the girls? Go away!'

When alone under the wagon with her friend, Ústenka suddenly put both her arms round her, and clinging close to her began kissing her cheeks and neck.

'Darling, sweetheart,' she kept repeating, between bursts of shrill, clear laughter.

'Why, you've learnt it from Grandad,' said Maryánka, struggling. 'Stop it!'

And they both broke into such peals of laughter that Maryánka's mother shouted to them to be quiet.

'Are you jealous?' asked Ústenka in a whisper.

'What humbug! Let me sleep. What have you come for?'

But Ústenka kept on, 'I say! But I wanted to tell you such a thing.'

Maryánka raised herself on her elbow and arranged the kerchief which had slipped off.

'Well, what is it?'

'I know something about your lodger!'

'There's nothing to know,' said Maryánka.

'Oh, you rogue of a girl!' said Ústenka, nudging her with her elbow and laughing. 'Won't tell anything. Does he come to you?'

'He does. What of that?' said Maryánka with a sudden blush.

'Now I'm a simple lass. I tell everybody. Why should I pretend?' said Ústenka, and her bright rosy face suddenly became pensive. 'Whom do I hurt? I love him, that's all about it.'

'Grandad, do you mean?'

'Well, yes!'

'And the sin?'

'Ah, Maryánka! When is one to have a good time if not while one's still free? When I marry a Cossack I shall bear children and shall have cares. There now, when you get married to Lukáshka not even a thought of joy will enter your head: children will come, and work!'

'Well? Some who are married live happily. It makes no difference!' Maryánka replied quietly.

'Do tell me just this once what has passed between you and Lukáshka?'

'What has passed? A match was proposed. Father put it off for a year, but now it's been settled and they'll marry us in autumn.'

'But what did he say to you?'

Maryánka smiled.

'What should he say? He said he loved me. He kept asking me to come to the vineyards with him.'

'Just see what pitch! But you didn't go, did you? And what a dare-devil he has become: the first among the braves. He makes merry out there in the army too! The other day our

Kírka came home; he says: What a horse Lukáshka's got in exchange! But all the same I expect he frets after you. And what else did he say?'

'Must you know everything?' said Maryánka laughing. 'One night he came to my window tipsy, and asked me to let him in.'

'And you didn't let him?'

'Let him, indeed! Once I have said a thing I keep to it firm as a rock,' answered Maryánka seriously.

'A fine fellow! If he wanted her, no girl would refuse him.'

'Well, let him go to the others,' replied Maryánka proudly.

'You don't pity him?'

'I do pity him, but I'll have no nonsense. It is wrong.'

Ústenka suddenly dropped her head on her friend's breast, seized hold of her, and shook with smothered laughter. 'You silly fool!' she exclaimed, quite out of breath. 'You don't want to be happy,' and she began tickling Maryánka.

'Oh, leave off!' said Maryánka, screaming and laughing. 'You've crushed Lazútka.'

'Hark at those young devils! Quite frisky! Not tired yet!' came the old woman's sleepy voice from the wagon.

'Don't want happiness,' repeated Ústenka in a whisper, insistently. 'But you are lucky, that you are! How they love you! You are so crusty, and yet they love you. Ah, if I were in your place I'd soon turn the lodger's head! I noticed him when you were at our house. He was ready to eat you with his eyes. What things Grandad has given me! And yours they say is the richest of the Russians. His orderly says they have serfs of their own.'

Maryánka raised herself, and after thinking a moment, smiled.

'Do you know what he once told me: the lodger I mean?' she said, biting a bit of grass. 'He said, I'd like to be Lukáshka the Cossack, or your brother Lazútka ——. What do you think he meant?'

'Oh, just chattering what came into his head,' answered Ústenka. 'What does mine not say! Just as if he was possessed!'

Maryánka dropped her head on her folded *beshmet,* threw her arm over Ústenka's shoulder, and shut her eyes.

'He wanted to come and work in the vineyard to-day: father invited him,' she said, and after a short silence she fell asleep.

CHAPTER XXXI

The sun had come out from behind the pear-tree that had shaded the wagon, and even through the branches that Ústenka had fixed up it scorched the faces of the sleeping girls. Maryánka woke up and began arranging the kerchief on her head. Looking about her, beyond the pear-tree she noticed their lodger, who with his gun on his shoulder stood talking to her father. She nudged Ústenka and smilingly pointed him out to her.

'I went yesterday and didn't find a single one,' Olénin was saying as he looked about uneasily, not seeing Maryánka through the branches.

'Ah, you should go out there in that direction, go right as by compasses, there in a disused vineyard denominated as the Waste, hares are always to be found,' said the cornet, having at once changed his manner of speech.

'A fine thing to go looking for hares in these busy times! You had better come and help us, and do some work with the girls,' the old woman said merrily. 'Now then, girls, up with you!' she cried.

Maryánka and Ústenka under the cart were whispering and could hardly restrain their laughter.

Since it had become known that Olénin had given a horse worth fifty rubles to Lukáshka, his hosts had become more amiable and the cornet in particular saw with pleasure his daughter's growing intimacy with Olénin.

'But I don't know how to do the work,' replied Olénin, trying not to look through the green branches under the wagon where he had now noticed Maryánka's blue smock and red kerchief.

'Come, I'll give you some peaches,' said the old woman.

'It's only according to the ancient Cossack hospitality. It's her old woman's silliness,' said the cornet, explaining and apparently correcting his wife's words. 'In Russia, I expect, it's not so much peaches as pineapple jam and preserves you have been accustomed to eat at your pleasure.'

'So you say hares are to be found in the disused vineyard?' asked Olénin. 'I will go there,' and throwing a hasty glance through the green branches he raised his cap and disappeared between the regular rows of green vines.

The sun had already sunk behind the fence of the vineyards, and its broken rays glittered through the translucent leaves when Olénin returned to his host's vineyard. The wind was falling and a cool freshness was beginning to spread around. By some instinct Olénin recognized from afar Maryánka's blue smock among the rows of vine, and, picking grapes on his way, he approached her. His highly excited dog also now and then seized a low-hanging cluster of grapes in his slobbering mouth. Maryánka, her face flushed, her sleeves rolled up, and her kerchief down below her chin, was rapidly cutting the heavy clusters and laying them in a basket. Without letting go of the vine she had hold of, she stopped to smile pleasantly at him and resumed her work. Olénin drew near and threw his gun behind his back to have his hands free. 'Where are your people? May God aid you! Are you alone?' he meant to say but did not say, and only raised his cap in silence.

He was ill at ease alone with Maryánka, but as if purposely to torment himself he went up to her.

'You'll be shooting the women with your gun like that,' said Maryánka.

'No, I shan't shoot them.'

They were both silent.

Then after a pause she said: 'You should help me.'

He took out his knife and began silently to cut off the clusters. He reached from under the leaves low down a thick bunch weighing about three pounds the grapes of which grew so close that they flattened each other for want of space. He showed it to Maryánka.

'Must they all be cut? Isn't this one too green?'

'Give it here.'

Their hands touched. Olénin took her hand, and she looked at him smiling.

'Are you going to be married soon?' he asked.

She did not answer, but turned away with a stern look.

'Do you love Lukáshka?'

'What's that to you?'

'I envy him!'

'Very likely!'

'No really. You are so beautiful!'

And he suddenly felt terribly ashamed of having said it, so commonplace did the words seem to him. He flushed, lost control of himself, and seized both her hands.

'Whatever I am, I'm not for you. Why do you make fun of me?' replied Maryánka, but her look showed how certainly she knew he was not making fun.

'Making fun? If you only knew how I ——'

The words sounded still more commonplace, they accorded still less with what he felt, but yet he continued, 'I don't know what I would not do for you ——'

'Leave me alone, you pitch!'

But her face, her shining eyes, her swelling bosom, her shapely legs, said something quite different. It seemed to him that she understood how petty were all things he had said, but that she was superior to such considerations. It seemed to him she had long known all he wished and was not able to tell her, but wanted to hear how he would say it. 'And how can she help knowing,' he thought, 'since I only want to tell her all that she herself is? But she does not wish to understand, does not wish to reply.'

'Hullo!' suddenly came Ústenka's high voice from behind the vine at no great distance, followed by her shrill laugh. 'Come and help me, Dmítri Andréich. I am all alone,' she cried, thrusting her round, naïve little face through the vines.

Olénin did not answer nor move from his place.

Maryánka went on cutting and continually looked up at

Olénin. He was about to say something, but stopped, shrugged his shoulders and, having jerked up his gun, walked out of the vineyard with rapid strides.

CHAPTER XXXII

He stopped once or twice, listening to the ringing laughter of Maryánka and Ústenka who, having come together, were shouting something. Olénin spent the whole evening hunting in the forest and returned home at dusk without having killed anything. When crossing the road he noticed her open the door of the outhouse, and her blue smock showed through it. He called to Vanyúsha very loud so as to let her know that he was back, and then sat down in the porch in his usual place. His hosts now returned from the vineyard; they came out of the outhouse and into their hut, but did not ask him in. Maryánka went twice out of the gate. Once in the twilight it seemed to him that she was looking at him. He eagerly followed her every movement, but could not make up his mind to approach her. When she disappeared into the hut he left the porch and began pacing up and down the yard, but Maryánka did not come out again. Olénin spent the whole sleepless night out in the yard listening to every sound in his hosts' hut. He heard them talking early in the evening, heard them having their supper and pulling out their cushions, and going to bed; he heard Maryánka laughing at something, and then heard everything growing gradually quiet. The cornet and his wife talked a while in whispers, and someone was breathing. Olénin re-entered his hut. Vanyúsha lay asleep in his clothes. Olénin envied him, and again went out to pace the yard, always expecting something, but no one came, no one moved, and he only heard the regular breathing of three people. He knew Maryánka's breathing and listened to it and to the beating of his own heart. In the village everything was quiet. The waning moon rose late, and the deep-breathing cattle in the yard became more visible as they lay down and

slowly rose. Olénin angrily asked himself, 'What is it I want?'
but could not tear himself away from the enchantment of the
night. Suddenly he thought he distinctly heard the floor creak
and the sound of footsteps in his hosts' hut. He rushed to the
door, but all was silent again except for the sound of regular
breathing, and in the yard the buffalo-cow, after a deep sigh,
again moved, rose on her foreknees and then on her feet,
swished her tail, and something splashed steadily on the dry
clay ground; then she lay down again in the dim moonlight.
He asked himself: 'What am I to do?' and definitely decided
to go to bed, but again he heard a sound, and in his imagination there arose the image of Maryánka coming out into this
moonlit misty night, and again he rushed to her window and
again heard the sound of footsteps. Not till just before dawn
did he go up to her window and push at the shutter and then
run to the door, and this time he really heard Maryánka's deep
breathing and her footsteps. He took hold of the latch and
knocked. The floor hardly creaked under the bare cautious
footsteps which approached the door. The latch clicked, the
door creaked, and he noticed a faint smell of marjoram and
pumpkin, and Maryánka's whole figure appeared in the doorway. He saw her only for an instant in the moonlight. She
slammed the door and, muttering something, ran lightly back
again. Olénin began rapping softly but nothing responded. He
ran to the window and listened. Suddenly he was startled by a
shrill, squeaky man's voice.

'Fine!' exclaimed a rather small young Cossack in a white
cap, coming across the yard close to Olénin. 'I saw . . . fine!'

Olénin recognized Nazárka, and was silent, not knowing
what to do or say.

'Fine! I'll go and tell them at the office, and I'll tell her father! That's a fine cornet's daughter! One's not enough for her.'

'What do you want of me, what are you after?' uttered
Olénin.

'Nothing; only I'll tell them at the office.'

Nazárka spoke very loud, and evidently did so intentionally,
adding: 'Just see what a clever cadet!'

Olénin trembled and grew pale.

'Come here, here!' He seized the Cossack firmly by the arm and drew him towards his hut.

'Nothing happened, she did not let me in, and I too mean no harm. She is an honest girl ——'

'Eh, discuss ——'

'Yes, but all the same I'll give you something now. Wait a bit!'

Nazárka said nothing. Olénin ran into his hut and brought out ten rubles, which he gave to the Cossack.

'Nothing happened, but still I was to blame, so I give this!— Only for God's sake don't let anyone know, for nothing happened . . .'

'I wish you joy,' said Nazárka laughing, and went away.

Nazárka had come to the village that night at Lukáshka's bidding to find a place to hide a stolen horse, and now, passing by on his way home, had heard the sound of footsteps. When he returned next morning to his company he bragged to his chum, and told him how cleverly he had got ten rubles. Next morning Olénin met his hosts and they knew nothing about the events of the night. He did not speak to Maryánka, and she only laughed a little when she looked at him. Next night he also passed without sleep, vainly wandering about the yard. The day after he purposely spent shooting, and in the evening he went to see Belétski to escape from his own thoughts. He was afraid of himself, and promised himself not to go to his hosts' hut any more.

That night he was roused by the sergeant-major. His company was ordered to start at once on a raid. Olénin was glad this had happened, and thought he would not again return to the village.

The raid lasted four days. The commander, who was a relative of Olénin's, wished to see him and offered to let him remain with the staff, but this Olénin declined. He found that he could not live away from the village, and asked to be allowed to return to it. For having taken part in the raid he received a soldier's cross, which he had formerly greatly desired. Now he was quite indifferent about it, and even more indifferent about his promotion, the order for which had still not

arrived. Accompanied by Vanyúsha he rode back to the cordon without any accident several hours in advance of the rest
of the company. He spent the whole evening in his porch
watching Maryánka, and he again walked about the yard,
without aim or thought, all night.

CHAPTER XXXIII

It was late when he awoke the next day. His hosts were no
longer in. He did not go shooting, but now took up a book,
and now went out into the porch, and now again re-entered
the hut and lay down on the bed. Vanyúsha thought he was ill.

Towards evening Olénin got up, resolutely began writing,
and wrote on till late at night. He wrote a letter, but did not
post it because he felt that no one would have understood
what he wanted to say, and besides it was not necessary that
anyone but himself should understand it. This is what he
wrote:

'I receive letters of condolence from Russia. They are afraid
that I shall perish, buried in these wilds. They say about me:
"He will become coarse; he will be behind the times in everything; he will take to drink, and who knows but that he may
marry a Cossack girl." It was not for nothing, they say, that
Ermólov[1] declared: "Anyone serving in the Caucasus for ten
years either becomes a confirmed drunkard or marries a loose
woman." How terrible! Indeed it won't do for me to ruin myself when I might have the great happiness of even becoming
the Countess B——'s husband, or a Court chamberlain, or a
Maréchal de noblesse of my district. Oh, how repulsive and
pitiable you all seem to me! You do not know what happiness
is and what life is! One must taste life once in all its natural
beauty, must see and understand what I see every day before
me—those eternally unapproachable snowy peaks, and a majestic woman in that primitive beauty in which the first woman

---

[1] General A. P. Ermólov (1772-1861) was renowned for his firmness and justness as a ruler in the Caucasus and subdued Chéchnya
and Daghestán.

must have come from her creator's hands—and then it becomes clear who is ruining himself and who is living truly or
falsely—you or I. If you only knew how despicable and pitiable you, in your delusions, seem to me! When I picture to myself—in place of my hut, my forests, and my love—those draw-
ing-rooms, those women with their pomatum-greased hair
eked out with false curls, those unnaturally grimacing lips,
those hidden, feeble, distorted limbs, and that chatter of obligatory drawing-room conversation which has no right to the
name—I feel unendurably revolted. I then see before me
those obtuse faces, those rich eligible girls whose looks seem to
say: "It's all right, you may come near though I am rich and
eligible"—and that arranging and rearranging of seats, that
shameless match-making and that eternal tittle-tattle and pretence; those rules—with whom to shake hands, to whom only
to nod, with whom to converse (and all this done deliberately
with a conviction of its inevitability), that continual ennui in
the blood passing on from generation to generation. Try to
understand or believe just this one thing: you need only see
and comprehend what truth and beauty are, and all that you
now say and think and all your wishes for me and for yourselves will fly to atoms! Happiness is being with nature, seeing
her, and conversing with her. "He may even (God forbid)
marry a common Cossack girl, and be quite lost socially," I can
imagine them saying of me with sincere pity! Yet the one thing
I desire is to be quite "lost" in your sense of the word. I wish
to marry a Cossack girl, and dare not because it would be a
height of happiness of which I am unworthy.

'Three months have passed since I first saw the Cossack girl,
Maryánka. The views and prejudices of the world I had left
were still fresh in me. I did not then believe that I could love
that woman. I delighted in her beauty just as I delighted in
the beauty of the mountains and the sky, nor could I help de-
lighting in her, for she is as beautiful as they. I found that the
sight of her beauty had become a necessity of my life and I
began asking myself whether I did not love her. But I could
find nothing within myself at all like love as I had imagined it
to be. Mine was not the restlessness of loneliness and desire

for marriage, nor was it platonic, still less a carnal love such as I have experienced. I needed only to see her, to hear her, to know that she was near—and if I was not happy, I was at peace.

'After an evening gathering at which I met her and touched her, I felt that between that woman and myself there existed an indissoluble though unacknowledged bond against which I could not struggle, yet I did struggle. I asked myself: "Is it possible to love a woman who will never understand the profoundest interests of my life? Is it possible to love a woman simply for her beauty, to love the statue of a woman?" But I was already in love with her, though I did not yet trust to my feelings.

'After that evening when I first spoke to her our relations changed. Before that she had been to me an extraneous but majestic object of external nature: but since then she has become a human being. I began to meet her, to talk to her, and sometimes to go to work for her father and to spend whole evenings with them, and in this intimate intercourse she remained still in my eyes just as pure, inaccessible, and majestic. She always responded with equal calm, pride, and cheerful equanimity. Sometimes she was friendly, but generally her every look, every word, and every movement expressed equanimity—not contemptuous, but crushing and bewitching. Every day with a feigned smile on my lips I tried to play a part, and with torments of passion and desire in my heart I spoke banteringly to her. She saw that I was dissembling, but looked straight at me cheerfully and simply. This position became unbearable. I wished not to deceive her but to tell her all I thought and felt. I was extremely agitated. We were in the vineyard when I began to tell her of my love, in words I am now ashamed to remember. I am ashamed because I ought not to have dared to speak so to her because she stood far above such words and above the feeling they were meant to express. I said no more, but from that day my position has been intolerable. I did not wish to demean myself by continuing our former flippant relations, and at the same time I felt that I had not yet reached the level of straight and simple relations with her. I asked myself despairingly, "What am I to do?" In foolish dreams I imagined her now as my mistress and now as my wife, but rejected both ideas with disgust. To make her a wanton woman would be dreadful. It would be murder. To turn her into a fine lady, the wife of Dmítri Andréich Olénin, like a Cossack woman here who is married to one of our officers, would be still worse. Now could I turn Cossack like Lukáshka, and steal horses, get drunk on *chikhir*, sing rollicking songs, kill people, and when drunk climb in at her window for the night without a thought of who and what I am, it would be different: then we might understand one another and I might be happy.

'I tried to throw myself into that kind of life but was still more conscious of my own weakness and artificiality. I cannot forget myself and my complex, distorted past, and my future appears to me still more hopeless. Every day I have before me the distant snowy mountains and this majestic, happy woman. But not for me is the only happiness possible in the world; I cannot have this woman! What is most terrible and yet sweetest in my condition is that I feel that I understand her but that she will never understand me; not because she is inferior: on the contrary she ought not to understand me. She is happy, she is like nature: consistent, calm, and self-contained; and I, a weak distorted being, want her to understand my deformity and my torments! I have not slept at night, but have aimlessly passed under her windows not rendering account to myself of what was happening to me. On the 18th our company started on a raid, and I spent three days away from the village. I was sad and apathetic, the usual songs, cards, drinking-bouts, and talk of rewards in the regiment, were more repulsive to me than usual. Yesterday I returned home and saw her, my hut, Daddy Eróshka, and the snowy mountains, from my porch, and was seized by such a strong, new feeling of joy that I understood it all. I love this woman; I feel real love for the first and only time in my life. I know what has befallen me. I do not fear to be degraded by this feeling, I am not ashamed of my love, I am proud of it. It is not my fault that I love. It has come about against my will. I tried to escape from my love by self-renunciation, and tried to devise a joy in the Cossack

Lukáshka's and Maryánka's love, but thereby only stirred up my own love and jealousy. This is not the ideal, the so-called exalted love which I have known before; not that sort of attachment in which you admire your own love and feel that the source of your emotion is within yourself and do everything yourself. I have felt that too. It is still less a desire for enjoyment: it is something different. Perhaps in her I love nature: the personification of all that is beautiful in nature; but yet I am not acting by my own will, but some elemental force loves through me; the whole of God's world, all nature, presses this love into my soul and says, "Love her." I love her not with my mind or my imagination, but with my whole being. Loving her I feel myself to be an integral part of all God's joyous world. I wrote before about the new convictions to which my solitary life had brought me, but no one knows with what labour they shaped themselves within me and with what joy I realized them and saw a new way of life opening out before me; nothing was dearer to me than those convictions . . . Well! . . . love has come and neither they nor any regrets for them remain! It is even difficult for me to believe that I could prize such a one-sided, cold, and abstract state of mind. Beauty came and scattered to the winds all that laborious inward toil, and no regret remains for what has vanished! Self-renunciation is all nonsense and absurdity! That is pride, a refuge from well-merited unhappiness, and salvation from the envy of others' happiness: "Live for others, and do good!"——Why? when in my soul there is only love for myself and the desire to love her and to live her life with her? Not for others, not for Lukáshka, I now desire happiness. I do not now love those others. Formerly I should have told myself that this is wrong. I should have tormented myself with the questions: What will become of her, of me, and of Lukáshka? Now I don't care. I do not live my own life, there is something stronger than me which directs me. I suffer; but formerly I was dead and only now do I live. To-day I will go to their house and tell her everything.'

CHAPTER XXXIV

Late that evening, after writing this letter, Olénin went to his hosts' hut. The old woman was sitting on a bench behind the oven unwinding cocoons. Maryánka with her head uncovered sat sewing by the light of a candle. On seeing Olénin she jumped up, took her kerchief and stepped to the oven.

'Maryánka dear,' said her mother, 'won't you sit here with me a bit?'

'No, I'm bareheaded,' she replied, and sprang up on the oven.

Olénin could only see a knee, and one of her shapely legs hanging down from the oven. He treated the old woman to tea. She treated her guest to clotted cream which she sent Maryánka to fetch. But having put a plateful on the table Maryánka again sprang on the oven from whence Olénin felt her eyes upon him. They talked about household matters. Granny Ulítka became animated and went into raptures of hospitality. She brought Olénin preserved grapes and a grape tart and some of her best wine, and pressed him to eat and drink with the rough yet proud hospitality of country folk, only found among those who produce their bread by the labour of their own hands. The old woman, who had at first struck Olénin so much by her rudeness, now often touched him by her simple tenderness towards her daughter.

'Yes, we need not offend the Lord by grumbling! We have enough of everything, thank God. We have pressed sufficient *chikhir* and have preserved and shall sell three or four barrels of grapes and have enough left to drink. Don't be in a hurry to leave us. We will make merry together at the wedding.'

'And when is the wedding to be?' asked Olénin, feeling his blood suddenly rush to his face while his heart beat irregularly and painfully.

He heard a movement on the oven and the sound of seeds being cracked.

'Well, you know, it ought to be next week. We are quite ready,' replied the old woman, as simply and quietly as though Olénin did not exist. 'I have prepared and have procured everything for Maryánka. We will give her away properly. Only there's one thing not quite right. Our Lukáshka has been running rather wild. He has been too much on the spree! He's up to tricks! The other day a Cossack came here from his company and said he had been to Nogáy.'

'He must mind he does not get caught,' said Olénin.

'Yes, that's what I tell him. "Mind, Lukáshka, don't you get into mischief. Well of course a young fellow naturally wants to cut a dash. But there's a time for everything. Well, you've captured or stolen something and killed an *abrek!* Well, you're a fine fellow! But now you should live quietly for a bit, or else there'll be trouble." '

'Yes, I saw him a time or two in the division, he was always merry-making. He has sold another horse,' said Olénin, and glanced towards the oven.

A pair of large, dark, and hostile eyes glittered as they gazed severely at him.

He became ashamed of what he had said. 'What of it? He does no one any harm,' suddenly remarked Maryánka. 'He makes merry with his own money,' and lowering her legs she jumped down from the oven and went out banging the door.

Olénin followed her with his eyes as long as she was in the hut, and then looked at the door and waited, understanding nothing of what Granny Ulítka was telling him.

A few minutes later some visitors arrived: an old man, Granny Ulítka's brother, with Daddy Eróshka, and following them came Maryánka and Ústenka.

'Good evening,' squeaked Ústenka. 'Still on holiday?' she added, turning to Olénin.

'Yes, still on holiday,' he replied, and felt, he did not know why, ashamed and ill at ease.

He wished to go away but could not. It also seemed to him impossible to remain silent. The old man helped him by asking for a drink, and they had a drink. Olénin drank with Eróshka, with the other Cossack, and again with Eróshka, and the more he drank the heavier was his heart. But the two old men grew merry. The girls climbed onto the oven, where they sat whispering and looking at the men, who drank till it was late. Olénin did not talk, but drank more than the others. The Cossacks were shouting. The old woman would not let them have any more *chikhir*, and at last turned them out. The girls laughed at Daddy Eróshka, and it was past ten when they all went out into the porch. The old men invited themselves to finish their merry-making at Olénin's. Ústenka ran off home and Eróshka led the old Cossack to Vanyúsha. The old woman went out to tidy up the shed. Maryánka remained alone in the hut. Olénin felt fresh and joyous, as if he had only just woke up. He noticed everything, and having let the old men pass ahead he turned back to the hut where Maryánka was preparing for bed. He went up to her and wished to say something, but his voice broke. She moved away from him, sat down cross-legged on her bed in the corner, and looked at him silently with wild and frightened eyes. She was evidently afraid of him. Olénin felt this. He felt sorry and ashamed of himself, and at the same time proud and pleased that he aroused even that feeling in her.

'Maryánka!' he said, 'Will you never take pity on me? I can't tell you how I love you.'

She moved still farther away.

'Just hear how the wine is speaking! . . . You'll get nothing from me!'

'No, it is not the wine. Don't marry Lukáshka. I will marry you.' ('What am I saying,' he thought as he uttered these words. 'Shall I be able to say the same to-morrow?' 'Yes, I shall, I am sure I shall, and I will repeat them now,' replied an inner voice.)

'Will you marry me?'

She looked at him seriously and her fear seemed to have passed.

'Maryánka, I shall go out of my mind! I am not myself. I will do whatever you command,' and madly tender words came from his lips of their own accord.

'Now then, what are you drivelling about?' she interrupted, suddenly seizing the arm he was stretching towards her. She did not push his arm away but pressed it firmly with her strong hard fingers. 'Do gentlemen marry Cossack girls? Go away!'

'But will you? Everything . . .'

'And what shall we do with Lukáshka?' said she, laughing.

He snatched away the arm she was holding and firmly embraced her young body, but she sprang away like a fawn and ran barefoot into the porch: Olénin came to his senses and was terrified at himself. He again felt himself inexpressibly vile compared to her, yet not repenting for an instant of what he had said he went home, and without even glancing at the old men who were drinking in his room he lay down and fell asleep more soundly than he had done for a long time.

CHAPTER XXXV

The next day was a holiday. In the evening all the villagers, their holiday clothes shining in the sunset, were out in the street. That season more wine than usual had been produced, and the people were now free from their labours. In a month the Cossacks were to start on a campaign and in many families preparations were being made for weddings.

Most of the people were standing in the square in front of the Cossack Government Office and near the two shops, in one of which cakes and pumpkin seeds were sold, in the other kerchiefs and cotton prints. On the earth-embankment of the office-building sat or stood the old men in sober grey, or black coats without gold trimmings or any kind of ornament. They conversed among themselves quietly in measured tones, about the harvest, about the young folk, about village affairs, and about old times, looking with dignified equanimity at the younger generation. Passing by them, the women and girls stopped and bent their heads. The young Cossacks respectfully slackened their pace and raised their caps, holding them for a while over their heads. The old men then stopped speaking. Some of them watched the passers-by severely, others kindly, and in their turn slowly took off their caps and put them on again.

The Cossack girls had not yet started dancing their *khorovóds*,[1] but having gathered in groups, in their bright-coloured *beshmets* with white kerchiefs on their heads pulled down to their eyes, they sat either on the ground or on the earth-banks about the huts sheltered from the oblique rays of the sun, and laughed and chattered in their ringing voices. Little boys and girls playing in the square sent their balls high up into the clear sky, and ran about squealing and shouting. The half-grown girls had started dancing their *khorovóds,* and were timidly singing in their thin shrill voices. Clerks, lads not in the ser/ice, or home for the holiday, bright faced and wearing smart white or new red Circassian gold-trimmed coats, went about arm in arm in twos or threes from one group of women or girls to another, and stopped joking and chatting with the Cossack girls. The Armenian shopkeeper, in a gold-trimmed coat of fine blue cloth, stood at the open door through which piles of folded bright-coloured kerchiefs were visible and, conscious of his own importance and with the pride of an oriental tradesman, waited for customers. Two red-bearded, barefooted Chéchens, who had come from beyond the Térek to see the fête, sat on their heels outside the house of a friend, negligently smoking their little pipes and occasionally spitting, watching the villagers and exchanging remarks with one another in their rapid guttural speech. Occasionally a workaday-looking soldier in an old overcoat passed across the square among the bright-clad girls. Here and there the songs of tipsy Cossacks who were merry-making could already be heard. All the huts were closed; the porches had been scrubbed clean the day before. Even the old women were out in the street, which was everywhere sprinkled with pumpkin and melon seed-shells. The air was warm and still, the sky deep and clear. Beyond the roofs the dead-white mountain range, which

---

[1] The *khorovód* is a ring formed by the girls, who move round in a circle singing.

seemed very near, was turning rosy in the glow of the evening sun. Now and then from the other side of the river came the distant roar of a cannon, but above the village, mingling with one another, floated all sorts of merry holiday sounds.

Olénin had been pacing the yard all that morning hoping to see Maryánka. But she, having put on holiday clothes, went to Mass at the chapel and afterwards sat with the other girls on an earth-embankment cracking seeds; sometimes again, together with her companions, she ran home, and each time gave the lodger a bright and kindly look. Olénin felt afraid to address her playfully or in the presence of others. He wished to finish telling her what he had begun to say the night before, and to get her to give him a definite answer. He waited for another moment like that of yesterday evening, but the moment did not come, and he felt that he could not remain any longer in this uncertainty. She went out into the street again, and after waiting a while he too went out and without knowing where he was going he followed her. He passed by the corner where she was sitting in her shining blue satin *beshmet*, and with an aching heart he heard behind him the girls laughing.

Belétski's hut looked out onto the square. As Olénin was passing it he heard Belétski's voice calling to him, 'Come in,' and in he went.

After a short talk they both sat down by the window and were soon joined by Eróshka, who entered dressed in a new *beshmet* and sat down on the floor beside them.

'There, that's the aristocratic party,' said Belétski, pointing with his cigarette to a brightly coloured group at the corner. 'Mine is there too. Do you see her? in red. That's a new *beshmet*.' 'Why don't you start the *khorovód*?' he shouted, leaning out of the window. 'Wait a bit, and then when it grows dark let us go too. Then we will invite them to Ústenka's. We must arrange a ball for them!'

'And I will come to Ústenka's,' said Olénin in a decided tone. 'Will Maryánka be there?'

'Yes, she'll be there. Do come!' said Belétski, without the

least surprise. 'But isn't it a pretty picture?' he added, pointing
to the motley crowds.

'Yes, very!' Olénin assented, trying to appear indifferent.
'Holidays of this kind,' he added, 'always make me wonder
why all these people should suddenly be contented and jolly.
To-day for instance, just because it happens to be the fifteenth
of the month, everything is festive. Eyes and faces and voices
and movements and garments, and the air and the sun, are all
in a holiday mood. And we no longer have any holidays!'

'Yes,' said Belétski, who did not like such reflections. 'And
why are you not drinking, old fellow?' he said, turning to
Eróshka.

Eróshka winked at Olénin, pointing to Belétski. 'Eh, he's a
proud one that *kunak* of yours,' he said.

Belétski raised his glass. '*Allah birdy*,' he said, emptying it.
(*Allah birdy*, 'God has given!'—the usual greeting of Caucasians when drinking together.)

'*Sau bul*' ('Your health'), answered Eróshka smiling, and
emptied his glass.

'Speaking of holidays!' he said, turning to Olénin as he rose
and looked out of the window, 'What sort of holiday is that!
You should have seen them make merry in the old days! The
women used to come out in their gold-trimmed *sarafáns*.[2] Two
rows of gold coins hanging round their necks and gold-cloth
diadems on their heads, and when they passed they made a
noise, "flu, flu," with their dresses. Every woman looked like a
princess. Sometimes they'd come out, a whole herd of them,
and begin singing songs so that the air seemed to rumble, and
they went on making merry all night. And the Cossacks would
roll out a barrel into the yards and sit down and drink till
break of day, or they would go hand-in-hand sweeping the
village. Whoever they met they seized and took along with
them, and went from house to house. Sometimes they used to
make merry for three days on end. Father used to come home
—I still remember it—quite red and swollen, without a cap,

---

[2] A kind of gored dress worn over a blouse of different material.

having lost everything: he'd come and lie down. Mother knew what to do: she would bring him some fresh caviar and a little *chikhir* to sober him up, and would herself run about in the village looking for his cap. Then he'd sleep for two days! That's the sort of fellows they were then! But now what are they?'

'Well, and the girls in the *sarafáns*, did they make merry all by themselves?' asked Belétski.

'Yes, they did! Sometimes Cossacks would come on foot or on horse and say, "Let's break up the *khorovóds*," and they'd go, but the girls would take up cudgels. Carnival week, some young fellow would come galloping up, and they'd cudgel his horse and cudgel him too. But he'd break through, seize the one he loved, and carry her off. And his sweetheart would love him to his heart's content! Yes, the girls in those days they were regular queens!'

CHAPTER XXXVI

Just then two men rode out of the side street into the square. One of them was Nazárka. The other, Lukáshka, sat slightly sideways on his well-fed bay Kabardá horse which stepped lightly over the hard road jerking its beautiful head with its fine glossy mane. The well-adjusted gun in its cover, the pistol at his back, and the cloak rolled up behind his saddle showed that Lukáshka had not come from a peaceful place or from one near by. The smart way in which he sat a little sideways on his horse, the careless motion with which he touched the horse under its belly with his whip, and especially his half-closed black eyes, glistening as he looked proudly around him, all expressed the conscious strength and self-confidence of youth. 'Ever seen as fine a lad?' his eyes, looking from side to side, seemed to say. The elegant horse with its silver ornaments and trappings, the weapons, and the handsome Cossack himself attracted the attention of everyone in the square. Nazárka, lean and short, was much less well dressed. As he rode past the old men, Lukáshka paused and raised his curly white sheepskin cap above his closely cropped black head.

'Well, have you carried off many Nogáy horses?' asked a lean old man with a frowning, lowering look.

'Have you counted them, Grandad, that you ask?' replied Lukáshka, turning away.

'That's all very well, but you need not take my lad along with you,' the old man muttered with a still darker frown.

'Just see the old devil, he knows everything,' muttered Lukáshka to himself, and a worried expression came over his face; but then, noticing a corner where a number of Cossack girls were standing, he turned his horse towards them.

'Good evening, girls!' he shouted in his powerful, resonant voice, suddenly checking his horse. 'You've grown old without me, you witches!' and he laughed.

'Good evening, Lukáshka! Good evening, laddie!' the merry voices answered. 'Have you brought much money? But some sweets for the girls! . . . Have you come for long? True enough it's long since we saw you. . . .'

'Nezárka and I have just flown across to make a night of it,' replied Lukáshka, raising his whip and riding straight at the girls.

'Why, Maryánka has quite forgotten you,' said Ústenka, nudging Maryánka with her elbow and breaking into a shrill laugh.

Maryánka moved away from the horse and throwing back her head calmly looked at the Cossack with her large sparkling eyes.

'True enough you have not been for a long time! Why are you trampling us under your horse?' she remarked dryly, and turned away.

Lukáshka had appeared particularly merry. His face shone with audacity and joy. Obviously staggered by Maryánka's cold reply he suddenly knitted his brow.

'Step up on my stirrup and I'll carry you away to the mountains, Mammy!' he suddenly exclaimed, and as if to disperse his dark thoughts he caracoled among the girls. Stooping down towards Maryánka he said, 'I'll kiss, oh, how I'll kiss you! . . .'

Maryánka's eyes met his and she suddenly blushed and stepped back.

'Oh, bother you! you'll crush my feet,' she said, and bending her head looked at her well-shaped feet in their tightly fitting light blue stockings with clocks and her new red slippers trimmed with narrow silver braid.

Lukáshka turned towards Ústenka, and Maryánka sat down next to a woman with a baby in her arms. The baby stretched his plump little hands towards the girl and seized a necklace string that hung down onto her blue *beshmet*. Maryánka bent towards the child and glanced at Lukáshka from the corner of her eyes. Lukáshka just then was getting out from under his coat, from the pocket of his black *beshmet*, a bundle of sweet-meats and seeds.

'There, I give them to all of you,' he said, handing the bundle to Ústenka and smiling at Maryánka.

A confused expression again appeared on the girl's face. It was as though a mist gathered over her beautiful eyes. She drew her kerchief down below her lips, and leaning her head over the fair-skinned face of the baby that still held her by her coin necklace she suddenly began to kiss it greedily. The baby pressed his little hands against the girl's high breasts, and opening his toothless mouth screamed loudly.

'You're smothering the boy!' said the little one's mother, taking him away; and she unfastened her *beshmet* to give him the breast. 'You'd better have a chat with the young fellow.'

'I'll only go and put up my horse and then Nazárka and I will come back; we'll make merry all night,' said Lukáshka, touching his horse with his whip and riding away from the girls.

Turning into a side street, he and Nazárka rode up to two huts that stood side by side.

'Here we are all right, old fellow! Be quick and come soon!' called Lukáshka to his comrade, dismounting in front of one of the huts; then he carefully led his horse in at the gate of the wattle fence of his own home.

'How d'you do, Stëpka?' he said to his dumb sister, who,

smartly dressed like the others, came in from the street to take
his horse; and he made signs to her to take the horse to the
hay, but not to unsaddle it.

The dumb girl made her usual humming noise, smacked her
lips as she pointed to the horse and kissed it on the nose, as
much as to say that she loved it and that it was a fine horse.

'How d'you do, mother? How is it that you have not gone
out yet?' shouted Lukáshka, holding his gun in place as he
mounted the steps of the porch.

His old mother opened the door.

'Dear me! I never expected, never thought, you'd come,'
said the old woman. 'Why, Kírka said you wouldn't be here.'

'Go and bring some *chikhir*, mother. Nazárka is coming
here and we will celebrate the feast day.'

'Directly, Lukáshka, directly!' answered the old woman.
'Our women are making merry. I expect our dumb one has
gone too.'

She took her keys and hurriedly went to the outhouse.

Nazárka, after putting up his horse and taking the gun off
his shoulder, returned to Lukáshka's house and went in.

CHAPTER XXXVII

'Your health!' said Lukáshka, taking from his mother's hands a
cup filled to the brim with *chikhir* and carefully raising it to
his bowed head.

'A bad business!' said Nazárka. 'You heard how Daddy
Burlák said, "Have you stolen many horses?" He seems to
know!'

'A regular wizard!' Lukáshka replied shortly. 'But what of
it!' he added, tossing his head. 'They are across the river by
now. Go and find them!'

'Still it's a bad lookout.'

'What's a bad lookout? Go and take some *chikhir* to him to-
morrow and nothing will come of it. Now let's make merry.
Drink!' shouted Lukáshka, just in the tone in which old
Eróshka uttered the word. 'We'll go out into the street and

make merry with the girls. You go and get some honey; or no, I'll send our dumb wench. We'll make merry till morning.'

Nazárka smiled.

'Are we stopping here long?' he asked.

'Till we've had a bit of fun. Run and get some vodka. Here's the money.'

Nazárka ran off obediently to get the vodka from Yámka's.

Daddy Eróshka and Ergushóv, like birds of prey, scenting where the merry-making was going on, tumbled into the hut one after the other, both tipsy.

'Bring us another half-pail,' shouted Lukáshka to his mother, by way of reply to their greeting.

'Now then, tell us where did you steal them, you devil?' shouted Eróshka. 'Fine fellow, I'm fond of you!'

'Fond indeed . . .' answered Lukáshka laughing, 'carrying sweets from cadets to lasses! Eh, you old . . .'

'That's not true, not true! . . . Oh, Mark,' and the old man burst out laughing. 'And how that devil begged me. "Go," he said, "and arrange it." He offered me a gun! But no. I'd have managed it, but I feel for you. Now tell us where have you been?' And the old man began speaking in Tartar.

Lukáshka answered him promptly.

Ergushóv, who did not know much Tartar, only occasionally put in a word in Russian:

'What I say is he's driven away the horses. I know it for a fact,' he chimed in.

'Giréy and I went together.' (His speaking of Giréy Khan as 'Giréy' was, to the Cossack mind, evidence of his boldness.) 'Just beyond the river he kept bragging that he knew the whole of the steppe and would lead the way straight, but we rode on and the night was dark, and my Giréy lost his way and began wandering in a circle without getting anywhere: couldn't find the village, and there we were. We must have gone too much to the right. I believe we wandered about well-nigh till midnight. Then, thank goodness, we heard dogs howling.'

'Fools!' said Daddy Eróshka. 'There now, we too used to lose our way in the steppe. (Who the devil can follow it?)

But I used to ride up a hillock and start howling like the wolves, like this!' He placed his hands before his mouth, and howled like a pack of wolves, all on one note. 'The dogs would answer at once. . . . Well, go on—so you found them?'

'We soon led them away! Nazárka was nearly caught by some Nogáy women, he was!'

'Caught indeed,' Nazárka, who had just come back, said in an injured tone.

'We rode off again, and again Giréy lost his way and almost landed us among the sand-drifts. We thought we were just getting to the Térek but we were riding away from it all the time!'

'You should have steered by the stars,' said Daddy Eróshka.

'That's what I say,' interjected Ergushóv.

'Yes, steer when all is black; I tried and tried all about . . . and at last I put the bridle on one of the mares and let my own horse go free—thinking he'll lead us out, and what do you think! he just gave a snort or two with his nose to the ground, galloped ahead, and led us straight to our village. Thank goodness! It was getting quite light. We barely had time to hide them in the forest. Nagím came across the river and took them away.'

Ergushóv shook his head. 'It's just what I said. Smart. Did you get much for them?'

'It's all here,' said Lukáshka, slapping his pocket.

Just then his mother came into the room, and Lukáshka did not finish what he was saying.

'Drink!' he shouted.

'We too, Gírich and I, rode out late one night . . .' began Eróshka.

'Oh bother, we'll never hear the end of you!' said Lukáshka. 'I am going.' And having emptied his cup and tightened the strap of his belt he went out.

CHAPTER XXXVIII

It was already dark when Lukáshka went out into the street.
The autumn night was fresh and calm. The full golden moon
floated up behind the tall dark poplars that grew on one side
of the square. From the chimneys of the outhouses smoke rose
and spread above the village, mingling with the mist. Here
and there lights shone through the windows, and the air was
laden with the smell of *kisyak*, grape-pulp, and mist. The
sounds of voices, laughter, songs, and the cracking of seeds
mingled just as they had done in the daytime, but were now
more distinct. Clusters of white kerchiefs and caps gleamed
through the darkness near the houses and by the fences.

In the square, before the shop door which was lit up and
open, the black and white figures of Cossack men and maids
showed through the darkness, and one heard from afar their
loud songs and laughter and talk. The girls, hand in hand,
went round and round in a circle stepping lightly in the
dusty square. A skinny girl, the plainest of them all, set the
tune:

> From beyond the wood, from the forest dark,
> From the garden green and the shady park,
> There came out one day two young lads so gay.
> Young bachelors, hey! brave and smart were they!
> And they walked and walked, then stood still, each man,
> And they talked and soon to dispute began!
> Then a maid came out; as she came along,
> Said, 'To one of you I shall soon belong!'
> 'Twas the fair-faced lad got the maiden fair,
> Yes, the fair-faced lad with the golden hair!
> Her right hand so white in his own took he,
> And he led her round for his mates to see!
> And said, 'Have you ever in all your life,
> Met a lass as fair as my sweet little wife?'

The old women stood round listening to the songs. The little boys and girls ran about chasing one another in the dark.
The men stood by, catching at the girls as the latter moved

round, and sometimes breaking the ring and entering it. On the dark side of the doorway stood Belétski and Olénin, in their Circassian coats and sheepskin caps, and talked together in a style of speech unlike that of the Cossacks, in low but distinct tones, conscious that they were attracting attention. Next to one another in the *khorovód* circle moved plump little Ústenka in her red *beshmet* and the stately Maryánka in her new smock and *beshmet*. Olénin and Belétski were discussing how to snatch Ústenka and Maryánka out of the ring. Belétski thought that Olénin wished only to amuse himself, but Olénin was expecting his fate to be decided. He wanted at any cost to see Maryánka alone that very day and to tell her everything, and ask her whether she could and would be his wife. Although that question had long been answered in the negative in his own mind, he hoped he would be able to tell her all he felt, and that she would understand him.

'Why did you not tell me sooner?' said Belétski. 'I would have got Ústenka to arrange it for you. You are such a queer fellow! . . .'

'What's to be done! . . . Some day, very soon, I'll tell you all about it. Only now for Heaven's sake arrange so that she should come to Ústenka's.'

'All right, that's easily done! Well, Maryánka, will you belong to the "fair-faced lad," and not to Lukáshka?' said Belétski, speaking to Maryánka first for propriety's sake, but having received no reply he went up to Ústenka and begged her to bring Maryánka home with her. He had hardly time to finish what he was saying before the leader began another song and the girls started pulling each other round in the ring by the hand.

They sang:

Past the garden, by the garden,
A young man came strolling down,
Up the street and through the town.
And the first time as he passed
He did wave his strong right hand.
As the second time he passed
Waved his hat with silken band.

But the third time as he went
He stood still: before her bent.

'How is it that thou, my dear,
My reproaches dost not fear?
In the park don't come to walk
That we there might have a talk?
Come now, answer me, my dear,
Dost thou hold me in contempt?
Later on, thou knowest, dear,
Thou'lt get sober and repent.
Soon to woo thee I will come,
And when we shall married be
Thou wilt weep because of me!'

'Though I knew what to reply,
Yet I dared not him deny,
No, I dared not him deny!
So into the park went I,
In the park my lad to meet,
There my dear one I did greet.'

'Maiden dear, I bow to thee!
Take this handkerchief from me.
In thy white hand take it, see!
Say I am beloved by thee.
I don't know at all, I fear,
What I am to give thee, dear!
To my dear I think I will
Of a shawl a present make—
And five kisses for it take.'

Lukáshka and Nazárka broke into the ring and started walking about among the girls. Lukáshka joined in the singing, taking seconds in his clear voice as he walked in the middle of the ring swinging his arms. 'Well come in, one of you!' he said. The other girls pushed Maryánka, but she would not enter the ring. The sound of shrill laughter, slaps, kisses, and whispers mingled with the singing.

As he went past Olénin, Lukáshka gave a friendly nod.

'Dmítri Andréich! Have you too come to have a look?' he said.

'Yes,' answered Olénin dryly.

Belétski stooped and whispered something into Ústenka's ear. She had not time to reply till she came round again, when she said:

'All right, we'll come.'

'And Maryánka too?'

Olénin stooped towards Maryánka. 'You'll come? Please do, if only for a minute. I must speak to you.'

'If the other girls come, I will.'

'Will you answer my question?' said he, bending towards her. 'You are in good spirits to-day.'

She had already moved past him. He went after her.

'Will you answer?'

'Answer what?'

'The question I asked you the other day,' said Olénin, stooping to her ear. 'Will you marry me?'

Maryánka thought for a moment.

'I'll tell you,' said she, 'I'll tell you to-night.'

And through the darkness her eyes gleamed brightly and kindly at the young man.

He still followed her. He enjoyed stooping closer to her.

But Lukáshka, without ceasing to sing, suddenly seized her firmly by the hand and pulled her from her place in the ring of girls into the middle. Olénin had only time to say, 'Come to Ústenka's,' and stepped back to his companion. The song came to an end. Lukáshka wiped his lips, Maryánka did the same, and they kissed. 'No, no, kisses five!' said Lukáshka. Chatter, laughter, and running about, succeeded to the rhythmic movements and sound. Lukáshka, who seemed to have drunk a great deal, began to distribute sweetmeats to the girls.

'I offer them to everyone!' he said with proud, comically pathetic self-admiration. 'But anyone who goes after soldiers goes out of the ring!' he suddenly added, with an angry glance at Olénin.

The girls grabbled his sweetmeats from him, and, laughing, struggled for them among themselves. Belétski and Olénin stepped aside.

Lukáshka, as if ashamed of his generosity, took off his cap and wiping his forehead with his sleeve came up to Maryánka and Ústenka.

'Answer me, my dear, dost thou hold me in contempt?' he said in the words of the song they had just been singing, and turning to Maryánka he angrily repeated the words: 'Dost thou hold me in contempt? When we shall married be thou wilt weep because of me!' he added, embracing Ústenka and Maryánka both together.

Ústenka tore herself away, and swinging her arm gave him such a blow on the back that she hurt her hand.

'Well, are you going to have another turn?' he asked.

'The other girls may if they like,' answered Ústenka, 'but I am going home and Maryánka was coming to our house too.'

With his arm still round her, Lukáshka led Maryánka away from the crowd to the darker corner of a house.

'Don't go, Maryánka,' he said, 'let's have some fun for the last time. Go home and I will come to you!'

'What am I to do at home? Holidays are meant for merry-making. I am going to Ústenka's,' replied Maryánka.

'I'll marry you all the same, you know!'

'All right,' said Maryánka, 'we shall see when the time comes.'

'So you are going,' said Lukáshka sternly, and, pressing her close, he kissed her on the cheek.

'There, leave off! Don't bother,' and Maryánka, wrenching herself from his arms, moved away.

'Ah my girl, it will turn out badly,' said Lukáshka reproach-fully and stood still, shaking his head. 'Thou wilt weep be-cause of me . . .' and turning away from her he shouted to the other girls:

'Now then! Play away!'

What he had said seemed to have frightened and vexed Maryánka. She stopped, 'What will turn out badly?'

'Why, that!'

'That what?'

'Why, that you keep company with a soldier-lodger and no longer care for me!'

'I'll care just as long as I choose. You're not my father, nor my mother. What do you want? I'll care for whom I like!'

'Well all right . . .' said Lukáshka, 'but remember!' He moved towards the shop. 'Girls!' he shouted, 'why have you stopped? Go on dancing. Nazárka, fetch some more *chikhir*.'

'Well, will they come?' asked Olénin, addressing Belétski.

'They'll come directly,' replied Belétski. 'Come along, we must prepare the ball.'

CHAPTER XXXIX

It was already late in the night when Olénin came out of Belétski's hut following Maryánka and Ústenka. He saw in the dark street before him the gleam of the girl's white kerchief. The golden moon was descending towards the steppe. A silvery mist hung over the village. All was still; there were no lights anywhere and one heard only the receding footsteps of the young women. Olénin's heart beat fast. The fresh moist atmosphere cooled his burning face. He glanced at the sky and turned to look at the hut he had just come out of: the candle was already out. Then he again peered through the darkness at the girls' retreating shadows. The white kerchief disappeared in the mist. He was afraid to remain alone, he was so happy. He jumped down from the porch and ran after the girls.

'Bother you, someone may see . . .' said Ústenka.

'Never mind!'

Olénin ran up to Maryánka and embraced her.

Maryánka did not resist.

'Haven't you kissed enough yet?' said Ústenka. 'Marry and then kiss, but now you'd better wait.'

'Good-night, Maryánka, to-morrow I will come to see your father and tell him. Don't you say anything.'

'Why should I!' answered Maryánka.

Both the girls started running. Olénin went on by himself thinking over all that had happened. He had spent the whole evening alone with her in a corner by the oven. Ústenka had not left the hut for a single moment, but had romped about with the other girls and with Belétski all the time. Olénin had talked in whispers to Maryánka.

'Will you marry me?' he had asked.

'You'd deceive me and not have me,' she replied cheerfully and calmly.

'But do you love me? Tell me for God's sake!'

'Why shouldn't I love you? You don't squint,' answered Maryánka, laughing and with her hard hands squeezing his. . . .

'What whi-ite, whi-i-ite, soft hands you've got—so like clotted cream,' she said.

'I am in earnest. Tell me, will you marry me?'

'Why not, if father gives me to you?'

'Well then remember, I shall go mad if you deceive me. To-morrow I will tell your mother and father. I shall come and propose.'

Maryánka suddenly burst out laughing.

'What's the matter?'

'It seems so funny!'

'It's true! I will buy a vineyard and a house and will enroll myself as a Cossack.'

'Mind you don't go after other women then. I am severe about that.'

Olénin joyfully repeated all these words to himself. The memory of them now gave him pain and now such joy that it took away his breath. The pain was because she had remained as calm as usual while talking to him. She did not seem at all agitated by these new conditions. It was as if she did not trust him and did not think of the future. It seemed to him that she only loved him for the present moment, and that in her mind there was no future with him. He was happy because her words sounded to him true, and she had consented to be his. 'Yes,' thought he to himself, 'we shall only understand one another when she is quite mine. For such love there are no

words. It needs life—the whole of life. To-morrow everything
will be cleared up. I cannot live like this any longer; to-
morrow I will tell everything to her father, to Belétski, and to
the whole village.'

Lukáshka, after two sleepless nights, had drunk so much at
the fête that for the first time in his life his feet would not
carry him, and he slept in Yámka's house.

CHAPTER XL

The next day Olénin awoke earlier than usual, and immediately
remembered what lay before him, and he joyfully recalled
her kisses, the pressure of her hard hands, and her words,
'What white hands you have!' He jumped up and wished to go
at once to his hosts' hut to ask for their consent to his marriage with Maryánka. The sun had not yet risen, but it
seemed that there was an unusual bustle in the street and side-
street: people were moving about on foot and on horseback,
and talking. He threw on his Circassian coat and hastened
out into the porch. His hosts were not yet up. Five Cossacks
were riding past and talking loudly together. In front rode
Lukáshka on his broad-backed Kabardá horse. The Cossacks were all speaking and shouting so that it was impossible
to make out exactly what they were saying.

'Ride to the Upper Post,' shouted one.

'Saddle and catch us up, be quick,' said another.

'It's nearer through the other gate!'

'What are you talking about?' cried Lukáshka. 'We must
go through the middle gates, of course.'

'So we must, it's nearer that way,' said one of the Cossacks
who was covered with dust and rode a perspiring horse. Lukáshka's face was red and swollen after the drinking of the
previous night and his cap was pushed to the back of his head.
He was calling out with authority as though he were an officer.

'What is the matter? Where are you going?' asked Olénin,
with difficulty attracting the Cossacks' attention.

'We are off to catch *abreks*. They're hiding among the

sand-drifts. We are just off, but there are not enough of us yet.'

And the Cossacks continued to shout, more and more of them joining as they rode down the street. It occurred to Olénin that it would not look well for him to stay behind; besides he thought he could soon come back. He dressed, loaded his gun with bullets, jumped onto his horse which Vanyúsha had saddled more or less well, and overtook the Cossacks at the village gates. The Cossacks had dismounted, and filling a wooden bowl with *chikhir* from a little cask which they had brought with them, they passed the bowl round to one another and drank to the success of their expedition. Among them was a smartly dressed young cornet, who happened to be in the village and who took command of the group of nine Cossacks who had joined for the expedition. All these Cossacks were privates, and although the cornet assumed the airs of a commanding officer, they only obeyed Lukáshka. Of Olénin they took no notice at all, and when they had all mounted and started, and Olénin rode up to the cornet and began asking him what was taking place, the cornet, who was usually quite friendly, treated him with marked condescension. It was with great difficulty that Olénin managed to find out from him what was happening. Scouts who had been sent out to search for *abreks* had come upon several hillsmen some six miles from the village. These *abreks* had taken shelter in pits and had fired at the scouts, declaring they would not surrender. A corporal who had been scouting with two Cossacks had remained to watch the *abreks,* and had sent one Cossack back to get help.

The sun was just rising. Three miles beyond the village the steppe spread out and nothing was visible except the dry, monotonous, sandy, dismal plain covered with the footmarks of cattle, and here and there with tufts of withered grass, with low reeds in the flats, and rare, little-trodden footpaths, and the camps of the nomad Nogáy tribe just visible far away. The absence of shade and the austere aspect of the place were striking. The sun always rises and sets red in the steppe. When it is windy whole hills of sand are carried by the wind from place to place. When it is calm, as it was that morning, the silence, uninterrupted by any movement or sound, is peculiarly striking. That morning in the steppe it was quiet and dull, though the sun had already risen. It all seemed specially soft and desolate. The air was hushed, the footfalls and the snorting of the horses were the only sounds to be heard, and even they quickly died away.

The men rode almost silently. A Cossack always carries his weapons so that they neither jingle nor rattle. Jingling weapons are a terrible disgrace to a Cossack. Two other Cossacks from the village caught the party up and exchanged a few words. Lukáshka's horse either stumbled or caught its foot in some grass, and became restive—which is a sign of bad luck among the Cossacks, and at such a time was of special importance. The others exchanged glances and turned away, trying not to notice what had happened. Lukáshka pulled at the reins, frowned sternly, set his teeth, and flourished his whip above his head. His good Kabardá horse, prancing from one foot to another not knowing with which to start, seemed to wish to fly upwards on wings. But Lukáshka hit its well-fed sides with his whip once, then again, and a third time, and the horse, showing its teeth and spreading out its tail, snorted and reared and stepped on its hind legs a few paces away from the others.

'Ah, a good steed that!' said the cornet.

That he said *steed* instead of *horse* indicated special praise.

'A lion of a horse,' assented one of the others, an old Cossack.

The Cossacks rode forward silently, now at a footpace, then at a trot, and these changes were the only incidents that interrupted for a moment the stillness and solemnity of their movements.

Riding through the steppe for about six miles, they passed nothing but one Nogáy tent, placed on a cart and moving slowly along at a distance of about a mile from them. A Nogáy family was moving from one part of the steppe to another. Afterwards they met two tattered Nogáy women with high cheekbones, who with baskets on their backs were gathering dung left by the cattle that wandered over the steppe. The cornet, who did not know their language well, tried to question them, but they did not understand him and, obviously frightened, looked at one another.

Lukáshka rode up to them both, stopped his horse, and promptly uttered the usual greeting. The Nogáy women were evidently relieved, and began speaking to him quite freely as to a brother.

'*Ay-ay, kop abrek!*' they said plaintively, pointing in the direction in which the Cossacks were going. Olénin understood that they were saying, 'Many *abreks*.'

Never having seen an engagement of that kind, and having formed an idea of them only from Daddy Eróshka's tales, Olénin wished not to be left behind by the Cossacks, but wanted to see it all. He admired the Cossacks, and was on the watch, looking and listening and making his own observations. Though he had brought his sword and a loaded gun with him, when he noticed that the Cossacks avoided him he decided to take no part in the action, as in his opinion his courage had already been sufficiently proved when he was with his detachment, and also because he was very happy.

Suddenly a shot was heard in the distance.

The cornet became excited, and began giving orders to the Cossacks as to how they should divide and from which side they should approach. But the Cossacks did not appear to pay any attention to these orders, listening only to what Lukáshka said and looking to him alone. Lukáshka's face and figure were expressive of calm solemnity. He put his horse to a trot with which the others were unable to keep pace, and screwing up his eyes kept looking ahead.

'There's a man on horseback,' he said, reining in his horse and keeping in line with the others.

Olénin looked intently, but could not see anything. The Cossacks soon distinguished two riders and quietly rode straight towards them.

'Are those the *abreks*?' asked Olénin.

The Cossacks did not answer his question, which appeared

quite meaningless to them. The *abreks* would have been fools to venture across the river on horseback.

'That's friend Ródka waving to us, I do believe,' said Lukáshka, pointing to the two mounted men who were now clearly visible. 'Look, he's coming to us.'

A few minutes later it became plain that the two horsemen were the Cossack scouts. The corporal rode up to Lukáshka.

CHAPTER XLI

'Are they far?' was all Lukáshka said.

Just then they heard a sharp shot some thirty paces off. The corporal smiled slightly.

'Our Gúrka is having shots at them,' he said, nodding in the direction of the shot.

Having gone a few paces farther they saw Gúrka sitting behind a sand-hillock and loading his gun. To while away the time he was exchanging shots with the *abreks*, who were behind another sand-heap. A bullet came whistling from their side.

The cornet was pale and grew confused. Lukáshka dismounted from his horse, threw the reins to one of the other Cossacks, and went up to Gúrka. Olénin also dismounted and, bending down, followed Lukáshka. They had hardly reached Gúrka when two bullets whistled above them. Lukáshka looked around laughing at Olénin and stooped a little.

'Look out or they will kill you, Dmítri Andréich,' he said. 'You'd better go away—you have no business here.'

But Olénin wanted absolutely to see the *abreks*.

From behind the mound he saw caps and muskets some two hundred paces off. Suddenly a little cloud of smoke appeared from thence, and again a bullet whistled past. The *abreks* were hiding in a marsh at the foot of the hill. Olénin was much impressed by the place in which they sat. In reality it was very much like the rest of the steppe, but because the *abreks* sat there it seemed to detach itself from all the rest and to have become distinguished. Indeed it appeared to Olénin that it was the very spot for *abreks* to occupy. Lukáshka went back to his horse and Olénin followed him.

'We must get a hay-cart,' said Lukáshka, 'or they will be killing some of us. There behind that mound is a Nogáy cart with a load of hay.'

The cornet listened to him and the corporal agreed. The cart of hay was fetched, and the Cossacks, hiding behind it, pushed it forward. Olénin rode up a hillock from whence he could see everything. The hay-cart moved on and the Cossacks crowded together behind it. The Cossacks advanced, but the Chéchens, of whom there were nine, sat with their knees in a row and did not fire.

All was quiet. Suddenly from the Chéchens arose the sound of a mournful song, something like Daddy Eróshka's 'Ay day, dalalay'. The Chéchens knew that they could not escape, and to prevent themselves from being tempted to take to flight they had strapped themselves together, knee to knee, had got their guns ready, and were singing their death-song.

The Cossacks with their hay-cart drew closer and closer, and Olénin expected the firing to begin at any moment, but the silence was only broken by the *abreks'* mournful song. Suddenly the song ceased; there was a sharp report, a bullet struck the front of the cart, and Chéchen curses and yells broke the silence and shot followed on shot and one bullet after another struck the cart. The Cossacks did not fire and were now only five paces distant.

Another moment passed and the Cossacks with a whoop rushed out on both sides from behind the cart—Lukáshka in front of them. Olénin heard only a few shots, then shouting and moans. He thought he saw smoke and blood, and abandoning his horse and quite beside himself he ran towards the Cossacks. Horror seemed to blind him. He could not make out anything, but understood that all was over. Lukáshka, pale as death, was holding a wounded Chéchen by the arms and shouting, 'Don't kill him. I'll take him alive!' The Chéchen was the red-haired man who had fetched his brother's body away after Lukáshka had killed him. Lukáshka was twisting his arms. Suddenly the Chéchen wrenched himself free and fired his pistol. Lukáshka fell, and blood began to flow from his stomach. He jumped up, but fell again, swearing in Russian and in Tartar. More and more blood appeared on his clothes and under him. Some Cossacks approached him and began loosening his girdle. One of them, Nazárka, before beginning to help, fumbled for some time unable to put his sword in its sheath: it would not go the right way. The blade of the sword was blood-stained.

The Chéchens with their red hair and clipped moustaches lay dead and hacked about. Only the one we know of, who had fired at Lukáshka, though wounded in many places was still alive. Like a wounded hawk all covered with blood (blood was flowing from a wound under his right eye), pale and gloomy, he looked about him with wide-open excited eyes and clenched teeth as he crouched, dagger in hand, still prepared to defend himself. The cornet went up to him as if intending to pass by, and with a quick movement shot him in the ear. The Chéchen started up, but it was too late, and he fell.

The Cossacks, quite out of breath, dragged the bodies aside and took the weapons from them. Each of the red-haired Chéchens had been a man, and each one had his own individual expression. Lukáshka was carried to the cart. He continued to swear in Russian and in Tartar.

'No fear, I'll strangle him with my hands. *Anna senil'* he cried, struggling. But he soon became quiet from weakness.

Olénin rode home. In the evening he was told that Lukáshka was at death's door, but that a Tartar from beyond the river had undertaken to cure him with herbs.

The bodies were brought to the village office. The women and the little boys hastened to look at them.

It was growing dark when Olénin returned, and he could not collect himself after what he had seen. But towards night memories of the evening before came rushing to his mind. He looked out of the window, Maryánka was passing to and fro from the house to the cowshed, putting things straight. Her mother had gone to the vineyard and her father to the office.

Olénin could not wait till she had quite finished her work, but went out to meet her. She was in the hut standing with her back towards him. Olénin thought she felt shy.

'Maryánka,' said he, 'I say, Maryánka! May I come in?'

She suddenly turned. There was a scarcely perceptible trace of tears in her eyes and her face was beautiful in its sadness. She looked at him in silent dignity.

Olénin again said:

'Maryánka, I have come——'

'Leave me alone!' she said. Her face did not change but the tears ran down her cheeks.

'What are you crying for? What is it?'

'What?' she repeated in a rough voice. 'Cossacks have been killed, that's what for.'

'Lukáshka?' said Olénin.

'Go away! What do you want?'

'Maryánka!' said Olénin, approaching her.

'You will never get anything from me!'

'Maryánka, don't speak like that,' Olénin entreated.

'Get away. I'm sick of you!' shouted the girl, stamping her foot, and moved threateningly towards him. And her face expressed such abhorrence, such contempt, and such anger that Olénin suddenly understood that there was no hope for him, and that his first impression of this woman's inaccessibility had been perfectly correct.

Olénin said nothing more, but ran out of the hut.

CHAPTER XLII

For two hours after returning home he lay on his bed motionless. Then he went to his company commander and obtained leave to visit the staff. Without taking leave of anyone, and sending Vanyúsha to settle his accounts with his landlord, he prepared to leave for the fort where his regiment was stationed. Daddy Eróshka was the only one to see him off. They had a drink, and then a second, and then yet another. Again as on the night of his departure from Moscow, a three-horsed conveyance stood waiting at the door. But Olénin did not confer with himself as he had done then, and did not say to himself that all he had thought and done here was 'not it'. He did not promise himself a new life. He loved Maryánka more than ever, and knew that he could never be loved by her.

'Well, good-bye, my lad!' said Daddy Eróshka. 'When you go on an expedition, be wise and listen to my words—the words of an old man. When you are out on a raid or the like (you know I'm an old wolf and have seen things), and when they begin firing, don't get into a crowd where there are many men. When you fellows get frightened you always try to get close together with a lot of others. You think it is merrier to be with others, but that's where it is worst of all! They always aim at a crowd. Now I used to keep farther away from the others and went alone, and I've never been wounded. Yet what things haven't I seen in my day?'

'But you've got a bullet in your back,' remarked Vanyúsha, who was clearing up the room.

'That was the Cossacks fooling about,' answered Eróshka.

'Cossacks? How was that?' asked Olénin.

'Oh, just so. We were drinking. Vánka Sítkin, one of the Cossacks, got merry, and puff! he gave me one from his pistol just here.'

'Yes, and did it hurt?' asked Olénin. 'Vanyúsha, will you soon be ready?' he added.

'Ah, where's the hurry! Let me tell you. When he banged into me, the bullet did not break the bone but remained here. And I say: "You've killed me, brother. Eh! What have you done to me? I won't let you off! You have to stand me a pailful!"'

'Well, but did it hurt?' Olénin asked again, scarcely listening to the tale.

'Let me finish. He stood a pailful, and we drank it, but the blood went on flowing. The whole room was drenched and covered with blood. Grandad Burlák, he says, "The lad will give up the ghost. Stand a bottle of the sweet sort, or we shall have you taken up!" They bought more drink, and boozed and boozed——'

'Yes, but did it hurt you much?' Olénin asked once more.

'Hurt, indeed! Don't interrupt: I don't like it. Let me finish. We boozed and boozed till morning, and I fell asleep on the top of the oven, drunk. When I woke in the morning I could not unbend myself anyhow——'

'Was it very painful?' repeated Olénin, thinking that now he would at last get an answer to his question.

'Did I tell you it was painful? I did not say it was painful, but I could not bend and could not walk.'

'And then it healed up?' said Olénin, not even laughing, so heavy was his heart.

'It healed up, but the bullet is still there. Just feel it!' And lifting his shirt he showed his powerful back, where just near the bone a bullet could be felt and rolled about.

'Feel how it rolls,' he said, evidently amusing himself with the bullet as with a toy. 'There now, it has rolled to the back.'

'And Lukáshka, will he recover?' asked Olénin.

'Heaven only knows! There's no doctor. They've gone for one.'

'Where will they get one? From Gróznoe?' asked Olénin.

'No my lad. Were I the Tsar I'd have hung all your Russian doctors long ago. Cutting is all they know! There's our Cossack Bakláshka, no longer a real man now that they've cut off his leg! That shows they're fools. What's Bakláshka good for now? No, my lad, in the mountains there are real doctors. There was my chum, Vórchik, he was on an expedition and was wounded just here in the chest. Well, your doctors gave him up, but one of theirs came from the mountains and cured him! They understand herbs, my lad!'

'Come, stop talking rubbish,' said Olénin. 'I'd better send a doctor from head-quarters.'

'Rubbish!' the old man said mockingly. 'Fool, fool! Rubbish. You'll send a doctor!—— If yours cured people, Cossacks and Chéchens would go to you for treatment, but as it is your officers and colonels send to the mountains for doctors. Yours are all humbugs, all humbugs.'

Olénin did not answer. He agreed only too fully that all was

humbug in the world in which he had lived and to which
he was now returning.

'How is Lukáshka? You've been to see him?' he asked.

'He just lies as if he were dead. He does not eat nor drink.
Vodka is the only thing his soul accepts. But as long as he
drinks vodka it's well. I'd be sorry to lose the lad. A fine lad—
a brave, like me. I too lay dying like that once. The old
women were already wailing. My head was burning. They
had already laid me out under the holy icons. So I lay there,
and above me on the oven little drummers, no bigger than
this, beat the tattoo. I shout at them and they drum all
the harder.' (The old man laughed.) 'The women brought
our church elder. They were getting ready to bury me.
They said, "He defiled himself with worldly unbelievers; he
made merry with women; he ruined people; he did not fast,
and he played the *balaláyka*." "Confess," they said. So I began to confess. "I've sinned!" I said. Whatever the priest said,
I always answered "I've sinned." He began to ask me about
the *balaláyka*. "Where is the accursed thing," he says. "Show
it me and smash it." But I say, "I've not got it." I'd hidden
it myself in a net in the outhouse. I knew they could not find
it. So they left me. Yet after all I recovered. When I went for
my *balaláyka*—— What was I saying?' he continued. 'Listen to
me, and keep farther away from the other men or you'll get
killed foolishly. I feel for you truly: you are a drinker—I love
you! And fellows like you like riding up the mounds. There was
one who lived here who had come from Russia, he always
would ride up the mounds (he called the mounds so fun-
nily, "hillocks"). Whenever he saw a mound, off he'd gallop.
Once he galloped off that way and rode to the top quite
pleased, but a Chéchen fired at him and killed him! Ah, how
well they shoot from their gun-rests, those Chéchens! Some of
them shoot even better than I do. I don't like it when a fellow
gets killed so foolishly! Sometimes I used to look at your soldiers and wonder at them. There's foolishness for you! They
go, the poor fellows, all in a clump, and even sew red collars
to their coats! How can they help being hit! One gets killed,

they drag him away and another takes his place! What foolishness!' the old man repeated, shaking his head. 'Why not
scatter, and go one by one? So you just go like that and they
won't notice you. That's what you must do.'

'Well, thank you! Good-bye, Daddy. God willing we may
meet again,' said Olénin, getting up and moving towards the
passage.

The old man, who was sitting on the floor, did not rise.

'Is that the way one says "Good-bye"? Fool, fool!' he
began. 'Oh dear, what has come to people? We've kept company, kept company for wellnigh a year, and now "Good-bye!"
and off he goes! Why, I love you, and how I pity you! You
are so forlorn, always alone, always alone. You're somehow so
unsociable. At times I can't sleep for thinking about you. I am
so sorry for you. As the song has it:

> "It is very hard, dear brother,
> In a foreign land to live."

So it is with you.'

'Well, good-bye,' said Olénin again.

The old man rose and held out his hand. Olénin pressed it
and turned to go.

'Give us your mug, your mug!'

And the old man took Olénin by the head with both hands
and kissed him three times with wet moustaches and lips,
and began to cry.

'I love you, good-bye!'

Olénin got into the cart.

'Well, is that how you're going? You might give me
something for a remembrance. Give me a gun! What do you
want two for?' said the old man, sobbing quite sincerely.

Olénin got out a musket and gave it to him.

'What a lot you've given the old fellow,' murmured Vanyúsha, 'he'll never have enough! A regular old beggar. They
are all such irregular people,' he remarked, as he wrapped
himself in his overcoat and took his seat on the box.

'Hold your tongue, swine!' exclaimed the old man, laughing. 'What a stingy fellow!'

Maryánka came out of the cowshed, glanced indifferently at the cart, bowed and went towards the hut.

'*La fille!*' said Vanyúsha, with a wink and burst out into a silly laugh.

'Drive on!' shouted Olénin, angrily.

'Good-bye, my lad! Good-bye. I won't forget you!' shouted Eróshka.

Olénin turned round. Daddy Eróshka was talking to Maryánka, evidently about his own affairs, and neither the old man nor the girl looked at Olénin.

[Finished Dec. 19, 1862.]